Time for Trouble

The Blake Brothers Trilogy

Book 3

Susan Sey

Other Titles by Susan Sey

For Jody, who finally took me up on my offer (okay, my desperate plea) to share a table at the coffee shop. I have wanted a co-worker for years. I'm so glad it's you.

For Bryan, who loves me enough to read outside his genre. And is brave enough to offer notes.

And for Claudia and Greta, who teach me more than I could ever teach them, and who still love to see their names in my books. For now.

Chapter 1

Andrew Blake didn't necessarily believe in heaven but supposing such a place existed? And supposing he was eligible for entry when his time came? He expected it would look a lot like Friday night at Declan's Pub.

The heavy oak door whispered shut at his back and Drew took a moment to savor the welcome warmth. Fiddles and accordions hummed low under the buzz of happy hour, and he inhaled the comfortable musk of spilled beer and polished wood while his ears thawed out. There was a nasty snap in the air tonight. Fall was hanging on here in northern Virginia but winter would drag it out back and steal its lunch money any minute now.

But not inside Declan's. No, inside Declan's winter held no sway. It was friendly and comfortable year round, just the way Drew liked things.

Yeah, he thought happily while his eyes adjusted to the low light. Heaven was probably just like this. Except with dead people. Drew had been assured that heaven was chock-full of the dearly departed, and while there were a few folks he was looking forward to seeing again—his mom and dad foremost among them—he was glad Declan's had missed that particular note. Dead people would be weird at a bar. Plus he was more concerned with the living this evening.

With one live person in particular.

The crowd shifted and rolled like an ocean of tipsy goodwill, and he scanned the waves for Meghan Wise's bright golden head. It would be hard to miss. She wore all that sleek hair of hers twisted up high and tight, giving her cheekbones you could cut diamonds with. It also gave her a solid six inches on every other woman in the room—and a few of the men. Which was just a bonus to Meg's way of thinking.

He grinned. God love the girl, she didn't believe in hiding her light under a bushel. Any man that wanted to date his Meggy would need balls of stainless steel. Not many had them, which suited Drew just fine. Not that he wanted his best friend in the world to be single, alone and unhappy. Certainly not. That would be petty and selfish. But who would meet him at Declan's every Friday night if Meg got all cozied up with somebody?

He tossed himself into the ocean of liberated office drones ringing in the weekend with a beer or two, and let the current loop him willy-nilly through a small forest of two-and four-tops. When he eventually neared the long, polished bar lining the back wall, he stepped out. He hooked an elbow over the edge and smiled at Lila, the curvy little brunette manning the tap who—in Drew's humble opinion—was the very reason God had invented jeans. She gave him a friendly nod and hiked one pierced eyebrow in silent question. Drew held up two fingers.

He unwound a yard or two of the scarf around his neck and kept an eye on the door. A moment later, Lila slid a couple of foam-topped pints onto the bar at his elbow.

"Either Meg's running late, or you're drinking for two tonight." Ireland was a faint whiff in her voice, like smoke from a distant campfire.

"Running late, I think. Even Meg can't control the traffic."

"Though I'm sure it galls her."

"Oh, it does. Eternally." Drew sampled the beer. He hadn't even asked what she'd served him. "God, that's good. Help me out here, will you? Meg would want us to honor this beer." He lifted his pint. "To the weekend."

"*Slainte.*" Lila picked up Meg's glass and tapped it to Drew's. She pointed her chin toward the door. "And there she is now."

Drew turned and found Meg coming his way. She arrowed through the crowd, burning a line straight through it rather than flowing with it the way Drew did. It seemed like a lot of work to him, but he could still admire it. There wasn't a guy alive who wouldn't admire that stride—each long, long leg slung out from the hip, fast and confident, as if those ice pick heels were hiking boots or something.

She arrived at the stool next to Drew's, peeled out of a sharply tailored trench coat and pointed at the beer he wasn't drinking. "Tell me that's for me."

"That's for you," Drew said obligingly.

"Thank Christ." She dumped her coat on the stool and picked up the pint for a long swallow.

Lila lifted that studded brow again. "Somebody had a rough day."

"Looks that way, doesn't it?" Drew watched with equal parts admiration and interest while half of Meg's beer disappeared. "Tough day in the dog-eat-dog world of cyber security entrepreneurs, Meggy?"

"You have no idea." Meg set down the glass with a gusty sigh. "Thank you, Lila, oh provider of life sustaining beer. I may be in love with you."

"Hey," Drew said mildly. "I ordered it."

"I love you, too." Meg handed Drew her purse. "Now hold this, because I have to pee in the worst way. Traffic was a stone-faced bitch. And don't even get me started on the tool I just decided not to work for."

"Got it." Drew tossed her bag onto the bar next to her beer. "Go pee."

"Oh no you don't." Meg narrowed those bottle green eyes and aimed a finger at him, the nail murder red and as sharp as her cheekbones. "You hold that thing. Cradle it like your firstborn child. That's my purse. What kind of security expert are you?"

"I'm not a security expert." He offered her a charming grin. "I tweet for a living. It says so on my business card." He made a marquee of his hands. *"Drew Blake, making social media your bitch since—"*

"Screw your business card." She danced from heel to heel, that strong-boned face caught somewhere between exasperation and impatience, with a dash of desperation thrown in. She really must have to pee. "My business card says expert security consultant, so if I hire shit out to you—which I do—you're an expert security consultant, too. And if your screwed-up version of self-esteem forces you to criminally low-ball your skills—"

Drew pulled out his phone and snapped a quick photo.

"What?" Meg froze. "Oh, hell, don't post that."

She snatched at his phone but Drew was faster. "Meg pees her pants at the bar," he said. "The internet thanks you for your business."

"Damn it." Meg glared at him.

Drew treated himself to a long, easy swallow of icy beer. "Mmmmm." He gave Meg's beer a pointed look. "So good."

"Hold the purse, Drew." She pushed the words through her teeth.

"James and Will trust me with their offspring, you know." He patted the purse at his elbow. "More importantly, so do their wives. I think I can babysit a purse."

"Nice try. I know your nephews, Drew. I've babysat them myself. They're animals. No criminal in his right mind would want them. That, however—" She gave her purse a loving stroke. "—is a Birkin bag. Everybody wants that purse. Criminals have wet dreams about that purse. Women make sex noises when they see that purse."

Drew gave it a more respectful look. "Sex noises? Really?"

"Damn it, Drew, will you just—"

"Jesus, Mary and Joseph." Lila snatched up Meg's purse and dumped it behind the bar. "Go, before you wet yourself."

"Thank you, Lila," Meg said sweetly. She gave Drew a last glare, spun on one lethal heel and strode off. Drew turned his stool lazily back toward the bar and tracked Meg in the mirror at Lila's back. Her hair knot sliced through the crowd like a shark fin.

"I really do love that girl," he said, deeply satisfied with the exchange.

"I believe you." Lila gathered up an armload of empty pint glasses, dumped them into a tub and swept up the damp rings with a white cloth, all in one efficient motion. "Even if you do show it like a thirteen-year-old boy."

A server slid into the gap at Drew's side, a compact kid with black curls and the easy grace of an athlete. "Four pints and a black and tan, Lila," he said.

"On it." Lila racked up some fresh pint glasses and started drawing.

"A guy can't hold a girl's purse just because she asks, Lila." Drew settled more comfortably onto his stool, ready to expound on his theory. "You might as well just beg her to take you shoe shopping."

"Or to marry you," the server put in.

Drew shot a finger at the guy. "Thank you! Exactly my point."

Lila scowled at the kid.

"What?" The server shrugged. "It's true."

"It's totally true," Drew said. "My brothers carry their wives' purses all the time. *All the time.*" He and the server shook their heads in a mutual moment of wonder and despair.

"As well they should." Lila handed off a couple of full pints and squatted to heave another rack of glasses, still steaming from the dishwasher, onto the work surface behind the bar. "Have you had a look at their wives lately?"

"I have," the server said wistfully. Drew cut him a sideways look, which he returned with a cheerful smile. "What? I'm a fan. James and Will are the best thing that's happened to ESPN's soccer coverage since *Men in Blazers*." The smile broadened. "Bel and Audrey are just a bonus." He released an admiring breath. "A very, very hot bonus."

Drew shook his head. "You wouldn't say that if you lived with them."

The server's eyes went wide and respectful. "You live with them?"

"With Will and Audrey, yeah, in the Annex." Which, despite the name, was a damn mansion and a half. Possibly two whole mansions shoved together. His wing alone covered more real estate than some small nations. "And James and Bel are right next door at Hunt House." He sighed as if oppressed. "And Bel keeps trying to put me on TV."

"The nerve." Lila angled him a look of deeply false sympathy.

Drew chose to take the sympathy and leave the rest. "I know, right?"

She rolled her eyes. "My point, Drew, is that your brothers' wives are women of looks, brains, heart and ambition."

"Stubborn as twelve mules, too." Drew hunched and drank.

"Moreover," Lila went on serenely, "they're willing to give their hearts and a passel of gorgeous children to their men. It seems the least a man could do in return is to hold a damn handbag on occasion." She divided a hard look between Drew and the server, who sidled to the left and gave Drew a look that clearly said *on your own, dude*. "Simply in payment for the labor and delivery, if nothing else."

Well, damn. Drew had to give her that one. "When you put it that way, it seems petty to disagree."

"And surely you're not so small."

"Not that anybody's ever said." He grinned at the server who gave a muffled snort and held up his fist for the knuckle bump. Drew obliged.

"Well, not to your face, anyway," Lila said mildly. The server yelped out a laugh, this one not muffled at all.

Drew blinked at him, then at Lila. "Wait, did somebody say—"

"I'll not be violating the bartender code," Lila said primly, "so don't ask me." She pushed the last of the order toward the server, who took it and moved off into the crowd with the élan of a world-class striker, still chuckling.

"Damn," Drew said, momentarily distracted. "Kid's got moves."

"He does. We make a point of recognizing talent, Declan and I do. And speaking of moves." Lila propped her elbows on the bar and aimed an amused look into the crowd behind Drew's shoulder.

"What?" Drew tried to turn around for a better look but Lila slapped a hand over his on the bar.

"Don't look, for heaven's sake. You'll distract her."

"Distract who? Meg?"

"Of course, Meg. Don't be dense. Use the mirror now, and be subtle." She grinned, amusement deepening into delight. "Well, now, isn't that interesting?"

"Isn't what interesting?"

"That fellow chatting up our Meg?" Lila said. "The one with the shoulders and the suit, looks like he should be having his picture taken?"

"Shoulders?" Drew focused on the mirror, found Meg and a guy who did, indeed, have some shoulders on him. Drew straightened his own reflexively. The guy's back was to the bar, but he had dark hair and enough height that even Meg had to look up to meet his eyes. The flirtatious angle at which she did so, however? The angle that forced her to peep up through her lashes at him? That was gratuitous. "What about him?"

"Well, he looks quite eager to hold our Meghan's purse, now, doesn't he?" Lila smiled.

"He does not." Drew scoffed and finished off his beer. But he frowned at the mirror. "No guy is eager to hold a chick's purse in public."

Lila's smile spread as Meg continued to make a spectacle of herself. "And she might be after letting him."

"Oh, cripes," Drew said, "she's doing the hair flip." He felt his lip curl. "Her hair's not even down. You can't flip a damn bun."

"She's doing fine, isn't she?" Lila murmured. "Mr. Shoulders certainly seems to think so."

Drew scowled. Mr. Shoulders, his ass. He rolled his own defensively as the guy leaned close to Meg's ear to say something. Meg threw back her head and cut loose with a naughty, bawdy laugh as distinctive as a fingerprint. It was the kind of laugh that wrapped itself around a guy's dick, whether kissing was on the table or not. Sex was in that laugh's DNA and Mr. Shoulders—Christ, now he was doing it—was digging it.

Even as Drew watched, the guy leaned in again, touched her elbow, said something else. Meg unleashed that laugh again—the one that had no effect on Drew's dick whatsoever. None.

And suddenly Drew couldn't take it. He needed to see this better.

He spun on his stool and squinted into the puddle of amber light that made Meg's hair knot glow like a beacon. Mr. Shoulders turned, angled in a little closer—definitely getting Meg's green light—and gave Drew his profile. And the mild irritation in Drew's gut fled, replaced by a flash of memory so deep and so sudden that Drew fell back against the bar as if punched.

"Holy Christ," he murmured. "He's dead."

"Dead." Lila snorted and flapped a disgusted hand. "Don't be dramatic, Drew. If you don't want to hold the girl's handbag, I don't see how you can possibly object if somebody else does."

"What?" Drew glanced at her, distracted, then rolled his eyes. "Jesus, Lila, I didn't mean I was going to kill the guy. He gets handsy, Meg knows how to put him down. No, I meant—" He glanced back at that profile, gave it a good hard look. He knew it couldn't be who he thought it was. Knew it. But the bells ringing in his head wouldn't shut up and his lizard brain insisted. And Drew wasn't one to overthink things. When your gut pinged, you paid attention.

"You meant what?" Lila said.

"It's just, well—" He stopped, lifted a baffled hand. "That's Ian Sheffield."

"You know him? Mr. Shoulders?" Lila gave the guy a more thorough study.

"Yep." Drew frowned. "Only he's dead. Has been for years."

"Is that right?"

"At least ten. Maybe fifteen?" Drew picked up his pint, found it empty and set it back down. "Except—" Cripes. Maybe Declan's really was heaven. He suppressed the urge to look around for his mom and dad. Because that was nuts. Wasn't it? "Except...there he is."

Lila frowned. "I must say, he doesn't look dead."

"No." He frowned as well. "He doesn't."

"Which leaves just the one question, then, doesn't it?"

"When did the zombie apocalypse happen?"

"For heaven's sake, Andrew. A dead man is putting the moves on your Meg." Lila arched that pierced brow. "I think the question is, what are you going to do about it?"

Chapter 2

"I—" Drew stopped, unsure what he'd been about to say. "I have to do something?"

"Well, of course you do! Meg's your best girl, isn't she?"

"She's my best friend," Drew allowed. "She just happens to also be a girl."

"Don't split hairs. It's unattractive." Lila waved that away. "Besides, gender has no bearing on your obligation in this matter."

"I have an obligation?" he asked automatically. He was distracted but not so much that he couldn't dodge an obligation. He honored the ones he took, so he took them damn sparingly.

"For goodness' sake, Drew, focus." Lila snapped her fingers beside his ear.

"I'm focused." Drew gave his glass a pointed look. "I'm very aware that I have no more beer, for example."

Lila ignored that. "It's in the friendship rules," she insisted.

"What is?"

"Your obligation." She gave him a glare that Drew ignored. Because damn if that guy wasn't Ian. Who had been dead for fifteen years. Or so Drew had believed. Meg fingered an earring and gave the guy another sideways peep through her lashes. Might-be-Ian's answering smile slid from interested to something warmer, and a prickly knot gathered in Drew's stomach.

"Supposing you know something about a potential romantic interest," Lila went on. "Like maybe they're married. Or gay. Sociopathic. Dead. You say something."

"Of course you do." He nodded slowly while unfamiliar

fury slid sickly up his throat. Ian had everything. Had had everything, anyway. Not that it had ever stopped him from wanting what was Drew's. And now he wanted Meg? "Especially that last one."

"Especially," Lila agreed. "Men comfortably dead these past fifteen years don't rise from the grave and turn up at happy hour for no good reason, Drew."

"They don't, do they?" He circled his glass between his palms. It was cool and smooth but something inside him screamed for the jagged and bloody. "Ian Sheffield, Jesus."

They paused to watch while Ian leaned in to say something in Meg's ear. She tossed back that shiny head and gave another delighted laugh that leapt into the rage kindling in Drew's stomach, pulled it tighter, uglier.

"Are you sure it's him?" Lila asked. "Certain?"

"Nope." Drew handed her his glass and rose, his head light and strange. He never lost his temper. Never. Mostly he pretended he didn't have one. "Only one way to find out, though, isn't there?"

* * *

Meg knew Drew was watching her. She'd always been able to feel his eyes on her. She'd gotten used to it over the years, and moreover she'd developed a darn good gauge for the intent of that attention. Mostly it wavered between affectionate interest and mischievous needling, which was fine with her. Drew was as lazy as he was brilliant, and if he ever stirred himself up to more than mischief, the world might have a problem on its hands.

Thankfully he didn't stir himself up that often. Or, you know, ever. Not that she'd ever witnessed, anyway.

Not until right this minute.

A whole-body tingle shot from the crown of her head to her fingertips and she laid a hand on the sleeve—mmm, the very nice sleeve—of the guy who was apologizing prettily for bumping into her. She nudged him just a smidge to one side and angled herself just a bit toward the other side. She wanted a better look at whatever had caused her Drew-dar to red-line so alarmingly.

The suit took the invitation to put his mouth closer to her ear. It was loud, after all, and again, *mmm*. But Meg didn't hear a word he said. Because once her sight line cleared his shoulder, she got a load of Drew. And one hell of a shock.

Because Andrew Blake, who didn't stand when he could sit, who didn't sit when he could lie down, was steaming through the crowd in a straight line, his eyes fixed on the guy whose warm hand was on her elbow, whose pretty mouth was next to her ear.

Meg jumped back as if Mr. Well Cut Suit was on fire. Judging from the murder in Drew's normally easy face, he might as well be. She'd never seen Drew throw a punch—she hadn't thought he actually knew how—but unless she was seriously misjudging the situation, he might be looking to try it out.

She gave up on subtlety and shoved the flirty stranger behind her, put her body between him and whatever madness Drew was serving up.

"Drew, whoa!" She went for authority, both in tone and in posture. Fists on hips, feet spread, chin down, eyes narrow. "What the hell?"

Drew didn't even glance at her, and that full-body tingle went nuclear. It flashed down her back, wrapped around her hips and punched somewhere low in her stomach. Because Drew always listened to her. Always. It was just the way they rolled. It wasn't that he couldn't be in charge; it was just that he never wanted to be. Claimed it was too much work. And Meg liked to drive, so they suited one another perfectly.

Or had. Until Drew had snapped the leash without warning. Without so much as a reason as far as Meg could see.

He strode past her, and she stood there gaping, every nerve ending in her body alive and struggling to figure out how to play this one. She shot a panicked look at Lila at the bar—*what the hell?* Lila just shrugged and nodded her back toward Drew.

Who now had Mr. Well Cut Suit by the shirt front and was hauling him...where? The stranger had his hands up and open.

"Easy, mate," he said. "I didn't touch her."

"Easy, my ass," Drew snarled. *Snarled.* Another shudder of shock and heat rocked her and Meg shook it off to scamper after them. "Drew, my God! What are you doing? He didn't do anything!"

Drew said nothing, only drove the guy into the nearest two-top. Mr. Suit's head knocked the pendant light above it into a wild arc, and the occupants of the table wisely grabbed their beers and bailed out. Drew plastered the guy across the tabletop and grabbed his jaw in one hand. A very big hand, Meg realized suddenly. She swallowed. How had she never noticed before that Drew had hands the size of catcher's mitts? He was six-five, easy, though a very skinny six-five. Of course he had big hands. She'd just never seen them doing violence before.

The guy clawed at Drew's forearm while Drew used his free hand to snatch at the swinging light above them. For one horrified second Meg thought he intended to smash it over the stranger's head.

"Drew!" She latched onto his elbow with some desperation. "For God's sake, knock it off!"

He didn't so much as glance her way, but he didn't swing either. He only aimed the bulb straight into the guy's face like he was staging a bad interrogation, throwing all those pretty bones into harsh relief. They stood there for a frozen instant, Drew staring down into the man's face while the man blinked back, his eyes silvery and startled.

"God damn it, Ian," Drew said finally. "You died."

Meg said, "You know this guy?"

Ian said, "Jesus Christ on the cross." He stared, stunned. "Drew?"

"I saw you," Drew said tightly, his fingers white on the jaw he'd yet to release. "I saw you die."

"You were supposed to." Ian let go of Drew's forearm slowly, his hands going open, harmless. "That was the deal."

"What deal?"

13

Ian hesitated and Meg stepped in. She kept the one hand hooked in Drew's elbow—just in case—and laid the other tentatively between his shoulder blades. Violence pumped tangibly under her palm. It sent an electric shock clear up to her shoulder and she stifled a hiss.

"Drew," she murmured. Slid that tingling hand up and down the tight line of his spine. "Drew, take it easy. I think we need to take this easy."

"Easy. Right." He sucked in a breath. "Right. Jesus." He released the stranger—Ian, evidently—and shook himself like a wet dog. "Fuck it, that one slipped away from me." He dropped his eyes and offered Meg a crooked smile from under his brows. "Sorry."

She only stared, utterly beyond words. It got away from him? What got away from him? And how often did he struggle with keeping it in, whatever it might be? And how the hell had she never noticed him doing it?

He extended a hand to Ian, who was still cautiously extricating himself from the table. "Sorry," he said. "You, uh, startled me."

"Back at you, mate." Ian accepted the help up, then wiggled his jaw side to side. "Didn't think you had that in you."

"I don't." Drew lifted lazy shoulders, violence utterly erased. Meg blinked uneasily. Two minutes ago, she'd have agreed wholeheartedly. Drew had never exhibited anything like a capacity for violence. He wasn't built for it, physically or emotionally. But what had she just seen if not a murderous rage, evidently triggered by betrayal? Or dishonesty. Disloyalty? Something. She had one hand still latched into the crook of his elbow, the other between those tight shoulders, but for the first time in their long friendship, the touch wasn't easy. An electric wariness sparked underneath it, danger just waiting for its moment. She let him go, stepped back.

"I don't know," Ian said, shooting Drew an adorably crooked smile. "My jaw says maybe you do."

Drew grinned. "Still worried about that pretty face of yours, huh?"

"It's a priority," Ian agreed. He leaned around Drew to aim that smile Meg's way. "Speaking of pretty."

Drew shook his head. "One foot out of the grave and still charming the ladies."

"*I'm not dead*," Ian deadpanned, his accent sliding from crisply British to a broad Cockney, though the silvery eyes stayed seriously pinned to Meg.

Drew barked out a startled laugh. "*I'm getting bettah!*"

"*I think I'll go for a walk!*" Meg said, rolling her eyes. "And now that the Monty Python tribute is over, can I please know what the fuck is going on?"

Ian turned to Drew. "I think I love her. Is she yours?"

"Yes," Drew said and that shock of heat and terror went off again at the top of Meg's skull. "Hands off."

Ian turned back to Meg with a slow smile and held out a hand. "Ian Sheffield, dead man." He leaned in confidentially. "Though reports of my death have been greatly exaggerated."

"Meg Wise, best friend." She took his hand for a brisk shake. It was wide and warm, but not as warm as the melting invitation in his eyes. They were shockingly light against that olive skin, that mass of dark, curly hair. Real attention getters. And she bet he knew it.

"Ooh." One dark brow arched Drew's way. "She friend-zoned you."

Drew arched a brow right back. "She's about to punch-zone you."

Ian let her hand go. "Is she?"

"Considering it," Meg said, sharpening up her smile. "I believe I asked a question, and all I'm getting is banter."

"Flirty banter," Ian said winningly.

Meg showed him her teeth.

"Right." He stepped back. Drew laughed.

"Answers, boys." Meg folded her arms. "Now."

"Wow," Ian breathed. "I can see why you like her."

"She is so going to kick your ass." Drew gave him a shoulder shot. "If she beats me to it, that is. Because I'm still thinking about taking that swing myself."

Ian sobered.

"You haven't answered my questions yet either, Ian," Drew pointed out.

"I will." He held up peaceable hands. "I absolutely will. Though this likely isn't the appropriate place for a...complicated conversation."

Drew opened his mouth and Meg shot him a warning look. He would invite this guy back to his place over her dead body. Not that his address wasn't public info—everything was public anymore—but this guy was supposed to be dead. Or had let Drew believe so, evidently. And that struck her as more than a little sketchy. The kind of sketchy you didn't bring home when home included the rich, the famous, and all the security concerns that went along with them. Not to mention a tribe of wild-ass children.

Her dilemma evidently wasn't lost on Ian, who said, "I'm at the Prince George Hotel. It's not but five miles from here."

"I know where it is," Meg said.

"Why don't we talk there?"

"Sounds good," Drew said. "I'll ride with—"

"—me." Meg renewed her grip on Drew's elbow and pulled him to her side. "We'll meet you there in ten minutes."

Drew blinked at her in a way that made her immediately smooth out her expression and wonder what exactly he'd seen there. "Right." He nodded slowly, then turned to Ian. "Ten minutes."

"All right." Ian turned and melted into the crowd with impressive speed, given that he was probably only a couple inches shorter than Drew's six-five. Meg let go of Drew's arm.

"What," she said carefully, "was that?"

Drew was still staring at the door through which Ian had disappeared. "That was Ian fucking Sheffield," he said, shaking his head. "Holy shit."

"I didn't mean him." Meg gave him an impatient shot to the shoulder. "I meant this." She swung an arm toward the empty table beside them, lamp still swaying gently above it. "I meant you charging over here like a raging bull, like you

16

were going to kill somebody. Like you not only knew how—which would be a shocker in and of itself—but like you were planning to go for it." She threw both arms out, baffled and pissed. "Who were you just now?"

"Yeah, that was weird, wasn't it?" He put his hands on his hips and shook his head at the floor, a sheepish half-smile on that long, angular face. "Honestly, I'm not sure what that was." He opened both hands in front of him, inspected them like they weren't quite attached. "One second I was explaining the ban on purse-holding to Lila, then she said how that guy looked like he wouldn't mind holding your purse. I turned around and saw Ian there, only Ian can't be there because he's dead, right?"

"Right," Meg murmured.

"Yeah, only not so much." Drew continued to frown at his hands. "So there he is, right, chatting you up like—"

He broke off, glanced up at Meg. That weird electric awareness went off in Meg's chest again, but in slow motion this time. It cracked open slowly, sent out sparkly runners to body parts best left unmentioned and pulsed there. She swallowed.

"Chatting me up like what?"

"Like...God, Meg, like I don't know what." He hooked a hand around the back of his neck and blew out a breath, a sure sign that he was thinking hard. "All I know is that I saw him there and I was suddenly angry. Beyond angry. Furious."

"Why?" she asked softly, her heart thudding harder than it probably should. Because she was alarmed, she told herself. Because her best friend was clearly having some kind of crisis, a crisis that had put a serious crack in a *laissez-faire* attitude toward life that she'd previously considered bone-deep. And that was concerning. Of course it was. "What made you so mad about seeing him there with me?"

"It wasn't about you," he said quickly. "It wasn't your fault."

"Well, of course not," she said briskly. "Why would it be?" But that funny, sparkly glow dimmed, the warmth

17

backed off, her throat loosened.

He narrowed his gaze on her face. "Did you think it was?"

"I didn't see how it could be," she said with deliberate evenness. "But I'll admit, it gave me a moment's pause. For a second, I thought you were coming for me."

"Coming for you." Drew held her gaze for a moment, considering it. "Coming for you?" He tipped his head. "To do what?"

The heat flashed back, punishing, intense. She put a hand to her throat automatically. What had she thought he might do to her? She pressed her knees together and cleared her throat again. "I couldn't imagine. I just knew you were mowing through the crowd like the damn Terminator and you were heading my way."

She shrugged, suspected it looked as jerky as it felt and hoped he didn't notice. Drew always noticed more than people thought he did, and how could she explain what she didn't understand?

"Which would probably give anybody who knows you a bad moment, Drew. So..." She lifted an expectant brow, satisfied that she'd put that uncomfortable ball back in his court where it belonged. "...what were you thinking?"

"I honestly don't know."

She considered that for a moment, added in the troubled bafflement in that sweet, expressive face of his.

"Fine. Tell me this, then: Who the hell is Ian Sheffield?"

"Now? I have no idea." He frowned at the floor between them. "Then?" He shook his head. "Even then it was complicated."

"Thumbnail it for me."

He sighed. "You drive. I'll talk."

"Deal."

Chapter 3

Drew strapped himself into the passenger seat of Meg's little Audi. She pulled out of the lot in thoughtful silence, but something elusive and dark moved behind the skeptical green of her eyes. Dismay pinged in his chest

"So I made kind of a scene, huh?" He linked his fingers between his knees, bounced a heel restlessly. "Think they'll ban me for life?"

"From Declan's? Unlikely." She tilted him a sideways look. "Surprised a few folks, though."

"Yeah." He closed his eyes, shame unspooling in his gut. "Damn it. I'm sorry, Meg."

"For what?"

"For freaking out. For losing my shit. For tackling a guy while you were trying to get your flirt on."

"I accept your apology." She primmed up that generous mouth of hers. "I mean, my goodness. All that macho pushy-shovey?" She gave her chest a delicate pat. "My maidenly sensibilities are just a-flutter."

He worked up the smile she'd been aiming for. "A-flutter, huh?" Threw in a brow waggle for good measure. "What kind of flutter, exactly?"

"Not that kind. Geez." She dropped the damsel-in-distress routine to send him a sidelong look. "Tell me, do all roads lead to sex when you're a guy?"

"Well, yeah. We're guys."

"And there's no fixing it?"

"Please don't say fixed. Not after you friend-zoned me in front of a guy I was beating up."

"Ah, yes. The mysterious Ian Sheffield." She lifted a brow across the snug darkness of the car. "Speaking of whom."

"Speaking of whom." Drew paused to assess his mental state. Something he should have done, he realized now, before he'd gotten up to say hello—or something—to the Ghost of Ian Past. But he was fine. The ugly pressure in his chest had eased back. God bless Meg, she'd smoothed him out, hadn't she? Steered them right back onto comfortable, well-trodden ground. A wave of affection for her rose up inside him, tightened his throat ridiculously. He poked her shoulder. "He had your maidenly sensibilities doing the cha-cha, though, didn't he?"

"He had potential." She gave a nostalgic sigh. "Those shoulders were yummy. Plus the accent?" She made the kind of noise Drew had only ever heard her make over Bel's cinnamon rolls, and even then only when they were hot out of the oven.

He frowned. "I have an accent."

"You do not. You're just a word slut."

"I beg your pardon."

"I've heard you bust out a *y'all,* a *you guys*, and a *blokes*, all in the same conversation. Your accent says *I grew up in twenty-nine countries; I can go whatever way you want, just let me know.* Ian's says *I might be Patrick Stewart when I grow up.*"

Drew stared at her. "Patrick Stewart is old. And bald."

"Jean Luc Picard," she said dreamily, and made that yummy noise again.

"You're an accent whore," he told her, disgusted.

"Guilty." She smiled without shame. "Now. Tell me about Ian."

"Right." Drew gripped both knees—they were bouncing again—and let Meg pilot them through the night while he threw his mind back across the decades. "Ian was...Ian was my brother."

"Your brother?" She blinked, startled. "Like for real your brother?"

"What? No. No blood involved. But I was ten when my folks died. Car wreck. James was sixteen, Will was eighteen. Kids themselves, really. But they stepped up. Worked like hell to keep us together."

"I know they did," Meg murmured. "I know it."

"James had had an offer to play soccer for a Premier League farm team in England right before the accident. Mom wasn't going to let him take it." He lifted a shoulder. "So I don't think it was quite as bad for him. He was hurting the same as the rest of us, but he was playing his ass off. Living the dream, you know?"

"Hell of a price."

"Tell me." He sighed. "But Will? He kissed college goodbye to manage James into soccer super stardom."

"And to parent you."

"And to parent me." He stared at the backs of his hands against his knees. "Can you imagine? Eighteen years old, and it's all *hey, welcome to orphanhood and parenthood, all in the same fucked-up moment! Oh and guess what, super genius? No college for you!* Brain like Will's? Giving up his education must've been like cutting off his right arm." He thought about that. "Worse, maybe."

"No lie."

"Screwed him up something fierce. He kept us together but putting himself back together? It took years."

"It took Audrey," Meg said.

"Well, yeah. Her, too." He smiled, fondness blooming warm inside him for his brother's wife. "That girl's a miracle, no question." As was James' wife, Bel. In spite of her efforts to put him on TV. "But prior to the Audrey-and-Bel era, there were some difficult times in the Blake household."

He paused and she let him, though her hands tightened on the wheel.

Finally she said, "How difficult, Drew?"

"More difficult than they had to be, and a lot of it was my own stupid fault." He rolled shoulders that had hunched on him somewhere along the line. "And, damn, I hate talking about this."

"Why?"

"Because I was such a little shit."

"No." She arched an amused brow his way. "You?"

"Shut up."

She laughed and gave his forearm one of those brisk pats. "Spill it, Drew."

"God. Fine." He gave the back of his neck a good scrub and blew out some of the shame and guilt still clutching at his gut. "So Will and James are out there, bleeding and sweating and slaving away to keep us together, right? Family first. Your fight is our fight. What we have we share."

"The Blake brothers' battle cry," Meg said. "I've heard it many times."

"Yeah. Me, too. And when I was ten, it was awesome. Knowing who you are, where you belong, who you belong to? That's what a grieving kid needs the most, and my brothers gave it to me. In spades." He looked out the window. Couldn't face her when he told this part. Couldn't face anybody. The dark speeding past his window was unconcerned. Easier to look there.

"But eventually you get past the shock. You get past just blinking and eating and sleepwalking through your new life, and you realize that the old one's never coming back. You have to live this one forever. And that's going to mean figuring out how the hell to survive in a place where everybody sounds like Patrick fucking Stewart, and your *y'all* just paints a huge fucking target on your back, hillbilly." He paused, startled to find bitterness still thick on his tongue. "By the time I was eleven, I'd figured it out."

"Figured what out?"

"How to get along."

"And how was that?"

"Easy."

"It was easy?"

"No, you *be* easy. Easy for everybody." He rubbed a hand over his mouth, tried to push away the faint sickness still there. "You smile, you agree, you go along. You do your homework without complaining and you pack yourself a nutritious lunch every day. You mind your manners with the adults, and with the kids you figure out when to say *blokes* and who'd rather be charmed by your backwater *y'all*. You learn to expect nothing and be delighted by everything."

"Love the one you're with?" she murmured.

"So you don't miss the ones you're not with, and won't ever be with again." He released a deep breath, hoped the shame would go with it. "I made myself easy to please, easy to raise. I never argued with my brothers. I never argued with anybody. I never gave them a moment's worry."

"Ah," she said, and there was a wealth of understanding in that little syllable. "But not because they shouldn't worry. More because they had no idea what you were doing and who you were doing it with."

"Exactly." He didn't turn away from the window. Still couldn't. "Family was everything to them. I was everything to them. If it hadn't been for me, they'd have just grown up. They'd have been sad to lose our folks that way—okay, pretty fucking wrecked—but they'd have been okay. Will would've gone to college and become whoever he was meant to be. James would've filed for legal emancipation and launched his career, free and flexible. But because of me, they weren't free. They weren't flexible. They were my family instead. Not that I appreciated it."

"You were a child, Drew. You were grieving."

"I was loved," he said flatly. "And I was ungrateful for it."

She let that pass without comment and Drew dragged his mental shit together.

"So I stole my first password when I was twelve," he said finally. "Sister Angelica Marie's. I was the charity case at the local poshy-posh public school—which is what the British call private school for reasons I still don't quite understand. Anyway, they had primo computer equipment— the way rich people do—and a wide-open internet connection, as we trust the little angels. I had the nuns eating out of my hand by 8th year." He sent her a sideways look. "Did you know that Episcopalians have nuns? They do. No on popes, yes on divorce. No on celibate priests, yes on nuns. Good ol' Church of England."

"Fascinating. Get back to the stealing."

"Right. So by the time I was fifteen—this would be tenth year, according to the British educational system—I'd moved up from basic password theft to trading stolen programs in chat rooms and writing 'bots to phish for credit card numbers."

"Credit cards, huh?" She tipped her head. "What did you want to buy?"

"Nothing in particular. I just liked the buying. That's what poor people want, you know. Not the things themselves, but the buying. Wanting is like an itch you can't reach. Buying is scratching it." He shook his head. "But the secret, the thing they don't tell you? You can't actually end the wanting. The wanting is endless. You can always want more. And come to find out, I didn't really want the things or the buying."

"What did you want?"

"The rush. The thrill. Turns out? I like stealing." He gave a weary laugh. "No, that's a lie. I don't like stealing. I like lying. Or maybe I like disobeying. By-product of all that easy I perfected, I guess." He shrugged. "I like giving the rules a salute with one hand and fucking them with the other. Fucking them hard, too." He leaned his forehead against the cool glass of Meg's window. "It was a double life and I got off on it, sure. But it was lonely. At a certain point, you want somebody to know you. To understand who you are. After all, what's the point of being the best at what you do if nobody knows you do it? If nobody's there to appreciate it?"

"I'm not sure your brothers would've appreciated your burgeoning talent for cyber crime."

"Like I wanted them to? They'd have killed me. And worse, they'd have ended the fun. Quick, fast and in a hurry." He huffed out a half-laugh. "Believe me, my brothers were the last people I wanted to know about my shiny new skills. Maybe I'm not as smart as Will—"

"Who is?" she murmured, and in a tone that knocked him off his thread for a second. Meg had a thing for smart boys, he knew. Had toyed with having a thing for Will when they'd all first met. Then Audrey had happened, and Meg was a pragmatic soul. She'd shrugged and let it go. But it still pinched a little to know that Meg had looked there first. First? Hell, only. She'd never looked Drew's way at all. Not seriously.

Which was exactly as it should be, he reminded himself. Because if she had, he'd have taken her up on it in a red-hot second. And would that sweaty, delicious couple of hours— days, if they'd been lucky—have landed them here? Now? Would she still be his dependable Friday night date? The friend who played with him, argued with him, worked with him? The one he called whenever he didn't know who to call? Who came whenever he did? Who told him the truth, the whole truth and nothing but the truth no matter what?

He seriously doubted that.

"Nobody's as smart as Will," he conceded, and without rancor, because nobody was. "But nobody's ever called me stupid, either."

"Not unless you wanted them to."

He laughed again, startled this time. "True enough." He closed his eyes. "You're a sharp one yourself, Meggy."

"None sharper," she said. "And don't call me Meggy."

"Sorry."

"No, you're not." She flicked that away and dug back into the subject at hand like a goddamn terrier. "I'm assuming your grades were stellar, and your teachers loved you?"

"Yes, ma'am. I made sure of it. I had a screen habit, sure, but there are way worse things to be addicted to than the internet, right? It was the perfect babysitter. It kept me home, it kept me quiet. And when we were on the road, it kept me in school. And I was smart enough to keep my stolen goods small and explainable, so the situation was relatively stable."

"Until?" Meg slanted him a look. He felt as much as saw the flash of her eyes reflected in the window. "I'm hearing an until coming."

"You have very good ears. The situation was stable until I met Ian."

CHAPTER 4

"Ah." Meg digested that. "And Ian saw you? The real you?"

"Worse. Ian recognized me. And I recognized him."

"Another thief?"

"And a liar and an outcast. British father, Russian mother, both geologists for British Petroleum. He grew up everywhere and nowhere, either with them on location—wherever that happened to be—or at a fancy boarding school. But he didn't belong anywhere either, and I got that."

"Where did you meet?"

"James had an away series in the Ukraine. Ian's folks were there on assignment at the time. Ian had game tickets with locker room access because he was a fan and his parents were rich. I was there because there was nowhere else to put me. Let's just say we found each other."

"And embarked on a life of crime?"

"The way you do." He shrugged. "Geography is no big barrier when you're a super-hacker, as of course we were. Eventually Ian's folks finished up in the Ukraine and came back to London. We were able to hang IRL."

"In real life." Meg considered that. "Which is sometimes the worst thing ever to happen to a beautiful virtual relationship."

"Not to me and Ian." He closed his eyes again, leaned back into the headrest. Breathed in the buttery scent of good leather. "Well, it probably was but it didn't feel that way. Hanging out with him made me feel...I don't know, whole. Like I'd finally found my people." Shame pooled thick and ugly in his stomach. "Think of that, Meg. James was running himself literally into the ground for us. Will was working three jobs and going toe to toe with the Premier League's barristers over every letter of James' every contract, all on about four hours of sleep a night. And why? To keep what was left of our family together. Me, though? I'm off thinking Ian's my brother because we like to steal shit together over the internet."

"Jesus, Drew, cut yourself some slack, why don't you?" Meg snapped. Drew blinked himself upright, startled out of the memory. "You were, what, fifteen by this time?"

"Sixteen."

"Fine. Sixteen, and you'd lost your parents, your home, your life and anything resembling stability. You met somebody who made you feel normal. Any kid—hell, any person—would glom onto that. Onto whoever or whatever made them feel that way again. Let's just be grateful it wasn't heroin, okay?"

"Heroin?"

"It's a classic for a reason, Drew. And does one hell of a lot more damage to the innocent bystanders than a bad influence."

"You're...right."

"As I so often am." She smoothed a stray hair back into her shiny topknot. "So if you're going to keep telling me this story—and you definitely are—you're going to want to lay off the judgment. If there's any judging to be done, I'll do it. Trust me."

"I do." And he did. Meg was nothing if not up front with her opinions. "There's nobody I trust more."

"Aren't you sweet." Her tone was pure acid and she lifted one hand to make a puppet mouth: *blah blah blah*. Drew had to smile. No wonder he adored her.

"Start talking, buddy. Only hold the commentary and skip right to the part where Ian dies. Or appears to. I'm getting bored."

"Right." He sucked in a breath and focused. "Ian was better than I was. I don't mind admitting it. I was good; he was better. He was better connected, too. He spoke some Russian, thanks to his mother, and had pulled off a couple exploits while he was in the Ukraine that impressed some major players in that part of the world. Once he was back in the UK, his Ukrainian buddies made contact with...let's call it a job offer."

"To do what?"

"Oh, well, let's see. Here we have a half-Russian British citizen with impressive hacking skills, a pretty face, and the best education money could buy. He's also got a gap year to burn and an accent that says *I'm going to be Patrick Stewart when I grow up*." He shot Meg an impatient look across the car. "What do you think they wanted?"

"A minion," she said instantly. "Of course. They wanted a minion."

"They did indeed."

"Ah, but where to position him?" Meg tapped the wheel and thought it over, clearly enjoying herself now that she had the scent. She did love her work. "Now where would a bunch of Ukrainian hackers want to place an inside man? I'm thinking a government agency or a bank. All that sensitive customer information, protected from the employees by nothing but a password." She angled him a look. "How am I doing?"

"No flies on you, sweet pea."

"If you hadn't distracted me with your pity party I'd have seen it sooner." She cast her eyes toward the ceiling, disgusted with herself. "It says *security expert* right on my business card."

"So it does. Which is why you won't be surprised to hear that we landed ourselves a couple of summer jobs in the cafeteria of a major bank."

"The cafeteria, huh? They keep account numbers on the salad bar in jolly old England, do they?"

"Wouldn't that have been nice? But no." He huffed out a laugh. "We were young and stupid but we didn't want to go to jail. Ian decided it would be better for all parties concerned—by which he meant himself and the Ukrainians, of course—if the information leak couldn't be traced to him."

"Which meant he needed to sweet-talk a password out of somebody else." Meg nodded. "Somebody disgruntled and abused, who wouldn't mind watching his asshat of a boss get shit-canned over a security breach."

"Which is exactly how we ended up in aprons and hairnets all summer, tossing salads and chatting up bank tellers."

"Ian in a hairnet." She frowned. "Why can't I picture that?"

"Because his trust fund is in the easy seven figures, and money has a shine you can't rub off."

"He does have a certain dazzle."

"And no hairnet in the world can contain it. Which was handy, actually, as girls like Cinnamon always require some dazzle."

Meg blinked. "Cinnamon? You conned a bank clerk named Cinnamon?"

"Would you believe that she had two older siblings named Anise and Basil?"

"Oh my God. Were her parents just working their way through the spice cabinet?"

He thought about it for a moment. "Alphabetically, I guess."

Meg gave that the moment of horrified silence it deserved.

"So, yeah," Drew went on. "Cinnamon. Girl was built like Jessica Rabbit and sounded like Betty Boop, but her brain ran like a damn Ferrari. She was perfect."

"Of course she was." Meg's lips twisted. "Put a beer in her hand and you're talking about every man's dream girl."

"Every hacker's dream girl, for sure," Drew allowed. "Because after the fact? When it became clear that somebody had breached security at a major bank? Somebody on the inside?" He shook his head. "Who's going to look at Betty Boop?"

"Nobody," Meg said, with some bitterness, and Drew wanted to smooth a hand over that sleek bun of hers. He could read her mind as easily as she could read his. Sometimes.

"Next thing I know Ian's banging ol' Cinnamon like a drum, and in all sorts of creative places." He paused. "Her boss' desk among them."

"And her boss was?"

"The bank's Chief Technical Officer, of course."

"Of course." Meg snorted. "Guy was an asshat, I assume?"

"Naturally. And way more concerned with Cinnamon's cleavage than with securing his password. So when Ian suggested a little post-coital mischief one night—uploading a fun little program that would slide the line *I'm an incorrigible wanker* into every tenth email sent, for example?—Cinny logged him right in."

"Got what he deserved, then, didn't he?" Meg said. "Jerk."

"Guess so. You know what Ian got?"

"Root access without leaving a finger print?"

"Yep. Keys to the kingdom, data-wise." Drew sighed. "And a blow job along with it."

"Spare me the details," Meg muttered. "And you don't have to sound so impressed."

"Well, it's a fantasy of mine," Drew said easily.

"A particularly unoriginal fantasy."

"It's a classic for a reason."

"You're so gross."

"Oh, I am." He linked his fingers over his belly, oddly satisfied by the exchange. "I really, really am."

Meg just rolled her eyes. "And what did our buddy Ian do with this unprecedented access to the bank's highly secured and extremely sensitive information?"

"The usual." Drew waved an expansive hand. "Downloaded passwords and account numbers on a shit-load of high rollers. Inflated credit limits, eliminated overdraft fees and alerts. The Ukrainian boys wanted to keep the fun going as long as possible, you know, which means you don't want the mark getting tagged with all kinds of *you're over your limit* notices."

"And what was your job in all this?"

"I was the bag man." He smiled. "I was bitter as fuck about it, too. I was as good as he was, or nearly. But a chick like Cinnamon was never going to look twice at me, with my don't-notice-me clothes and a twang that comes and goes under pressure. I wasn't the face. Ian was."

"Plus you were, what, sixteen?"

"Almost."

"And he was..."

"Eighteen. But he told her he was twenty-four, and of course she bought it. Which only made it worse for me, because I couldn't pass for twenty-four until...well, now-ish. And I'm thirty this summer."

"Yeah." She thought about that. "I can see how that would suck."

"So I was supposed to meet him at the loading dock out back of the cafeteria at, I don't know, oh-dark-thirty or something. He would tell Cinny that he needed something from his bag in his locker downstairs—probably condoms. I'd be waiting outside for him, and he'd hand off the thumb drive with the goods he just stole from the asshat CTO. He'd go back upstairs and continue to screw Cinny sideways. My job was to put the thing into an envelope—unmarked—and drop it into a specific postal box on a specific corner. He'd cut me a little percentage for the work, but it was his deal. I was never in contact with his Ukrainians." He stopped, amazed that he could still feel the sting of the slight, the burn of his best friend's mistrust.

"That must've chapped your ass," Meg observed.

"Oh, it did. Might've saved my life, too."

"Yeah?"

"Yep. I was on foot—nobody drives in London—so I was sitting across the alley in an all-night café, drinking coffee and playing on the Gameboy I couldn't use at home because my brothers would wonder where the hell I'd gotten it, and when I'd learned to use it. I got absorbed I guess, because when the shitstorm went down across the alley I was still sitting there diddling my damn video game instead of standing next to Ian. Who was in the middle of said shitstorm."

He stopped, brought back the memory like it was a photograph. "I busted ass out the back door—along with half the staff and every other customer in the place, mind you— and the loading dock across the alley is lit up like high noon.

Spotlights, the whole deal." He swallowed. "Ian's standing on the loading dock, hands in the air, eyes the size of saucers. Probably a dozen burly dudes all around him, weapons drawn, Secret Service plastered across the back of their jackets."

"Well, crap." Meg frowned. "What was the US Secret Service doing in London?"

"They do more than just protect the president, you know."

"Cyber crimes and financial fraud, I know." Meg pulled into the Prince George Hotel, angled into a spot and killed the engine. "They'd been tracking the Ukrainians?"

"Evidently. They wanted to bust up that ring—bad—and Ian must've looked like the weak sister. He'd have been a right handy inside man, too." He paused. "If they hadn't shot him."

"They shot him?" Meg's eyes were huge in the darkness. "Why the hell would they shoot him when they could've turned him into a mole?"

"Because he was eighteen," Drew said bitterly. "Eighteen and stupid along with it. They had him surrounded, guns drawn, remember? And they're all shouting at him to get the fuck down, down on his face, hands up, get down. They were very, very clear on that. And what does Ian do? What does that stupid fucker do?"

Meg didn't answer. He hadn't expected she might. Meg knew when to shut up. It was a particular gift of hers.

"He reached into his jacket," Drew told her. "He reached into his goddamn jacket, probably for the thumb drive. He was just going to give it to them. Here you go, boys. Shit got real, game over, you know? He was just a kid. A kid. Only the feds didn't know what he was reaching for, now did they? How could they?"

"What happened?" Meg asked softly.

"They opened fire is what happened." Bile rose in his throat at the memory, at his brain's helpful replay of Ian's body jerking like a puppet on its strings. "They killed him right there in front of me. I watched it happen." He swallowed it down, the grief and rage and cowardice. "I watched it happen and I didn't say a word." He forced himself to look at her across the car, to meet her eyes directly in the darkness. "I went home."

"And you think that was the wrong choice?" She didn't look away. "What do you think you should've done instead? Jumped out of the bushes and let them shoot you, too? Gotten your ass arrested so they could use you as their inside man with the fucking Ukrainians, who were clearly nobody to screw with? Or, no, wait, maybe you could've used your god-like powers to revive your dying friend while the Secret Service looked respectfully on?"

He scowled and looked away. "He was my brother," he said flatly. "Next thing to it, anyway. I shouldn't have left him. I shouldn't have been able to."

"Oh, fuck that." She pushed into his space. "First of all, you were sixteen and powerless. You saved yourself. You survived. Don't ever apologize for surviving, Drew."

He opened his mouth and she said, "Shut up."

He shut his mouth.

"Second, you obviously didn't see your friend die. Because he's inside right now, waiting for us. Waiting to tell you what really went down that night. And I'm willing to bet it's not anything like what you thought it was. What you thought you saw? Fiction. And you've been beating yourself up about it for nearly half your life. So before we go in there, Drew, you'd better leave all that guilt and shame and misinformation right here. Because you're not going to hear the truth—you're not going to be able to hear the truth—if you drag that shit in there."

She pushed a finger into his chest, hard enough that he could feel the sharp bite of her nail through his sweater. "Do you hear me, Andrew? What you think you know, what you think you saw? Leave it here. Forever. It was wrong, and you need to reassess. Got it?"

He studied her in the darkness, the fierce light in her eye, the hard set of that curvy mouth of hers. Those strong bones, and the unapologetic opinion.

"Yeah," he said slowly. He released a breath, let it all the way out. It was the first time he'd really breathed in an hour. "Yeah. I got it."

"Now, are you ready to get in there or do you need another minute to pull it together?"

He considered that. Considered her. "Nope. No, I'm good."

"Then let's go hear what the dead man has to say."

CHAPTER 5

They found Ian in the hotel bar. He sat in the far corner, his back to the wall, frowning into the beer between his elbows. The instant Meg's eyes landed on him, his head came up with a quick, animal-like awareness. The kind of awareness, she thought, that kept a guy alive when other people wanted him dead. The kind that made her wonder what exactly he'd been up to these past fifteen years.

The kind that made her wonder if she really wanted to know.

He raised a hand to them and Meg, suddenly uneasy, snatched at Drew's sleeve before he could respond.

"Drew, wait," she said. "Are you sure you want to do this?"

"What, talk to him?" He frowned down at her. "I have questions, Meg. He's got answers. I deserve to hear them, don't you think?"

"Well, yeah, of course." She hesitated. "But what if you're better off—safer—not knowing those answers?"

He grinned. "What, you think he's going to pull one of those *I could tell you, but then I'd have to kill you* deals?"

She scowled at him. At the laugh lurking in his voice. "I'm just saying. Normal people don't have the skills to fake their own deaths quite so effectively. Nor do they have friends—or enemies—who do. We don't even know which camp you fall into yet. Maybe we should sleep on this."

"Sleep on it." A skeptical brow flew up into the nut-brown bramble of his hair. "Like I could sleep?" He took her hand from his sleeve, twined his fingers through hers and shook his head. "The curiosity alone would kill me, Meg. You know it would. I don't think it's much of a risk, but I'm going to take it. I have to."

She blew out a breath, one she hoped would erase the dread still wriggling around in her belly. It didn't. "How did I know you were going to say that?"

"Because you know me." He gave her hand a warm squeeze.

"Which makes me wonder why I even bothered asking in the first place."

"Because you love me."

She shook her hand free, irritated by his impenetrable serenity.

"And the fact that you did," he went on calmly, "is why I love you right back."

She closed her eyes. Drew's love was the one constant in her life. The one thing that never shifted, moved, or went high-drama on her. He viewed life as one big semi-comic show that ought not to be taken too seriously, and that was exactly why she loved him. She had no idea why he loved her back. She knew only that he kept showing up. So she would too. Always.

"Just..." She lifted her eyes to his, to the warm laughing brown and let them hold a moment. "Let's try not to get killed tonight, okay?"

He spread easy hands. "Works for me."

What didn't, she wondered? But she didn't demur when he put a hand in the small of her back to start them forward. Warmth bloomed where he touched her and she wondered if he knew he did things like that. Opened doors for her, nudged her through them ahead of him. Such a gentleman for a guy who refused to hold her damn purse.

The hotel lounge was a long, rectangular bump-out attached to the back of the lobby. A skinny bar ran down the left side and a line of narrow red velvet booths ran down the right, all of it snug under a slanted, heavily beamed ceiling. The whole place whispered *upscale antique* in a way peculiar to northern Virginia, where age conferred prestige. Meg's heels clicked over the uneven floorboards with a confidence she only wished she felt.

Ian slid out of the booth when they arrived. "You made it. I was starting to think you were going to stand me up."

"No chance of that." Meg slid into the booth and sent him a bright smile that was more teeth than warmth. Drew slid in beside her. "Drew was just bringing me up to speed. It took a minute."

"Yeah." A look passed between the two men as Ian took his seat across the table. "I'll bet."

A waitress appeared at the edge of the booth in a droopy sweater and thick-soled shoes that said she'd put nonsense in the rear-view a solid twenty years ago.

"Y'all drinking tonight?" Her tone suggested they should give it up as a bad plan, go home and watch TV.

Drew smiled at her with the slow charm he gave all womankind. "Matter of fact, we are."

She shook her head like she'd been afraid of that. "What'll it be then?"

He dropped his eyes to the name tag on her nubby sweater. "Well, what's on tap tonight, Tracy?"

She pointed at Ian's glass, stone-faced.

Meg grinned in spite of herself. "Who could refuse an offer like that?" she asked Drew.

"Not us," Drew said.

"Certainly not." She gave Tracy a brilliant smile and pointed at Ian's glass. "I'll have what he's having."

"Make it two," Drew said.

Tracy sighed deeply and wandered off. Meg turned back to Ian. "Did you know this place is one of the oldest businesses in the country?"

"Is it?" He linked his fingers and gave her his attention.

"Yep. Been in continuous operation since the 1700s. We're sitting in what used to be the stables." She patted the table. "These booths were converted from horse stalls."

Ian looked around respectfully. "Is that so?"

"It is." She leaned in, her smile sharp and bright. "So there's been enough shit shoveled up in here to last several lifetimes. We'd just as soon not shovel any more."

"I see." He shifted those startlingly pale eyes to Drew. "So you have filled her in."

"As much as I knew," Drew said. "The rest?" He shrugged. "I figured you could fill us both in at the same

37

time."

The waitress stumped over, plunked down a couple napkins and planted the pints on them.

"Thanks, Tracy," Drew said. She stumped off again without a word. Drew watched her go. "I might love that lady," he said absently.

Ian grinned, amusement transforming his face from perfect to breathtaking in a lightning-quick flash. "No, you just want her to love you." He turned that grin on Meg. "Fifteen years and he hasn't changed a bit."

Meg maintained a pointed silence. She didn't trust breathtaking any more than she trusted perfect.

Ian's grin faded and he cleared his throat. "Then again, fifteen years is a long time."

"It is," Meg agreed. "It really is."

"Let's bridge the gap, then." Drew lifted his beer in a toast. "To old friends."

"To fresh starts." Ian lifted his glass. They both looked to Meg. She wasn't particularly excited about either one but dutifully lifted her glass to theirs.

"Cheers."

"Amber lager," Drew announced as he set down his glass. "Little bit of fruit on the backside. Nice."

"Wouldn't have killed Tracy to mention it, though," Ian said.

"I don't know," Drew mused. "It might've."

"Speaking of getting killed." Meg nudged her glass aside and folded her arms on the table in front of her. "Drew tells me he watched you get shot to pieces."

"He did." Ian met her eyes steadily.

She exchanged a look with Drew. "Sounds like a story to me."

"And I'm going to tell it to you. All of it." He put his elbows on the table, fitted his fingers together and frowned. Then he lifted his eyes to Drew's and smiled with a ferocity that took Meg aback. "But I just have to say first? Goddamn it's good to see you, Drew." He shook his head on a chuckle that was part bewilderment and part delight. "Of all the bars in all the world, I had to walk into yours."

"Yeah," Drew said, his gaze admirably even. "What were the chances?"

Ian's smile dimmed. "Not good, I'll admit. And given the whole faked-my-death thing, you have every right to be suspicious. But honest to God, Drew, I had no idea you would be there. Or anywhere in this part of the world, for that matter."

"What are you doing in this part of the world?" Drew asked.

"New job," Ian said. "It's just one fresh start after another tonight."

"Congratulations," Meg said. "But I think we're getting ahead of ourselves. We should get back to how you're not dead, Ian. Because, unless I'm misinformed, my buddy Drew here attended your funeral."

"I didn't, actually." Drew didn't look away from Ian's face. "There wasn't one. His parents were too distraught. They just posted the obit in the *London Times* and moved away." He narrowed his eyes on Ian's face. "Didn't they?"

"They did. But they weren't distraught. And I wasn't dead." His eyes didn't waver. "Those were simply the terms of the deal."

"What deal?"

"The Secret Service had a laundry list of my misdeeds." He shrugged. "I'd been a very bad boy, Drew."

"Yeah," Drew murmured. "I know. God knows I tried to keep up."

"Didn't, though." Ian's lips curved. "Lucky you. After the Americans shared my—let's call it my resume, shall we?—with MI6, staying in England wasn't an option. They wouldn't revoke our citizenship but my parents were advised—strongly—to make their home base in Moscow. As for me? I moved to Las Vegas—by way of Toronto—where I became Ethan Silver, ex-pat. Pleased to meet you."

"Ethan, huh?" Drew considered that.

"You can call me E, if it's easier. Most do."

"I'll try to remember that." He shook his head. "E. My God."

Meg frowned. "Why Vegas?"

"Why Vegas?" E arched a brow. "Have you ever been?"

"No. If I want to see naked women dancing, I can just go to Maxwell's." She held his gaze. "It's closer."

"But it's not Vegas." Drew's smile flashed quick and bright. "And believe me, I've done my comparison shopping." He turned to E. "My brothers are family men these days but once upon a time—" His sigh was deep and nostalgic.

"They were legends," Meg told E solemnly.

"We were." He shook his head. "We really were. At Maxwell's for sure. Possibly Vegas, too. But this would've been, what, ten years ago?" He glanced at Meg for confirmation.

"About that." And she ought to know, because eight years ago, they'd been handcuffed together in a dingy police station while Drew explained to the sheriff that he and his brothers were reformed men and this was all a grave mistake. Drew was quite convincing when he wanted to be. Lucky for Meg, he'd also been telling the truth.

"After my time," E said, squinting at the mental math. "Just, though. I only spent four years in Vegas—long enough to graduate college—then jumped over to southern California. You Blakes cut quite the swish, I take it?"

"Quite," Meg said. "I understand Vegas was their favorite weekend get away for a while there."

"Well, then. Perhaps I'm glad I missed it." E sent her a rueful smile. "I was under strict instructions to keep a low profile at the time. I'm sure the jealousy would have killed me. Not that it would've been anything new." He turned back to Drew. "I always envied you, you know."

"Did you?" Drew shot Meg a sidelong look she couldn't read.

E lifted a brow. "You must've known it."

"I knew there was a rub somewhere." Drew shrugged. "I wouldn't have called you envious, though."

"No? What then?"

"Competitive, maybe." He kept thoughtful eyes on E, but turned to speak to Meg. "E never liked being bested," he told her. "Especially not by me."

"Did you best him often?" she asked.

"Are you kidding?" Drew laughed. "Jesus, Meg, look at him."

Meg made a show of inspecting E, who returned the regard soberly. Finally she said, "He is pretty."

"Pretty?" Drew snorted. "He smiles and girls' panties fall off."

"Oh, nice."

"And let's not even get into his trust fund." Drew shook his head. "He's the original Guy Who Has Everything." He turned his attention back to E. "And yet he envied me. Imagine."

"You had family," E said quietly.

"Half of one, anyway," Drew shot back. "The other half died in a car crash when I was ten." Those warm brown eyes weren't laughing now, and Meg's heart squeezed in her chest. "How are your folks, anyway, E? I hope you'll give them my best."

"It sounds ungrateful, I know." E didn't look away from Drew's scorn, though Meg had the impression that it cost him. "Maybe it was ungrateful. I wasn't neglected, not by any means. I certainly wasn't abused. I was just...unnecessary." He shifted those big shoulders again. "Extraneous. I had a beautiful home, my own line of credit and a staff to look after me. But you? You had something else entirely."

Drew gave a quick bark of incredulous laughter. "Tell me about it."

"That's not what I mean." E leaned back, stretched one arm across the back of the bench seat, studied Drew closely. "You might've been badly supervised and occasionally overlooked but you mattered, Drew. Your brothers loved the hell out of you."

Drew didn't move, didn't shift, not visibly. But Meg could all but hear the thud of that arrow finding its mark. The fucker across the table still knew how to hit Drew where it would hurt the most.

"Yeah," Drew said finally. "They did."

"And I wanted that. What you had. What they gave you." E didn't flinch away from the bald avarice in the words. "But I knew I couldn't have it." He turned to Meg. "My parents are good people, mind you, but intellectuals. They simply weren't capable of strong emotion. It wasn't that they didn't love me. It was more that they couldn't." He shrugged and turned back to Drew. "Being so denied, I felt entitled to take other things. Your things, especially. Anything you had that I could win, cheat or steal away, I did. Because you had the one thing I wanted most, and couldn't ever have."

He spread his lips in a smile now, fierce and ugly. Meg wondered how she'd missed this piece of him. He wasn't *that* shiny and sparkly.

"I was a royal shit, Drew. I pushed us both into dangerous waters, simply for the pleasure of proving myself your superior. In dress, in looks, in skill. For the thrill of making you aware that I was welcome in circles where you were nobody."

"It was never enough, though, was it?" Meg asked. The sound of her own voice startled her; she hadn't meant to speak. But recognition sat like a cold brick in her stomach. She knew what it was to be stuck in a family that simply had no room for you. Patient neutrality was far worse than bitter hatred. "Taking what wasn't yours," she clarified. "It didn't fill the hole, did it?"

E cut her a shrewd look and she carefully blanked her face. "It didn't. I was on the verge of figuring that out for myself. I like to think I was, anyway. Getting shot to death sped up the process considerably."

CHAPTER 6

Meg greeted this statement with patient silence, the sort that took apart bullshit statements like cheap appliances. The sort that broke down lying clients with devastating efficiency. The sort that E, Drew noted with amusement, was no more immune to than the incompetent tech people Meg eviscerated on a daily basis. A beat or two of Meg's skeptical eyebrows and E was shifting in his seat and dropping his eyes.

Was it any wonder, Drew thought, that he adored her? Hell of a game face, his Meggy.

"Well." E cleared his throat. "Perhaps it was the actual arrest that was so edifying."

"Really?" Now Drew sat forward, interested. He'd been arrested a handful of times himself. It had taught him what not to do the next time he broke that specific law, but in terms of personal growth? He hadn't found it particularly enlightening. "How so?"

"Cinnamon liked you." E smiled but it looked bitter around the edges. "Did you know that? It drove me mad. I was better looking, a better hacker, and definitely better off. Why would she even notice you?"

"Because he's not a dick?" Meg suggested helpfully.

Drew pointed at Meg. "What she said."

She leaned in and rounded her eyes at E, as if imparting a grave secret. "Girls are kind of smart sometimes."

"Yes, Cinnamon mentioned as much when she arrested me." E gave the table a rueful pat. "Lesson learned, believe me."

"She arrested you?" Drew's mouth fell open, shock erasing all amusement. "Cinnamon did? Holy hell, she was Secret Service?"

"Near enough. She was on loan from MI6. Laid a pretty little trap for me and I walked right into it."

"Dick-first, too." Meg snorted. "Which is absolutely what you deserved for being one."

"No argument." E gave her a puckish grin. "I was a dick, and struggle with dickish tendencies to this very day."

Meg gave him a stony stare. "No. You?"

E laughed. "Oh, I do like you, Meg."

More stony staring. E sobered and Drew bit back a grin. Ah, Meg. He was going to lay a big fat one on her at his earliest possible convenience, friendship be damned.

"Fresh starts are rare beasts," E said to Meg, all sincerity. "Seldom cheap and never easy, as I have good reason to know. Cinnamon handed me one fifteen years ago—along with a Kevlar vest and instructions on how to take a barrage of rubber bullets—and I took it. Fate handed me another one tonight. I'll not be screwing it up. It'll be full disclosure from here on out."

"Full disclosure." She leaned back, folded her arms. "This should be interesting."

"Wait, wait, wait." Drew waved a hand to cut off the byplay. "Back up. I need to understand this." He pointed at E. "You're telling me you were doing an *MI6 agent*? On the CTO's desk?"

E cleared his throat. "Oh, well, as to that? Not precisely."

Drew lifted a brow. "Not precisely?"

"Or, you know, at all." He gave them a winning smile. "The same dickish tendencies that led me to covet your family? They also led me to, ah, imply that my relationship with Cinnamon was a bit warmer than it actually was."

"Damn it. I was afraid of that." He sighed. "I spent years fantasizing to those stories."

"As well you should've done. They were excellent stories. I was lacking in morals, Drew, not imagination. Plus? She was a walking wet dream."

"Amen," Drew said with near-reverence. He really had enjoyed those stories. He tried to decide if it made a difference to his enjoyment that they weren't true. Nope. He grinned. Still good. "My sixteen-year-old self appreciated them a great deal, even as he seethed with jealousy."

"Well that was part of the attraction for me, wasn't it?" E's smile was crooked, rueful. Honest. Meg frowned at him with palpable skepticism but Drew's gut was reading this as straight-up. "Lording my fictional conquests over you was delicious. Not as delicious as Cinnamon would've been, of course, but as I'd not be tasting any of that—she'd been quite clear on that score—I had to make do, didn't I?"

"Did you ever," Drew murmured.

"And then she arrested me." E's lips twisted. "She had me dead to rights, you know. Caught me with my proverbial pants down, if not my actual pants. Pity, that." He paused. "I offered her you instead."

Meg's eyes went hot and narrow. "You what?"

"I offered her Drew." E didn't look at her but kept his eyes pinned to Drew, his fingers knitted neatly together on the tabletop as if in prayer, though the knuckles showed white. Confessing, Drew understood suddenly. Admitting his sins. For what, though? Absolution? Did he think that was within Drew's power to grant?

"For the first time in our history," E said, his voice low and steady, "I gave you full credit for your skills, your brains, your accomplishments. I told her you were a brilliant hacker with a gift for endearing yourself to all and sundry. I explained in excruciating detail what a valuable asset you could be to the Secret Service, and that I could deliver you. Hell, that I would gift wrap you and hand you over. But she was having none of it."

"Why the hell not?" Meg frowned at him, switching mental tracks with her usual blistering speed. "She didn't need to choose, not with the way you were running your mouth. Which—sidebar—only means you're a dick and an idiot. Upon arrest? You shut up. Immediately."

"Thank you. I know that now." E studied his linked fingers with deep concentration. "And believe me, I've wondered the same over the years. In my haste to offer up a tastier alternative, I babbled out all sorts of incriminating details on our friend Drew here. She could've easily had us

both on the strength of that alone—a two for one special."
He lifted baffled shoulders. "End of the day? She wanted
me, not him."

The truth of that settled on Drew's shoulders with a
familiar weight and he suppressed a sigh. Because, fuck it, E
was right. People liked Drew just fine. And why wouldn't
they? If likeability was an art, he'd perfected it. So, yeah,
people liked him. They enjoyed him. Appreciated him. But
nobody had ever wanted him. Not really. Not even the
arresting officer, evidently.

"You're disgusting." Meg bit off the words with an icy
rage that had Drew blinking at her. She leaned toward E with
cool deliberation, her hand spread on the table between
them. Her voice was even, her face smooth, and yet each
word was a lethal blade. "You're a disgusting worm of a
human being, E. He thought you were his brother."

Drew's chest went tight and hollow, and he simply
stared. Meg was...furious. Utterly enraged. And he'd never
seen anything like it. Not that she was one to hold back. It
was the rare thought that passed through Meg's mind
without bulleting out of her mouth. But when it came to the
contents of her heart, she played a much tighter game. So
this simmering fury, just under the surface, barely controlled
and on his behalf? It was out of bounds. Way out.

"Easy," he murmured and touched her knee with his
under the table. "It was a long time ago."

"What the fuck does that matter?" she snapped, still
glaring at E. "You gave this jerk your loyalty and he sold
you out! And now he thinks there's a fresh start on the
table?"

"Tried to sell me out." Drew nudged her with his elbow
this time, waited for her to turn the laser-eyes on him. She
did and the shock of it sang straight through his skull. Damn,
Meg gave good glare. "And failed."

"And that absolves him? That Cinnamon-the-Secret-
Agent thought she could get more mileage out of his perfect
face and superhero shoulders without a sidekick?"

"Why shouldn't it?" He studied the man draped
casually across the bench seat opposite, all chiseled

46

cheekbones, striking coloring, and—fuck, he had to admit it—great shoulders. He shifted, uncomfortable with the novel pinch of envy. He was too lucky, he reminded himself, too damn fortunate to waste time on envy. Usually.

"We can't all be superheroes, Meggy. I never even wanted to be." He forced an easy shrug. "We sidekicks get way better lines. Also? We don't have to wear tights and nobody shoots at us. And when it comes down to brass tacks—or arresting officers—we're not the one the ladies want. It's a sad little fact that works in his favor ninety-nine percent of the time." He hooked a thumb E's way, though he aimed his smile at Meg. "When it doesn't? It's kind of awesome, so let's not ruin it with a bunch of yelling."

She gave the glower another moment, her curvy lips pinched flat, and he leaned in. Gave her another cajoling nudge with his elbow. "Come on, Meg. You have to admit it's kind of delicious. I mean, look at him over there. Of course the ladies love him. He takes it for granted. Did you hear him just now? He didn't say as much but he's still sort of surprised—genuinely—that Cinnamon declined to screw him silly."

"Oh, well, now—" E began.

"You know? You're right." Meg turned, peered at E like a scientist studying a smear on a slide. And not a particularly nice smear, either. "He was."

E sighed and those shoulders sagged. "Dickish tendencies," he mumbled. "Daily struggle."

"Keep struggling," Meg advised. "Only harder."

"Right." He straightened, tried a grin. And it was, Drew felt compelled to acknowledge, charming. Did this guy never quit? "Faint heart never won fair lady, what?"

Meg shook her head but Drew could see the smile tugging at her mouth, trying to curl up those wicked lips of hers. That weird, envious pinch twisted inside him again, startlingly sharp, but why? He had a darn charming grin himself; he had it on good authority and from multiple sources. He might not have quite E's luck with the ladies, but he was no pariah. He did just fine. And he'd never been one to waste time begrudging others their successes. Much better to just concentrate on your own.

"Peace?" E extended a hand across the table to her. "I meant what I said earlier, Meg. Regarding fresh starts. I'm certainly not perfect but I've come a long way from the boy I was. I know a bit more now about how to appreciate what I've been given, how to keep it safe. Drew was a rare friend, and Fate's dropped him back into my lap for some reason. I'll take care."

Meg studied that outstretched hand for a long moment. Then she put hers into it. "I'll be keeping an eye on you."

E's smile flashed bright and wicked. "You can keep anything on me you like."

She rolled her eyes and took back her hand, but flushed prettily. "You just never quit, do you?"

"When there's such a lovely prize to be won?" E leaned forward, elbows on the table, invading her space just enough that the color on Meg's cheekbones deepened. "Oh, dear, no. I never do. Faint hearts, fair maidens, etc., etc."

She stared. "You're not even delivering the lines anymore," she said. "You're just referencing them." She cast Drew an incredulous look. "Was he always this...smarmy?"

"Oh, no." Drew waved that off, but the pinch in his gut bloomed into a clenched fist. Because, holy hell, Meg was attracted to E. For reals. She was. Roses in her cheeks, sexual awareness buzzing all around her. Drew could practically smell the pheromones. He rubbed a casual hand over his chest, hoping to ease that ridiculous cramp. "He used to be worse. This is quite restrained, from what I remember."

"Really?" Meg turned her attention back to E, tipped her head and considered him. "Wow."

E gave her one last melting look, then turned to Drew. "I'm sorry, mate. For everything. But mostly for hating you."

Drew lifted a shoulder. "Nothing wrong with hating a guy. Some bastards deserve it."

"Ah, but I hated you while pretending to be your friend."

"Yeah." Drew studied him, searching. It had been years,

but once upon a time they'd been as close as brothers. Nearly, anyway. Which meant that Drew had always been able to read him. E hadn't known that, of course. He probably thought he'd well and truly concealed his gleeful superiority but Drew hadn't survived—hell, thrived—in rich-kid-landia by misreading people. He knew exactly how much E had savored his superiority, how he'd gloried in the ugly thrill of rubbing Drew's nose in it. Nothing new there, not to this scholarship kid. That shared delight in mischief, though? That mutual gift for e-based larceny? Being utterly himself with somebody? That didn't come along every day, and more than made up for the dickish tendencies. It had at the time, anyway. "I guess you did."

"And that was unforgiveable," E said, regret in every line of that I'm-so-handsome face. "But I'm hoping you'll forgive me anyway."

He stretched a hand across the table for Drew to shake, and Drew only barely concealed a start. It was a damn risky move. He could totally leave the guy hanging. Right in front of a pretty girl, too. The old E—Ian, he supposed—would never have risked it. Drew eyed that hand, wondered if E really had risked it, or if those dickish tendencies of old simply hadn't allowed him to realize that rejection was even a possibility.

Then he brought his eyes back to E's. And saw pure self-loathing. It was right there in the rueful twist of his lips, in the knowledge in his eyes as his peace offering hung in the air between them, the moment stretching from awkward to uncomfortable. E knew exactly what he'd risked. It was a peace offering. Not the handshake itself, but allowing Drew to choose—right here in public, and in front of a potential sexual conquest—whether or not to accept it.

The clenched fist inside Drew finally released. He put his hand in E's. Not Ian's, he told himself. E's. Shook.

"Fresh start," he said.

Relief bloomed on E's face and his grin was brilliant. "Damn," he said. "I thought you were going to leave me hanging."

"Thought about it," Drew said, grinning back. "You

deserved it."

"I know."

Meg studied them with folded arms and a cocked brow. "You're not going to hug it out, are you? Because if you are, I want out."

Drew laughed. "Just when I think you're a total guy."

She drew back, offended. "You think I'm a guy?"

"Well, of course not." He patted her hand and shared a laughing look with E. "I'm just saying, if the genders at this table had been reversed, you—the guy—would not have minded hanging around while the two girls hugged it out."

"In fact," E said, "you'd have waited for it with bated breath, praying the whole time that somehow our clothes would fall off and we'd begin wrestling."

"Ew." Meg wrinkled her nose. "There's a mental picture I'll never be rid of."

"You're welcome," E said solemnly and lifted his glass in salute. Meg sighed and just that fast, everything inside Drew that had been out of place slid back home. He hadn't really even known himself how fucked up his insides had been until it had all fixed itself. Until Meg fixed it, really. Until she'd restored normalcy by being so dependably normal.

"Ah, Meggy." He clinked his glass to E's and smiled at her fondly. "You're such a girl sometimes."

"For which I thank God routinely," she said, and clinked her glass to theirs. "But don't call me Meggy."

"Right," Drew said with patent insincerity. "Sorry." They all threw back the last swallow of their collective beers and Drew peered around the bar. "Now where do you suppose the lovely Tracy has gotten off to? I do believe we could use another round."

CHAPTER 7

Three hours later, Meg was on her third cup of coffee and Tracy's fourth marriage. Or was it the fourth cup of coffee and the third marriage? She couldn't remember, but she definitely had a new insight into Tracy's less-than-sunny outlook on life.

The waitress gave the bar between them a desultory swipe with a damp rag. "So then he tells me—get this—he tells me that if I'd been a little livelier in the sack, he might not have had to look elsewhere." Tracy sighed. "Like it was my fault he fell into bed with that man-stealing slut-whore."

"Jackass," Meg said and sipped her truly awful coffee. A sudden burst of laughter rang out from the back booth and she turned to see Drew and E slapping each other's shoulders and howling like idiots over yet another hilariously illegal exploit from the good old days.

"I know, right?" Tracy huffed out a sour laugh. "Jason the jackass."

"It does have a certain ring," Meg said absently, her attention still on the bromance blooming in the back booth.

"Truth usually does." Tracy narrowed her eyes. "I mean, honestly. He thought I'd buy that shit? Just because I drew a few hard lines in bed he thinks it gives him the green light to do my daughter?"

"Whoa." Meg jerked her attention back to Tracy. "The man-stealing slut-whore was your daughter?"

Tracy flapped her rag dismissively. "Step daughter. She was Ray's girl—"

"Ray was husband number two?"

"Three."

"Jason was four, then?"

"And two. Pay attention, chickie."

51

"Right." Meg paused, blinked. "Wait, two and four? Really?"

Tracy slumped inside her saggy sweater. "Really."

"Okay." Meg shrugged. "Elizabeth Taylor gave Richard Burton two tries, too."

Tracy brightened. "She did, didn't she?"

They both indulged in a moment of silent appreciation for Richard Burton, then Tracy sighed. "She always was a trashy little thing."

Meg cocked her head. "Elizabeth Taylor?"

"No, Carly. The man-stealing slut-whore." Tracy shook her head gravely, dragged the coffee pot out from under the bar and topped off her cup. She jacked a thinly plucked brow at Meg in silent question.

"Yeah, hit me." Meg had hung with the boys for three rounds and endless tales of remembered glory. She'd switched to coffee maybe an hour ago, the better to drive Drew's drunk ass home. Somebody had to think about logistics, after all, and lord knew it wasn't going to be Drew. No, he was too busy with his new best friend Ethan—E, Meg reminded herself sourly—to think that far ahead. To think at all. Because as far as Meg could tell, he hadn't even noticed that she wasn't right there in the booth anymore, matching him drink for drink, story for story.

She fought the scowl but evidently didn't win because Tracy patted her hand.

"Men suck, baby girl. Break your heart, take your money." She nudged the creamer Meg's way. "Better to just keep your legs closed and your PIN private."

"My legs are closed." She lightened her coffee and gave in to the scowl. It felt marvelous. "And he doesn't want my money. Or my heart."

"Now that's a shame."

Meg frowned at her. "But you just said—"

"I said you should keep your bed to yourself. I didn't say he shouldn't be trying to get into it." She went back to dragging her rag over the bar at random. "That's the good part, you know." Something almost wistful softened her face. "When they try."

"Try." Meg snorted. "Like he ever tries at anything."

More hilarity ensued in the back booth and Tracy glanced up. "Smile like that?" She shook her head. "Don't expect the boy has to try at all. Or not very hard, anyway."

"I know, right?" Meg couldn't help it. She looked, too. Drew had simply surrendered to laughter, his face buried in the crook of his elbow while he pounded the table with the other fist. It was E who still sat up, gesturing widely, his beautiful face lit up like a priceless painting.

"Oh," she said. "I wasn't talking about him."

"Who, the pretty boy?" Tracy abandoned the rag again and leaned a hip into the bar. "Neither was I." She lifted her coffee for a leisurely sip. "I was talking about that long, tall one with the slow smile and the eyes."

"The eyes?" Meg blinked. "Don't they both have eyes?"

"Not the same, they don't." Tracy did smile this time. Tiny, crooked, grudging. But it was definitely a smile. "You wait tables as long as I have, you get used to people looking at you but not seeing you. Pretty boy there? He just looks. Your fella?"

"Drew," Meg supplied, mildly fascinated. "His name is Drew."

"Your Drew, then."

"Not mine. Just Drew."

Tracy waved this off. "Whatever. He sees."

"Sees what?"

"Not what. Who."

"Who, then?"

"The folks who serve up his fries and change his oil, that's who." She sipped her coffee contemplatively. "Asks our names, and not because he's a hipster shithead who makes an ironic point out of name checking the staff. He actually wants to know who's bringing his beer, even if she's bringing thirty extra pounds and twenty extra years along with it. He just likes people, that kid. All people, right, and not only the hotties like you."

"I'm not a hottie," Meg said automatically. "I'm the ugly twin. And I have very large feet."

Tracy leaned forward for a look. "Sure do, sugar. But

you're what, six feet tall?"

"Nearly."

"And you wear heels." Tracy gave her a look that approached admiring. "Bless you, child. Legs up to your earlobes and he's not trying?" She sipped her coffee in wonder.

"He did try." Meg felt compelled to admit this. "Once. A long time ago."

"Yeah?" Tracy's brows went up. "What happened?"

"He kissed me."

"Did he now?" Her eyes danced over the rim of her cup. "And?"

"And nothing." She gave a jerky shrug and pushed aside her own coffee. Her stomach was already jumping; there was no point throwing more caffeine at it. And if there was a hot pulse of something more dancing with the caffeine, something old and long-buried that had sparked to life when Drew had stalked across a crowded bar, his hot eyes pinned to her, fury all over his face? Well, she wasn't going to think about that. "I told him to knock it off."

"Aw." Tracy's nose wrinkled with disappointment. "That bad?"

She wanted to say yes but again, honesty compelled her. "No, actually. It was fine." Better than fine. Sort of mind-blowing, actually. "He was...good at it."

"But you told him to stop?"

"Yep."

Tracy cast her eyes to the ceiling. "Why?"

"Because—" She blew out a helpless breath. Ah, hell. "Because I liked him."

The waitress stared at Meg for a long moment, then set aside her coffee cup. She put both elbows on the counter and leaned in. "So let me get this straight. The guy is kind and funny, has a smile that lights up the damn room, and has some skills in the sack."

Meg's cheeks went hot. She wasn't totally sure about that last one, but she suspected. "Well, I haven't given it a lot of thought but—"

Tracy cut that off like the nonsense it was. "And you

told him to stop kissing you how long ago?"

"Eight years," Meg mumbled.

"Eight years." Tracy snorted with disbelief. "So he's hung in there for eight solid years of cheerful, sex-free friendship?"

"Well, yeah, but it isn't like I forced him to—"

Tracy's hand went up like a stop sign. "And he isn't interested in your money, you say? Has his own?"

"Plenty." She fought a squirm. Why did she want to squirm? This had been a good decision. A very good decision. Hadn't it? "I said he was smart, didn't I?"

"Trust me, sweet pea, it's not *his* brains I'm questioning."

Meg scowled. "It's just better this way."

"Yeah?" Tracy folded her arms across that droopy sweater and leveled her a look of deep skepticism. "How's that?"

"Because Drew loves women, all right?" It burst out of her, surprising in its vehemence. "All women, just like you said. Doesn't care if they're fat or thin, old or young, pretty or ugly. He loves them all, unconditionally."

"Bless his heart," Tracy said promptly. "Why not let him love you, too?"

"Because he wouldn't love just me, would he?" Meg shot back. "He'd love me and you and the pretty sales clerk and the next woman who happens to sit beside him on the Metro. Because that's how it is when you love something. You can't resist a shiny new one, not even if the one you've already got is awesome. There's always a next one, isn't there? Always a better one, or a different one, or just a more interesting one. Why limit yourself when there's a whole world of women out there to enjoy?" She was talking too fast. She forced herself to stop, to take a calming breath before she went on. Slower. "It's like you said—the guy sees people. He can't not see them. It's just who he is, and I'm not going to change him. Why would I want to? I like him. Everybody does. He's a great guy."

Tracy lifted a dubious brow. "A great guy who goes through women like Kleenex?"

"Yeah, that shouldn't work, should it?" She shrugged lightly. "It does though. He totally makes it work."

"Really." It didn't sound like a question. "How?"

"I have no idea." She smiled brilliantly. "But he does. He never hurts anybody's feelings. Not on purpose, or even otherwise." Meg felt compelled to make her understand this for some reason. "He falls in love twice a week, and falls out just as often. Nobody takes it seriously, though. Not even him. Because that's the thing, right there. He doesn't want to be taken seriously. Not by women, anyway. Not by anybody, now that I think about it." She reached for her coffee cup again. It was cold, but she didn't care. She wasn't going to drink it. She just wanted something in her hands. "But, Tracy, you know what he does take seriously?"

"What?"

She lifted her eyes and found the other woman's steady on hers and full of something perilously close to sympathy. "Family." She forced herself to meet all that blunt understanding without a flinch. "Women come and go but his family? That's forever."

"And you like him," Tracy said softly.

"I do," Meg said simply. "I love him. I always have. He's my brother. Closest thing to it, at least." Raucous laughter rang from the booth again and Meg let her lips curve along with it. For the first time that evening, the smile came naturally. "Which is why I'm going to do us all a favor and get his drunk ass home." She patted the bar and rose. "Thanks for the coffee."

Meg turned and strode off toward the back booth, prepared to part Drew from his new bestie by whatever means necessary.

"Meg, wait."

She turned, found Tracy standing there, head cocked, eyes shrewd and weary.

"It was a good move." She lifted her rag in a curiously helpless gesture. "Telling him to knock it off with the kissing, I mean. You're a smart girl. Damn smart."

Something inside her chest protested like a rusty gate so she slapped on a jaunty grin. "I am, aren't I?"

"Too smart, I hope, to believe your own bullshit."

Her grin wilted. "Excuse me?"

"That boy's not your brother, honey. And you know it." Tracy went back to wiping the counter. "You don't have to tell him so. But don't lie to yourself."

"I'm not lying." Meg stared at her. "He's my best friend."

"Of course he is. Any fool can see that." She scooped up Meg's abandoned mug and emptied it into the sink. Met Meg's eyes very directly. "But he's more than that. Much more. I can see it, and I think you can, too."

Meg opened her mouth but no words presented themselves. She only stared blankly at Tracy, mouth open, mind empty, tiny wings of panic beating inside her chest.

Tracy's smile was sad and knowing as she hefted a dish tub onto her hip. "Y'all drive safe now."

"Yeah," Meg said faintly, frowning as the woman disappeared through the swinging door to the kitchen. "Thanks."

She turned and walked slowly down the row of booths.

"Meg! You're back!" Drew beamed at her with the charmed delight of a man not one hundred percent sober. "Where've you been?"

"With our fair Tracy at the bar," E told him. "I saw them chatting."

"Chatting?" Drew scoffed. "Right. Like Meg chats."

Meg stiffened. "I chat."

"Please. You hate conversation."

"No, conversation is fine. Tracy gave good conversation." She frowned, still chewing on that parting shot of hers. "Pretty good," she amended. "It's small talk I hate."

"Really?" E surveyed her with interested eyes. "Why?"

"Well, it's just so small." She smiled sweetly at him. "If I have to indulge, I like something I can sink my teeth into."

Something hot and focused flashed into those silvery eyes. "Is that so?" he asked softly. A slow prickle crawled over her skin and she couldn't decide if it was sex or fear. Hard to tell the two apart sometimes, in her experience. Then she realized that she'd taken an involuntary step away from E. Closer to Drew.

And, damn it, that was probably her answer right there. E was like a panther, sex and danger dripping from every sleek line, and she responded to that. Of course she did. She was female and he was very, very male. But there was something slippery and not quite right underneath that, a menace slipping around under all the dazzle, and she didn't trust it. Didn't trust him.

To be fair, she didn't trust anybody. But she actively distrusted this guy.

"Nothing personal." She kept her smile firmly in place, let that unsettling shimmer of sexual awareness surface in it. Guy like E would expect that, would need the proof that he was hitting the mark. It was better to give him what he expected for the next little while. Just until she figured out what the hell was going on. "I just get bored. Make it worth my while or let me go home, you know?"

Drew laughed. "There's my little introvert."

"What can I say?" Meg lifted airy shoulders. "I'm task oriented."

"No," E said, utterly deadpan. "You?"

"I know. Shock, awe, et cetera." But she had to smile at his perfect mimicry of her earlier shot. "You know what I really find tedious, though?"

"What?"

"Small talk with drunk people." She slid a hand into Drew's elbow and tugged. "Come on, big boy. Bed time."

"You're taking me to bed?" He punched the air with his free hand. "All right."

E snorted out a laugh and Meg rolled her eyes. "For heaven's sake, Drew."

"All right, all right. I was just teasing you, Meggy."

"Why don't you make up for it by cooperating?" She tugged on his arm again. "And don't call me Meggy."

"Right. Sorry." He slid her a sideways grin with a wicked edge on it, and she realized that he was closer to sober than she'd first thought. "You're ready to take off?"

"Have been," Meg said. "For about two hours."

"Aw." His mouth drooped. "Why didn't you say something?"

"And break up the happy reunion? You were having such a good time with your little friend."

"My little friend." Drew grinned across the table at E. "She thinks you're little."

E shrugged easily. "Most people find me large enough to suit when the, ah, rubber meets the road."

"That's what she said," Meg said automatically and E blinked at her. Drew just roared. He slung out an arm—why was she always surprised by how fast he moved?—caught her by the shoulders and suddenly she was snuggled into his side on the bench seat of the booth.

"I love this girl," Drew told E, giving Meg an enthusiastic squeeze. "Love, love, love her."

"I can see why," E murmured.

Meg gave him a half-apologetic look while Drew continued to chuckle and side-hug the life out of her. "Knee jerk," she said. "Sorry. I spend too much time with this idiot."

"Lies!" Drew snatched at her chin with his free hand and brought her face to his. "Dirty lies! You work every day, and for hours."

"That's true," Meg said, her cheeks squished between his fingers. She lifted her voice to E, as she couldn't turn her head his way. "I insist on working at least an hour each day. I'm funny like that."

"Slave driver!" Drew snarled, as if she didn't work for herself. "Run away with me, Meggy! Make me the happiest man alive."

Meg pursed her lips. Did the best she could, anyway, given Drew's grip on her face. The subject was a well-trodden path between them. "You'd support us, then?"

"Support us?" Drew tossed his head. "Who needs support when you have love?"

"Well, call me prosaic, but I like to eat."

"We would eat! We'd eat pizza and play *World of Warcraft* all day and watch soapy porn on HBO all night! And when we got stinky, Audrey would come upstairs and turn the hose on us." A naughty gleam came into his eye. "I'd scrub your back."

"Gosh, you make it sound so appealing." Meg pretended to consider it. "I think I'll pass this time."

"I'll ask again later," he assured her.

"Great. I'll look forward to—"

Then he kissed her.

CHAPTER 8

To be fair, it wasn't exactly a romantic kiss. How could it be, when the guy was gripping her face hard enough to give her fish lips? He just planted his mouth on hers and delivered a beery, enthusiastic kiss, complete with a hearty *mmmmm-WAH*!

Her brain recorded all this from behind a glaring sheet of shock. Because Drew hadn't kissed her—joking or otherwise—since she'd told him to knock it off eight years earlier. She thought she'd forgotten what it was like.

She hadn't.

She'd remembered, she realized as she stared at him, ears ringing, lips tingling. (Still pooched up, too, thanks to the grip he'd yet to release.) She'd remembered the clean, vaguely piney scent of him. He always smelled green, somehow. Underneath the beer, it was all mowed grass and sunny fields with a shot of toothpaste thrown in for good measure. And when he kissed her, when his mouth was on hers, warm and firm and assured, the scent of him enveloped her. Just wrapped her up in a mind-numbing overdose of Drew. She could live inside that smell, she thought before she could stop herself.

"For Christ's sake," she heard herself say. "What was that for?"

And she sounded absolutely right—impatient, brisk, incredulous. Practice really must make perfect because her voice betrayed not a hint of the chaos roiling around inside her, dampening her palms, unstringing her knees. For fuck's sake, her stomach was trying to jump onto the table where it would probably flop around like a damn fish.

"That, Meggy?" Drew's eyes laughed down at her. No, he wasn't anywhere near as drunk as he should be for having

61

put down half a dozen beers over the course of a single evening. "That was a kiss."

"Yeah, I got that." She knocked his hand away from her face and glared up at him.

"It was a perfectly friendly, utterly non-sexual token of my appreciation for your particular brand of awesome." He smiled, slowly, and she wanted to press a hand to her twitching stomach. "What can I say? I was overcome."

She leveled him a skeptical look. "You were overcome by my awesome."

He nodded soberly. "As I so often am."

She studied him for a long moment, Tracy's challenge floating through her mind like a song fragment you can't get unstuck. *That boy's not your brother, honey. And you know it.* But he'd kissed her like a brother. She had to admit it; there had been absolutely nothing sexual in that kiss. He could've given that same kiss to Bel or Audrey or, hell, even one of the kids. He could've given it to Will or James, for that matter. He'd have gotten punched for his trouble, but that was because there were standards to maintain among brothers, not because he'd put an actual move on anybody.

So this unsettling shot of pure sexual adrenaline she was staggering under? That was all on Meg. That was her deal, and hers to deal with. Certainly nothing Drew needed to know about. And if she had anything to say about it, he never would.

"Well, try to resist in the future, will you?" she said briskly. "I tend to punch when surprised and I'd hate to lay you out for being overcome by my awesome."

"I do try, Meggy." Drew laid a hand on his heart, all sincerity. "It's a daily struggle but I do."

"Do it harder," she advised him and slid out of the booth, relieved to find her knees were up to the challenge.

"That's what she said," E put in, and looked pleased with himself. "I like this game."

Drew barked out a laugh. "Okay, I love you, too." He held out his arms to E across the booth. "Come here."

Meg's stomach settled a bit further. If Drew was offering the same kiss to E, she'd clearly been reading it right.

"Ah, no." E slid out to stand next to Meg. "Thanks."

"Don't take it personally." She sent E a sideways look. "We've just moved into the *I love everybody* phase of Drew's evening."

E sent her an amused look. "He still does that, hey?"

"Oh, yes." She and E watched Drew maneuver his endless legs out of the booth. "Somewhere after the third drink but before the sixth. He's a friendly drunk."

"I am." Drew stood and slung an arm around each of their shoulders. "I really am, but I'm not drunk. I mean, I tried. We both did, but Tracy liked you—" He gave Meg a fond squeeze. "—better than us. She pretty much abandoned the table when you did, and that was what, two hours ago?"

"About," E said as Drew steered them both toward the door.

"We missed several rounds."

"So we did." E went along under Drew's other arm. "We had a good time in spite of the lack of social lubricant, however."

"Yeah, I got that," Meg said dryly. "Everybody in the entire hotel probably got that. You weren't keeping it down like sober people."

"I didn't say we were sober, Meg." Drew gave her another one of those warm squeezes, snugging her up against the lean line of his body from shoulder to knee. There was an answering squeeze somewhere low in her belly, a hot flutter that wanted to bloom into something more. She ignored it. "I just said we weren't drunk."

"You sounded drunk."

"Well, we were having fun."

"Yeah? Doing what?"

He stopped so suddenly that she stumbled. He caught her by both shoulders and spun her to face him. "I'm so glad you asked." A whiff of sunbaked fields drifted her way and she tried not to suck it in like a greedy, pathetic slob. "We need you, Meg."

"You do?" She narrowed her eyes at him, then tried to peer over his shoulder. She wanted to see what E's part in all this was. "Why?"

"Because we're plotting adventure!"

"Oh, God."

"The kind that requires hot girls with mad tech skills." He beamed down at her. "As the best adventures always do."

"Okay, you can stop right there." Meg frowned up at him. "The last time we had an adventure—" She put the word in sarcastic finger quotes. "—we got arrested."

"No risk, no adventure. Besides, what do we say about that in the Blake house?"

"About adventure?"

"About arrest."

She raked her mind for the appropriate line of the Blake family motto. "What we have we share? Because I'm not up for sharing your jail cell, buddy."

"Meg, Meg, Meg." He smiled indulgently at her. "Arrested isn't charged. That's what we say in the Blake house."

"He does have a point," E said from behind Drew's shoulder. "I should know."

"You're not helping, E," Meg told him.

"Right. Sorry. I'll just let you two...work this out."

"Work what out?" Meg asked Drew.

"The adventure we're all about to have." He gave her a confiding little squeeze. "Come on, Meggy. We need you."

"For what?"

"Well, for your technical skills, first of all. They're superior, and for what we have in mind, we'll need the very best. Which is, of course, you."

"And second?" She stepped back and folded her arms. Gave him a deeply disapproving look that bounced off him entirely. "You said *first of all*, which implies a second of all, and possibly a third."

He spoke over his shoulder to E. "Did I mention that I love this girl?"

"Repeatedly."

"I do."

"Cheers."

Drew shifted his attention back to Meg and spread

engaging hands. "Secondly, while neither of us is exactly drunk, neither are we exactly sober. Not sober enough to pull this off, probably." He leaned in. "But we might give it a go, as we're highly motivated for adventure."

She stared, appalled.

He grinned back. "Our judgment is impaired. Save us from ourselves."

She shook her head in pure wonder. "I should leave your drunk asses here and let Tracy have you."

"But you won't." He edged closer, so close that the warmth of him reached out to her, wafted over her lips, her hair. She wrapped her arms around her stomach and looked away. "I know you won't, Meg. Because deep down inside?" He touched the arms banded over her stomach, and something pulsed hot and shocking inside her. "Deep down inside, you like adventure. That's why you like me. We balance each other out. I push you toward the edge and you pull me back. We're better together. Always have been, always will be." He dipped his head until she had no choice but to meet his eyes under that shaggy fall of nut-brown hair. Until she had no choice but to see the affection there, the laughing promise. That razor thin streak of reckless adventure inside all the friendly and harmless that had always called to her just like he said.

"Come on, Meggy," he said softly. "Come play with me."

The ends of his enormous scarf dangled down his chest, and she took it in her hands. Wrapped both fists in it and considered—briefly—strangling him to death with it. Instead, she tugged on the ends until he bent obligingly. She put her mouth next to his ear and said, "Fine."

He all but jumped up in his delight but she'd been ready for him and held the scarf firm. He gave a strangled *aaaack* and stopped jumping. She tugged until he put his ear next to her mouth again.

"But if you call me Meggy even one more time, I'm calling the cops myself and leaving your not-exactly-drunk self in lock up where I will personally make sure that arrested becomes charged as soon as humanly possible. You hear me?"

"Loud and clear, Megg...han." He gave a small cough. "Can I, uh, have my scarf back?"

She opened her hands and he sucked in a grateful breath. She smiled, sharp and mean. "Now. Where are we going?"

* * *

Drew peered out the windshield of Meg's car at a massive rectangle of concrete that squatted sullenly in the center of a vast parking lot. Despite a complete lack of windows, Northern Virginia Data glowed from the bottom up like some malevolent alien war craft sliding in under cover of night to decimate the human population and appropriate the planet. And Drew ought to know. He played a lot of video games that began with exactly this plot device. Probably it was just landscaping lights, though.

"This is it?" He turned to E in the back seat. "This is your new job?"

E leaned forward, one elbow on either of the seatbacks in front of him. He rested his chin on his linked fingers and gazed out at the building. "This is it."

Drew turned back to consider it. "It looks like a bunker. A really good one. In the event of a nuclear holocaust, you're set."

"Better than you know. It goes down six additional stories," E told him. "My office is on the second floor from the bottom."

"Really?" Meg draped an arm over the wheel and leaned forward herself. "Why?"

Drew blinked at her. "Why is his office on the second floor?"

"No. Why does a private company that sells server space need a six-stories-underground bunker?" She turned to E, her face grim in the watery light of the dashboard. "What's on those servers, E?"

He shrugged. "How do I know? It's not our business, is it? Our business—see how I'm doing that? Already identifying the company's goals as my own?" He grinned at her. "I'm going to be an excellent employee."

"You are." Drew patted his arm. "You're going to kill this."

"Your business?" Meg prompted. She really was task oriented, God love the girl. No radar for subtle crises of confidence, no talent for the there-theres or the hair patting that came as naturally as breathing to most women. Luckily, Drew's self-confidence was such that his hair rarely needed patting. Other portions of his anatomy appreciated a good pat, but he didn't look to Meg for that.

Memory flashed, hot and sharp, of her lips under his in that cramped little bar booth half an hour ago. She'd tasted like coffee and surprise, the edge of her jaw sharp and uncompromising under his fingers. Fingers that had wanted—for the briefest of instants—to soften. To trace and learn and explore. Because Drew knew what she looked like, what she sounded like. He even knew what she smelled like—warm and woodsy and achingly feminine, which was weird because he happened to know that she wore men's cologne. Said she'd rather smell like power and sex than flowers and sugar. Meg was full of odd ideas but he had to admit, she might be onto something with that one. She smelled incredible.

Which was maybe why it had occurred to him suddenly that he didn't know what she felt like. He knew her with his mind and his heart—and, obviously, with his nose—but he didn't know her with his hands. And for one brief moment, his palms had literally itched to change that.

It had sobered him up right quick. He'd only been half in the bag anyway, his mind just clouded enough to have laid one on her in the first place, even that half-assed, chicken-shit smackeroo he'd opted for. But then his lips were on hers, and the urgency of his need to touch, to learn, to know had shocked him into instant clarity.

A clarity that Meg, evidently, had never lost sight of, judging by the epic eye roll with which she'd greeted his efforts. Which was why, he reminded himself, he and Meg didn't kiss.

Wasn't it?

"Our business," E said, "isn't asking what's on the servers. Our business is keeping it secure for our clients."

"I see." Meg nodded wisely. "Which is why we're breaking in? To demonstrate said security?"

"We're not breaking in," Drew said quickly. "Not technically. E signed his employment contract this afternoon, right?"

"I did." E patted the briefcase at his side. "As of three-forty-five this afternoon, I'm officially the Chief Security Officer at Northern Virginia Data. Would you like to see the contract? I have a copy."

"You know, I wouldn't mind." Meg held out a hand. E rustled in the briefcase and laid it on her. She didn't turn on the interior lights—affection for her filled him; his Meggy was no dummy—but held the papers up to the glow of the dash and squinted.

"Think of it as a penetration test," Drew said. "Nothing you haven't done a million times."

"With full knowledge of the company concerned," Meg murmured. "That's actually the difference between a routine pen test and breaking and entering, you know. That the people in charge of security are paying us to break and enter, just to see if we can. It's a technicality, true enough, but an important one. Makes all the difference between arrested and charged."

"But E is in charge of security. He's the new CSO. It says so right on those papers in your hands."

"Sure does." Meg handed them back to E. "Tell me again why you want to kick off your tenure as CSO by breaking into your own office in the dead of the night?"

"Because at this point I'm still anonymous. But come Monday, I'm officially on the clock and the announcement will go out, company-wide. By noon, anybody I haven't met face-to-face will have seen my picture, gotten my name, and Googled me into infinity."

Meg's brows rose. "You think? Why would the average employee care about a new fat cat upstairs?" She paused. "Or downstairs, as the case may be."

"Because the average employee spends a significant portion of work time each day enjoying social media, internet shopping or—everybody's favorite—watching porn. If the new CSO's a git, well, that fun could end, now couldn't it? They'd be curious about me. Possibly even concerned, depending on exactly how they entertain themselves on the internet."

Meg took that in, and Drew understood that she'd known the answer before she'd asked the question. She'd just wanted to see if he'd give her the right one. She was interviewing him, like late-night borderline-illegal hijinks were a corporate position and she was choosy about her colleagues. He wondered if E knew how much was riding on this conversation.

"I should look familiar, at the very least, to every single employee by Monday afternoon, latest," E went on, as if unaware of Meg's scrutiny. "But tonight? This weekend? I'm still a stranger. Nobody in that building has ever so much as heard my name, let alone clapped eyes on me."

"You didn't interview here?" Meg's brows went up. "Surely you at least came in to sign your contract this afternoon."

"Well, as to that." E smiled engagingly. "Not precisely."

Drew knew that smile. There was more to the story. Fuck, when wasn't there more to the story when it came to E? "How precisely, then?"

"As it turns out, my predecessor doesn't actually know he's getting the boot." E dropped his elbows to his knees, leaned between their seats to chat more comfortably. "He's a bit...volatile. It's part of the reason he's about to become the former CSO, and the board of directors isn't at all confident that he'll take the news with any grace. They're keeping it quiet until the very last minute."

"It's midnight on Friday, and the guy doesn't have a job come eight a.m. Monday," Meg observed. "Hasn't the last minute already come and gone?"

"Not quite. My first task on Monday morning will be sliding into Valor's office—that's his name, by the way,

Edward Valor—"

"Really?" Drew laughed, delighted. "He sounds like a hero."

"Doesn't he?" E shook his head. "And that's the salient question here, isn't it? Whether our friend Valor is a hero or a villain? Because he's slated to meet with the CEO at 8:30 Monday morning, at which time he'll be given the news of his termination, effective immediately."

"Here's your box, here's your escort, thanks for the memories?" Drew shook his head. "Harsh."

"But effective." Meg studied E. "That's what I'd have recommended."

"It's what I recommended, too."

"You're the mastermind on this?" Drew asked, startled.

E smiled at him. "I interview quite well."

"No kidding." He was acing Meg's, whether he knew it or not. Drew gave an admiring whistle.

"And what will you be doing while Valor's getting canned?" Meg asked.

"Me? Why, I'll be sitting in Valor's own office chair, busily changing his passwords and revoking all permissions. Closing any nasty little backdoors he may have left open for himself." E's smile went sharp and ugly. "Any hacker worth his salt leaves himself backdoors, of course. It's just what they do, as automatically as breathing. Sneaky little weasels like Valor, though? They build bombs. The kind they can rig to blow for maximum damage when they themselves are safe and away. But bombs can't be blown if the system doesn't recognize the trigger." E's face was stony in the faint light, the lines harsh and uncompromising. "So I'm going to erase the bastard."

Drew stared. "Remind me never to go up against you when a job is on the line."

"*Never go up against a Sicilian*—" Meg murmured.

"*—when death is on the line*," Drew finished. "Truer words."

E looked back and forth between them, then shrugged, the menace sliding off his face between one breath and the next. That was new, Drew thought, that ability to shift

70

mental states as easily as changing a shirt, and it reminded him yet again that E wasn't Ian anymore. At least not precisely, as E himself would say. It would bear watching but for now Drew just grinned at Meg. They'd come a long way if she turned to *The Princess Bride* for moral guidance. She didn't grin back but her eyes did. That clear bottle green warmed right up with humor and shared knowledge, and something deep inside him preened and opened at this tangible proof of her affection.

"The fear," E went on, "is that Mr. Valor isn't going to be taken by surprise. As the CSO, he's got his fingers in any number of pies that are off limits to mere mortals. And he strikes me as the sort to keep an ear to the ground and a bobby in his pocket."

Meg looked at Drew. "Do we know what that even means?"

"He's got minions," he translated. "Paid—or compensated somehow—to keep him informed."

E nodded. "As a result of which, it's entirely possible that he's aware of his pending termination and has primed any number of nasty little explosions."

"A pre-emptive strike?" Meg asked, gazing thoughtfully at the weird glow of the building.

"Or perhaps a demonstration of his indispensability. What better way to ensure his job security than to light a fire that only he can put out, after all? I imagine he's prepared to keep doing just that until the Board of Directors comes to its senses and stops trying to seize back what he views as his own personal fiefdom."

"Yeah." Meg nodded slowly. "I see where you're going with this."

"So you'll help us?" Drew asked. "We need one more set of hands for what we have in mind, and nobody's are better than yours."

"Then there's your legs," E murmured.

"Also nobody's better," Meg said.

"Truer words," E said, grinning. "And there's no quicker way to short circuit higher-order thinking in a building full of geeks than to present them with a hot girl."

"Yeah, only I'm not a hot girl. I just have good legs." Meg frowned. "I usually don't have to explain that so much over the course of a single evening." She paused. "Or, you know, at all."

Drew didn't know about that, but he reached over to pat her knee. Her bare knee, as her skirt was very straight and her seat was very low. A funny little thrill zipped from his palm straight to his dick and he added it to the growing list of things to think about later.

"Hot's in the eye of the beholder," he assured her. "And with the amount of leg you've got on display there? Believe me, nobody's going to be beholding anything else."

CHAPTER 9

Meg sighed but didn't argue. Hadn't she discovered the same thing herself? She was basically and temperamentally a pessimist—as all good security experts should be—but when it came to personal grooming, she knew how to accentuate the positive. She was never going to be short, so she owned being tall. High heels, endless legs, unapologetic hair. She worked that action.

Much to her surprise she'd discovered that people—in their surprise that a woman would take such a flagrant pass on self-effacement—were usually suckered into believing in the illusion of her...well, if not her beauty, at least her appeal. They somehow overlooked the prairie-flat chest, and the sharp-boned face that missed pretty by a country mile, and saw only what she wanted them to—excellent legs, a sharp mind and a sharper tongue.

Not that she had any choice as far as the sharp tongue went. That was just how she was wired. Good thing, too, as her chosen profession was still very much an old-boys club. Blatant misogyny was nothing but white noise in the high-tech world, a background buzz that conveniently drowned out the sound of women's voices, no matter how expert. Happily, Meg had been throwing her thoughts into conversations like live grenades since she'd learned how to speak.

It was hard to ignore a live grenade.

It was also hard to like a live grenade. Meg knew this. Just like she knew that—like it or not—you never ignored one. And Meg would rather be hated than ignored any old day.

"Gosh, Drew, thanks," she said tartly. "You can take your hand off my knee any time."

He gave it a fond squeeze, then withdrew his hand. Slowly. Awareness crawled up her thigh with a sneaky heat that she carefully ignored.

"So." She turned to E, who was watching the byplay with unreadable eyes. "How are we getting in?"

"I was thinking about tailgating."

"It's a classic for a reason." She glanced around. The parking lot was starting to fill. Not *fill* fill, as it was nearly midnight and the lot could easily hold the population of a small city, but cars had begun to filter in as they'd sat there, discussing breaking and entering. Or least entering. "Shift change?"

"At midnight, yes. We're an eight-to-four, four-to-twelve, twelve-to-eight company." He smiled. "We. I did it again."

"Way to go, bro." Drew patted his forearm.

"ID badges?" Meg asked.

"No, as I didn't imagine I'd be doing this tonight. I'd reckoned on tomorrow but then I ran into Drew and—"

"And you both ran face-first into several beers and here we are."

"Yes, well, liquid courage and all that."

Meg only stared at him.

He cleared his throat. "I did, however, take the liberty of snapping a photo of the ID badge of the admin with whom I met—off site, of course—this afternoon to take care of the employment paperwork." E dug into his pocket, came up with his phone. "It's not the best photo but it'll serve."

Meg squinted at it. "Generic."

"Quite."

They both shook their heads. Meg didn't like to think that companies victimized by hackers got what they deserved, but really, was it that hard to take basic precautions? She said, "Be right back."

Drew all but clapped his hands. "Here comes the bag of tricks. I love this part."

"Bag of tricks?" E lifted a brow.

Drew grinned. "Just wait for it."

Meg stepped out of the car and circled to the trunk.

Pulled out the black valise that doubled as her rolling office.

"Okay." She settled back into the driver's seat and wedged the bag into the space between her and Drew. "Let me see that photo again."

E handed over the phone and she gave it to Drew. "Hold that for me, will you?"

He obligingly held up the phone displaying the photo of the ID badge while she unzipped the valise and spread wide the vast array of compartments and trays and pockets.

"Bag of tricks," Drew said in tones of deep satisfaction while Meg sorted through a stack of ID badges for the closest match to Northern Virginia Data's.

E blinked at her extensive collection of badges. "Not your first rodeo, Meghan, darling?"

"Hardly." She selected three badges and clipped them to the lanyards she pulled from a different pocket. "I do this for a living. Didn't Drew tell you?"

Those guarded silver eyes shifted Drew's way. "Not precisely."

Drew gave him big, innocent eyes. "I didn't want you to be sad if she said no. It would've been a big blow. Meg's the best."

"It certainly looks that way." E eyed her valise with respect. She handed him a lanyard, looped another around her own neck and dropped the third over Drew's head herself. "Wait, we're all going in?"

"What did you think?" Meg asked, her tone deliberately cool. "That one of us would assume all the risk?"

"Well, yes. I assumed it would be me, of course. Why expose all of us?"

"Because one person is memorable. Even a pair of men you don't recognize sticks with you. Toss a woman into the mix, though, and the harmless factor jacks right up. Who's going to worry about holding the door for—" She checked their ID badges quickly. "—Ben and Max and Kaitlyn, jogging in a couple minutes late for shift, chatting about the wonky fan on stack 86?" She smiled thinly. "There's safety in numbers, remember? So smart thieves come in threes."

"And we're smart thieves," Drew said cheerfully.

E divided a glance between them. "You two've done this before, haven't you?"

"Well, not like every other day or anything—" Drew began modestly.

"—but yes. I occasionally employ his lazy ass." She let her fingers drift over the contents of her valise, took the usual comfort in the military-grade organization that allowed her to select her tools without the benefit of the dome light. She tucked various bits of gadgetry into various pockets of her trench coat. She cast a look at E's briefcase. "I assume you're at least minimally equipped for this little assault on your own company?"

"Minimally." She zipped her valise shut and he leaned forward a bit, as if reluctant to lose sight of the contents. She fought a grin. "Last minute, as I said."

"Right." She checked her watch. Five after twelve. Perfect. "Okay, we're officially running late. Let's get this party started."

They stepped out of the car and started across the parking lot at a motivated hustle. The bulk of entering employees had already gone in but there were a handful of stragglers streaming toward the building.

"Let me do the talking," Meg murmured. "You two idiots smell like beer."

"Still?" Drew cupped a hand in front of his mouth, gave an exaggerated *haw* and inhaled. "Wow. We do." He reached for Meg, as if he were going to do a breath check on her, too. Her heart did a quick shimmy so she gave his hand a crisp smack.

"I smell like coffee."

"Oh, yeah." He rubbed his insulted hand and sent her a sunny smile. "I remember."

She remembered what he smelled like, too. And what he felt like. His mouth, his hands...God. She had to snap out of this. "Shut up and focus, will you?" She wondered if she was talking to him or herself.

E strode along behind them, briefcase in hand like a good little employee, and gave Drew a watchful eye. "Is he always this much trouble?"

"Oh no," Meg said grimly. "Sometimes he's more."

"Trouble's my middle name," Drew told him cheerfully.

"Your middle name is Shelley," Meg informed him.

"Oh, yeah. It is." Drew considered that. "Maybe that's why I tell people it's trouble."

"I can see why you would," E said.

Drew sighed. "Mom did like her poets."

"Could've been worse," E said sympathetically. "What if she'd liked monster trucks? Your middle name could've been *Gravedigger* or some such."

"Are you trying to make it worse?" Drew frowned reproachfully. "Because that would've been awesome. I mean, think about the possibilities! I could've been *Bigfoot* or *Snakebite* or—"

"Or sitting in the car because you won't shut up and focus," Meg said.

E said, "That's rather a long one, isn't it? For a middle name?" Drew yelped out a laugh and Meg just shook her head and lengthened her stride. They were closing in on the building, and she wanted them to hit the door just behind the guy hustling in from their right.

A quick glance at the security set up showed a number pad for entering an access code mounted under a NoVD placard but no scanner of any sort. Meg sighed. Passwords and PINs were notoriously insecure. All it took was one chatty idiot and there went the entire building's security. E frowned at the key pad, which she really hoped meant that NoVD—and holy Christ, was that really their acronym? NoVD?—would be splashing out sooner rather than later for an upgrade.

The guy ahead of them punched in his code. The door issued a mechanical buzz, and he shifted his backpack to open it. Meg broke into a trot and grabbed the door just before it swung shut behind him. The guy—practically still a kid, she saw now, maybe mid-twenties at best—turned to give her a look that was mostly surprise with just a whiff of suspicion. Good for him. Then his eyes drifted south and glazed. She could almost hear his brain derail. *Legs*. Poor kid. He probably hadn't been this close to a bare pair of female legs in his life. In real life, anyway. His gaming avatar probably looked like a UFC champion wearing naked women like bandoliers but in real life, he had the pasty complexion and soft build that pointed toward a serious lack of sunlight in his life. And an even more serious lack of cardio. If he had any hobbies that didn't involve staring slack-jawed at a screen for hours at a pop, Meg would start calling Drew *Gravedigger*.

So she appreciated the effort it must've taken for him to drag enough brain cells together to mumble, "You're supposed to key in your own code."

Meg shot him a brilliant smile. "I know but, God, I'm so late." She groped at her own chest—why not give the kid another dirty little thrill while she was at it?—until she snagged the lanyard. She waved the ID badge his way— close enough for him to see, not nearly close enough for him to inspect. He barely glanced at it before his eyes drifted back to her legs.

"I'm legit, swear to God. But if the fan on 86 bites it and I'm not babysitting that thing, my supervisor is going to have my ass." She leaned in confidentially. "He can be kind of a prick about punctuality."

The kid continued to stare but said, "Stack 86, that's..." With an effort he dragged his eyes back to hers, waiting for her to supply the right name. A wave of motherly affection filled her. He was working so hard to do the right thing. Was he actually sweating? She thought maybe he was. She almost hated to take him this way.

"Balzac," E said, swinging in behind her. His American accent was absolutely spot-on. He could deliver the network news and not inspire a single call from a xenophobic hater. "And he's totally going to have your ass, Kaitlyn." E gave her a snotty smirk. "Seeing as you're five minutes late."

"So are you, Maxwell," she shot back with an eye roll. "But you're a man so you get a pass. God, I hate—"

Drew shoved in behind E. "We're all late," he announced with a brisk impatience that startled Meg even more than E's perfect Americanese. "I doubt we have time to get into gender politics in the workplace at this particular juncture. So unless you want Balzac to have all our collective asses, I suggest we move it."

The kid was still blinking glassily at Meg's legs. "You're all supposed to key in your codes," he told her calves.

"I appreciate your attention to security—" Drew leaned in for a close study of the kid's badge. "—Justin. But when protocol and efficiency are in conflict, the thinking man must choose. I give precedence to efficiency." He held up his badge briefly then let it drop. "Benjamin Keillor. I'm sure my fellow employees—bickering fools though they are—will vouch for me. Max? Kait?"

E shrugged. "Stick up his ass that size? Believe me, we wish it wasn't so. But, yeah. Ben's ours."

"Right," Justin mumbled to Meg's legs. "'kay."

"Thanks, Justin!" She gave his arm a warm squeeze. "You're a doll!" She hurried off down the hall, E and Drew at her heels. "Unlike some other people I could mention." She threw this over her shoulder at E, who muttered, "Here we go again with the war on women."

Damn. He was good. They both were.

They strode down hallway after hallway, E giving subtle directions with nothing but his eyes and the occasional jerk of his chin. They kept up the bickering with Drew murmuring *children, children* every now and then—even in the elevator that descended with an efficient and ear-popping swish—until E nodded them into a darkened conference room on the second floor.

The door whispered shut behind them, leaving them in a dimly lit rectangle of a space. It smelled like dry erase markers and was filled nearly to capacity with an enormous, glossy conference table. Drew punched E's shoulder with giddy delight. "I didn't know you could do an American accent!"

"Yes, well, I've had several years to work on it." E grinned and returned the shoulder punch. "Speaking of, when did you learn to do an impression of a grown up?"

Drew buffed his nails on his shirt. "It's just a little

something I picked up."

"He pulls it out without warning," Meg told him. "It's always good for a shock." At least that's what she was telling herself. Because something about Drew getting all business-like had unsettled her, and it had been a very unsettling night already. She didn't need anything else screwing with her balance.

Drew grinned. "For what it's worth, it's always fun to see you pull off the whiny chick routine, too."

"We're all just full of surprises tonight, aren't we?" E said, studying them both. She wondered what he was seeing, and carefully composed her face to show nothing but neutral interest.

"And I do love surprises," Drew said, rubbing his hands together with anticipation. Good for him, Meg thought. That made one of them. "What's next?"

"Valor's office," E said. "Which is, of course, locked up tight."

"Of course," Meg said. "What's your thinking on that?" But she figured she knew. E had been too specific in directing them to this particular conference room for this to be anything but well-planned.

"Well, we can't very well stand about in the hallway picking the lock, now can we?" E said.

"It would be a little obvious," Drew admitted.

"We'll need to go in through the ceiling," E said firmly.

"Of course we will," Meg murmured.

Drew said, "Excellent." His eyes danced with unholy anticipation. Easy for him, Meg thought sourly. He was all jeans-and-sweater comfy while she was wearing a skirt that restricted knee movement to a brisk walk. And she figured she knew exactly where E was going with this.

They all lifted their eyes to study the ceiling. It was the usual—an endless mosaic of 18 square inch acoustic panels, punctuated by sheets of cheap, rattle-prone plastic over long fluorescent lights.

"It's simple," E said. "We'll slide aside one of the panels, and two of us will boost the third up into the crawl space. That person will make their way—carefully, of course, as it's a dropped ceiling and I'm not entirely sure of what local building codes specify in terms of structural strength—to Valor's office. At which point that person will slide aside another panel and drop into the office. A quick phone call to the other two, and they'll skip down the hallway and be let into the office by the third." He spread engaging hands. "Easy peasy."

"Yeah," Meg said darkly. "Easy peasy. Except who's the lucky crawler?"

"Well, as to that." E scratched his chin and exchanged a look with Drew.

"I'm wearing a skirt and heels, for God's sake," Meg said. "I'm nearly six feet tall."

"Which is at least three inches shorter than E, and six inches shorter than me." Drew gave her an encouraging look. "And you weigh, what, one-ten? One-twenty?"

She shot her chin into the air. "None of your damn business." Plus it was more like one-thirty. Christ, she was five-eleven. And she worked out.

"One-thirty, then," Drew said and she scowled at him. "Which is still like fifty shy of me, and at least sixty shy of E. If not more." He gave her what he probably thought was a sympathetic look but Meg knew him. Laughter lurked behind those solemn brown eyes. He was going to enjoy this. "You're the smart choice here."

"I'm afraid he's right," E said. "I think it really has to be you." He took her hand, patted it. "And that's a brilliant suit. I'm really sorry."

"Screw it." Meg closed her eyes and said a prayer for her seams. She peeled off her coat, dropped it on the nearest chair and stepped out of her shoes. "How will I know which office?"

CHAPTER 10

"It's a private office rather than a cubicle," E told her. "He has a Baltimore Ravens mug serving as a pencil holder and a *Go Army, Beat Navy* pennant on the wall behind the desk."

"He's ex-army?" Meg asked. Drew watched with interest while Meg rolled aside a couple of the chairs that hugged the long table in the center of the conference room. "Or just a fan?"

"Ex-army," E told her. "Special forces vet, played for West Point. Goes to the game every year in person. Ravens season ticket holder, too. Fifty yard line."

"Lucky him." She boosted her bottom up onto the table's edge. She tucked her knees to one side, her bare feet to the other and executed one of those neat female maneuvers that Drew couldn't possibly have described afterwards. He only knew that one second she was sitting on the edge of the table and the next she was standing in the center of it, inspecting the ceiling tiles. And she hadn't so much as flashed him her panties.

Not, he told himself, that he was disappointed. He wasn't an ogler. He wouldn't ogle Meg's panties. And if they happened to present themselves, he'd look away immediately. Almost immediately. He was just curious, that was all. It was such a severe suit. Did she balance it out with slutwear underneath? Enquiring minds wanted to know. It was nothing personal. Not really.

He cut a guilty look at E, who was paying him not the least bit of attention. He was too busy gazing at Meg's legs with an air of disappointed expectation that perfectly summed up Drew's own mental state.

He punched E's shoulder.

"Ow," E said, scowling at him. "What?"

"Knock it off." Drew scowled back. "Pervert."

"What, like you weren't hoping, too?" E sighed and went back to the legs. "We're only men."

"No," Meg said idly, pushing a ceiling tile up into the crawlspace and boosting up onto her tiptoes to have a look inside. "You're boys. Horny, juvenile boys who are such losers that an accidental glimpse of a woman's underwear is the biggest thrill they can hope for." She angled a look Drew's way. "Pathetic."

"What are you looking at me for?" Drew spread innocent hands. "I wasn't the one trying to sneaky pete your unders! That was him." He gave E's arm a backhanded slap. "If I wanted a gander up your skirt, I would've asked for one." He paused. That didn't sound great out loud. "Nicely." Still not great. "And probably, like, years ago."

"When I was young enough to be worth ogling, presumably?" Meg went back to peering into the ceiling.

E laughed. "For what it's worth," he said to Meg, "I wasn't sneaky pete-ing anything. I was quite open. You're hot and I thought I might get a look at what's under that skirt of yours. Which, for the record, is also hot." He shrugged. "I didn't."

She angled him a look this time, sharp and cool. "No. You didn't."

"Forgive me if I don't apologize." He returned that look with a slow, wicked smile, and suddenly he was the lady killer Drew remembered from the days of old, right down to the piratical gleam in his eye. Drew's stomach clenched inexplicably. Women loved pirates. Meg probably did, too. Which was totally her business, he reminded himself. If Meg wanted to take E for a spin, what did it matter to him? It didn't. It wouldn't. And yet that fist in his stomach refused to let go, damn it.

E said, "I'll try again later."

Meg paused, both hands hooked over the edges of the hole in the ceiling, still jacked up on her toes. She was little more than a silhouette in the dimness, but Jesus, what a silhouette. She was one long, elegant line from that tight hair

83

knot all the way down to the delicate scoop of her ankle bones, with a whole lot of interesting curves in between.

Not that Meg was the curvy sort. She wasn't. Not exactly. Well, not at all. Her blouse was crisp and white and hugged every strong, straight line of her body. But that was the cool thing about Meg; she didn't waste time trying to camouflage or apologize for the fact that the puberty fairy had forgotten to deliver her boobage. She just wore skirts that made Drew suspect that not only did God exist but that He wanted Drew to be happy.

"You do that," she murmured and went back to inspecting the ceiling. The fist in Drew's stomach tightened one more brutal degree and he frowned. Wait, had she just invited E to try to get up her skirt? He threw a glance E's way, found that piratical gleam firmly in place.

"Yeah," E said. He tucked his fingers into his pockets and rocked back on his heels, a considering eye on that skirt of hers. "I'll do that."

For the second time that night, Drew considered hitting the guy.

"Drew," Meg said, and he jumped, guilty. "Give me a leg up."

E started forward. "I'll do it."

"No," Meg said. She pointed. "I want Drew." His stomach eased a bit and he sent E a smirk.

"She wants me." He got a knee up on the table and Meg slapped his head. "Ow. What was that for?"

"Because you're not even interested in what's up my skirt but you looked anyway." She slapped him again. "Jerk."

"What, it would be better if I were interested?" He gained his feet and frowned down at her, his head inside the crawl space. He bent a bit, just enough to get into her face. "What if I said I was?"

"I'd slap you again," Meg said promptly, "only harder because you'd be lying."

Would he? He gazed down at her for a moment, honestly perplexed. Because this was Meg. He wasn't exactly not attracted to Meg—she was a woman, after all, and Drew just loved that—but he'd spent so many years purposely not seeing her that way. It had become a habit, one he'd cultivated at her particular request. When had he forgotten what she really looked like? When was the last time he'd looked at her and really seen her? Seen *her* and not just who she wanted him to see? Who she said he should see?

Well, he was looking at her now. And he was seeing everything. And Meg's everything, he realized suddenly— uncomfortably—looked pretty damn good.

For a long moment, she gazed back at him, that pugnacious chin of hers just daring him to disagree. He almost did, just for fun, and because he couldn't ever resist tweaking Meg. She was so much fun to fight with. She was just so darn certain all the time. Who could resist? Not him.

His mouth was open to do just that, in fact, when she blinked, an instant of uncertainty flitting across her face. And that strange tension inside him seized savagely. Meg? Uncertain? Of him? Suddenly he couldn't breathe. Couldn't speak. Couldn't even think. He just stared down at her, completely at sea and vibrating with an awareness that was both breathtakingly new and somehow familiar. Like it might've been there all along, bubbling away under the surface, just waiting for its moment to hijack Drew's brain. And body.

She rolled her eyes and the moment broke.

"Yeah," she said, shaking her head. "That's what I thought." Normalcy dropped back in but landed just slightly askew. Drew rolled his shoulders, trying to get back under it. "Okay, come on. Give me that boost, will you?"

"Right," Drew said, giving himself a stern mental slap. He threaded his fingers together and offered it to Meg like a stirrup. "Ready to ride?"

She looked up into the ceiling with an air of grim determination. "Ready as I'll ever be." She grabbed her skirt and hiked until it barely covered the promised land. She put one bare foot in his palms and a hand on either shoulder.

"Drew?"

Her voice seemed to come from a long way off, as his

85

complete attention was now focused on the fact that his face was all but buried in her skirt. The inside of her thigh was practically next to his chin, for crying out loud. If he so much as turned his head, he'd be able to put his lips right there on the shallow inner curve of her thigh.

And, oh for God's sake, now he was half-hard. He'd seen these thighs before, he reminded himself grimly. What, maybe six or seven thousand times over the past eight years? And a lot more of them, too, given that they lived in fucking Virginia and Meg did like her bikinis. *Nothing new to see here, Drew. Move along.*

"What?" His face was all but in her lap and he thanked Christ that it was relatively dark. He and his dick were going to need some privacy pretty soon.

"*Drew*." She flicked his ear.

"What?" He blinked and met her eyes. "*What*?"

She smiled at him, sharp and mean. "If you look up my skirt, I'm going to kick you in the face."

The vicious fist of tension inside him uncurled suddenly in a gush of pure lust. He went from half-hard to raging boner in the space of a nano-second, and didn't know if it was from the purely genuine threat or the slick smile that went with it. Or the idea of looking up her skirt. Probably the combination of all three.

He'd always been a sucker for honesty, probably the result of his peripatetic childhood. Friendships tended to be short and shallow when you moved as often as he had, rarely getting to the point where truth telling was either necessary or desired. But his Meggy didn't have any other speed. And he fucking loved that about her. He never ever had to guess where he stood with her. Nobody did. She just told them.

"Do you want me to close my eyes?" he asked, appreciating the crap out of her. "I can't promise I won't throw you into the wrong hole in the ceiling but I'll be a gentleman about it."

She sighed and gave a few testing bounces. "Oh, to hell with it. Just get me up there."

"You got it, sister. On three?"

"On three." She folded her lips down tight. "One. Two."

"Three," Drew said and boosted. She disappeared into the black hole in the ceiling with a neat jackknife. Like an Olympic diver, if Olympians dove up. After a moment, her face appeared above him.

"I'm in," she said.

E grinned at her. "You two work well together. Done that before, have you?"

"Once or twice," she said. "Which way am I going?"

E made a clock of his hands. "If twelve o'clock is here?" He ticked a hand a couple notches to the right. "Aim for two o'clock, perhaps twenty yards out. Across the hall and down three doors."

"Got it." She disappeared.

"And now?" E dropped into the rolling chair at the head of the conference table. "We wait."

"Fine by me." Drew didn't hop down to join him. His legs just folded and he sank down on the tabletop, flat out on his back, one hand to his heart, the other over his eyes. His heart knocked against his ribs like it was trying to get out and his dick was keeping the beat inside his jeans.

Because, God forgive him, he'd looked. He was only a man, after all, and her skirt had been right there. So, yeah, he'd looked for the panty flash. And nearly had a heart attack.

Because Meg hadn't been wearing any panties at all.

* * *

Meg fixed two o'clock on her mental compass and prayed that she wasn't about to crash through the ceiling like some doomed cartoon character. Drew and E wouldn't abandon her—she hoped—but they would find her out cold, face-planted in the middle of the hall, wearing her skirt like a cape, her bare ass hanging out for all the world to see, thanks to this morning's laundry crisis. Which she very much hoped was still her little secret even after Drew's helpful boost into the ceiling.

It would be better, she decided, to just go slowly and take care.

There was about two feet of space between the pipes above her and the ceiling under her hands and knees. The tiles were suspended by some sort of thin metal grid-work that she didn't trust. At all. So she eased over onto her back, hooked her hands and feet into the much sturdier pipes above and Spidermanned her way in the direction E had indicated.

Ten yards into the estimated twenty, her abs were screaming. Fifteen yards in, her glutes and pecs joined the chorus. Twenty yards and her whole body was vibrating like a damn sewing machine, every muscle reduced to a sloppy whimper. She finally lowered her back to the flimsy grid-work and lay there for a moment, sweating and cursing, while she composed a mental thank you note to her personal trainer. Who was an evil bitch, but evidently did excellent work.

When she stopped panting, she eased back over onto her stomach. She picked a tile at random, dug her fingernails into the soft edge and carefully lifted it a bare three inches. Just enough to put an eye to the crack to see where she'd landed.

Satisfaction zipped through her, along with a healthy dose of relief, because there was the *Go Army, Beat Navy* pennant, right on the wall. She'd overshot the desk so couldn't verify the mug situation, but what were the chances that anybody else on this particular hallway had the same pennant? This had to be the right office.

She let go of the tile and tucked it neatly back into place, then army-crawled back three tiles. That should put her right over the desk. If she lifted out the tile, she could then use the overhead pipework to lower herself to the desk. She added a mental P.S. to her personal trainer's note— *thank you also for the pull ups but I still hate you*—and selected her tile.

She had the corner in her hands and was preparing to slide it out of the way when somebody said, "The fuck you will."

Chapter 11

She froze. Heart, body, mind—it all just seized up on a blinding white flash of shock. She stared down through the lifted tile while a man in an office chair rolled up to the desk—the desk she'd have landed on in about thirty seconds, give or take. He glared at an array of screens sprawling across the enormous L-shaped surface—tablets, laptops, desktops, smart phones—all of them blinking and flashing and scrolling.

He yanked one of the laptops closer to him and went to work on the keyboard, typing at a blistering rate and muttering under his breath.

"Yeah, I don't think so, motherfucker. Don't bring that weak-ass shit up in here." He punched the enter key and turned to a second screen. "Yeah, see how you like that. Asshole. This is my house."

Meg's throat convulsed on an unauthorized swallow, the excruciatingly audible kind. Thank Christ the guy— Valor, she had to assume—was too busy smack-talking his screens to hear her. She eased the tile back into place with sweaty hands and lay there for a moment, her cheek on the cool tile, her pulse hammering in her ears. Then she rolled— with exquisite care—onto her back and gave herself one more moment to just breathe. Then she hooked her hands and feet back into the plumbing and crawled.

Aiming was easier this time, as she'd left the original tile out and a square of ambient light filtered faintly upward. She muscled her way toward it, dropped her feet through the hole and lowered herself into the conference room where she'd left E and Drew.

Drew was still flat out on the table where she'd left him, lying there like somebody had shot him. Probably sleeping off his beer, the jerk, while she had a heart attack in the ductwork. She considered kicking him awake but didn't think she had enough left in the tank for a fight. So she slid to her knees instead, then flopped over onto her back beside him. She gazed up at the black hole in the ceiling from which she'd just dropped.

"Wakey wakey, buddy." She managed a weak flail of her hand, landed it somewhere in the area of his gut and just left it there. "We've got trouble, gentlemen."

Drew muttered something that sounded like, "Tell me about it." He removed her hand from his stomach without opening his eyes, and placed it on the table between them. But he gave it a friendly pat before resuming his nap, or whatever.

E's face loomed into her field of vision. "What kind of trouble?"

"Valor's working late."

Drew blinked and came up on one elbow. "He's in there?"

"Bollocks," E said. He shoved his hands into his pockets and stalked off. "Did he see you?"

"What, like did I drop down onto his desk like a ceiling ninja?" Meg closed her eyes. "Of course not." Okay, so she nearly had. But E didn't need to know that, now did he?

"What's he doing?" E asked.

"How the hell should I know?" Meg opened her eyes and swung her legs over the edge of the table to sit up. Her abs whined pathetically. "He had, like, eight screens going. I couldn't even tell which one he was swearing at." She frowned. "Though based on the one side of the conversation I could hear, I'd guess he was either gaming or hacking. It sounded...competitive."

"Damn it," E said. He pushed splayed fingers though his hair. "If he's onto us—to NoVD, I mean, not *us* us—" He circled a finger between the three of them. "If he suspects what's coming on Monday, that is, this could be bad. Very bad." He stalked off to pace the perimeter of the room.

"NoVD." Drew swung his legs to the side as well and sat up next to Meg, chuckling. "I almost died when I saw that on the key pad at the door." He lifted his voice as E paced by. "Do you really want to work for a company that forbids venereal disease? What fun could that possibly be?"

E paused, frowned. "Forbids...what now?"

"NoVD," Drew said, and grinned. "Your company—Northern Virginia Data?—calls itself NoVD. Said so on the door."

"NoVD." E stared at him for a moment, then shook his head. "I hadn't noticed."

Drew gave Meg a friendly elbow shot. "He hadn't noticed."

Meg's triceps wept. "Easy on the arms. I just gave my personal trainer an orgasm." But she eyed E skeptically. "You really didn't notice the giant placard that said NoVD in all caps above the key pad at the door?"

"I saw it, of course." He gave an impatient shrug and resumed pacing. "But I didn't pay mind to the double entendre. I was rather more focused on getting in."

"God bless Justin," Drew said, pressing his hands together as if in prayer and lifting his eyes to the ceiling. "May he someday get the chance to kiss a real live girl."

"May he also remember to wrap it before he taps it," Meg added. "Or risk being in violation of stated company policy."

"No glovin', no lovin'," Drew said solemnly. "That's our motto here at NoVD, and Justin strikes me as a company man." He patted her knee. "He'll remember."

"Will you two please be serious?" E stopped pacing to scowl at them. "We're having a crisis here. Valor could be over there at this very moment planting enough bombs to well and truly fuck my nascent career straight into the hereafter."

"Nascent career?" Meg asked, startled. "Like newborn?"

"It's a late start, I know." He started pacing again. "But I only just shook free of the Secret Service, didn't I?"

Drew bumped her with his shoulder, though more gently this time. "You didn't think they'd just relocate him, give him a fresh ID and let him go, did you?" He shook his head. "Poor E's spent the last fifteen years playing bitch to the Secret Service."

"What does that mean exactly?" Meg watched him pace. "Playing bitch."

"Developing multiple on-line personas, keeping an ear to the ground, keeping my handlers apprised of anything that rose above the level of scurrilous gossip to actual information." He waved an irritable hand. "That sort of thing."

"Keeping tabs on the Ukrainians?" Meg added. It was only a guess but a good one judging from the cool look E sent her.

"That, too." He gave a shrug. "It paid for college. Which wasn't cheap, by the way. Capitalism does allow for a certain amount of government regulation, you know. Tuition cap isn't a dirty word. One of you citizen types ought to inform a congressperson or something."

Meg ignored this. "And they just let you go, did they? The Secret Service?"

"After fifteen years of paying my debt to society, yes." E resumed pacing, both hands jammed into his hair again. "Fuck me, what's he doing over there?"

Drew shoved off the table and dusted his hands. "There's only one way to find out."

E tipped his head. "What's that?"

"Have a look ourselves."

"Oh, sure. I'll just go knock on his door and ask him, shall I?" E rolled his eyes.

"I was thinking we'd get him out of his office first," Drew said, unperturbed.

"How? Fire drill? Bomb threat?" E clasped his hands and rounded his eyes. "Oh, I know, let's mail him some anthrax!"

"All good suggestions but I think we can do better." He smiled gently at E. "Did you happen to grab a password while you were photo-stalking the admin this afternoon?"

"Of course," E snapped. "When they take absolutely no trouble to enter it privately one feels almost obligated to take note."

Meg cocked a brow his way. "You stole the admin's log in and password?" she asked. "As a matter of principle?"

"Certainly." E turned his frown on her. "Doesn't everybody?"

Drew shrugged. "I do."

"Well so do I but—" Meg pressed a thumb to the frown forming between her brows.

Drew patted her shoulder with some sympathy. "If it makes you feel any better, I doubt that we're representative of the general populace."

"Of course we are." Meg sighed and dropped her hand. "That's why I can afford a personal trainer." She turned to E. "You have your work cut out for you here. This place leaks like a sieve."

"I know it, believe me." Irritation melted into weariness, and he pulled a hand down his face, blew out a breath. "I may be throwing you some work in the future if you impress me tonight." He flashed her a sudden, wicked smile. "Impress me, why don't you?"

Meg gave him a cool stare. "I already did."

"Mmm." His eyes dropped to her skirt. "Yes, you did."

She cleared her throat and pointed to the ceiling.

"Oh. Right." He and Drew exchanged a swift look. "Of course."

"It's Drew's turn now." She waved an imperious hand his way. "You heard the man. Impress him."

"Right." Drew jerked his chin at the briefcase E had left on the floor by the door. "Laptop me. I have an idea."

Five minutes later, Drew was logged into the company's network as Phillip Masters, executive administrative assistant to the CEO.

"Okay, there we go." He punched a flurry of keys and leaned back, satisfied. "Everything *p_masters* has ever stored to the company servers."

Meg leaned over one of his shoulders while E leaned over the other, and they all peered at the list on the screen. "Which is...God, everything."

"Every file helpfully named for exactly what's in it, too." E closed his eyes, pained. "Holy hell, it's worse than I thought."

Meg tapped the screen. "Oh, look. Here's one called *User Names and Passwords*. Handy."

E dropped into the chair next to Drew and put his head down on the table. Drew gave him a there-there on his perfectly tousled head. "People forget that shit all the time," he said. "I'm sure the guy thinks he's being helpful."

E only moaned. Drew shrugged and went back to the screen. He scrolled at the speed of light and Meg hunched lower, until her chin was practically resting on his shoulder. Drew's hands paused over the keyboard.

"What?" she asked, scanning the screen. "Did you find something?"

She turned her head and found her nose about half an inch from his. She inhaled involuntarily and got an intoxicating blast of green grass and clean man. And a little beer. Her brain promptly went bright and blank and she just stared. He arched a brow.

"You're crowding me, Meg."

"Hmm?" She blinked slowly, a little lost in the warm brown of his eyes.

He lifted a single finger from the keyboard, put it deliberately into her deltoid—ow—and nudged her back six inches. "You're breathing up all my air."

"Oh." She cleared her throat. "Right. Sorry. Small screen." She straightened and folded her arms across her leaping stomach. Gripped her own elbows like they were trying to escape. "What are you looking for?"

"Don't know." He resumed scanning. "Know it when I see it."

"You said you had an idea." She found herself sidling closer, trying to get back into his space, trying to catch another whiff of him. Cripes. She ordered her feet to stay put. "You said—"

"Ha." Drew stabbed a finger at the screen and grinned up at her in triumph. She grinned back automatically. That was the thing about Drew. He was so damn contagious. He smiled, you smiled. He laughed, you laughed. He relaxed, you relaxed. For a guy who didn't want to drive, she realized with a start, he spent an awful lot of time at her emotional wheel. "There you are."

"There who is?" She gave herself a shake and tuned back in.

"Not who. What." Drew leaned back in his seat and linked satisfied hands over his belly. "And in this case, what is an inventory of all cars authorized for executive parking, complete with makes, models, license plates and owners." He flexed his fingers and approached the keyboard like a hungry man at a buffet. "What are you driving tonight, Mr. Valor? Let's just find out, shall we?"

E's head came off the table. "What does that matter?"

"It might not matter," Drew said, completely focused on the screen. His fingers flew and Meg's mouth went dry. God, she loved a guy who knew his way around a keyboard. "But my gut's saying that our buddy Valor is the sort to compensate."

"Compensate? For what?" She stared at those big hands of his, moving with such precision and certainty.

"Who knows?" Drew didn't look away from the screen, utterly absorbed even as he held up his end of the conversation. "Little dick? Limited intellect? Short stature? Maybe mommy didn't love him? Everybody's got something, and we all fill the gap somehow. Guy like Valor? I'm thinking car."

"What do you know about Valor?" Meg asked automatically. Arguing with Drew was second nature; she didn't even think about it. It just happened all by itself, which was great because she was staring at his hands like she'd never seen them before. They were so big to move with that kind of delicacy. It made her wonder what else he could do with them, what other sorts of intricate machinery he knew how to operate. Heat bloomed in her cheeks and—oh, hell—parts farther south. "Like you've ever met the guy?"

Drew shoved away from the keyboard, punched both fists in the air in triumph. "Brand new Range Rover Supercharged, black, Virginia plates." He grinned up at Meg. "That would be the one with the 5 liter V8 engine and the 21 inch alloy wheels standard."

"Christ, he'll bankrupt himself in petrol alone." E leaned in for a look. "Plus a Supercharged is a bit...obvious, isn't it?"

"I know, right?" Drew lifted one hand, put a scant half-inch between his thumb and forefinger and shook his head sadly. "Poor guy."

Meg pulled out the chair on the other side of Drew and sank down into it. "Great. So we know what he drives, and his approximate dick size. What we don't know is what we're going to do with this information."

"Where's the executive garage?" Drew asked E.

"Below ground."

"Access via elevator?"

"Of course."

Drew smiled, and it spread across his face like a slow, wicked sunrise. Meg pressed her knees together and looked away. "We're going to get Mr. Valor out of his office."

Chapter 12

Twenty minutes later, Drew had root. For the next hour or so, there was nobody in the universe—or at least in NoVD's universe—more powerful than he. The only thing that could've made it sweeter was getting a blow job along the way.

He gave himself a moment to sigh over that little dream—it was a long-standing favorite—then let it go. It was always good to leave something on the table, right? Something to strive for. Not that Drew was much of a striver. But hey, he had goals. Just not as many or as lofty as most people. Or so Meg informed him.

Then again, it was the dead of the night and he was in an underground conference room (which he'd broken into) with both hands (electronically speaking) deep in the guts of a company he didn't work for. His oldest friend in the world was tucked into the crawl space above a potentially rogue CSO's desk, waiting for Drew's word to drop in and hijack the guy's little kingdom. Meanwhile his best friend in the world was en route to the parking garage three floors down where she would—again, upon Drew's command—violate the guy's SUV. And every security camera in the building answered to him and him alone.

What more could a guy want?

Well, that blow job still sounded good.

He thought about Meg's skirt, about what was under Meg's skirt. About what wasn't under Meg's skirt. He shifted in his chair but there just wasn't any more room in his pants. He sighed and advised his dick to forget about it. Forget about her. His dick told him to fuck off. It was going to stand at attention and aim itself at Meg and that damn skirt until it got what it wanted.

He left his dick to its doomed vigil and flicked through various security cams, waiting for the woman of the hour— hours? How long could a boner last, anyway?—to stroll into the frame. He wondered idly if it was even a Meg-specific boner. What if it was just a generic thing? Because attractive female plus no underwear plus real e-based mischief for the first time in forever? Do the math on that and you could totally end up with "equals raging boner."

He keyed through the security cams again—hallway, elevator, garage. Garage. Bingo. Valor's Range Rover crouched in its parking spot like some sleek, glossy beast ready to spring. Meg strode down the aisle toward it fast enough to send her trench coat flying open behind her like a cape. She threw out each leg from the hip, eating up the distance on those brutally high heels of hers with utter confidence and athletic grace. His dick gave a hungry leap and Drew blinked.

Okay. So the boner was Meg-specific. His dick wanted her. He shifted uncomfortably. It really, really wanted her.

She stopped next to the Range Rover and dug in her purse as if fishing out her keys. Inside the confines of her purse, however, Drew knew she was triggering one of those neat little gadgets Meg always packed. Within seconds, she'd reverse-engineered the radio code of Valor's key fob. The Ranger Rover beeped obediently and unlocked itself. Meg looked up at the security cam and gave it a smile of such silky satisfaction that Drew wondered if he was going to disgrace himself.

She opened the door, slid into the seat and disappeared under the dash. Drew tried to breathe. Just breathe. Because when a girl disappeared under the dash, a guy's fancy turned naturally to thoughts of blow jobs. And Drew's self-control was already stretched pretty thin. If he made it through this evening without putting his hands—let alone his lips or, God help them all, his optimistic dick—on this girl, it would be a bona fide miracle. How was he supposed to resist, when she was all sleek and mean and skilled and smart? Not to mention smoking fucking hot, a tiny fact that he'd somehow missed or ignored for the past eight years.

How the hell was he supposed to resist?

He didn't know. But he'd try. He'd try, he told himself grimly, because that was what Meg wanted. Because that was what Meg had asked him for, and it was the only thing she'd ever asked him for in all the years he'd known her. So he'd give it to her. And he'd keep giving it to her if it killed him.

Which it might.

But he'd be a stand up guy for her or die trying.

Stand up, his dick mused. *Well, we've got that part covered.*

Drew barked out a laugh at his own expense. God. He was so screwed. Then Meg's head poked cautiously over the dash, and he tuned back in. Watched her sweep the horizon with her eyes. Drew flipped through screens until he found the security guard putting along on a golf cart on the other side of the garage.

He shot a message to Meg's phone. *Clear. Move it.*

The Rover's door swung open, and Meg popped out. She crossed the aisle with her usual air of purpose, head high, hips swinging, as if she owned the place. As if she was the queen of the place. It was intentional, he knew. He'd gone on enough late-night adventures with Meg to know her philosophy on breaking the rules: Never hesitate. Own it or don't even touch it.

Meg owned it.

She stopped beside another car across the aisle from Valor's Rover and didn't even bother to duplicate the key fob signal. She just tried the door. It opened easily. Drew could see her disgusted sigh even via the grainy black-and-white video feed. He smiled and watched her fold those endless legs of hers into the driver's seat. She slouched down until even her hair knot was invisible behind the headrest.

All set, she texted to Drew's phone. *On your go.*

Stay tuned, he texted back.

He sent a message to E: *All systems go. Set?*

E shot back, *Set.*

"Show time," Drew said to himself and flexed his fingers. He pulled up the screen from which he controlled

NoVD's mechanical system—HVAC, electrical, the whole shebang—and found the sector he was looking for. He flipped back to the garage cam and waited until the security guard was an aisle or two away from Meg and the Rover.

Hit it, he texted her.

He couldn't hear the car alarm go off, but the Rover lit up like the Fourth of July—headlights, tail lights, fog lights, hazards. It all but sat up on its hind legs and danced. The security guard jumped like somebody had slapped him. He nailed the golf cart's accelerator, took the corner toward the Rover on two wheels and came in hot. Left the cart parked at an angle in the center of the aisle and drew his Mag Light to scan the darker corners. The whites of his terrified eyes showed even on the crappy video feed. When he didn't find anybody, he approached the Rover. Drew gave him credit. Guy didn't cheap out but did the job—peered inside, underneath, all around. Frowned and pulled out his radio.

Pay dirt. Drew smiled and flipped back to the security camera monitoring the hallway outside Valor's office. Within thirty seconds, Valor strode into the shot, his phone to his ear, his mouth moving in short, hard bursts. Like he was really giving it to the security guard on the other end. Drew didn't figure the poor kid was being paid enough to be deafened by the alarm on a dick-car. For sure he wasn't being paid enough to put up with the dick it belonged to.

Speaking of whom. Drew studied Valor as he headed for the elevator. He wasn't a tall guy. Wasn't short, either. He moved like a fighter, though. Efficient, tight, light on his feet in khakis and an open-throated shirt. Toss in that to-the-skull buzz cut and Edward Valor looked like exactly what he was: ex-military, and not a grunt either. This was a guy used to giving orders rather than taking them, to winning rather than losing. This was a guy who knew how to blow shit up and wasn't at all averse to pulling the trigger, whether the situation required heavy explosives or not.

Drew didn't like him on principle.

Valor punched the elevator button like it had personally offended him and shoved the phone into his pocket. His mouth continued moving, though, and Drew didn't need to be a lip reader to get the gist. The doors slid open and Drew shifted to the elevator cam. He wasn't surprised to see that Valor didn't stand still to watch the numbers count down like an ordinary person. No, he stalked and paced and talked to himself, hands in fists on his hips. The instant the doors opened, he leapt out, the key fob in his hand already aimed at the SUV like a gun.

Back to the garage cam where Drew watched Valor stalk into the shot. The Rover went dark and—presumably— silent. The security guard sidled foot to foot, practically wringing his hands in apology. Valor waved a hand—*hey, man, forget about it*—which absolutely did not go with the *I'm an assassin* demeanor. He strode back to the elevator and once again punched the call button as if it had slapped his mother.

Drew waited until he was in the elevator but before the doors slid shut. Then he texted Meg: *Again.*

The Rover jumped back into its frantic dance. Valor got off the elevator.

Drew texted E: *Status?*

E shot back: *Fucking wanker. I need more time.*

Drew had to assume that Valor was the wanker in question. Texted back: *You got it.*

He eyed the video feed of Valor going back to the elevator after having silenced his beast of a truck. He texted Meg: *Again.*

The SUV danced. Valor's scowl went from irritated to incredulous. He stalked back, keyed it off.

Again.

Again.

Again.

Finally, Valor just slapped his key fob into the hand of the security guard, who couldn't have looked more startled if he'd been given the cash value of the Rover instead of just the keys.

Drew texted *Again* to Meg, purely for the comedic value of watching the guard—whose frantic Adam's apple was clearly visible even via bad video—lift the key fob tentatively toward the Rover and cut cautious eyes to Valor.

Valor nodded tersely. The Rover went dark.

He texted E: *Return trip impending. ETA?*

Stall him, from E. *Something's here.*

Fuck. *You got it*, to E.

Again, to Meg. He kept one eye on the garage cam. The guard gave Valor the questioning eyes. Valor nodded. The guard pointed the fob and the Rover shut up.

10 seconds, then again, he texted Meg. He kept one eye on the garage cam. Valor stood there, eyes narrowed, arms folded, with a stillness that told Drew he knew how to wait when he needed to. Drew wondered if that was going to work for or against them. The guard kept his eyes on Valor, the keys aimed at the SUV. The Rover did its little dance, and the guard keyed it off. Finally Valor shook his head in disgust and stalked back toward the elevator.

Keep spacing them out, he texted Meg. *Keep him busy for 5-10*. He pulled up the mechanical system again and zeroed in on the elevator. He let Valor climb into the carriage and begin the ascent. Then he killed the power.

The carriage jerked to a halt and emergency lights flooded the tiny space. It turned the security cam feed a weird filmy brown. Drew didn't need audio to catch Valor's thoughts on this development. Guy's fist actually dented the metal wall. Damn.

Drew flipped back to the garage feed and saw the guard standing vigil at the rear bumper of the SUV. It was obediently dark. To Drew's amusement, the kid began actually pacing back and forth in front of it, like he was on duty at Buckingham Palace. Chest out, chin tucked, eyes narrow, key fob at attention.

The Rover leapt into distress and the kid spun, shot it with the key fob like a gunslinger. Drew grinned. He liked this kid. Back to pacing, very serious. Minute and a half later, the SUV danced into action and he shot it again. This time, he spun the keys, blew on them like they were a smoking gun, and tucked them into his belt with his Mag Light. Drew laughed outright. If he ever needed anything guarded, this kid was getting a job offer.

"And how's our buddy Valor doing?" he asked himself.

"Punched himself out yet? Broken a metatarsal or two?" He shifted back to the elevator cam and said, "Ah, fuck me."

Because Valor wasn't punching shit. Valor was climbing the fuck out.

The adrenaline rush was pure and beautiful and Drew rode it like the best wave in the world. His fingers were magic, and they flew across the keyboard almost independent of thought or command. They simply manifested the intentions of his brain without any messy relays mucking things up in between.

To both E and Meg: *Containment fail. Get out. You have 5.*

He restored power to the elevator with a single key stroke then killed it just as fast. The carriage jerked like it meant business. Valor, already halfway out the ceiling panel, paused.

"Yeah, that's right," Drew murmured to him. "Think twice about getting on top of that thing, Valor. Show Daddy how you can wait. Let's see all that special-ops patience of yours."

Valor dropped back into the dim carriage to examine the control panel.

"Good boy," Drew told him.

He shifted displays, got back to the hallway outside Valor's office.

Hall's clear, he texted E. *Screw the ceiling crawl.*

Two minutes, E sent back. *Holy goatfuck.*

Get. Back. Drew's fingers flew and he switched back to the garage. The kid had abandoned the palace guard routine and was now watching the Rover from—oh, hell—from the back bumper of the car across the aisle. The car in which Meg was hidden.

Chapter 13

Small problem, Meg texted Drew.

Yeah, he sent back. *I see.*

She eased her skirt yet farther up her thighs, prayed for the seams and sank down another precious inch. Her knees were in grave danger of turning on the hazards—the car was a compact and Meg decidedly wasn't—but cripes, the security guard was sitting on her bumper.

Can you get him off me? She was folded practically in half at this point, so could only sort of see her own screen. Which was fine, because did she really want this kid catching sight of her glowing screen and turning that Mag Light of his on this car? No, she did not. She did, however, hope that she was thumb-typing with reasonable accuracy.

Your wish is my command, Drew told her.

Meg contemplated the muscle screaming in her neck. Her wish at this very moment was a glass of wine, a full body massage, and to get the hell out of this garage without being arrested. Or conked over the head by an anxious guard and his very heavy flashlight.

She had wine aplenty at home, and she had confidence that Drew—in his own wacky way—would secure her release from the Prison of the BMW Coupe. That left only the full body massage which, given the round trip ceiling crawl and this unexpected bit of car yoga, she felt she deserved.

Her mind leapt to Drew's hands—those big, dexterous, curiously capable hands of his—and everything in her cramped body flashed hot. She wanted to squeeze her knees together in defense but they were splayed on either side of the steering wheel so she suffered this excruciating blast of lust as vulnerably as if she were giving birth. She wondered if she sort of was. Because this thing she was suddenly nursing for Drew? This awareness, this obsession, this whatever? It reminded her of the time she'd accidentally attended the birth of one of his nephews.

Had Meg had even the slightest idea that she was about to witness labor and delivery, she'd have fled like the coward she was. Unfortunately, there had been no warning. One second she'd been hanging out in the kitchen of Hunt House with Drew's hugely pregnant sister-in-law Bel, watching her crimp a pie crust, although badly. This should have been her first clue because Bel took pie crust very, very seriously. The next second, Bel was inexplicably squatting by the refrigerator door, swearing. Which should have been her second clue because Bel didn't normally curse.

Next thing Meg knew, she was on her knees front of America's favorite domestic diva, who was still cursing a blue streak but also giving fucking birth. So she'd done what anybody whose brain had gone completely numb with terror and shock would have done. She'd snatched a dishtowel from the drawer—a dishtowel!—and caught the damn baby. It had been, what, four years since then? And it still surprised her.

Not the birth, though that had definitely been surprising. No, it was more the fact of the baby. Because an honest-to-God human being had slithered out from between Bel's thighs, red, bloody and squalling like a demon. And she remembered thinking, *Where the hell did this come from?*

One second she'd been alone with Bel—just them and a pie crust and cups of tea. The next second there'd been somebody else in the room. A person had arrived, and not gradually, either. Hadn't walked in the door. Hadn't called on the phone. A whole human being—who had previously not even existed as far as Meg was concerned—was suddenly right there.

Her desire for Drew felt strangely like that moment. One second it wasn't there, the next it inarguably just was. It wasn't a question; it was a fact. It wasn't going to go away, either, any more than the baby had. Micah. She smiled at the memory. She'd cried over him, over the gorgeous anger in his wail. He was here, damn it, and not happy about it. Meg hadn't been thrilled herself. Not particularly. But her hands—okay, her dishtowel—had welcomed him into the world. She'd been the first person to touch him, to hold him, to prove to him that he could fall but it was possible to be caught.

She had a soft spot for that kid to this day.

She wasn't so sure about Drew. She had something for him but it didn't feel soft. Didn't feel warm. She wondered if it, too, would make her cry those hot, jagged tears, the kind that ripped aside pretense and cool and just poured out of your darkest, most primitive places.

She fucking hoped not. She'd never been a crier and she didn't intend to start now. That said, she might overlook a tear or two of pure gratitude if Drew managed to get this guard off her ass. Her spine was never going to be the same.

Wait for it, Drew texted her.

For the longest five seconds of Meg's life, there was nothing. Then a wail ripped through the silence and the little BMW gave an enthusiastic bounce. She had to assume that the guard had launched himself off the back bumper, thanks be to God. Or to Drew, and whatever he'd done to trip the fire alarms. Or whatever that was, screaming through the night. She heard the golf cart spin its teeny tires and risked a cautious peep out the window. She was just in time to see the cart disappear around the corner at top speed.

You're clear, Drew texted. *Go.*

She didn't bother texting back. She knew he'd catch her on the security cam. She shoved out of the car, grateful when she unfolded properly and didn't have to crawl. She blew a kiss at the camera, threw her shoulders back and headed for the elevator at a confident clip.

She knew the elevator was currently serving as a between-floors holding cell for Valor—or should be if they were on plan—so she bypassed it. She hit the stairwell instead. It was dim and smelled faintly of pee, the way all stairwells did, no matter how swanky the company. She hitched her purse more securely under her arm and started to climb.

She'd climbed out of the garage and nearly to the bottom floor of offices when her phone buzzed frantically in her hand. She glanced at it.

Valor just escaped the elevator, Drew texted. *Heading for the stairs.*

She froze. Didn't move, didn't breathe. She just focused with every fiber of her being on listening. Somewhere— above her? Below?—a door banged open. She could hear him, Valor, his footsteps ringing quick and assured in the air all around her. Oh hell, he was in the stairwell. He must've climbed out of the elevator like the ex-special ops guy he was, shinnied down the cable or something and pried open the doors to whatever floor was closest. She knew Drew would've pulled out every stop to keep him in that elevator as long as humanly possible—and with great glee if she knew Drew—so she had no idea how high or low his elevator had been when he'd busted out.

As for herself, she'd come from *Parking 2*, had passed *Parking 1*, and was now staring at a big black *Level 1* painted on the door in front of her. That meant only one more flight of stairs stood between her and the relative security of *Level 2* where Drew and E were waiting for her.

Then again, Valor was heading for *Level 2* as well.

On L1, she texted. *Do I go up or down?* She put a hand on the door handle and, in spite of the key pad next to the knob, gave it a cautious jiggle. Locked. Of course. She suppressed a groan. *Now* NoVD decided to take security seriously. Damn it.

Go up, Drew texted. *L3. NOW*.

She reached down, snatched off her shoes and sprinted up the stairs as silently as she could. The stairs were cold and sticky under her bare feet—she refused to think about that, given the pee smell—but her breath stayed smooth and quiet even as she maintained a controlled sprint. She'd have to add interval training to her trainer's growing thank you note, damn it.

Still, Valor's footsteps dogged her like a shadow, and she couldn't gauge whether they were growing closer or farther away. Was she putting distance between them? God, she couldn't tell. But she could practically feel his eyes, nicking her like a bullet as she flew around the landing between floors and sailed up to *L2*. She shot past that landing, too, grabbed the railing on the next turn and took the corner on the fly. There was *L3* above her, one more flight up. Her lungs wept with relief, but her thighs were no longer even speaking to her. They just burned with sullen defeat. Her shoulder blades ached with the exquisite anticipation of Valor's gaze. *Don't look back*, she commanded herself. *He's not there. Just run.*

She ran. It took every ounce of her self-control not to fling herself at the door with wild abandon, sucking wind like a wreck survivor. She skidded to a halt, her bare feet slipping on the concrete, and she took the door handle between two delicate fingers. She gave it an all but silent nudge only to find that it was locked.

Of course it was.

Valor's footsteps filled the air around her, the soft shush of leather soles jogging up—definitely up—the stairs. Toward her.

Stay put, Drew texted her. *He'll get off at 2.*

Meg pressed the phone to her chest, muffling even the quiet *you've got a text!* buzz the phone made in silent mode. He'd better be goddamn right.

Trust me, he texted, as if he were right in her head with her. *I've got you.*

He'd better.

She stood there, completely exposed. If Valor decided to get a little middle-of-shift exercise and take a few extra flights, she was well and truly screwed. She might as well just get herself fitted for her orange jumpsuit. She pressed her back to the door and shot a glance at the stairs. They ascended to her right and called to her irresistibly. Screw Drew's instructions. He was safe in the conference room, pulling strings from a distance. It was her ass on the line, and she wanted one more level, just a couple more feet of space, between her and danger. What thinking person wouldn't?

She didn't move. Her entire body trembled, and she didn't know if it was from fear, from the sprint, or from the effort of overriding her instincts.

Trust me, he'd texted. *I've got you.*

Drew had her. Did she trust that? Did she trust him?

The staircase descended, too, and she told herself not to look there either. The desire to see Valor hit the landing, to confirm with her own eyes that he got safely off at *L2* was almost overwhelming. But it was a risk, a truly stupid one. Especially when Drew had her. Said he did, anyway.

She heard the beeps of Valor punching in his ID number outside the door one level down, and relief threatened to put her on her knees. She leaned back against her own door, closed her eyes and let the adrenaline crash over her like a rogue wave. Blood beat in her ears, and she just caught the click and shush of the door opening below her, then the pneumatic hiss of it easing slowly closed. And then she was alone in the stairwell, her heart knocking against her ribs, her knees like water.

She wondered for one awful moment if she was going to throw up or pass out. Her phone buzzed against her sternum—she was still trying to suffocate it in her wholly inadequate cleavage—and she eased it back for a look.

I'm coming for you, Drew texted. *Stay put.*

She wanted to laugh; it bubbled up in her throat, all edgy and uncomfortably hysterical. Stay put? Like she was going somewhere? Like she was just going to take a walk or something? Her feet and hands were ominously numb and her head was light and floaty. She was hyperventilating, or dangerously close to it. She wanted to sink down and put her head between her knees but she liked this skirt. Bad enough that she had stairwell stink all over her feet. She'd be damned if she'd sacrifice her skirt in the name of girlie vapors.

She closed her eyes, tipped back her head and let the door hold her up while she concentrated on breathing. In and out, nice and even.

Three minutes later there was a scratch at the door behind her. She eased herself off it and suddenly, Drew was right there. She squinted at him in the sudden blast of the hallway's overhead fluorescents, and was seized with the unexpected urge to fling herself at him. To throw herself into his arms and squeeze the ever-living crap out of him.

"Meg!" He stared at her, as if he'd just found her on his doorstep in the middle of the night. "You're here."

"I sure am." She stepped into the hallway, wiggling her bare toes against the industrial-grade carpet like it was meadow-fresh grass. "Why so surprised?"

"Because, um." He let the door ease shut while he studied her. "Because you're...here."

"What, right where you told me to be?"

"Yes, exactly." A smile crawled slowly across that long, funny face of his with all the dazzle of a sunrise. "I mean, I told you to stay put, sure. But I didn't expect that you actually would."

She scowled at him. "I know how to follow instructions, Drew."

"No, you don't. Not when your ass is on the line. Your ass, your decisions." He shot her with an imaginary finger gun. "That's how Meggy rolls."

"Don't call me Meggy." He had a point, actually. Not that she'd let him have it. "I'm here, aren't I?"

"Yeah, you are." He tipped his head like a perplexed dog. "And I'll admit, it's throwing me a little."

"Oh, for heaven's sake. Pull yourself together." She bent to hook a foot into a shoe. "Valor's back in his office?"

"Yep." Drew offered her his elbow and she took it while she did the second shoe. "Got off on *L2* like the good little soldier he is."

"Who did you watch?" She straightened and gazed up at him, exquisitely aware that he'd wrapped a hand over hers, keeping her hand snuggled in the crook of his elbow. "On the security feed, I mean. His stairwell or mine?"

"His." He stood there, his long, expressive face tipped down to hers, uncharacteristically serious and searching. "I had to make sure I was sending you good intel so you could make good choices. In case you forgot how to follow instructions."

He'd watched Valor. Not her. So he hadn't seen her struggle. He didn't know how close she'd come to ignoring him, how hard she'd fought to give herself over to his authority. He hadn't seen what it had cost her to cede control that way.

It washed over her again, hot and uncomfortable, this new awareness of him, and she prayed that he stayed blissfully unaware of it.

"Well if I did, who could blame me? You won't even babysit my damn purse, Drew." She scowled at him. "But you expect me to trust you with my life?"

"Of course not. That's what I just said." He leaned in, grinned at her. "And yet here you are."

She sighed. "Here I am."

"And you're surprised that I'm surprised." His grin went wicked. "Which one of us is irrational now, huh?"

"It's not that big a deal, Drew." She pulled her hand free of his elbow, ignored the tiny pang of loss. She wanted to keep touching him. "You said you had me. I believed you. End of story."

She had the petty pleasure seeing him blink at her, startled, before he smiled. Smugly.

"You should." He dropped his hands to her shoulders and planted a smacking kiss on her forehead. The kind you'd give to a favorite niece, which made the dirty little thrill that zipped through her all the more shameful. "You should definitely believe that."

It took a great deal of effort but she gave him a fairly credible eye roll. "So I'm good, but my purse—the purse in which I keep my life—is on its own?"

He slung an arm over her shoulders and started them down the hallway. "See how well we understand each other?"

"Oh, yeah." She matched her stride to his with the ease of long practice but shrugged out from under his arm. Because about the only thing she understood was that—in a night filled with dead men come back to life, ceiling crawls and stairwell chases with GI Joe—nothing had been more dangerous to her than the way she wanted Drew's arm around her shoulders.

Chapter 14

It was after three in the morning when Meg followed Drew's Blazer onto the massive estate that he and his brothers called home. That she herself had called home these past five years. She threw a longing glance at the Dower House—the sweet little cottage she rented from James and Bel—as she shot by. Everything in her weary system yearned toward the cheerful front door of that tiny, white-slatted house. Toward that pretty front porch flanked by a pair of cherry trees and a pointy hedge of hollyhock stalks. Toward the comfy bed and the sixteen straight hours of sleep that she so richly deserved.

God, she was tired.

But she wasn't going to sleep. Not yet. Not when she and Drew had just performed what amounted to a penetration test, and on some damn questionable authority. Not when the guy on whose questionable authority they'd done it was refusing to account—in detail—for the fifteen minutes of alone time their crimes had bought him with a stranger's computer.

But when Meg had made a very reasonable request for more information, had Drew backed her up? Had he followed up her very pertinent questions with a few of his own? Hell, no. He'd just shaken E's hand, slapped his back and agreed to table the discussion until daylight like civilized people. Nobody had actually said that Meg was tired and cranky and not fully reasonable at the moment, but as subtext went, it hadn't been particularly subtle. And while Meg was willing to allow that she hadn't exactly used her best judgment in all situations today, she was not willing to let the men pat her hair and dismiss her concerns. Not in this lifetime or any other.

So she clung stubbornly to Drew's bumper and let Hunt House roll past her window, too. The pink-bricked manor house that Bel and James called home was smack in the center of the former plantation. Once upon a time it had been a chilly monument to good taste and old money, famous to one and all as the home of the lifestyle show *Kate Every Day*. Then Belinda West had taken charge of both the show and the house—and Drew's soccer-star brother James—and transformed them all.

Now the house was a home and James was a husband, a father and a desperately happy man. At least as far as Meg could tell. She was no expert on desperate happiness but thought it was as good a phrase as any. And aside from whatever questionable sporting activity had led to the odd collection of hockey sticks, soccer balls and athletic socks scattered across the lawn like fallen soldiers, Hunt House was the very picture of post-midnight domestic bliss.

She followed the Blazer around a gentle bend in the drive, and the Annex loomed into view. The third spoke of the massive estate the Blake brothers had reunited, the Annex was a sprawling white mansion that made up in size and splendor what it lacked in dignity. Which was, Meg thought, what happened when you ripped a family inheritance down the center and gave the best half to the Confederate son and the crappy half to the Union son. Prodigal sons sometimes made good and rubbed your nose in it. Or at the very least, they built tacky mansions under your genteelly impoverished nose so they could throw lavish balls and not invite you.

She didn't get why more kids didn't enjoy history. It was so petty and violent. Good stuff.

All this meant in modern terms, however, was that the Annex was big enough to contain the entire Blake family for a holiday dinner with enough space left over to prevent fisticuffs. Usually. Spreading the brothers out across the entire estate was a better long-term solution, and the Blakes had embraced it.

At this moment in time, Drew lived in the east wing of the Annex while his brother Will (plus wife Audrey and their pack of boys) lived in the west wing. Both of which were as dark and quiet as the hour would suggest. It was in the north wing that a single light burned.

Jillian, Meg thought. Probably up conquering the world via the internet. Or at least knitting another yards-long scarf.

Jillian was Audrey's niece. She'd been eight when they'd come to live at the Annex, on the run from an ugly domestic situation. A domestic situation that Meg's mom— in her usual inexplicable way—had fixed. Well, not *fixed* fixed. Meg knew better than most that there was no fixing some families. But Hildy Wise had provided a certain clarity for all parties involved, and the end result had been that Jillian had been raised by Audrey and Will here at the Annex. And she'd been loved to pieces by every single soul on the property.

Now sixteen with the brains of a nuclear physicist, the legs of a supermodel and a fashion sense Meg didn't know who to blame for, Jillian was testing her wings and killing her de facto parents—especially Will—by abandoning the family nest. She'd only moved as far as the north wing so far, but it was still sort of fascinating to watch Will, for whom family was nothing short of a religion, grapple with letting go of the girl he'd raised as his own. Even by degrees.

Drew's Blazer disappeared around the corner of the Annex and Meg blinked herself back to the moment. Back to full wakefulness. She shook herself. Cripes. Asleep at the wheel, contemplating the meaning of family or some shit when she should have been reviewing her talking points. Because arguing with Drew was never as easy as it should be. The guy was cheerful and agreeable and whimsical, but he was also smart as hell, and slippery as a snake. Arguing with him required skill, grit and unwavering focus. Winning an argument took all that plus unassailable logic.

Because Drew was, underneath all the hair and the charm, a reasonable man. If she had the better argument— and she did—she'd win. So long as she stayed in the game. So it was time to get her head in the damn game.

She pulled around the Annex to the carriage house, and found Drew already parked on the cement apron. She followed, nosed up to his bumper and killed her engine. Outside the passenger window, the lawn sloped down to the pretty pond at the heart of the estate. All three back yards hugged its banks, and all three had been given over to an exquisitely formal garden. At the heart of the garden was an elaborate hedge maze, each entrance marked by a wrought iron arbor dripping with winter-spindly vines. Hunt House presided over the whole thing like a gracious queen.

It was a sight so familiar that Meg hardly even saw it anymore. She probably walked the maze between the Dower House and the Annex every single day, most days more than once.

But the moonlight made it strange and new, and all of a sudden it struck Meg like a fist to the chest. It was beautiful. This whole place, it was astonishingly beautiful. And she lived here, right inside it.

Sometimes she didn't know how she'd ended up living this life. It was more than she'd ever expected, better than she deserved. She knew this like she knew her own name. And she also knew that she'd trade her last breath to keep it.

Drew's tail lights flashed as he cut his engine and stepped out of the Blazer. The moonlight trailed across him, too, throwing his eyes into deep shadow. And suddenly he was strange, too. All cheekbones and jawline, broad shoulders and long legs. He reached out a careless hand to shove his rusty truck door shut, and realization hit her like a second punch to the chest.

She didn't love her sweet little cottage, the hollyhocks or the hedge maze. She didn't love her fucking landscaping, for sweet Christ's sake. She loved Drew. He was her home. He was what she came back to over and over. He was her touchstone, the steady beating heart of her life. After a nasty set-back at work or an ugly go-round with her dad, she didn't want a drink. She didn't want a punishing run, a sweaty bout of anonymous sex, an unconscionable amount of chocolate, or any of the other things people comforted themselves with.

She wanted Drew.

She negotiated a literal maze every morning to get to

his side, for God's sake, and it wasn't because he made excellent coffee. Though he did.

It was because she wanted him, she realized now. She wanted Drew. No, she needed him. She was addicted to him. To the easy generosity of his affection, to the astonishing gift of his loyalty. Even to the criminally sneaky punch of his brains. At this point, she doubted she could function without a daily dose of the whole package. Without him.

Oh, Christ. This was a disaster. A complete, epic, world-destroying disaster.

Her heart rattled inside her chest like a pebble in a can and she gripped the wheel with slippery hands. Groped her frantic mind for a plan here. Because what she'd said to Tracy the barmaid earlier had been absolutely true: Drew loved his family forever. Everybody else was fun but disposable. And Meg would no more allow herself to be disposable than she'd allow herself to be dismissed when the men were talking.

Which was why, she reminded herself, she'd put herself firmly in the family camp in the first place. Which was why, she now understood, she'd so diligently suppressed the volcanic lust that had hijacked her tonight, body and soul. Nothing made Drew hit the eject button faster than some girl falling in love with him. The second fun veered toward love, it was all *thanks for coming, there's the door*. She'd watched it happen a million times, and with a smug superiority, too, because she was too smart to be that girl, wasn't she?

Bitter amusement filled her. Meg was totally that girl right now, and it served her right.

Quite the day she was having.

She glared out the windshield at Drew who stood waiting for her, all limned in silvery moonlight, wearing that knowing smirk he always wore for arguing. And looking good enough to eat, damn it.

To hell with it. She gave herself a hard shake. She had a game face, and it was a darn good one. She'd just have to use it until she figured out how on God's green earth she was getting out of this mess.

In the meanwhile, she settled for getting out of the car.

"Ah, Meg." Drew stood on the moon-dappled pavement grinning at her, hands on his hips. "Such manners! You didn't have to see me home."

She stalked across the crushed shell drive to join him on the carriage house apron. "He's keeping secrets," she snapped, fists on her own hips. Picking up the argument as if they'd never left off. As if there were nothing bigger to argue about, God help her. "He's keeping secrets and you're letting him."

Drew gave a lazy shrug. "His to keep."

"No." She stabbed him with a single, sharp finger. "They aren't. They were his, but the instant you and I put our asses on the line to help him? They became our secrets, too. We deserve answers, Drew. Why won't he give them to us?"

"He will." He tipped his head, studied her in the moonlight. "In the morning."

"Yeah, so he said." She glared. "But this guy let you think he was dead for the better part of two decades. Why are we taking his word for it? Why would we take his word for anything?"

Another shrug, and fury crawled into her bloodstream. She welcomed it with shameful relief.

"Stop overreacting, Meg. It was just a favor between friends, okay?"

"An illegal favor."

That charming smile bloomed across his face. "Performed with the new CSO's permission. I think we're in the clear."

"If he really is the CSO." She stuffed her fists into her elbows because he was being deliberately stupid about this. She didn't imagine a punch would straighten out his thinking but it sure would relieve her emotions. Because she hadn't exactly played it smart this evening herself. "Loyalty doesn't equal stupidity, Drew." She wondered if she was talking to him or to herself. "Do you have any idea what we've done?"

"Helped out an old friend?"

Her palms itched with violence so she clenched her fists until they ached. "We broke into a company. We used stolen passwords to hack into their database. We hijacked the building systems, violated the sitting CSO's vehicle and lured him into the parking garage while your old buddy E did God knows what all by himself in the guy's office."

She stepped forward, put her toes practically on top of Drew's and leaned in close enough to whisper, although why she felt the need she had no idea. They were the only two people awake within five miles. "And we have no idea what he did. We don't know if he took something, if he planted something, if he learned something. And why not?" She poked his chest again. "Because he won't tell us!"

"He will, Meg." Drew smiled at her again. "In the morning. When we're all rested and...reasonable."

She breathed through a surge of impotent fury. He was deliberately baiting her now. He knew how much she hated being patronized. When she spoke, her voice was very cool and exquisitely calm. "But what if he doesn't? What if he disappears? What if, instead of meeting us for coffee bright and early as promised, he takes off for parts unknown? What if we then discover that he faked his employment contract? What if it turns out that he's not NoVD's new CSO?" She knew her voice was rising but found that she didn't care anymore. The more she talked, the more she made sense. The kind of sense that concerned the hell out of her.

"What's on those servers anyway, Drew?" She glared at him. "What if E's still working for the Secret Service?" Her eyes widened. "Or, Jesus, what if he's not?" She threw out her hands in frustration. "We put our asses on the line for him. He owes us, but he won't even answer us. How the hell are you not concerned about this?"

"Okay, see, there's your problem." He narrowed his eyes and aimed a finger at her. "You think he owes us."

She stared. "He does."

"No, he doesn't." Drew caught her hands before she could stab them into her hair. Or punch him. God. Her head wanted to explode. "We did a favor for a friend, Meg. You don't put conditions on a favor."

"We damn well should have," she muttered.

"He's a friend," Drew said simply. He gave her hands a

warm squeeze. Something deep inside her gave an answering squeeze—a hot one—and she closed her eyes. Tugged on her hands. He kept them.

"And I suppose you don't believe in putting conditions on friendship any more than on favors, do you?" she asked.

"I don't."

She made a disgusted noise and tugged on her hands again. He kept them again. Tugged back, actually. She stumbled forward a step, caught by surprise.

"That," he said, "would be you."

She blinked up at him. "What's me?"

"Putting conditions on friendship."

She frowned. "I do not."

"You did on ours." He let go of her hands only to slide his palms—wide and warm—up her arms. She shivered. "Cold?"

"No." Hardly. Because that warm clutch inside her was spreading, burning, uncurling in hot licks. "Yes. No?" His hands moved slow and lazy up her arms. Down again. As if he were trying to warm her up. *Bull's eye*, she thought and choked back a bark of semi-hysterical laughter. Because certain parts of her were feeling very warm indeed.

He smiled. "So you're hot."

Another shiver seized her, and she wanted to close her eyes against the swamping wave of high-octane lust. She didn't let herself, though. She forced herself to gaze straight back into his laughing eyes. *Game face, Meggy.*

"I'm not cold," she said evenly, and with perfect honesty. "And I don't put conditions on our friendship."

"No?" The humor continued to sparkle in those warm, dark eyes, but something else joined it. Something dangerous, something wild.

Oh Christ, she thought. *Adventure.*

The lust in her belly exploded into something punishing and vicious. Something hungry and desperate. Something that had his name and *big mistake* written all over it.

He said, "Then it'll be totally okay for me to do this."

"This?" she asked, though her own voice sounded far away and unimportant. She was having some difficulty

119

caring about conversation when his hands were sliding, smooth and silky, from her wrists to her elbows. Then farther. Suddenly his palms were hot on the backs of her arms, burning through the sheer sleeves of her blouse, his fingers curling around her biceps. "What this?"

Those big hands lifted her with a startlingly easy strength that put her on her toes in spite of the very ambitious heels she'd picked out that morning. "*This* this."

And he kissed her.

Chapter 15

Drew had tried to talk himself out of this. God, how he'd tried.

He'd tried to ignore the pressing urgency inside him. The building, inexorable pressure. He'd told himself to play it cool. To be easy, just the way he'd trained himself all those years ago. He and Meg were friends, best friends. And that was how things were going to stay.

Then he'd stood there and watched the door of her Audi open. He'd watched one long, long leg emerge, smooth and pale and endless. His dick had given a hungry pulse and whatever this was that Meg had sparked to life inside him?

It just bloomed.

It had gone up in a rush of flame and intention and desire. It had opened and devoured and Drew knew he wasn't going to fight it anymore. Knew he couldn't.

He'd listened with half an ear to the crush of gravel under her shoes as she stalked toward him on those ridiculous heels of hers. He would always remember it, he knew. The toothy grind of it under her soles, the noise flying into the air as she sailed to him through the chilly air. Air that should've slapped him back to his senses.

Only it didn't.

It had just pressed itself on his memory, this moment, this night, this noise. The crisp snap of impending winter on the air, the scent of frost-touched plants giving themselves to the soil so that something old and outgrown could be replaced with something new and unknown.

The parallels weren't lost on Drew.

Then Meg's mouth had been moving, all sharp words and soft curves. He'd made appropriate noises—he thought he had, anyway—and waited for his moment. And when it had finally come along, he'd seized it.

Seized her.

He'd just wrapped his hands around the curiously delicate bones of her upper arms, lifted her to her toes and straight into his mouth.

He was glad now that he'd given her that half-assed peck in the bar earlier. Because if he'd suffered this exquisite blast of pure Meg without a warm up, he didn't know if he'd have stayed on his feet. Her mouth was soft and shocked under his, and he took shameless advantage. He curved a hand around the back of her head, and it fit there like it had been custom designed for his palm.

He dragged her closer and, oh good God, it wasn't just her head. It was her whole body, the whole long elegant line of her. She just fit. Her body snugged up against his like they'd been built together, one carved out of the other, and he simply fell into her.

It occurred to him, dimly, that they'd skipped the awkward. They'd blown right past the part where you had to figure out how exactly this was going to work between two bodies that had never touched before. Maybe it was because it wasn't really their first kiss—not technically. Maybe it was because they'd known each other, though not carnally, for years and years. Maybe it was because they were familiar with each other in ways that most people sharing their first kiss—or second, or whatever, depending on how you were scoring the situation—weren't.

All Drew knew with any certainty was that this was Meg. This was Meg in his arms, and she was absolutely and completely herself from the sleek heat of her hair to the startled surprise that had softened that sharp mouth under his.

He felt it, the moment she connected the dots. The instant that shock melted away and Meg realized what the hell was going on here. That he—Drew, her best friend and nothing more, not ever—was kissing her. Was kissing her— Meg, his best friend and nothing more, not ever. And he wasn't kissing her like a brother, either. Not like a brother, not like a friend, not even like a first date. He was kissing her with intent. With heat. He was kissing her like he was burning inside. Like he was on fucking fire. Like a guy who'd been driven to the slippery edge of his control, and had finally just jumped the hell over.

He'd known it couldn't last forever, that compliant shock. He'd known she'd wake up any second, and here it was. Now was the moment that she'd pull back and shred him with a look, an eye roll, a cutting remark. He had seconds, heartbeats, before she pulled herself together and destroyed him.

He was going to make them count.

So he took her mouth like it was his. Like it belonged to him and always had. Like he'd never get another chance to prove it, because he probably never would.

Except then she was kissing him back. Oh holy hell, suddenly she was kissing him and all the blood in his body jumped up and crashed into motion. Everything he knew—thought he knew—all his facts and conclusions and ideas? They jumped the track and scattered into hot, jagged confusion, leaving him abruptly with nothing but need.

It was the only word left in his head, the only landmark remaining on his mental map. Need. It burned inside him, a sudden vast ocean of hunger. He had to get his hands on her. Had to feel her, had to know. His hands flew, fast and greedy, over her back, down the strong lines of her hips, landed on the curve of her bottom. It fit into his palm, too, with hot perfection—of course it did—and he lifted her into the throbbing ache of his need.

She made some kind of noise—or was that him?—and then her hands opened on his shoulders. He hadn't even been quite aware that they'd been there, fisted like tight little flower buds. But he knew when they opened. Knew the instant they loosened and bloomed. One slid slowly up, stopping his breath and blanking his mind. Her fingers sank into the hair at the base of his skull, and hot satisfaction thudded into him. God, she was touching him. He'd waited so long. Had he known he'd been waiting? Did it matter? She was touching him now and he wanted it to go on forever. He wanted her to touch more of him. All she wanted to touch.

He tipped, angled, nudged, and then her mouth was open under his and he wasn't waiting for anything anymore. He took her mouth with a greedy delight, learned her, stroked her, worshipped her. God, her mouth. It was the universe. It was everything.

But it wasn't enough. That edgy, hungry need crouched inside him, growled and demanded. He had more Meg than he'd ever expected, more than he'd ever dreamed of, and suddenly it just wasn't enough. He wanted more. Needed more. He needed her skin under his hands, under his lips. He wanted to see it, to feel it. To take it, take her, and mark her as his own.

He twisted, angled his mouth over hers and fell back. Took her with him. He let his back fetch up against the door of the Blazer, relished the startled stumble that put her body right up against his. He didn't let her catch her balance, either, but hooked an arm around her waist and spun, pushed her back against the driver's door instead.

He trapped her there with the hot press of his body. Sucked in a breath as if she'd burned him. She might as well have. His mind had registered the body-to-body contact with a sharp sizzle that he interpreted as his transformer blowing. Everything in his head went hot and white in a hungry blast that shoved him along ahead of it. He caged her in without thought, his feet on either side of hers, his hands flat on the roof of the truck just past her shoulders. Her head fell back, giving him the slender, vulnerable curve of her throat. He fell on it, just dropped his mouth to her skin and feasted. Gorged himself on the dizzying scent of her, of perfume and Meg, of sex and power.

She gave a startled squeak but her hands fisted in his sweater, and her head tipped yet further, giving him more. He took it with a dark satisfaction, dragged his teeth lightly down the curve of her throat until he could taste the rattle of her pulse on his lips. A prickly, punishing wave of want crashed over him, and he rode it with fierce delight. He slid his mouth, hot and open, to the secret curve of her shoulder inside the vee of her blouse, and used his teeth on her.

"Oh, Jesus," she said and Drew was startled to find that he could smile. Even racing that vicious, edgy want, he smiled against her skin. "Holy fucking hell," she said. "Do that again."

Delight bubbled up inside him. It ribboned into the raging lust, tempered it in some odd way. It was still vicious, still roaring just this side of uncontrolled, but God, Meg was just so...Meg. Her hands were twisted in his sweater now, tight and demanding, but her head lolled to the side like a sunflower too heavy for its own stem. His dick jerked and he pushed himself into her, circled the hungry ache of his desire into her.

More, he thought wildly. He needed more of her, in his mouth, in his hands. More of her skin, more of her scent, more of her heat, more of her demand. Just *more*.

He dragged a hand off the roof of the Blazer, slid it down the line of her neck, bumped it over the elegant wing of her collarbone. Traced the demure edge of her blouse. She hissed in a breath and Drew found the first button. Flicked it open.

"Drew," she breathed, and a fierce satisfaction roared through his veins at the sound of his name on her lips. His hand froze over that vulnerable button, over that pale trail of skin he'd just exposed. He lifted his head, brought his gaze to her face. Her eyes were screwed shut, her knuckles white against his sweater.

"Say it again." He hardly recognized his own voice. It was harsh, demanding. Impatient. She made an anguished noise that went straight to his crotch but he focused. "My name, Meg. Say it again."

She opened her eyes, and they were green and rainforest hot. She let go of his sweater, took up his scarf instead. Wrapped her hands in it and dragged him yet closer. He leaned into her, rubbed himself helplessly against her heat. "Drew?"

"Fuck, yeah." He circled and pushed and sought. "Just like that."

"No, I'm—" She broke off on a sharp moan and Drew grinned.

"Sweet spot?"

"Stop distracting me." But she closed her eyes.

"You want me to stop?" He let the grin grow, and circled his hips again. She stopped breathing altogether. "Are you sure?"

"Drew."

It was hardly more than a breath, hardly audible but it sank into his system like a drug. His blood gave a dangerous leap.

"Keep it up and this is going to be over before it starts," he told her.

"*Drew.*"

"Okay," he said and reached for another button. Flicked it open and dragged his finger down until he found the gorgeous shallow indent under her breast bone. "Have it your way." Her bra was pale and lacy and he wanted to bite it. "I'll last longer next time, promise."

He bent to see about that bra, but then her hands were in fists in his hair. Not gentle fists, either.

"Ow!"

She dragged his face up to hers and her eyes were open. Green. Hot. Aware. She said, "Damn it, Drew, I'm not talking dirty to you here." She glared at him and the sharp pain in his scalp dropped into the hot mix of affection and lust grappling around inside him. Everything went dark and topsy-turvy and he lost his breath. "I'm trying to talk to you!"

"Right." He slipped both hands into her blouse and filled his palms with lace and warm woman. Found tight little nipples with his thumbs and had to close his eyes and write code in his head until he was convinced he wasn't going to come right there.

"Go ahead," he said, when he could manage words. "Talk."

"Oh fuck it," she said. And shoved.

Drew fell back, had a fleeting moment to thank God he'd jumped when opportunity had knocked. He'd never forgive himself if he'd passed up what had probably amounted to his one and only chance to find out for himself what Meg's breasts felt like in his hands.

And they'd been perfect. Holy Christ, had they been perfect. Warm and pink and small and tight and eager. Regret grabbed him by the throat. He should've tasted them. He'd go to his grave wondering what her nipples tasted like.

It all flashed through his head in a millisecond, all the regrets and the wishes, the memory printing itself mercilessly on his brain in the single instant that they stood staring at each other in the moonlight.

Then Meg turned and walked away from him. Stalked to the front of the Blazer and spun to stare at him, her face strong and unreadable in the silvery light. He found himself going to her, his feet operating on instructions from his libido rather than his brain. Or so he assumed, because he didn't actually want to get his face slapped but he was helpless to resist. His palms still tingled, for heaven's sake. Still ached with the emptiness, and he wanted to fill them again. With her.

He stopped a prudent foot away and opened his mouth. Not that he had any idea what he was about to say. He knew only that he needed to pay this price. Whatever it cost to keep things right between him and Meg, to put their friendship back in place and leapfrog them over this...well, whatever this was? He'd pay it. So they could go back to being Meg and Drew again. If they couldn't have this, tonight's madness, they could at least have that back. Their precious usual.

Only Drew had no idea what words he could say that would do the trick.

He paused, mouth open, still groping for words, hoping that maybe Meg had them. He lifted helpless eyes to hers and waited.

She stared at him in the moonlight for a moment. A long, endless moment and Drew realized that he couldn't read her. For the first time in forever, he didn't have any idea what was in her mind. Loss was a panicked flutter somewhere deep inside him, even as lust continued to smoke and pulse.

He tried again for words but Meg just shook her head.

Then she boosted herself up onto the hood of the truck. She hooked those amazing heels over the bumper, grabbed him by the belt buckle, spread her knees and dragged him in.

And Drew remembered that she wasn't wearing underwear.

Chapter 16

"Oh thank Christ," Drew muttered, and his hands dove back into her blouse. "I thought you were going to punch me."

Meg slapped her palms onto the hood of the Blazer behind her, shoved back by Drew's enthusiasm and a punishing wave of pure need. His mouth latched onto that magic spot where her neck met her shoulder and a dangerous flutter seized her core.

"I was thinking about it," she managed. She let her head fall back to give him more room. "If you didn't put your mouth right back...ah, Jesus—" He'd done something wicked with his tongue and it was a serious effort to drag words out of a mind gone blank and bright. "—there—right Jesus help me *there*—I was totally going to punch you."

He bit her. Just flat out sank his teeth into the meat of her muscle, and followed it up with a sharp flick of his thumbs over her nipples. The smoking hunger inside her gave a hot, delicious clutch and reason faltered. Then it failed entirely, consumed by pure, roaring need.

It was a relief, she realized vaguely. Letting go of reason. Giving in to madness. Plus, she couldn't stop now, even if she wanted to. She could've laughed him off a minute ago, chalked that kiss up to hormones, impulse, the hour, whatever. Instead, she'd boosted herself up on the hood of his ugly truck and dragged him back in for more. Stopping now would be like writing *THIS IS A BIG DEAL* in a cartoon word bubble over her head. Which would make Drew ask why exactly it was such a big deal. Which was a question that she was ill-prepared to answer.

So, no. Stopping was no longer an option. Not that she wanted to. Maybe she'd regret it in the morning but right now? At this moment? Meg was officially lost to reason.

And it was delicious.

The night air licked across her bare belly suddenly, and she opened her eyes to find Drew undoing the last of her buttons. When had he tackled the others, she wondered wildly, and how had she not noticed? It seemed like the kind of thing a girl would notice.

Then she decided to think about it later because Drew wasn't stopping with the buttons. No, he'd moved right along to peeling open her blouse, though with the kind of reverent care you'd give particularly pretty wrapping paper. He eased the edges apart, nudged it over the knobs of her shoulders, and let it drift to her elbows, revealing...well, everything that her blouse usually covered. Her breath stopped in her chest and she watched him watch her. Watched those eyes go dark in the moonlight, watched his face go grave as he inspected what he'd uncovered.

Meg looked, too. She looked and found her own skin glowing whitely back at her, the thin light painting shadows below each plainly visible rib. A vague bitterness tightened her chest. It just figured, didn't it, that that whole magical-moonlight thing was bullshit? She didn't expect it to give her cleavage—that was a big ask by anybody's standards—but did it have to point out her goddamn ribs?

Shame spurted up inside her, vicious and familiar. It whispered to her—*ugly, plain, boyish, skinny, flat, ridiculous*—but she refused to give in. She refused to hide herself. Meghan Wise didn't hide from anybody, God damn it. It was a point of pride with her. It was also a matter of survival.

Because Meg wasn't bullet-proof, no more than anybody else. Far from it. She might not be pretty, but she had brains to burn. She knew very well what people liked, what men liked, and knew just as well that she didn't have it. Beauty? Charm? Curves? Nope. But she'd shared the womb with somebody who had been gifted with all three, and lavishly. Which meant that Meg had spent her entire childhood standing right next to everything people loved. And suffering by comparison.

She wasn't bitter about it, though. Not usually. She had her own gifts and wouldn't trade them. But she had learned to be careful about who she let matter to her. About whose opinions she let matter to her. As a result, she loved very, very few people. And let even fewer love her back.

But Drew did. He definitely loved her. Oh, he didn't *love her* love her, of course. She wasn't so much of an idiot that she thought an episode of hot sex would equal happily ever after. But Drew did love her. She knew he did.

And she loved him right back. More than she'd allowed herself to understand, but whatever. It hardly mattered how she loved him, only that she did. Which was exactly why she refused to let him give her that pity face. That careful blankness slapped over a steaming pile of *well, looks aren't everything*. She fucking refused to accept that. Not from him.

"Don't look like that," Meg said tightly. Her hands ached to fly up, to shield herself from those dark, frowning eyes. She forced them to stay flat on the hood of the truck behind her. "Don't you dare look at me that way."

"Shh." He flicked her a glance, then went back to gazing at her chest, his eyes very serious, his face very grim. "I'm having a moment here."

She stared at him. "I'm sorry, did you just shush me?"

"Meg, shh." He tucked his fingers into the back pockets of his jeans, rocked back on his heels and ran his eyes over her body. Slowly. "I'm concentrating."

"Oh, well, then. I'll just be quiet." She tossed up a trembling hand. "Do let me know if you need anything, okay?"

"Actually, can you unhook your bra?" He didn't even bother to look at her face this time. His eyes were fastened on what there was of her breasts. "I'd do it myself but I, ah..." His smile was faint. "I'm having that moment."

"You're having—" She stared at him, blank and amazed. "—a moment."

"Yeah. So I don't, you know..." He cleared his throat and her brain finally connected the dark focus in his eyes to blistering heat. It reached out and burned her. "I just need a minute, okay?"

Something uncurled deep inside her, something so tangled that the release of it was almost painful. "A minute you want to spend looking at my boobs?"

His smile was like lightning in the darkness. "See how well we understand each other?"

She paused, momentarily speechless. "I don't think I understand any of this."

"I didn't say that. Just that we understand each other."

She blinked at him. "What do you think it says about us that I actually got that?"

"Nothing as important as your getting rid of that bra, Meggy. Stat."

She studied him for one more long pulsing moment. He was still between her knees, the seam of his jeans rough against the bare skin of her inner thighs, his desire hard against her melting need. She eased herself upright, just until she could feel the heat raging off his chest. Her nipples stiffened and yearned but she didn't close the gap. Didn't give herself the thorny pleasure of contact. She shrugged out of her blouse and freed her arms, then put one finger in the center of his chest. She nudged him a step backward, and he went obligingly enough. His eyes slid down her body again, all the way to her skirt, to her open knees.

To her laundry crisis.

"The bra," he said, his voice thick. Rough. "For Christ's sake, Meg. I need to see you. All of you."

Joy fountained up inside her. He wanted to see her. He was desperate to see her. She put a hand on her own stomach, drifted two fingers lightly up her body. Smiled at the naked hope in Drew's face as he tracked the movement. "This bra?" She toyed with the lacy edge. Maybe she wasn't most men's sexual ideal but she'd learned to appreciate her body. She knew how it worked, she knew what she liked, and knew where to buy bras and panties that made the most of what she had. It was usually her secret and her pleasure to hide them under a strict no-nonsense suit. But now it was going to be Drew's pleasure, too, and the idea landed hot and low in her belly.

She kept her eyes on his face and dipped a finger into the cup of her bra. Pleasure bolted from her nipple to her core as she watched his hands go to fists in his back pockets. It pulled his jeans tight across the front and she suffered another debilitating blast of lust.

Drew wanted her. He wanted her exactly as much as he said he did. Possibly more. She sucked in a quick breath and it felt cool on her super-heated lips. She flicked out the tip of her tongue to check and sure enough, she was hot. She felt like she was on fire.

Drew made a noise, something harsh and guttural.

"Jesus, Meg. You want to play it like that?" He shook his head once, sharp and impatient. "Fine."

She never saw him move. Why did she never remember how fast he could be? One second he was standing there, devouring her with his eyes. The next second those big hands were wrapped around her hips, and he'd jerked her forward to the very edge of the hood. She squeaked and flailed backward.

"Take your time with the bra." His eyes were the strangest combination of amused and pissed that she'd ever seen. "I'll be right here whenever you're ready."

Then he dropped to his knees, shoved her skirt up to her hips and lifted her into his mouth.

Meg's heart exploded. It just detonated, overpowered by a glittery crash of shock and sensation and lust. His mouth was hungry on her, avid, merciless. She fell back, unstrung by a vicious punch of pure pleasure. Her back hit the warm hood and she slapped both hands to her heart, honestly concerned that it had leapt from her chest. He pulled back, just far enough to grin up at her, his eyes as hot and hungry as his mouth.

"Oh, now that's pretty. The bra, the hands, all together? Nice." He brushed a finger along the dark secret of her, played and learned and teased. Then he sank it into her, long and deep and knowing. She cried out and her hands fisted onto the edges of her bra cups.

"Oh, even better," he whispered, and she could feel his breath on the heart of her desire. "Let me see you now,

133

Meggy. Let me see you touch yourself." He worked her slowly, pressing with his thumb while his finger slid in and out of her. While he added another finger. She whimpered and obeyed, helpless to do otherwise. She pulled the cups of her bra down and exposed herself to the moonlight. To him. Slid her own hands over her modest curves until her nipples thrust greedily up between her fingers.

"God, that's pretty." He pulled her closer yet, hooked her helpless knee over his shoulder. And when he lowered his mouth to her again, she pinched both nipples. Hard.

She came in a blazing roar. She jerked and shuddered against his mouth and he rode it. Rode the spasm and clutch of her need, pumped his fingers into her without mercy or restraint. And when it was over, when she was sprawled across the hood of his truck, still wrung out and pulsing with what he'd done to her, he stood.

He reached for his back pocket again and she wondered if he was taking another moment. God knew she'd just had one. But he only pulled out his wallet and withdrew a condom. He watched her wordlessly as he unbuckled his jeans. As he shoved them open and sheathed himself. As he slid his hands around the shockingly hot skin of her thighs and spread her wide again.

Her core wept for him, pulsed and ached and yearned.

He sank into her, pushed himself straight into the needy heart of her. She cried out and wrapped herself around him. And this time she rode him. She rode the frantic thrusts of his need, matched the pace of his desire. And when he came apart over her, inside her, around her, she threw herself over the edge behind him.

Chapter 17

Drew had no real idea how long they stayed that way, sprawled across the hood of his truck like they'd been dropped there by a tornado. He wondered if they had been, actually. He felt bruised, fragile. As if he'd survived something, but barely. He wouldn't be surprised to open his eyes and find the surrounding trees impaled by playing cards and spoons and other unlikely items. He'd read about stuff like that. It didn't matter how harmless the object; accelerate it to 200 miles per hour and you had yourself a deadly fucking missile.

And Meg hadn't been exactly harmless to begin with.

He wasn't afraid of her, though. Not of Meg. Not of her temper, not of her tongue. Girl had a bark on her but Drew could take it. And if she wanted to bite him, well.

An edgy pulse of interest took him by surprise and he huffed out a laugh against her neck. Really? He was ready to go there again? She shivered underneath him, all soft skin and sharp bones, and he thought *yes*. He was definitely ready to go there again. It was probably a huge mistake—his specialty—but hell, it was already done. No point making a small mistake, right? Go big, or go home.

And Drew wasn't ready to go home yet. Not nearly.

"Cold?" He nuzzled his face into the crook of her shoulder, into the bold, woodsy warmth of her.

"Hardly. You just—" He touched his lips to her collar bone and she broke off on another shiver.

"Ah." He traced the delicate line of bone with his tongue, gratified by her sharp—and likely involuntary—gasp. "I did just." He gave his hips an experimental circle, slow and easy, and the pleasure spun out in lazy waves.

Then Meg made the noise. *That* noise. The cinnamon-rolls-hot-out-of-the-oven noise. The noise he'd last heard in response to another man's shoulders.

And suddenly, laziness flashed into heat. Into urgency. Into something possessive and demanding and...oh, hell, complicated. Which was a problem because Drew didn't do possessive. He didn't do urgent and he sure as hell didn't do complicated. Drew did light and easy. Drew did casual. It was his signature move; nobody did casual better than Drew.

So this sudden jag into *mine all mine* territory? It was bad. Very bad. Concern cut through the heat, and he shifted so he could lift himself off her. So he could run away, or make her run away, or something. He didn't know, exactly. But he needed space. He needed to breathe. To think.

But even that small movement sent pleasure spiraling through him again. He stopped, clamped his teeth together and breathed through the need as it rose, peaked and fell away in a perfectly mathematical arc. And suddenly Drew couldn't help himself. He'd deal with the complications later. Right now he wanted one more. Just one.

He sank into her again, deep and achingly slow. If this was it—and it obviously had to be—he wanted to remember it. Wanted to remember her. The hot give of her underneath him, the rich scent of her rising up to him, the dizzying clench and invitation of her body around him. One last taste, he thought. A souvenir.

That was the plan, anyway.

But then Meg moved, too. Maybe she shifted, or arched, or wiggled, or God only knew what she did. All Drew knew was that it wiped his mind as clean as a blackboard. And all his noble intentions had been on that blackboard.

He levered himself up on his elbows to stare down at her. Her hair knot sat crazily to one side. A handful of strands had escaped to spread themselves across the hood like a glittery spider web. Her hands had fallen to the sides, open and helpless, as if she were as wrecked as he was. Her bra was still under her breasts, offering them up like plump little apples. His mouth actually watered. Her eyes were closed, the moonlight painting her lashes blacker than black where they rested on her cheekbones. And her mouth—

Jesus, her mouth. Soft and wicked and utterly kissed.

Heat roared through him and he clenched his teeth against it. "This was a mistake," he told her.

"I know." She didn't open her eyes. Her mouth curved, though, slow and sharp.

"But we're going to do it again." He hadn't meant to say that, but he knew the truth when he heard it. Knew desperation when he heard it, too, God help him.

"Probably."

He blinked down at her, startled. His dick (mind of its own, as always) pulsed optimistically inside her.

"Oh," she said, "you mean like right now?"

Yes. The thought was right there on his tongue. Because Drew was ready to go there. Embarrassingly ready. Before he could manage to say the word, however, his brother stepped out of the hedge maze, a baby in his arms, amusement in his eyes.

"Fine by me," Will said. "Only keep it down this time, huh? Because I've been walking this kid around the maze for frickin' decades, and if you wake him up I'll murder you both. And there goes your happily ever after, you feel me?"

There went more than happily ever after, Drew thought bitterly. Because Meg would never—but never—make the same mistake twice. Not given a fully clothed moment to think it over. He'd rather Will *had* just murdered him.

He looked down at Meg, who had gone very still underneath him. "Yeah," he muttered. "I feel you."

She gazed up at him, cheeks flushed. "I'm pretty sure that's not your brother you're feeling there, Drew."

He startled himself with a crack of laughter. "No?"

"For Christ's sake," Will hissed. "The *baby*."

Drew ignored him, suddenly delighted by her. Because she'd just been caught *in flagrante delicto*, and by Will, for heaven's sake. But did she fall apart? Did she weep, snatch up her clothes or otherwise give in to hysteria? She did not. She only informed him—calmly—that what he was feeling was not, in fact, his brother's wrath but her vagina.

"I do love you, Meggy."

"You've always loved her." Will rolled his eyes. "And

137

don't call her Meggy. She hates that."

"I know." Drew grinned foolishly down at her. Because if even earth-shattering sex on the hood of his truck couldn't shake her, maybe nothing could. Maybe they were going to be okay after all.

"You know you love her?" Will asked, cradling the baby in his big hands like an incongruous football. "Or that she hates it when you call her Meggy?"

"The Meggy thing." His grin only spread. "But the love thing's not exactly a secret, either. I tell her I love her at least twice a day."

"That's true." Meg lifted her voice to Will. "He does." Drew stirred, as if to withdraw, to let her up, to gather up what was left of her maidenly dignity. She snatched the ends of his scarf, dragged him back. "If you move a muscle before Will is safely back in the house," she said, "I will kill you."

"I'll help you bury the body," Will told her, rubbing slow circles into his infant son's back. "Or I would if somebody else would hold the baby."

"Thank you." Meg renewed her hold on Drew's scarf, and Drew wondered if she was eying strangulation as the cause of death. He cleared his throat meaningfully but she didn't let up. He sighed and tried to stay as still as possible.

"Will?" he managed. "A little privacy?"

Will chuckled. "You might've thought of privacy before you decided to go for it *en plein air*," he told them. "You crazy kids." But he shifted the baby into the crook of one elbow and started for the back door at a rolling amble that suggested pirate captains or fathers of fussy babies. Drew knew it well. He was no father—nor was he a pirate—but he'd taken a shift or six with a howling kid on his shoulder. It didn't matter how big the house; you lived with babies, you took your turn.

Will threw him a laughing look on the way by.

"Congratulations," he said. "I think I speak for both myself and Audrey when I say it's about time. Just don't fuck it up, okay?"

Drew waited until the door had swished shut behind his brother, then looked down at Meg still pinned beneath him.

She was looking straight back up at him, as always. Meg didn't look away, he knew. Not ever. But he didn't let her up, because she *would* walk away.

"Come inside," he said. "Come inside with me. We need to talk."

She shook her head and sat up. Scooched her bottom up the hood and left him there. Dick out, heart pounding, abandoned.

Abandoned?

For God's sake, he was standing between her knees still. What business did he have feeling abandoned?

She shimmied her bra back into place with a quick maneuver that Drew found both sad and enchanting. There went the nudity, of course, but it was just so mysteriously female, that shimmy. She found her blouse and drew it up her arms. Ran the buttons together with a neat, steady competence that told him she wasn't feeling anything like abandoned. She didn't look like she was feeling much of anything, actually. He stepped back, unaccountably stung, and turned away. Dealt with the condom and his jeans. When he turned back, she was standing next to his bumper, all cool and elegant and collected. Except—

"Your hair," he said stupidly. He stared. Couldn't help it. Because her hair was loose. No pins, no pony, no knot. It fell straight down like unimpeded water, parting over her shoulders and flowing in two pale streams practically to her elbows.

"My hair?" Her brows flew up and she touched her head.

"It's down." Good God. What was he talking about? It was like his mouth was operating on autopilot or something.

"Oh. Yeah. The bun didn't actually survive the, uh—" She hooked a thumb over her shoulder at the truck behind her. "The sex." She met his eyes directly. "It didn't survive the sex on the hood of your truck."

Yeah, his Meggy didn't look away. Affection filled him, pushed out a few more ill-advised words. "I just didn't realize it was so—" So gorgeous. So glittery. So much. "—long." He swallowed. "I didn't realize it had gotten so

139

long. You never wear it down. Even when we go running, you do that—" He spun a hand in the air. "—thing. Where you loop up the ends?"

"Yeah." She folded her arms and studied him. "Do you really want to talk about my hair right now, Drew?"

"I could." One last blast of truth, courtesy of his unhinged impulse control. But he could. He could talk about her hair all night. It glowed like something fucking magical. And, Jesus, listen to him. He was losing it. "But we probably shouldn't." He studied her right back. "You probably want to talk about the whole sex-on-the-hood-of-Drew's-truck thing."

She sighed. "No, actually, I don't."

He blinked at her. "You don't?"

She waved an impatient hand. "Oh, I get that we have to, Drew. I just don't particularly want to."

He stared at her. "I never know when you're going to be a girl and when you're going to be a guy, Meg. It's confusing."

She startled him with a smile, sly and smoking hot. "You weren't confused a few minutes ago."

"A few minutes ago you were crying out my name in the throes of passion. It was pretty straightforward." He stepped toward her, hope blooming. "Want to be straightforward again?"

She laughed. "And now we're talking about the sex thing." She shook her head. "Sneaky, Drew. Very sneaky."

He found himself smiling back at her. He took the last step that closed the distance between them and slid a hand under her elbow. "Come inside, Meg," he said softly. "You're cold."

She wasn't actually cold. He knew that now. Hell, he'd always known that to some extent. He'd never been as fooled by that cool, slippery façade as most people. But even he hadn't suspected the molten lava she kept buried underneath it.

She shook her head. "It's nearly four in the morning, Drew. We're too tired to do anything effectively, even round two which I know you're angling for."

"Is round two on the table?" Some inner caveman he'd never met before lifted its head, sniffed hopefully at the air.

"It's not *not* on the table." But she stepped back, took her elbow with her. "Just not right now. We'll figure it out, Drew. We always do."

"Yeah." He didn't know what to do with his hands now that he wasn't touching her, so he shoved them in his pockets. Rocked back on his heels. "We do."

"But what we need to figure out first?" She arched a brow. "The E situation."

"The E situation." He frowned and wondered exactly which E situation she meant. Was she talking about the possibility—remote, as far as he was concerned—that they were both pawns in some intricate plot E had hatched? Or was this about the fact that she'd just had sex with Drew but might've been thinking about E's shoulders the whole time? Because she'd never made that cinnamon rolls noise over Drew's shoulders, now had she? "Meg, come on. There is no E situation."

"Of course there is." She folded her arms, lifted her chin. "We need answers, Drew."

"Which E has already agreed to provide." Drew folded his arms, too. Stared her down. "In the morning."

"So he says, but I really don't think—"

"Damn it, Meg, will you please just knock it off?" He glared at her, suddenly out of patience with the whole topic. Given what they'd just done together, what they'd just risked to do it, Drew figured they had better things to argue about than a guy who wasn't even there. Then again, Meg would hardly be the first girl Drew had slept with who'd maneuvered the conversation straight back to E at her earliest possible convenience. At least Meg had had the decency to get dressed first.

"He's the oldest friend I have," Drew snapped. "He was dead for fifteen years, and I just got him back. Do you mind giving me, I don't know, twenty-four hours to rejoice before you decide he's a criminal?"

She looked right back at him, unmoved. "Depends on whether or not he shows up for coffee with those answers he promised."

"Can't you just trust me?"

"You? Of course. Him? Not so much."

He tossed up his hands and growled—literally *growled*—in frustration.

She sighed. "Okay, we're getting nowhere here."

"No kidding."

"It's late," she said carefully. "We're tired. Tonight's been very...big."

He huffed out a laugh and scrubbed both hands over his face. "And in any number of ways."

"Amen." She smiled at him, a little amused and a lot sharp. Vintage Meg, in other words. "I'll come over in the morning and we'll see what we see, okay?" She patted his arm. "Until then, let's just try to get some—"

Her hand jerked, and her nails dug into his forearm.

"Hey, ow!" He tried to pull away but she was latched on like a leech. He frowned down at her but she wasn't looking at him. She was staring beyond his shoulder, her eyes huge and stricken, her face chalky white.

"What?" He whirled, threw a shoulder in front of her and scanned the darkness for whatever threat could cow his bullet-proof Meggy. "*What?*"

"Oh my God," she breathed and lifted a hand. She pointed past his shoulder, her finger all shaking accusation. "Drew, look."

He followed her finger to the upper corner of the carriage house, to the darkness under the eaves. To the tiny red light glowing there, indicating that the security system was live.

"What, the alarm's on?" Relief blasted through him, chased by a quick shot of anger. Jesus, she'd scared him to death. "Of course it's on, Meg. Will lives here. With his family. He'd have the kids implanted with those microchips like they put in stray dogs if Audrey let him. He'd have her implanted with one, too, but he's too smart to ask. So we're locked down like Fort Knox instead, and the marriage survives. Why are we suddenly panicking—"

She gave the back of his head a crisp smack and he

scowled. "Ow."

She took his jaw in her hand and aimed his face toward that tiny light again. "That's not a motion detector, Drew. That's a security camera. High powered, full color, internet capable, with 24/7 streaming. I installed it myself, I ought to know."

"Okay, so? I mean, it's just a camera—" He broke off, understanding dawning with a brutal flash. "Oh hell." He met her eyes in the darkness. "Oh shit." He swallowed, caught somewhere between a curse and a laugh. "Meg. Did we just make a sex tape?"

Chapter 18

"I told you he wasn't going to show up," Meg said to Drew's stiff shoulders the next morning. He didn't answer, only unlocked a set of pretty French doors at the rear of the Annex and let them into a vast, echoing ballroom. A ballroom, for Pete's sake. Meg often forgot exactly how rich Drew and his brothers were until a random bit of grandeur—like a ballroom—jumped up and slapped her in the face. The absurdity of it stalled her for a moment, and by the time she shook it off, Drew was already halfway across the dance floor. She jogged to catch up. "I told you E was going to stand us up. Didn't I tell you?"

"Calm down, cranky pants." He didn't slow the pace, or even turn to face her.

"Calm down? Calm *down*?" She was all but dancing with indignation. "Not even a remote possibility, buddy. And do you know why?"

He angled her a cool look. "Because you have about a pot and a half of high-test coffee in your system?"

"If I do, it's only because I spent a good chunk of my morning sitting around a coffee shop." She clung to his heels as he sailed through a warren of elegant parlors, nimbly dodging all the foot stools, wing back chairs and assorted priceless hoohahs. "Waiting for a guy who—did I mention?—didn't show up."

They hit the foyer—a lavish affair that looked like the bastard love child of Scarlett O'Hara and Elvis Presley—and he finally stopped.

"I guess you were right, Meg." He gave a gusty sigh and took her by both shoulders. Looked deeply into her eyes. Her heart leapt into a confused patter and she swallowed. "He must be a crime lord, after all. It's the only explanation." He shook his head sadly and turned away. He started up the double-barreled staircase that spiraled grandly to the second floor. Meg leapt after him.

"Unless—" he said, and stopped on the landing so suddenly that she almost crashed into him. She retreated a careful two steps. The landing had been designed to accommodate half a dozen hoop skirts, easy, but she felt safer with a few risers between them, given that his hands on her shoulders had nearly sent her into cardiac arrest just now.

She frowned up at him. "Unless what?"

"Unless he got a flat tire." He caressed his chin thoughtfully. "Or got hit by a car. Or even just overslept."

"Overslept?" She stared at him, astounded. It was hard to take a guy seriously when there was a zebra skin rug under his feet and a *Gone with the Wind* staircase at his back, but this was pushing it. "Drew, please. Consider the facts: A man rose from the grave last night to con us into committing a handful of very ugly felonies. He promised us an explanation at the time and the place of his own choosing, then didn't show up." She spoke with deliberate calm. "And you're suggesting it's because he overslept?"

"Why not?" His mouth went mulish and she pressed her fingers to the headache blooming at her temples. "He just moved here from California, which is, like, three hours behind East Coast time. A nine a.m. meeting to us is like six a.m. to him, plus he was up until after four, probably. Oversleeping is an entirely reasonable possibility."

"Oh, entirely." She nodded slowly. "So call him again. Maybe he'll answer this time. If he's awake."

He gazed down at her, and Meg didn't like what she saw in that face of his. Not even a little. "Yeah, I don't think so."

"Why not?"

He stepped forward, and suddenly she could smell the coffee shop where they'd spent the last few hours on his shirt. It mingled pleasantly with that sunshine-and-green-leaves smell that was pure Drew, and her stomach clenched on a surge of unauthorized desire.

"Because I don't want to talk to him right now," he said

softly. "I don't want to even talk about him." He slid a hand under her elbow and tugged her gently forward until she'd joined him on the landing of that ridiculous staircase. The urge to keep going until she'd pressed herself right up against that surprisingly solid chest of his was almost overwhelming. "I think we have other things to talk about, Meggy."

"You're right. We do." She swallowed hard and told herself to focus. Because they did have other things to talk about. And Meg was purely unwilling to discuss at least one of them. So she'd just have to direct the conversation toward the ones she was willing to get into. "Our accidental sex tape, for starters."

His brows shot up, then he chuckled. "How do you keep doing that?"

"What?"

"Surprising me."

"Oh, was I not supposed to mention the sex tape?" She blinked at him innocently. "Or just the sex? I'm sorry. Were we pretending that didn't happen?"

"I wasn't planning to." He studied her. "But when you accidentally get filmed banging a girl on the hood of your truck, she mostly either freaks out or pretends it didn't happen. And you didn't freak out, so—"

"So it didn't happen." She nodded slowly. "Only it did." Her blood gave an electric jump at the memory. "And I'm not most girls."

"Believe me, I know."

"Which means that—aside from getting some answers out of your old buddy E—destroying that tape is my top priority." She gave him a hard look. "Our top priority."

"Okay." He considered her thoughtfully. "But why?"

She stared at him. "Why?"

"Yeah. I mean, Will all but caught us in the act." He shrugged, like this was no big deal. Meg wondered if she was getting an ulcer. "Which means that everybody on the compound over the age of twelve will be fully briefed by noon at the latest. Why the big rush to kill footage of something everybody already knows about?"

She gazed at him, incredulous. "Because Will didn't catch us in the act, Drew. If memory serves—" And it did, dangerously. It smoked and pulsed and lingered, that memory. "—there was quite a lot of act that Will didn't catch at all. And I know he's the vigilant sort but given that it's a Saturday morning and that he was walking his baby around the yard until after three last night? There's still a possibility—remote, I know—that he isn't up yet. So maybe he hasn't reviewed his surveillance feed yet either. And if he hasn't, then it's possible—just possible—that the homemade porn is still our little secret." She glared at him. "So unless you want to see that tape in rotation at the family gift exchange for the next decade or so, we need to delete it right now."

"Hmm." Drew pursed up his lips and thought it over. "I see your point."

"Thank you. Can we go kill it now?"

He studied her. "Can we watch it first?"

Meg was saved from answering when the giant front doors at her back swung open. Good thing, too, as she had no idea what she'd been about to say. Suddenly, the foyer was filled with boys and noise. They spilled into the room, Drew's herd of nephews, ranging in age from six on down to diapers. They invaded in a cloud of shoving and thunder, the way boys did, their wet heads varying from silvery-white to jet black. The scent of chlorine wafted off them, which made some sense of the wet hair and the swim goggles they were shooting at one another like rubber bands.

"I totally got you, Ben!" Luke roared. Luke and Ben were the firstborns of their respective families. Luke belonged to James and Bel while Ben belonged to Will and Audrey but there wasn't a lot of daylight between brothers and cousins in the Blake clan. Luke delivered an open-handed smack to Ben's shoulder. "You're dead!"

"Merely a flesh wound!" Ben caught Luke's hand and gave it an enthusiastic twist. "I'm not dead yet!"

They fell across the stairs at Meg's feet, wrestling and yipping like a pair of puppies.

"*I'm getting bettah*," Meg murmured, watching them

147

with bemused affection.

Drew laughed. "*I think I'll go for a walk.*"

Audrey Blake stepped through the doors the boys had left hanging open behind them, her arms loaded with boxes. A gorgeous purse rode in the crook of her elbow and a pair of equally gorgeous sunglasses covered half of her perfect face. Shiny hair swung to her jaw in two impossibly perfect wings that she called her mommy do but that other people—normal mortals—paid vast amounts of money to achieve.

Not Audrey, though. No, Audrey just woke up that way. Meg knew this for a fact. The woman didn't dye her hair, either. It just came out of her scalp the exact color of fairy wings. Mother Nature had also provided the girl with some classic bone structure and a truly astonishing set of curves. Standing next to her made Meg feel eight feet tall and about as appealing as cottage cheese.

She adored the woman anyway. Nobody resisted Audrey Blake.

"Audrey!" Drew said. Then the man who wouldn't even hold Meg's purse bounded down the steps to scoop the pile of boxes out of his sister-in-law's arms. He planted an affectionate kiss on her cheek, too. Such a gentleman. Meg suppressed an eye roll. "Bought out Russia, I see."

"What?" Audrey blinked down at the...were those Cyrillic letters scrawled all over the packages in Drew's arms? "Oh, that." She waved a negligent hand. "I found them on the porch. They're probably for Jillian."

Meg cocked her head. "Jillian bought out Russia?"

"It's that style blog of hers." Audrey sighed. "She's all about the peasant dress these days, and some Ukrainian label keeps sending her clothes." She lifted an elegant shoulder. "I don't see the appeal of designer poverty myself, but the followers are multiplying like loaves and fishes. Evidently, Jilly knows what the cool kids are wearing these days before the cool kids do. And speaking of kids—" Audrey narrowed her eyes at the chaos in her foyer. "Boys!" She pitched her voice over the din with startling ease, given her snack-sized proportions. Silence fell. "Do we live in a barn?"

The dog pile at Meg's feet had grown by a four-year-old and a three-year-old since she'd last looked. At the sound of Audrey's question, they all froze. Even Luke's twin Joseph, who sat on the step beside her foot, his nose in his omnipresent book, looked up.

"Benjamin?" Meg said helpfully. She nudged him with the toe of her sneaker. "I believe your mother would like to know if you were, in fact, born in a barn."

Ben and Luke released one another and sat up, grinning. The four-year-old Micah got in one last lick, then followed suit. Meg smiled at him. She couldn't help it. He was the baby of her heart, and he had a damn good swing on him.

Luke pointed gleefully at his cousin. "Your mom's talking to you, Benny."

Belinda Blake strolled through the open door next and paused to survey the madness. The baby riding on her hip chewed wetly on its own fist with utter absorption.

"Good heavens," Bel said mildly. She blinked around the foyer as if taken aback, though Meg knew very well that she and James lived in the heart of their own hurricane over there at Hunt House. Her dark ponytail snaked over one shoulder and she stood hipshot in the doorway like some kind of lean, elegant race horse. Even in jeans and a long-sleeved tee with a baby now chewing on her ponytail, Bel exuded class. Money. Old money. If Meg had to pick one word to describe Bel, it would have to be *Mayflower*. That would take care of the whole vibe.

"Hey, Bel." Drew planted a kiss on this sister-in-law's cheek as well. The baby squealed and lunged for him, his little legs churning wildly.

"Oh, sure," Bel said to the baby. "It's all about Uncle Drew now. But what about when you're hungry? Or when you've loaded up your diaper? Who do you love then?"

"Mommy." Drew dumped Jillian's designer poverty onto a leopard print bench and scooped the baby off his mother's hip. He nuzzled his nose into the soft squish of the baby's neck. "You love your mommy best. But does Mommy do this?" He tossed the kid into the air like a droolly basketball and caught him with practiced aplomb. The baby shrieked with unhinged delight, and Meg's ovaries gave a startling little twinge.

She sat down abruptly on the riser beside Joseph and his book. Oh, no, she told herself. Bad enough that you're in love with him. You are not succumbing to baby madness, too.

"Are you okay, Miss Meg?" Joseph looked up from his book, his dark eyes large and concerned.

"I don't know."

He patted her elbow, scooted over to make room and went back to his book. Meg wanted to throw her arms around him. Because she was dying here—*dying*—and this thin, quiet boy was the only one who'd noticed. Who'd not only noticed, but offered any comfort.

"You're the best, Joe." She jostled him with her shoulder. "You know that?"

"Not at swimming, I'm not." He glanced at his twin and his cousin, happily grappling a few steps away. "Not at a lot of things."

"No, I guess not." Her heart squeezed for him. She knew exactly what it was to be the awkward twin. "But plenty of people can swim. And loads of people can talk. Geez, do they talk. But hardly anybody listens. Hardly anybody watches. But you do. And that means that you see stuff other people don't see. You know what they don't know. And that makes you—"

"A freak?"

"No, special." She gave him another shoulder nudge. "It makes you the best."

He hunched uncomfortably and went back to his book, a flush on his cheeks. She hoped it was because he was secretly pleased and not mortified.

Drew—evidently finished throwing the baby around like a Frisbee—was now flying him around the foyer like a fighter jet, with three-year-old Nicholas squealing at his heels.

"Does Mommy make you fly?" He zoomed the baby up to the steps and brought him in for a dramatic landing on Meg's knees. She automatically hooked her hands under those tiny armpits and the baby pushed himself up on surprisingly sturdy legs. "Take care of that one," Drew told her carelessly. "It's my favorite."

He snatched up Nicholas for an enthusiastic nougie—which the child endured in a fit of ecstasy—and abandoned Meg with the baby. Oh, she'd kill him. He knew very well that she didn't care for children until they could walk unassisted. Which was exactly why he was always plopping the fresh ones on her lap when she wasn't paying attention. She looked around for Bel—surely she'd take her own baby back—but the kid was having none of it. He put his two wet fists on either side of her face, put his nose about six inches from hers, and spoke to her at earnest length about lord only knew what. It sounded serious, though, and her ovaries wept. She wondered if it was possible to die of estrogen poisoning. Then she wondered if she could just kill Drew instead. Then she realized she didn't need to bother. His nephews were on the job.

Chapter 19

"I thought I was your favorite nephew!" Luke yelled and flung himself across Drew's back.

"You are!" Drew jabbed a finger into some unprotected ribs. Luke gave a happy shout and put his uncle in a headlock.

"But you said I was your favorite," Ben shouted, then threw himself onto Luke's back and put *him* in a headlock.

"Of course you are," Drew said obligingly, and went after his ribs, too.

"No, me!" Micah—evidently unable to reach anybody's head—launched himself at Drew's thigh. Nicholas, not to be left out, launched himself at the other one.

"Oh, that's right." Drew staggered dramatically and went slowly—carefully—to his knees under a pile of boys. "It's Micah who's my favorite. Or was it Nicky?" He paused. "Oh, no, wait, sorry. It's Joseph." He reached out and snatched Joseph into the heart of the madness, book and all. Demented laughter rang all the way to the cathedral ceiling.

The baby patted Meg's cheeks again and she returned her attention to those huge dark eyes. It appeared to be her turn to talk. "Boys are so weird," she told him. "I honestly don't know if you're worth the trouble."

"Believe me," Audrey said, "we wonder the same thing sometimes."

"Honestly." Bel joined her and—mercifully—took her baby back. "You'd think they'd been born in a barn and raised by wolves." She shook her head and turned to Audrey. "They didn't even shut the door before they fell on each other like wild dogs?"

Audrey pulled off her sunglasses and hooked them into

her collar. "They did not."

Ben scrubbed vigorous knuckles into Luke's head. "Your mom thinks you're a wild dog."

"Aaaarooooooo!" Luke's howl was somewhat muffled by Micah's armpit. Micah shouted and kicked Nicholas in the crotch. Things went, in Meg's opinion, somewhat predictably from there.

"And in front of company, too," Bel observed, unruffled. She dimpled down at Meg. "Good morning, Meg."

"Oh, yes," Audrey said and shifted her attention back to Meg. She smiled, too, and it spread across her perfect face, slow and knowing and amused. "Good morning, Meg."

Meg's heart dropped inside her. They knew. Of course they knew. Drew had been right. Will knew, therefore everybody knew. The question was, how much did they know? Hood of the truck? Sex tape? Both?

She smiled back, weakly.

"Good morning, ladies."

Drew scraped off the boys and dragged himself up to sit beside Meg as if exhausted but the twinkle in his eye said otherwise. The boys sprawled happily across the steps at their feet, exchanging desultory punches. Joseph, Meg noted with interest, had a pretty good swing for a bookworm.

"Okay, boys!" Audrey clapped her hands briskly. Meg jumped. "Shower time. Drew, do you mind making sure they don't drown each other?" She turned to Meg with a friendly smile and very shrewd eyes. "We girls are going to have some coffee."

"Oh," Meg said, alarmed, "I shouldn't. I'm fully caffeinated already." She shot Drew a look that said *don't you dare leave me*. "Plus, Drew and I have a...thing. A work thing we have to—"

"You go ahead and have coffee." Drew rose with cowardly alacrity. "I can get going on the...thing."

"You'd better," she muttered. Because if Bel and Audrey were going to grill her like a steak—and they definitely intended to—the least Drew could do was hack into his brother's security system and find that damn footage

"All right, men!" Drew scooped up an abandoned pair of swim goggles and shot it at the nearest boy. "Hit the showers!"

"Take those boxes up to Jillian on your way," Audrey called after them. "The peasants need their designer poverty."

They leapt up and swarmed the bench, snatched up various packages and clattered off up the stairs like that herd of wild dogs. Nicholas led the charge, then Ben and Luke, then Joseph and his book, then finally Micah. Drew gave a blood-thirsty yodel that inspired speed, shrieks and general delight, and bounded up the stairs after the boys.

Bel and Audrey watched them go with that odd mixture of affection and exasperation that Meg figured they must pass out to new mothers in the hospital. Especially mothers of boys.

Audrey turned bright eyes to Meg. "So how about that coffee?"

"Oh." Meg's mind, usually so agile, went blank. "I—"

"—could use a cup of coffee," Bel decided and hooked her free hand through Meg's elbow. "You had a very late night."

"Cripes," Meg muttered, her cheeks flaming. "You Blakes gossip like old ladies."

"We do." Audrey latched onto her other elbow and they began towing her toward the kitchen. "We absolutely do. Though Will was wise enough to wait until morning to tell me about the little eyeful he got outside the hedge maze last night."

Meg gave an internal sigh of relief. Blakes didn't bury the lead. If they knew about a sex tape, it would be the headline of this discussion, for sure. No mention meant no knowledge. Thank Christ.

"Well, that was smart," Bel said. "Your Owen's still got his days and nights mixed up."

"It's true." Audrey shoved them through a swinging door into the kitchen. "It was my night to sleep. If Will had woken me up—even for news this juicy—I'd have murdered him."

154

"Juicy?" Meg asked, humiliation sinking into her gut with a sickening squelch. "That's what we're calling it? Juicy news?"

She found herself being propelled across a gorgeous kitchen, all professional-grade appliances, copper-bottomed pans and yard upon yard of polished granite countertops. A hulking island took up the entire center of the room and Audrey nudged her onto one of the barstools beside it. Bel took a second stool. She plopped the baby onto the counter in front of her and spoke to Meg while addressing the baby.

"We *are* calling it juicy news, aren't we? *Aren't* we, sweet pea? Because that's what it is! Yes, it is! It's *news* when Miss Meg and Uncle Drew finally get their dirty on! And on the hood of Uncle Drew's ugly old truck, too!"

Meg folded her arms on the counter and slowly lowered her forehead to them. "Oh God."

"Well, it is," Audrey said calmly. She filled a kettle on the stove for Bel's preferred tea and set the burner aflame under it. She headed for the coffee maker. "We've been waiting for this for years, Meghan. Years."

Meg couldn't lift her head. Couldn't look them in the eye. "All of you?"

"Of course." Bel jiggled the baby, who gave a drool-filled guffaw of delight. "Yes, we have, haven't we? *Haven't* we, Bobby boy? What did your daddy say when we texted him the news this morning? He said *hot diggity*."

"He said that?" Audrey threw a skeptical look over her shoulder. "*Hot diggity?*"

"I'm paraphrasing," Bel said serenely. "For the baby." She gave Meg a laughing glance. "But it was hot diggity, wasn't it? I mean, you've waited long enough. It had to have been some pretty hot diggity. Right?"

"You texted your husband about this." Meg didn't lift her head—still couldn't—but twisted to stare at Bel, cheeks burning. Because holy hell she was not discussing the hotness of Drew's diggity with his sisters-in-law. And a baby. "You and James had a text conversation about the fact that I had sex on the hood of a car last night?"

"With Uncle Drew!" Bel told the baby. "That's the

important bit, don't forget."

Like she could forget.

"But you texted him. And he texted you back."
Acceptance started to trickle in around the humiliation, tied itself to the knowledge and sank it like a rock into her gut. Meg forced herself to sit up. Sit up, breathe it in, and pull herself together. "The two of you had an in-depth discussion of my sex life via text message while your boys learned to swim."

Audrey snorted. "Hey, you want privacy? Don't do it outside the hedge maze." Her hands flew like graceful birds over the coffee pot. "You know how Owen is. We spend more time carrying him around that garden after midnight than we do in our own bed."

"You want privacy?" Bel shot her a sideways look. "Don't fall for a Blake. Privacy is practically against the code."

"Family first," Audrey said cheerfully.

"Your fight is my fight," Bel told the baby, patting his little fists together. He crowed happily.

"What we have we share," Meg finished grimly. "Even the details of my sex life."

"Certainly not," Audrey said. "We're not animals. We only shared the broad strokes of your sex life."

"Strokes." Bel snickered to the baby. "She said strokes."

"Oh my God." Meg stared at her. "That was very nearly crude, Belinda."

"I know." She twinkled over at Meg. "James is a terrible influence. I used to be very proper."

"Don't tell anybody." Audrey set a cup of tea and a fat muffin on the counter, inside Bel's reach but outside the baby's. She put a cup of coffee and an even fatter muffin next to Meg's elbow. "She has a reputation to maintain."

"And a livelihood that depends on it," Bel told the baby. "Mommy's the queen of gracious living, did you know?" She rubbed her nose against the baby's, eliciting another delighted gurgle. "*Chat Magazine* says so."

Meg's phone jingled in her pocket and she snatched at it

like salvation itself.

"Hello?"

"Good morning, Meg!"

"Clara." She stared in horror at Audrey and Bel, at the baby. She'd already been in a hopeless situation, pinned down in the kitchen of the Annex, dancing just ahead of friendly fire. Now her psychic twin was calling?

"Guess where I am?" Clara sang cheerfully.

"Peru?" she asked with naked hope.

"Peru? No. I'm in your driveway."

She jerked around as if she could see Clara's neat little Jetta through several layers of drywall and brick. As if she could stop her arrival with the power of her mind. "My driveway?"

"Clara's here!" Audrey clapped her hands and leaned toward the phone in Meg's numb hand. "Hey, Clara," she called. "We're in the Annex having coffee. Come on over!"

"Is that Audrey?" Clara asked.

"Hey, Clara!" Bel leaned closer to the phone, too. "There's tea, too."

"You're having coffee with the girls and didn't invite me?" Clara's voice was the perfect combination of surprise and reproach.

"And muffins," Meg said, giving up. "There are muffins, too."

"I'll be there in two minutes."

Chapter 20

Meg's twin sister Clara walked into the kitchen bare seconds later, or so it seemed to Meg. It was hardly eleven in the morning, but her twin wore a curvy tweed suit that looked like it had walked off the set of a World War II movie. Not that Meg was surprised. Clara never dressed; she costumed.

"Good morning, Blakes," Clara chirped. "The door was open so I let myself in."

"Well, crap." Audrey poured another cup of coffee for Clara and looked at Bel. "We raised all that hell about it, then we forgot to shut the door. We really do live in a barn."

"And we're raising wolves!" Bel told the baby. She made little claws of his fists. "Rrrrahr!"

"I shut it for you." Clara settled on the stool beside Meg's as neatly as a little bird, and added a delicate stream of cream to her coffee. Her hands were tiny and fine-boned as she stirred, and her dark hair waved away from her face in a perfect victory roll. Meg had no doubt she'd scoured the internet for instructions the instant she'd bought the suit. Clara was nothing if not thorough.

"Thank you, Clara." Audrey plated up a pretty muffin and handed it over. "You're a doll."

Meg glanced over at her tiny, beautiful, charming twin. A doll. Wasn't she just?

"Oh, Audrey, thank *you*. I skipped breakfast." Clara beamed at her muffin with delight. "This is gorgeous." She broke off a minuscule crumb and slipped it between deep ruby lips. Christ, who wore lipstick at 11:22 on a Saturday morning? Clara closed her eyes, as if overcome. "And it tastes even better than it looks!"

"Thanks." Bel beamed back at her. She lived to reduce

people to helpless yummy noises. She wasn't the queen of domestic bliss for nothing. "You should take some home. I've been test-baking. We have dozens."

"Dozens of dozens," Audrey said, settling onto yet another stool and lifting her own coffee cup. "Save me from myself."

"Oh, goodness," Clara said, blinking open her enormous dark eyes. "I don't think I'll even be able to finish this one! It's so rich."

Meg sighed down at her own plate, at the scant crumb or two that remained of her own muffin. Her coffee cup was empty too. She was just a Piggy McPiggerson, wasn't she? All greedy wants and heedless satisfaction. Empty plates and hoods of trucks and squishy babies and—

"Oh, stop it," Clara said. "I'm on a tight schedule today, Meg. Don't waste my time on angst. I want details so start talking."

Bel blinked at Meg. "You told her already?"

Meg smiled grimly. "Nope."

Bel arched a brow at Audrey over the baby's bald head. "Did you call her?"

"Not me." Audrey studied Clara over her coffee cup. She tossed a glance Meg's way. "Is it a twin thing? Like one of those across-the-miles, great-disturbance-in-the-force deals?"

"No." Meg sighed. "We don't have that. I can't read her at all."

"So she really is a psychic, then?" Good old Audrey, blunt as always. It was just one of the many reasons Meg actually liked her. "She takes after Hildy?"

Meg sighed. Hildy Wise was the most famous ghost-buster in the tri-state area. She'd recently launched her own podcast on the subject, and it was hotter even than Jilly's style blog. She also happened to be Meg's and Clara's mother. "That's one way to explain it."

"Mom's gift is a little different from mine." Clara set down her cup and sent Audrey a twinkling smile. "She really feels the feels, you know?"

"Feels the feels," Bel said dubiously. "Right."

"It's messy." Clara shrugged delicately. "I don't care for messes."

"Not unless she's the one making them." Meg rose. "I'm having more coffee. Refill? Anybody?"

They ignored her.

"Whereas your gift?" Audrey prompted.

"Whereas my gift," Clara went on serenely, "is a bit less...personal. Mom connects. I'm more the observe and report type." Clara broke off another invisible particle of muffin. "Which is why the Secret Service and the FBI are kind enough to seek my opinion from time to time when they need a profile and the usual channels fail."

"That or the fact that you're a board-certified psychiatrist with a specialization in criminal profiling," Meg said from the coffee maker, still sort of shocked that it was true. Because emotionally speaking, Clara had been a hot mess straight through her early twenties. Then she'd figured out her gift, harnessed it to some serious intellectual firepower and blown through med school in about half the time it took ordinary humans. So now the girl was gorgeous *and* ridiculously accomplished. Not that Meg was bitter.

"I do like the bad boys." Clara folded tiny, smug hands. "Then again, who doesn't?"

"Bad?" Meg snorted. "Try homicidal."

"What can I say? Abnormal psychology fascinates me." She shot a sly smile Meg's way. "Maybe that's why I read you so well and with so little effort. The hood of his truck, Meg?"

Meg scowled at the coffee pot. "Why do you even bother asking for details when you already have them?"

"I don't have details. I have general impressions, one of which you just confirmed, so thank you." Clara fixed her with a look of sympathetic exasperation that Meg could feel between her shoulder blades. "I'd much rather have been wrong about that, though. Honestly, Meg, why do you have to make everything so damn easy for him? You couldn't even ask for a bed?"

Meg threw her a dark glance. "Tell me again what you're doing here?" she asked. "Because I'm pretty sure nobody invited you."

Clara smoothed her skirt with fond hands. "I did a crime-scene walk through this morning with the very yummy Special Agent Torrence—"

"Well that explains the outfit," Meg muttered.

"—and ended up practically next door. I thought we could have brunch."

"I'm sorry, I make it a firm policy not to brunch with extras in swing kids movies." Meg brought her coffee back to the counter and leaned hard into the subject change. "For Christ's sake, Clara, couldn't you impress Agent Prettyboy with your sparkling conversation? Did you really have to bust out the tweed?" She ran her eyes over the whole package. "And the hair?"

"Don't forget the shoes." Clara held out a tiny foot and Meg beheld a pair of hand-stitched spectator pumps in caramel and ivory, the leather polished to a soft glow. Either somebody had gotten themselves offed on a nice, dry sidewalk or Clara's Agent Torrence had spread his jacket over the mud puddles like a gentleman.

"They're good shoes," Bel announced.

"Very good," Audrey agreed. "Well played, Clara."

"I'm sure Agent Handsome was very impressed," Meg said bitterly, because the shoes were good. Of course they were.

"Oh, he was." Clara sipped her coffee and eyed Meg over the rim. "And I didn't even have to bang him on the hood of his Crown Victoria."

Meg's cheeks burned and she looked away. "Shut up."

Bel grinned. "You two are such sisters."

"That we are," Meg said with a resigned sigh. "That we are."

"So." Clara patted the counter and turned those huge dark eyes on Meg. Focused. Meg felt the impact all the way to her soul. "You finally slept with Drew, huh?"

Meg didn't answer out of principle. Clara already knew the answer, so why should she? She concentrated instead on the faint dizziness washing over her, fuzzy and alluring. It was one of the oldest sensations Meg could remember—her twin nibbling around the edges of her mind, of her heart. *Let me in, let me see, where are you,* what *are you*?

"Why now?" Clara murmured. "After eight solid years of no, what made you suddenly say yes? Something changed. It must've. What was it?"

Meg didn't have anything like her mother's or Clara's ability to perceive...more than normal people. But she had lived with them most of her life, and she knew how to protect herself. She imagined a lead vest, the kind they laid over you at the dentist's office to protect you from the x-ray machine. She pulled it up in her mind's eye in exquisite detail, right down to the grommets on the edges, then shrugged it on. The weight of it settled comfortingly over her body, over her soul. She was safe under it. Alone.

"Aw." Clara's lower lip poked out. "What's in there you don't want me seeing?"

"Maybe nothing," Meg said. "Maybe the most incredible, mind-blowing sex that's ever been experienced in the history of the world."

Bel's teacup paused halfway to her mouth. "Really?"

"My point is—" Meg kept her eyes on Clara's. "—you only get to know if I want you to know. And I don't."

Clara folded her lips into a dissatisfied line. "You never want me to know anything."

"I never want anybody to know anything," Meg corrected. "It's not about you. Not everything is."

"Oh yeah." Audrey lifted her cup. "Such sisters."

"Twins," Clara said her eyes dangerously bright. "Much to Meg's everlasting disgust."

"Oh, here we go." Meg threw up her hands and shot off her stool. "Here come the tears. It's the Clara show, everybody." She stalked the length of the kitchen and shoved her fingers into her hair. Tried to, anyway. Encountered a bunch of slick, smooth hair in a fat braid pinned low at the nape of her neck. She hit the stove and turned left. "I'm having a crisis, so she gets to cry. I'm the one who just blew eight years of solid friendship for one night—no, for twenty minutes. For twenty stupid, steamy minutes on the hood of his stupid, ugly Blazer."

She hit the door and jerked another left, stalked past a little breakfast nook and aimed for the fridge. "And Clara's right. I didn't even ask for a bed." She threw out disgusted hands. "I didn't make him buy me dinner, either, or even a drink. In fact, I'm pretty sure I picked up the bar tab last night." She paused, mid-stride. "Oh, hell, I did. *I* bought *him* drinks—him and his stupid, dangerous new best friend, or his old best friend or what the fuck ever—then we did a little breaking and entering—"

"Wait, you what?" Audrey's eyes were large and startled but Meg was too far gone to stop now. The cork was out and she was rolling.

"—after which we indulged in a side-dish of hacking, during which I flashed him my lady bits—"

Bel stared. "On purpose?"

"—then followed him home." She turned at the fridge and sailed back to the counter. She slapped both hands to the granite and leaned in. Was she shaking? She thought she might be shaking. "I followed him home and I screwed him silly outside the garage. Outside the *garage*." She dropped to her elbows. "Which is where your husband and your child, Audrey. Your precious baby, Owen, who doesn't know day from night? Yeah, that's where they found us. Found me. Skirt up, blouse gone, hair shot to hell. Just a pile of smoking rubble still pinned underneath the guy who'd wrecked me."

She lowered her forehead to the counter. Slowly. She simply deflated. "He wrecked me," she said softly. "Shattered me. I'm in pieces. I've been trying to be normal all day and I'm exhausted because I don't know how. I don't know how to be normal anymore."

Clara gave her arm a warm squeeze. "Oh, honey," she said. "You never knew how to be normal."

Meg laughed wearily. "For somebody who's made a profession out of feelings, you know shit-all about sympathy."

"You don't want my sympathy. You never want sympathy. You want to be cured, and you know that's impossible."

"Is it?" Hope sparked inside her. She lifted her head,

gazed at her twin. "Are you sure? What if I took off the lead vest? What if I let you poke around in there? Could you—"

"It's a lead vest?" Clara tipped her head. "You see it as a lead vest?"

"Yeah. Like at the dentist."

"A lead vest." She shook her head in wonder.

"Clara, focus." She leaned forward urgently. "If I took it off, could you—"

"Funny." Clara gazed into the middle distance. "It comes through as fire to me."

"What does?"

"The block." Clara blinked back to Meg. "When you drop the curtain on me, it feels hot. You practically burn my fingers."

"Well, you shouldn't reach for the stove," Meg said reasonably. "Now can we please talk about—"

"Whatever you are, Meggy," Clara said slowly. "Whatever you think you are? It's not cold."

Meg stared at her, at a loss.

"You didn't know, did you?" Clara's smile was faint, almost sad. "You've started to believe your own press. You think you're cold."

"But she's not," Audrey said, leaning in on her elbows.

"No," Bel said, eyeing her consideringly. "I've never thought so."

"She does, though." Clara nodded at her. "Poor Meggy."

"Don't call me that," Meg said automatically. They ignored her. "Plus, I'm not poor anything. I had mind-blowing sex last night. I had mind-blowing sex on the hood of a truck."

"It shattered you," Bel said softly.

"Wrecked you," Audrey put in.

"You lost your normal," Clara said.

Meg put her head back on her forearms, loss and fear swirling inside her, but strangely comforted. "Yes."

"You love him," Bel said simply.

"Of course I do," Meg said quickly.

"No, you *love him* love him." Audrey patted her

shoulder.

"Of course I do," Meg said, bitterly this time.

"You always have," Clara told her.

"Well, I wish somebody had told me."

"I just did." Clara ran her hand up and down Meg's arm, as if she could smooth out this horrifying wrinkle in her life as easily as she could iron a shirt.

"Gosh, thanks." She breathed, just breathed, inside the dark warmth of her folded arms. "Want to fix it now?"

Clara paused. "You really want me to do that? To take it out like mom takes out a ghost?"

"What, send it over the bridge?" Audrey asked, respect in her voice. She'd personally witnessed Hildy Wise sending an uncooperative spirit into the hereafter. "Are you sure that's a good idea?"

"Is that what you want?" Clara asked Meg again, her hand going still on Meg's arm. "Is that really what you want? For me to find this thing for Drew inside your heart? To pull it up by the roots and destroy it? Burn it down? Is that your answer?"

Meg just focused on the breathing. In and out. Fuck, it hurt. The very act of living, of taking in oxygen had become a chore, a conscious effort in the face of this impending pain.

"I can't lose him." The words came out bloody and jagged, torn unwillingly from beneath the lead she'd laid over her heart. "I can't—" Her throat closed and she had to swallow past the terror and something perilously close to hysteria. "I just can't," she said finally.

"But if you don't love him anymore," Bel said carefully, "haven't you lost him anyway?"

"Because you've always loved him." Audrey's voice was steady, merciless. "It's always been this way. You've always been in love with him. You just didn't know it."

"Which is why Clara can't fix it," Bel told her gently. "If she takes the love away, you're not going back to normal. Not if normal is being in love with him. You'd be going back to...nothing."

Tears gathered, hot and mortifying, in the back of her throat. "Can you make me not know, then?" Desperation grew inside her, clawed and crawled, and she turned frantic eyes on Clara. Snatched up her hands. "I've never asked you for anything in my life, but if you could do this—"

"God, Meg. You have no idea how long I've waited for you to ask me for something. For anything." She laughed, but it sounded so sad. "For you to need something from me. To need me, period."

"But you're not going to do it, are you?" Resignation washed over her, icy and final, and she withdrew her hands.

"I wish I could. Please believe that. I wish I could." Clara's hands hung in the air for a moment, abandoned and hurt. She folded them neatly and lowered them to the table. "Ask me for something else, Meg." Her lips curved, perfect and sad. "Anything."

"I don't need anything else." Meg met her eyes. "Just this."

She shook her head. "First do no harm."

"Stop being a psychiatrist," Meg snapped. It was petty but she didn't care. "Try being my sister for once."

"I am being your sister. This thing you want? It would do you harm," Clara said, her eyes on her linked fingers. "Irreparable harm, and I won't have your blood on my hands." She lifted her eyes, caught Meg's with a penetrating gaze. "Or his. I love him, too."

"Oh, please." Meg stared. "You hate Drew."

"Well, I'm not in love with him." Clara leaned in. "But my sister is. My twin sister. And he's taken that far too casually for my taste."

"He doesn't know, Clara." Meg pressed her lips together. "I didn't even know, so how could he—" She broke off, fresh horror flooding through her. "No." She chopped the thought off at the root. "No, I went over this last night in my head, very carefully. He doesn't know. He couldn't. If he did, he'd never have—" She broke off, swallowed. "—done what he did."

"Done you, you mean?" Audrey asked.

"Exactly." Meg nodded firmly. "He might not *love me* love me, but he loves me. And if he knew that I—"

She stopped. God, it was still so hard to plop it out

there.

"—love him?" Bel supplied. "If he knew that you were in love with him?"

"Yes, thank you." Meg sighed. "If he knew, he'd never have had sex with me. Because he'd have known how much it would hurt me. And he wouldn't do that. He's an irresponsible clown much of the time but when it counts, he comes through." She met Clara's eyes. "So he doesn't know."

Clara nodded slowly, then reached out to cover Meg's hand with her own. "But he should, Meg. That's my point. He doesn't. But if he wanted to know? If he just looked? He would know." Her smile was gentle for all that she'd just run Meg through with the truth like a fucking sword. "And this is why I love him. And why I hate him. He's got potential. A lot of it. But until he does know, and I see what he does about it? I won't know whether I love him or hate him."

Meg stared at her for a moment, then surprised herself with a laugh. A genuine laugh, straight from her belly.

"Yeah, you know what? Me, too." Meg laughed until tears gathered in her eyes. "I'm going to wait for that, too, then I'll decide which way to go with this."

Clara stood up—she only came up to Meg's chin, for God's sake—but she wrapped her arms around Meg, tight and strong.

"I'll kill him for you," she whispered. "If he doesn't choose the right way, I'll scramble his brains like an egg."

"You stay out of his head," Meg said, but she hugged her sister back. "If I need an egg scrambled, I'll scramble it myself."

The door swung open and Drew appeared in the threshold, clean wet boys hanging off him like barnacles. He looked like hell—two days worth of beard darkening his jaw, shampoo fluff clinging to his wild hair, his ancient t-shirt sopping wet. Meg could see a flash of belly through a hole in the cotton, for heaven's sake. His feet were big and bare and planted sturdily apart to accommodate Micah, who—naked as the day he was born—rode the left one like a pony.

Everything inside her leapt up and yearned.

God, she was a mess.

"I heard somebody say egg." He gave them a winsome smile. "I also heard scrambled. I'll marry the first woman who makes that happen."

Bel cut a glance Audrey's way. "He's proposing again."

"Over eggs." Audrey sipped her coffee with disgust.

"You're an egg slut," Clara told him.

"Good morning, Clara." Drew smiled at her, big and bright. "Nice to see you, too."

He cut hopeful eyes Meg's way.

"Oh, please," Meg said. She pulled that lead vest back into place with a breath and a wish. He looked so damn good. "Like I cook."

Chapter 21

"Well, since I'm already debasing myself with willy-nilly marriage proposals, let me make it clear that I would also marry whoever scrapes whatever this is off my foot." Drew lifted his left foot and gave it an experimental jiggle. Micah muffled his delight against Drew's shin. "I appear to have suffered an infestation of some sort."

"Well, that'll happen." Clara smiled sweetly at him. "The morning after is a real b—" She broke off, considered the boys in the crooks of his elbows, the two hanging off his back, the one on his foot. "—a bear. The morning after is just a bear, Drew."

As usual, it was all sugar and razor blades with her. Drew sighed. He'd never been able to figure out just what the hell Clara had against him. He didn't judge her or her mother on the ghost-busting-psychic thing. He was polite to her father, which was no easy task considering all the ugly water the guy had sent roaring under Meg's bridge. The one and only time Clara and Drew had ever even participated in the same kerfuffle, Drew had taken one for the team and gotten himself—and, okay, Meg—arrested in Clara's place.

Arrested, not charged.

So if Drew had ever done anything to offend Clara, he couldn't imagine what it was.

He'd done some things to Meg, though.

Awareness sparked through him with a bright shock, then settled down to cruise hot and glowy though his veins. He frowned. Sex was fun and Drew enjoyed it but he'd never had any trouble leaving it in the night before where it belonged. Not until today, anyway. But he'd been suffering these whole-body flashbacks all morning, and they were starting to concern him. One second he'd be enjoying a testy little back-and-forth with Meg, the next he was leaning into the scent of her hair, staring like a fool at the elegant line of her throat, or lost in the mystery of that lush, pretty mouth.

Yeah, Clara was right. The morning after was a real bitch.

But it wasn't anybody's business but his own.

"I'm going to have to widow you, Audrey," he said calmly. "It'll grieve me to do it, but I really have no choice."

Audrey laughed. "You can try. That's a fight I'd like to see, actually. I think they underestimate you, your brothers."

"No." Clara studied him with narrow eyes. "They don't."

He ignored her and spoke to Audrey. "I don't want to kill him, mind you. I love Will. But there's a code, you know. Between brothers."

Oh, we know," Audrey said. "That's how we know, uh, what we know."

"Family first," Bel murmured with equal parts apology and sympathy.

"What we have, we share," Audrey added, but her tone was less *I'm sorry we're hideous gossips* and more *don't disappoint us here, Blake*.

Drew only wished he knew how to not disappoint her. Or even what to do next. But given that Meg—while bluntly acknowledging the fact of last night—had thus far evaded any discussion on the topic, he was a little lost here.

"Your fight is our fight," he said. He knew the Blake family motto as well as anybody. "Yeah, yeah." He jiggled the boys hanging off him. "You don't have to tell the guy who just showered your offspring. I don't know if I have any fight left in me after that."

"Oh, Drew." Bel rose on a sigh, scooped her baby off the counter and onto her hip. "You've got plenty of fight left in you."

"You'd better," Audrey said. "You're going to need it." He wondered uneasily what exactly that meant. She jerked her chin at the kids on his back and said, "Boys."

Children fell off him like magic, leaving Drew with nothing but empty hands and a grimy t-shirt.

"I wish you'd tell me how you do that," he said to Audrey.

"It's all in the tone."

"I have got to learn that tone."

Bel sailed toward the door, kids falling in behind like she was the Pied Piper or something. Clara continued to study him like something unpleasant on the sole of her shoe, so he gave her a big, bright smile. She didn't return it.

Audrey herded the last kid toward the door but paused at Drew's elbow. "You have a huge heart, you know." Her eyes were deeply blue and very serious. "You're probably the kindest, most inherently generous person I know. And your moral compass, when you use it, is beyond question. They depend on you, you know. Will and James. For that heart of yours."

"I, uh—" He blinked down at her, startled. "Hmm?"

"Just follow it," she told him, "and you'll be fine."

"Oh."

She sighed. "You're totally going to screw this up."

"Will said that, too. Or something like it." He patted her shoulder. "Thanks, though."

She shook her head, scooped up one last very small human and disappeared through the door. Leaving him with Clara's glaring disapproval and...Meg.

She stood there, arms folded, brow arched, a faint air of derision still clinging to her, probably left over from his cockamamie suggestion that she might scramble him an egg. Drew couldn't fault her for that; Meg didn't cook and the suggestion that she would was pure craziness. Aside from that, though, she looked exactly like she had half an hour ago, from the smooth braid on her head to the worn jeans hugging those long, long legs. To the naked eye, nothing had changed. This was the same woman with whom he'd happily bickered away the morning.

Except it wasn't.

Something had changed. Something important.

He couldn't read her mind—not like Clara probably could—but they were close, he and Meg. Intimate. Not physically speaking, of course. Not before last night, anyway. But there was intimacy and there was *intimacy*, and even before last night, he'd been intimate with Meg. She'd given him access to the private space inside her head and—sometimes—a grudging glimpse of what was in her heart. She'd given him that, let him through a door she normally kept shut and locked. It was a gift, and Drew had never abused it. He'd cherished being inside the Fortress of Meg.

A fortress from which, unless he was very much mistaken, he had just been kicked out.

"Oh, no, you don't." He stalked across the kitchen to her, and she watched him come with the resigned calm of a woman whose decision—the one she'd evidently made without even consulting him—was final. "You don't get to withdraw. I've been trying to get you to talk to me about this since the minute it happened."

"It? You mean the sex?" She spoke with a precise dispassion that sent fury tumbling through his veins. Because how was it fair that she was all cool self-possession about it when he couldn't even think the words without suffering a debilitating flashflood of lust?

"Yes, I mean the sex." He scowled at her and suppressed the predictable bolt of want. She didn't scowl back, probably because she was purely unaffected. "And don't tell me you aren't blowing me off because you are. I know you, Meg, and you are." Fear bloomed under the fury, dark and unfamiliar. It crawled up his back and down his arms to settle in his sweating palms. "You want to be mad at me? You want to call me a jerk? An asshole? A heartless bastard? Fine." He flung his arms out to the sides, invited the blow. "Go for it. But you don't get to fucking leave. You're—" *Mine.* He swallowed it back. Not the right word. He knew this and groped his panicked mind for the right one. "—my best friend. You're my best friend, Meg, and that means you're not allowed to just walk out."

"I'm not going anywhere." She gazed up at him, her eyes green and distant, her arms folded tightly over her waist. "I'm right here."

"The hell you are." He sneered at her, enraged by the technical truth and the easy lie. "What, like I'm blind?

You've abandoned ship, Meggy. You've already snipped me out of your life like a stain on a table cloth."

"No, I didn't."

"Plus, nobody cuts up tablecloths," Clara put in. "A little seltzer, sometimes some dishwashing liquid if the stain is greasy, but you don't take scissors to a perfectly good—"

"I've followed your damn rules, Meg. I've spent eight years following them to the letter, okay? We've played this whole thing your way, and did I ever complain? Did I ever argue? No! I gave you exactly what you wanted and I never pushed for more. I never asked you for anything!"

"I know, Drew."

"He never asks anybody for anything," Clara pointed out. "What if he gets it? Then he'd be responsible for it, and God knows we can't have that."

Drew ignored her. "And, fine, okay, I kissed you. My bad. I'm sorry. I got carried away and didn't think it through. But, damn it, Meg, how much can you expect one guy to take? You walk around all day, all...*you*." He flung out a hand, swung it from her head to her feet. "With your hair and your skirts and that damn purse—"

"A purse!" Clara breathed, scandalized. "Meg, you trollop!"

He broke off to drag that hand down his face. He was getting sidetracked here. Meg was sharp as hell, and nothing about her was accidental—not the naughty librarian hair, not the you-only-wish skirts, not the burglar's paradise she carried around in her purse. It was all calculated for effect, and after last night, Drew doubted he needed to detail for her the effect she had on him. He could just point her to the instant replay, because, hey, they had video.

"So, yeah, I kissed you." Fear-laced anger shoved him on, had him firing the words at her like bullets. "But when you said stop, I stopped. I followed instructions, Meg. I obeyed the rules. I was a good guy. I did the right thing. Then you jumped me, remember?"

"I remember." The freckles stood out on that pixie nose of hers and guilt squirmed into the edgy bite of his rage. Why wasn't she fighting back? Meg always put up her dukes. "Believe me, I remember. I wish I didn't, but I do. I should never have—"

"So you made a mistake. Big deal!" He spread shaking hands. "People make them, you know. Normal human beings? They do. It's not the end of the world. So I've seen you naked. So what? You're just going to have to get over it because I'm not letting you kick me out of your life."

She sighed. "I'm not kicking you out of my life, Drew."

"No? Because it sure feels like you are."

"Well, I'm not." She cupped her elbows in her palms and chose her next words with a careful deliberation that put a knot in his already-tight stomach. "But we can't go back to the way things were, either."

"Why not?" Fear was slowly gaining on the anger, dragging it down, freezing it solid. Was he losing her? Really and forever? For the first time, it occurred to him that he might not actually be able to talk her down from this...this crazy overreaction. "Because we had sex?"

"Yes. Sex changes things. It—" She shrugged helplessly. "It matters."

He stared at her. "No, it doesn't."

And it didn't. It didn't matter at all. He would remember it for the rest of his life, sure. Dream about it every goddamn night. Fantasize about it with humiliating regularity. He would probably never look at his truck again without a twinge of regret and an instant boner. But he would live without it, and cheerfully, if it meant he could keep her. Keep the Meg he'd always known, the Meg who anchored his day, his life, his very self. She was the sturdy sun that set Drew's orbit and ordered his universe. He didn't want their friendship to evolve or whatever the hell she envisioned happening here. He didn't want something new. He wanted to keep exactly what he had. What he loved. What he fucking needed. What she was inexplicably taking away.

"Meg, it was just sex." He flicked a hand, like he could shoo those hot, amazing minutes away. Like a magician, waving his wand and erasing the past. Would he, he wondered? Erase last night? If he could?

Jesus, no. If he couldn't have that Meg—naked Meg, moaning Meg, open, hot, willing Meg? If he could only have the old Meg instead—best friend Meg, funny Meg, edgy Meg, and thank God for her? He was at least going to enjoy the memories. He'd be damned if he'd let her take it all away, just because she was having some regrets.

"It was nothing," he said, and even he could hear the bitterness in his voice. "Why are you making it matter so much?"

Clara gave a tiny sigh that sounded suspiciously like *asshole*. Meg only stared at him, pale and still, her eyes enormous and hollow. His mouth went arid and apprehension gripped him by the scruff.

"Okay, that sounded bad but Meg, come on." He reached for her and she stepped carefully back. A jagged crack snaked across his heart. He could all but hear the two halves creak apart. "You know what I meant. Sex is great and all, but it doesn't matter. Not like you do. You're my best friend." He dropped his hand helplessly. "I love you."

Clara hissed as if he'd tossed acid on her and Meg just closed her eyes. "Please don't say that."

"But it's true."

"I know it is." She opened her eyes again, met his, and something inside him took a steep, nasty slide. This wasn't going at all the way he'd imagined. "Please just stop saying it."

"I don't understand."

"I know. Just...please."

"Okay." He stepped back, hands open and harmless, even as they ached to touch her. To put right what he'd somehow put so miserably wrong. "I...okay. But why?"

"Because I believe you, Drew. I believe that you love me. I never doubted it. The problem is—" She pulled in a breath so deep he could see the rise of her chest. Clara made a soft noise he couldn't begin to interpret, then Meg released that breath, slow and even. She met his eyes squarely. "The truth is, I don't love you."

Chapter 22

Drew stared at her, that long, mobile face of his blank and shocked. Meg's heart jangled inside her like a bag of broken glass and she swallowed painfully. God. This was worse than she'd thought. "Of course you love me."

"No, Drew, I don't," Meg said with forced calm. "Not the way you mean."

"What way do I mean?" He blinked at her like he was trying to focus. Trying and maybe not doing a great job of it. Jesus, she did not want to do this right now. Or, you know, ever. At the very least she'd have preferred to wait until they'd escaped from the steaming heap of legal trouble they were probably in. But evidently, Drew would be satisfied with nothing less than right now. So now it was.

"You mean Drew-and-Meggy." The words came out vicious and sharp, and she tried to soften them. Tried to drag some compassion into them. It wasn't his fault that he didn't love her the way she loved him. It wasn't his fault that he loved her the way he loved Bel and Audrey. The way he loved Jilly. Like a sister, or a niece, or his sainted mother. It wasn't his fault. It was nobody's fault. But that didn't mean it didn't hurt like the fucking fires of hell. "You mean Drew-and-Meggy, just-like-the-old-days, nothing-ever-changes, best-friends-forever."

"What's wrong with that?" He put out a hand to her, and it was strangely tentative. And the pain was devastating. Icy and complete. Because Drew had never hesitated to touch her. He didn't hesitate to touch anybody. He was a hugger, a patter, a cheerfully-violate-your-personal-space kind of guy. And now he was afraid to touch her, because she'd sliced him to the bone. "What's wrong with being best friends forever, Meg?"

Tears tried to crawl up her throat but she swallowed them resolutely down and pushed on. There was no going back now. There was only forward.

"You want everything to be just like it was," she said again, desperately. "But life doesn't stay still, Drew. People don't stay still. And *just like it was* doesn't leave room for anything else. For anything new."

"Ah." For an instant, his face was raw and unguarded, his warm brown eyes filled with startled pain. Then the shutters came down and his face went carefully blank. "Or any *one* new?"

She allowed herself a moment—one desperate moment—to breathe through the pain of being outside. Of being evicted from the warm circle of Drew's regard. She hadn't been totally sure she could breathe under those circumstances, but found that she could. Which was a good thing, right?

Only she didn't know how to answer the question. Because the sea-change she'd suffered overnight—the love she'd become aware of? It had transformed her. Transformed how she understood herself, anyway. How she understood him, understood the two of them together. She was new. And she didn't know how much room there was in *just like the old days* for who she was now. For what she felt, or what she wanted. She just didn't know.

"Or any *one* new," she conceded carefully. "We have to make room, Drew." She met his eyes, willed him to understand what she wasn't saying. What she couldn't say just yet. "There has to be room for the new, or we're not going to make it."

He tucked his fingers into his pockets and rocked back on his heels. Frowned at his feet. "What if I don't want to make room? What if I liked the way things were?"

"Drew, come on." She sighed, suddenly weary all the way to her bones. "We need to be grown up about this. There's a lot at stake here, and we have to—"

"What?" Drew threw out his hands, frustrated and baffled. "What's at stake that's not completely under your control?"

She stared at him. "Under my control? You think anything in this situation is under my control?"

"I'm going to love you forever," he shot back, and her heart—her stupid, stupid heart—leapt with joy. Her brain knew better but, oh, how her heart loved those words. "You're family to me, and you know what that means around here." He stabbed a finger at her. "You're the one putting conditions on us. And if I don't fall in line with those conditions, I'm out. Voted off the island for insubordination." He raked both hands through his hair and laughed. "Jesus, wouldn't your dad be proud of you?"

"Dirty pool," Clara murmured. "For shame, Drew."

Meg waved that off. "No, he's entitled. It's a fair point." Joe Marshall and Hildy Wise hadn't been the world's greatest example of a functional marriage. Between Hildy feeling everybody's emotions for them, and Joe not even feeling his own, Meg still wasn't sure where normal fell, but she knew she tended to err on the side of stoicism. "I'm Joe's daughter, and I'm not going to apologize for it. I've thought it through, I understand what I feel—" she hoped "—and I know what I need. I'm asking for it. It's up to Drew whether or not he wants to try to give it to me."

She turned back to Drew, met his eyes and refused to flinch away from the accusation and the pain he wasn't bothering to conceal. "It's your call, Drew. That's the deal on the table. I don't know what's coming next for us, but I do know that it's all I have to give. So why don't you budge the hell over, make room and have some goddamn faith?"

Not her most persuasive speech—a little aggressive and snarly—but heartfelt and reassuringly in character, particularly the aggressive, snarly part. It was very her, she decided, and it would have to do. It was as close to the whole truth as she could get at the moment, and it cut right to the heart of it. He would either stick with her, or he'd abandon her for not feeling what he wanted her to feel. For not loving him the way he wanted her to love him. For not being the Meg he wanted her to be.

Now who was channeling her dad?

* * *

Meg decided to let Drew brood. Not many people knew he was a brooder—possibly not even his brothers—but Meg knew. Just like she knew to leave him alone when he went dark. Leave the guy alone with whatever was bugging him, and he'd emerge a couple hours later with the problem digested and his sunny disposition intact. It was a neat trick. She'd taken a couple runs at it herself over the years but unfortunately she just wasn't a brooder. Cutting sarcasm was more her speed. No help for it.

Meg wished like hell that Drew could take all the time he wanted to digest the ultimatum she'd dropped on him in the kitchen, but they could barely afford the couple hours she'd already given him. It was early afternoon now, E wasn't answering his phone, and as far as she was aware they hadn't destroyed that stupid sex tape yet.

It was time to get back on the job.

Maybe it would even help, Meg told herself as she gathered her courage and mounted the steps toward Drew's suite in the east wing of the Annex. Working together was a big part of their precious Drew-and-Meggy, just-like-the-old-days. It would be good to show him that that part at least didn't have to change. They could salvage some of the old days, maybe even the best part. She hoped. But there was only one way to find out.

She poked her head into the airy second-story parlor that served as Drew's home base. She knocked on the door frame and leaned in. "Hey."

Drew was slouched on the huge black leather sectional that held down the center of the room. He had a laptop on his stomach, crooked stacks of magazines and papers flanking both elbows and the coffee table under his bare feet.

"Hey," he said around the pencil in his teeth. The top of his head barely cleared the overstuffed cushions but his eyes moved across the screen in front of him at a blistering rate. He didn't look up. Meg sighed.

"Are you over it yet?"

The *go away* vibe pouring off him thickened. "Over

what?"

"Never mind." Definitely not over it. "So, hey, I'm about to hack into the house system and delete our accidental porno. Want to help?"

He consulted the mountain of papers on his left. "It's taken care of."

She frowned. "What do you mean, taken care of?"

"I mean it's taken care of." Still no eye contact.

"You got it?" She gripped the doorframe with slippery hands. "When?"

"Couple hours ago." He finally flicked her a glance and it licked at her skin like fire. "You obviously wouldn't eat, sleep or breathe until it was gone, so I took care of it."

"Took care of it how?" she asked, suspicious. "Is it *gone* gone? Like obliterated gone?"

"It's not even a shadow on the server, and the cloud was never even aware of its short, tragic life, okay?" He gazed at her impassively. "I'm no security expert, but I have my skills. Trust me. As far as the Blake compound's home monitoring system is concerned, last night never happened." His lips twisted into something approximating a smile, and it ripped at Meg's battered heart. "Jealous?"

She pushed the pain aside and focused on business. "Show me."

He arched a brow. "You're welcome."

She gave him an exaggerated eye roll. "Thank you, Drew."

He tipped his head in acknowledgement but stayed silent, his focus back on his laptop.

"But I still want you to show me." She stepped into the room despite his tangible disinclination to have her there. God, she hated this. Hated being awkward with Drew. It was like her whole life was off-beat and she couldn't get her footing. How was she supposed to? She had no practice at this kind of thing. She was never awkward with Drew. Nobody was. Putting people at ease was his particular gift.

No, she reminded herself slowly, it wasn't a gift. It was a skill. One he'd earned with years of childhood grief. How had he put it last night? *You smile, you agree, you go along.*

Expect nothing and be delighted by everything. Love the one you're with so you won't miss the ones you're not with and won't ever be again.

Her heart ached but there was relief, too. Because if he was angry enough at her to make her miserable, it was only because she'd hurt him, and you couldn't hurt somebody who didn't expect anything from you. So she hadn't been kicked out of his heart. Hadn't been relegated to the vast ranks of people he managed instead of loved. No, if he was still giving her shit, she still mattered. Not as much as she wished she did, but she still mattered. For now.

She hiked her chin into the air and crossed the cluttered room toward him as if she were welcome. A small army of half-assembled computers huddled companionably against the wall, spilling their guts all over the floor like puking frat boys. Screens flickered and scrolled all around her, and the floor was a scatter-shot mess of books, mugs, bottles, socks and snacks. She stopped at the coffee table by his feet and waited, letting expectant silence do the work for her. Nothing rubbed Drew raw like silence.

"Oh, fine," he muttered finally. He set aside his laptop and scooped up a second laptop from the couch cushions. He yanked it open and flicked through a series of commands.

Meg hastily straightened the avalanche of papers beside him into a pile and sat. She'd designed the security system herself, so she recognized the basic structure as he flew through the screens. She also knew exactly how hard she'd made it for anybody but Will to get their hands into the guts of the system, but Drew was in it up to his elbows, sifting through the complicated code like it was a day at the beach.

"Holy hell," she breathed. "How long have you had that little ace up your sleeve?"

"A while." He jerked a shoulder. "Will's the kind of guy it's good to have an ace on." He slowed down, pointed at the screen. "So there's where the file was stored. But as you can see, it's gone. As is every blip, bell and flag that might pique the interest of a curious bastard like my brother."

"What about—"

181

"Meg, relax." He flipped through several more screens, letting her see for herself every place she could imagine that a person might look for a file, a backup, a copy or even a shadow in the code. He turned to look at her and the breath caught in her throat. He was closer—much closer—than she'd realized.

"Last night never happened," he said. His mouth—inches from hers—curled into a bitter smile. Her heart knocked into her ribs like a mad thing. "As far as the internet is concerned, anyway."

"But it did happen," she heard herself say, unable to look away from that bitter smile. That expressive mouth.

"Yeah, don't remind me." He went back to his screen. She caught herself leaning toward him, trying to erase that distance, and eased back.

"Fine," she said briskly. "Let's focus on the work, shall we?"

"I am working."

"I see that." He was already typing again, his eyes stubbornly on the screen. "But I was talking about E. Now that the tape is behind us, we can focus on the next big threat to our safety and future happiness." She frowned. "And possibly our future liberty."

"And you think that's E."

"We need to figure him out, Drew." It was a masterful dodge of a leading question if she did say so herself. "What if he's not who he says he is? Because if last night wasn't about what he said it was about—"

"I talked to him half an hour ago."

"What?" She seized his arm. "He called? What did he say? Where was he this morning?"

"Buying a house." His fingers barely paused on the keyboard.

"A house?"

He shrugged. "It's a seller's market, Meggy. When the right house hits the market, you drop everything and make the offer. I know it wasn't exactly oversleeping but—" He flashed her a reproachful look. "—it does seem like a legitimate excuse for skipping coffee."

She maintained a skeptical silence. Drew just shrugged and went back to his keyboard.

"He's offered to take us out to dinner. An apology and a celebration, he said. I told him we'd pick him up at the Prince George at eight."

"Huh." The stack of magazines and papers between them started to crumble and she frowned as she nudged it absently back into place. A year or so ago, she'd toyed with buying a house herself. She knew very well that when the realtor called, you dropped everything and went. So it made perfect sense—a dream house trumped a coffee date. It just did. So why did her gut reject the excuse wholesale? "Well, good. That's...great."

"Isn't it?" He gave her a sour smile. "Now go away, will you? I'm working."

"So I see." She tossed her feet up onto the coffee table beside his with a nonchalance she didn't remotely feel. She plucked a *Sports Illustrated* off the pile between them and inspected the cover. "Garrett Dain, huh? You're getting him?"

"Trying to," he said shortly.

"Is he the one who punched out his girlfriend?" Meg flipped to the cover article and began scanning. "Or the one who beat his kid?"

"Neither. And, please, give me a little credit." He slid a notepad from the middle of the stack and consulted it. Scribbled something and tossed it aside. "I don't represent thugs."

She only arched a skeptical brow.

"Okay, I don't represent violent thugs. Dain's the soldier."

"That guy? Mr. West Point?" She blinked at him. "The one who, at twenty-one tender years of age, looked a five million dollar contract in the eye and said *screw football, my country needs me*? The one who then spent a decade getting shot at by terrorists instead of letting the NFL pay him by the concussion? The one who tweets like the concept of a social filter never occurred to him?"

"That's the one."

She shook her head, amazed. "What is it with you and problematic soldiers this weekend?"

He shrugged and Meg flipped back to the magazine's cover photo. Garrett Dain—blond, built and openly terrifying—glared off the page at her. An ugly scar sat below one cold eye, a scar he'd never spoken about or explained. He'd talk about anything else, though, from organized religion to the Oscars. Guy couldn't come within twenty yards of a Twitter account without setting the whole damn internet on fire.

Which was probably why—despite a towering talent that made all those twenty-year-olds he played against every week look like the children they were—the NFL was tossing him from team to team like a hot potato. If ever an athlete needed a ghost-tweeter, it was Garrett Dain.

Meg cut Drew a curious glance. "How are you going to play this one?"

Drew sighed and set down his pencil. "Hell if I know." He scrubbed both hands wearily over his face and dropped his head back to stare at the ceiling. *Finally*, Meg thought, hope flickering faintly inside her. A break in the brick wall.

"I mean, I like a guy with strong opinions. I can work with strong opinions. Only—" He rolled his head to the side, met her eyes and that little flicker of hope grew into a flame. A small one but the glow of it warmed her from the inside out. Not that they were out of the woods her ultimatum had landed them in, but at least he was talking to her. Talking shop, anyway. Which might not be a lot to most people but made up a huge part of what passed for normal between them. It was a small, grudging olive branch, and her throat went tight with emotion.

"Only those opinions are a little too strong sometimes?" she managed. "The kind of strong that doesn't sit well with your average football fan?"

"If only it were that simple. No, our buddy Garrett's opinions span the spectrum. At some point or another, he's rubbed everybody wrong." He sighed. "Remember when he punched out his own running back for making a gay joke?"

Meg smiled fondly. "Guy's an American hero."

184

"I agree. But then we finally got our first openly gay NFLer, and the kid—very reasonably—expresses some trepidation about how his fellow players might take to him. And what does Dain do? What does our favorite defender of the gays tweet?" He fished a paper from the stack between them and consulted it. "*It's the NFL, not a goddamn debutante ball.*" He handed it over. "Hashtag big girl panties. Hashtag pull 'em up."

Meg inspected the screen shot. "At least he can spell. But yeah, I see your problem. His fists say social justice but his mouth says reality bites, quit crying like a little girl. Not exactly the kind of dichotomy you really get across in 140 accessible, charming, kid-friendly, mother-approved characters."

"Tell me about it. But the guy's got a once-in-a-century arm, and he intends to get paid for it. And his brand new agent—a scary bastard himself—thinks he can make that happen."

"Ah." Meg smiled. "He signed with Will."

"He signed with Will." Drew sighed. "Which means the submission process for Dain's new PR team is blind because screw brotherhood, right?"

Meg shook her head. "Like you'd let Will throw you a contract. Especially one this juicy."

"That's neither here nor there. He should at least offer to throw me a contract so I could nobly refuse. But since he'd sooner let me kiss his wife, I'm going to have to bring my A game here." He handed her another magazine. "Get reading, Meggy. I need to get a handle on this guy."

"Don't call me Meggy," she murmured. And if she had to pretend-cough an aching lump of gratitude out of her throat, well. She wouldn't apologize for that. Their usual had taken the kind of hit it might never recover from. A brief return to the ordinary—even if it was just a Saturday afternoon of research on the couch—was a gift, and she was going to savor the hell out of it. And him along with it.

Chapter 23

Drew didn't remember falling asleep. He remembered the fat, golden squares of sunshine moving across his dirty floors while he and Meg worked. He remembered setting aside the morning's pain and panic, and opening himself to the companionable silence. To the easy wordless peace that was particular to Saturday afternoons on the couch with Meg. He remembered relaxing into it—into her, into the work, into the joy of recapturing even a slice of their precious normal—with a rush of gratitude and relief.

He remembered setting aside his laptop—just for a second—so he could rub his gritty eyes. It had been a very long and eventful night, after all, and a relatively early morning. He would just rest his eyes for a minute, then they'd get back to work.

When he woke up the sun squares on the floor had reinvented themselves as long, orange fingers pointing toward evening. The stack of source material on Garrett Dain that he and Meg had kept between them like a sleeping baby was history. It was now scattered like a mudslide on the floor, his laptop standing guard over it from its precarious post on the arm of the sofa.

As for him and Meg? Somehow they'd ended up snuggled into the deep corner of the sectional, her back to his chest, her bottom wedged against his crotch, her thighs companionably sandwiching one of his. Not exactly the usual—not by a long shot—but nothing Drew was going to complain about. He closed his eyes again and let himself sink luxuriously back into the warmth of her body, into the measured rise and fall of her breath.

Because Meg was asleep. He understood this with a slow ripple of wonder. He'd caught her cat-napping once or

twice but asleep? Like *asleep* asleep? The kind you dragged
yourself out of, stumbling and slurring? Nope. Never. He'd
actually sort of suspected that she slept like Will, in reluctant
fits and starts, twenty minutes here, forty-five minutes there,
her brain revving too high to ever completely let go of
consciousness. But Meggy was definitely asleep now.
Sacked the hell out.

Fondness glowed inside him, and something else.
Maybe...pride? But why? Because a woman who never let
her guard down was profoundly asleep in his arms? Drew
snuggled his cheek into the side of her neck, treated himself
to the secret scent she kept there in the curve of her throat.
And smiled. Yep. That was something to be proud of. He
kept his eyes closed and concentrated on soaking it all in,
every sensation—the weight of her sleek head pillowed on
his bent arm, the way she'd curled her entire self around his
other arm, the one he'd snaked around her waist to anchor
her body to his. The soft warmth of her...

Whoa. Of her breast in his hand. Her small, warm
breast. It filled his palm with that same freaky exactitude
with which her silence filled his soul and her shoulder fit
under his arm. With that unspoken *of course* that Drew
wasn't ungrateful enough to question or dissect. He just
appreciated it.

Heat spiraled into his bloodstream like a shiny ribbon,
scattering his thoughts. He snatched at one, caught it long
enough to wonder if he should take his hand off her breast.
He probably should. She was asleep, after all. He shouldn't
take advantage. He opened his fingers and gave his hand a
testing tug but she curled herself more tightly around his arm
and made some kind of noise, groggy and distressed.

"Shh," he said, instinctively shifting to hold her tighter.
He rubbed his chin against her shoulder. "Easy, Meggy. It's
only me."

"Drew?" Her voice was sticky, muddled. Rough with
sleep then warm with recognition. She threaded her fingers
through his and pressed his palm tighter to her breast.
"Drew."

"Just me." He swallowed and tried again. He flexed his

fingers carefully and only succeeded in pressing her pert nipple deeper into his palm. He wondered if she could feel his heart hammering against her back. He was pretty sure she could feel the boner he was cuddling against her bottom. "The guy with, uh, his hand on your boob."

She went still. "Drew." He didn't like the way she said it quite so much this time.

"Yeah?"

"You're holding my breast."

"I am."

She shifted, as if to leap off the couch and he went with instinct again. He didn't let her go. He kept his arm banded around her waist, her breast cradled in his palm like something precious and delicate. A bird, or a butterfly. Something worth taking care of. He hooked his chin over her shoulder and pressed his cheek to hers. Treated himself to one last lungful of that fascinating sleepy-Meg smell, to one more moment of standing guard over her vulnerability.

"Don't wake up." He snuggled her closer. "Please. Not yet."

"Drew. My breast is in your hand." But she didn't leap off the couch. He noticed that she didn't take his hand off her breast for him either.

"I know." He smiled into her neck. "Go back to sleep."

"Not with my breast in your hand."

"Why not?" he asked reasonably. "I tried to move it and you woke up. I put it back so you could sleep some more."

She paused. "You're quite the giver, aren't you?"

Her tone was pure acid and he couldn't help himself. He pressed his mouth to the pretty line of her neck. It was right there, after all. She sighed and let her head fall fractionally to the side. He slid his lips toward her ear while pleasure spun through him in slow, dizzy waves. "I am. I'm letting you keep my leg, too."

"Your leg—" She stiffened again. "Drew. Your thigh is in my crotch."

"I know," he said happily, and hooked his thumb into the placket of her oxford shirt. "This has been the best nap."

"Great. Good for you. I'm—"

He closed his mouth over her earlobe and flicked open a crucial button. Found the sweet thrust of her nipple with his fingers. She broke off on a half-strangled moan. And suddenly need was roaring through him like a brush fire. Just a few hours ago, he'd thought he might never be allowed into the Fortress of Meg again. Not even into the best-friends zone, let alone this blazing field of burn-me-down he'd discovered last night.

It wasn't a field she wanted him on. He knew that. No matter what they'd done to each other on the hood of his truck last night, she'd made her opinion of him as a lover abundantly clear. *I don't love you. Budge the hell over and make some goddamn room*. Evidently, she'd loved him enough to let him scratch last night's itch for her, but not enough to let him meet that need on the regular. No, unless he was greatly mistaken, she was eyeing E and his damn shoulders for that little job, no matter what kind of noises she made about his suspicious behavior.

Resentment smoked dark and tangled into the lust, but he ignored it. Because right now, in this moment? She wanted him. Him, not E. And he wanted her right back.

Moreover? He had her. He had her and he was going to take more. As much as he could grab. It might have to hold him a while. If not forever.

He worked a second button free and slid his whole hand into her shirt. And oh Christ, now there was nothing between them but the silky temptation of her bra. Need shifted abruptly into hunger, sharp and shocking and serious.

Serious. There was that word again. Drew didn't even like the concept, let alone the circumstance. But the sweet promise of Meg's breast in his palm had touched off an unholy tsunami of desire inside him, and if this wasn't serious, Drew didn't know what was. It whipped and flailed inside him, that want, like the severed end of a live electrical wire. Sparks fountained every which way, and suddenly there was this huge, ravenous emptiness inside him. A yearning, yawning blank that nothing would satisfy but Meg. Only Meg.

Which Drew did not understand. Meg's certainly wasn't

the first breast he'd ever touched. He'd touched lots of breasts, many of them objectively more likely to drive a guy around the bend, too. And that little moan of hers? It had been tiny, utterly reluctant, and not at all for his benefit. In fact, he'd guess she'd stifled it as best she could. She wasn't the demonstrative sort, his Meggy. She played her cards awfully close to the vest.

So maybe it was a combination deal? The sweet thrill of learning that long, pretty body with his hands (finally!) along with the shocking triumph of cracking a control he knew to be weapons-grade.

She squirmed against him with another half-voiced noise—part desire, part distress—and triumph vanished. It was simply swallowed whole by that driving, desperate hunger. That sharp-clawed craving that jostled and shoved inside him. And terrified him.

Because it wasn't supposed to be this way. At least it never had been before. Drew had been very, very careful about that. About keeping things light. Happiness was being able to replace any element of his life at any given moment without blinking an eye. So he drove old cars, owned dozens of computers, worked for himself, and dated pretty women by the boat-load. But whatever this was pounding in his head, crowding his heart, driving his body? (God, was it driving his body.) It was fucking serious.

And that was a problem. A serious one. (And oh, hell, there was that word again.) Because serious meant high stakes, falling rocks, dangerous curves. (*Curves*. Like the soft, warm one filling his palm.) And that was a road Drew was not interested in traveling. He'd lost enough at ten years old to last a lifetime. He didn't risk shit for fun. Nothing he was afraid to break, anyway.

So when it came to sex, Drew always picked women he liked, but nobody he was tempted to love. Certainly nobody he thought might love him back. He kept things perfectly transparent and patently easy. Casual. Light.

Unfortunately, there was nothing light about the feel of Meg's breast in his hand. Nothing casual, and definitely nothing easy. He rifled through his vocabulary—his extensive and impressive vocabulary—for a word to describe what he did feel, but couldn't come up with a thing that didn't begin with serious.

Then she sighed and arched. Maybe just stretched? Drew didn't really know. Didn't honestly care. Because the end result was that she simultaneously pressed her breast into his hand and her bottom into the raging erection he was sporting, and suddenly he was perfectly fine with serious. Suddenly, he was all about the serious. Suddenly, he was hooking his knee over hers and flipping her onto her back. Then he was on top of her, her body warm and long and perfect under his as he ground that aching need she'd lit inside him into the perfect cradle of her hips. And she was welcoming him. She was wrapping those endless legs around his hips, meeting his need and rolling into it.

The inside of his skull flashed white-hot, and his head emptied of everything but feeding that need, filling that space, feasting on the dark sweetness of her mouth. He tasted her, breathed her, gorged on her, conscious all the while of the shocking knowledge that she was letting him. Or that he'd somehow driven her so far beyond her usual control that she was helpless to do otherwise.

He smiled against her mouth, darkly satisfied by the idea, and went to work on that tight, all-business braid of hers. His life-long love affair with all things female paid off in spades, and in mere seconds the floor beside the couch was littered with little gold pins. Then he had the unexpected luxury of her hair in his hands.

It ran across his palms like living silk, warm and smooth and slippery and, Jesus, it smelled like her. It was concentrated Meg, a merciless punch of familiar scent and foreign abundance. There was just so damn much of it. Of her. More than he'd ever suspected. More than she'd ever allowed him to see, to know. More than she wanted to allow him, he knew, but something had happened to his Meggy.

Something had changed. He didn't know what but he understood that something had changed like he understood the fact of her hair in his hands. He had no idea what could have shattered a reserve so inherent that even Drew had never breached it but there was no doubt in his mind: Meg's regulator had blown and she needed.

Or maybe she'd always needed and just had never given in to something so human as the need to be touched? Whatever, however, Drew didn't care. All he knew was that she needed, and he was going to be the guy who provided. Him, not E. Because Drew needed, too. Needed her, needed this. He wondered vaguely if something inside him had broken, too. If her break had somehow triggered a similar break in him, because this sudden craving, this abrupt compulsion? It wasn't comfortable. It was sharp-edged and jagged, unlike any desire he'd felt before. It was drawing fucking blood.

But he didn't stop. Hell, no. It was pain but the sweetest pain he'd ever tasted. He dropped his face to the secret crook of her neck and put his mouth in the hollow of her throat where her pulse hammered. He buried his nose in the cool river of her hair and inhaled. He drew her into his lungs, into his heart, into himself. And when she lifted her mouth to his, he took it. He took and took and took, until there was nothing left.

Chapter 24

"Oh, damn it!"

Meg bucked under him as if somebody had tased her and Drew jerked out of a very happy post-coital drowse. He squawked, "What?" and fell off the couch.

She leapt to her feet—gloriously naked, because Drew was nothing if not thorough—and shoved both hands into the loose spill of her hair. "Damn it, damn it, damn it!" She gripped her skull and glared down at him, hair sprouting through her fingers in crazed tufts.

"What?" he said again, though more calmly this time. And without the pratfall as he was already lying on the floor. Naked, thank you very much.

"This wasn't supposed to happen! We weren't supposed to do this again!" She snatched up an armful of discarded clothes and began tossing them into his and hers piles. She came up with a pair of boxers and flung them at his head. "For God's sake, get dressed." She wriggled into her panties and blew the hair out of her face. "And where the hell are all my bobby pins?"

Drew rolled up to slide into the boxers, and winced. He lifted one bare butt cheek and inspected it. "Found them."

"Oh, ick." She curled her lip. "Keep them."

Drew nodded agreeably. "Thanks. I've always wanted a pin cushion for an ass."

"Serves you right." Meg hopped into her jeans one-footed and scowled at him while she hauled them up. "Screwing with a girl's hair like that."

A memory surfaced abruptly of Meg's hair wrapped around his hands and forearms, tangling them together in a web of hot silk while he sank into the sweet give of her body.

"Yeah, sorry." Total lie. "My butt has some serious regrets, if it's any consolation."

"It's not." She buttoned her jeans and shook all that hair back over her shoulders with an impatient wriggle that Drew found utterly and inexplicably riveting. He sat there, boxers forgotten in his hand, and watched her fish a bra out of a rumpled sleeve. "Because it's the walk of shame for me now." She aimed the bra at him like a switchblade. "You know that, right? That I have to skulk back to the Dower House, all hickeys and hair—"

"Wait, I gave you a hickey?" He blinked. "Where?"

She pointed silently to the pretty curve of her shoulder, to the faint purple bruise riding there. He grinned.

"Nice."

"No, Drew. Not nice. Because every Blake in this stupid house is going to see that and assume that we spent the afternoon going after each other like wild dingoes!"

"We did. Also? All dingoes are wild." He pointed this out with admirable calm given the insult stirring to life inside him. Because maybe she wasn't interested in adding a regular sexual component to the Meg-and-Drew show but she didn't need to make sleeping with him sound like a disease. "Saying *wild dingoes* is like saying *past history*. There's no other kind of history except past, and no other kind of dingo except wild. The modifier is built right into the word. Handy, right?"

"Thank you, Mr. Grammar." She hooked her bra with a shimmy and a snap. "But if we could just circle back to the point here for a moment?"

"What point? That we had sex again?" He rose to finish pulling on his boxers. "Or that you're ashamed of it?"

Her eyes narrowed. "Fuck you."

"You just did." He smiled at her with deliberate, knife-twisting cheer. Because he'd had about enough of her acting like he was a demerit on an otherwise spotless record. "It was fun, thanks."

She went perfectly still, and Drew paused, startled. Good God, had he hurt her? Then she scowled and threw his jeans at his head. He caught them neatly, and reality reasserted itself.

"I'm not ashamed, okay?" she snapped. "I just don't want your entire family watching this like a movie, that's all. Is a little privacy too much to ask?"

"If you wanted privacy, you probably shouldn't have had sex with me outside the hedge maze last night." He paused as if thinking it over. "Or, you know, in front of the security cameras." He ignored her small, pained moan. "You should definitely have skipped the part where we sat around the kitchen this morning, had coffee and discussed it with your sister."

She glared. "Believe me, there are any number of things I've done lately that I'd like to reconsider."

His emotional scales dipped dangerously toward insult, and a dismaying little flicker of anger leapt into the mix. "For Christ's sake, Meg, it was just sex." It took a little effort but he managed a credibly wry smile. "We didn't summon the last horseman of the Apocalypse."

"Are we sure about that?" She threw his t-shirt at him.

"Pretty sure, yeah." But even as he snatched it out of the air, even as he shoved into it, something twisted inside him. Something dark and mean and hurt. She was acting like he'd given her terminal cancer, for Christ's sake. And it hurt. The urge to hurt her in return bloomed inside him like a black flower. It wrapped razor-sharp tendrils around his bones and dragged itself toward daylight, but he pushed it back down. Reached deep for reason, for patience. For that easy he was so good at.

"Meg, come on. You didn't backslide on a crystal meth habit, okay? You grabbed some afternoon delight. And not with a scuzzy stranger, either, but with me." He threw out his arms and tried another smile. "With a guy who—"

"Don't say it." She jerked her blouse up her arms and started shoving buttons into buttonholes. The wrong buttonholes but he wasn't going to point it out. He didn't have a death wish. "Don't you dare say you love me."

She dropped her chin, ostensibly to focus on the buttoning job she was murdering but her voice had gone thin and shaky. As if she were fighting...tears?

He stared, shocked. Because Meg wasn't shaky. Not ever. She wasn't vulnerable and she wasn't uncertain. Meg was brilliant, Meg was tough, and Meg was absolutely dependable. You could count on Meg. Always. She said she'd do a thing? She did it. She had something on her mind? She said it. She had a plan? She worked it. She had a problem? She solved it. Every time.

But Meg didn't cry. Not ever. And she shouldn't be crying now.

That righteous outrage, his sense of having been ill-used somehow, filtered back in around the shock. Because, sure, maybe Drew had opened this can of worms. But he always opened cans of worms. That was his thing. Meg was supposed to say no. Because she always said no. That was her thing.

But he'd kissed her last night and she hadn't said no. She'd said yes instead. She'd said yes and blown away eight solid years of tradition without so much as a fire-in-the-hole. She'd changed all the rules, not him. But suddenly he was the asshole? He was an insensitive jerk and she was the walking wounded?

Well, fuck that. He shoved back against the fear and panic and clung tight to his anger. Maybe something had broken in her, but it had broken in him, too, damn it. And now every single thing he depended on had rearranged itself without warning, leaving him flapping in the fucking wind without the first idea what to do next. And it wasn't even his fault.

"Okay, Meg," he said, and if he was speaking through his teeth, at least he was smiling. "You're going to have to make up your mind."

She stopped with the buttons. Lifted her eyes to his. He'd braced himself to meet that terrifying and infuriating vulnerability but she'd reeled it in. Her eyes were cool and green and utterly dry.

"Am I?" She tipped her head and studied him. "About what?"

"About the sex." He studied her right back, pleased that he could do so without giving away the pulse thudding in his

196

ears, in his wrists. The fear-laced fury chasing it. "About the fact that we're having it. You seem...conflicted."

"Conflicted." She nodded slowly. "Yeah, I guess I am."

"Well, it's coming through loud and clear." Even he could hear the nastiness in his voice, so he took a moment. Held up a hand to forestall her interruption, though she hadn't made even the slightest twitch toward jumping in. "Which is understandable," he said, dipping deep into his wellspring of no-problem. "I mean, this is some complicated shit, given our history. But your friendship is the most important thing I have. I—" He broke off. *Love you* would get him punched, he was pretty sure about that. Plus that deep pool of crystal-clear fondness inside him, the one with Meg's name on it? It was gone. Transformed beyond recognition. He realized this with an unwelcome shock. The words were still there, as easy on his tongue as a bad habit, but the emotion behind them was gone. That tropically blue well of affection for her had gone oily and dangerous, its surface matte black, the depths impossible to gauge.

He hooked a hand around the back of his neck, tried to rub away the suppressed anger and the growing desperation collected there.

"Listen, I'll do whatever you want here, Meg. We can be friends, or we can be friends with benefits. On the regular or occasionally." He tried to smile. Didn't know if he pulled it off. "I just need you to tell me which way you want to go."

"Really?" She continued to study him, unblinking. "You can go either way on this?"

"Sure. I want to do whatever you need here, Meg." He spread his hands—Mr. Sensitively Cooperative—and pushed doggedly on. Because he had to get them through to the other side of this...whatever this was. It was dangerous out here, like walking on a half-frozen lake. The ice could give way at any moment, and then they'd both be in it, wouldn't they? He thought about the pretty, white-sand pool of his love for her, the way it had gone suddenly dark and unfathomable. Falling into it, he understood, would be death. Frigid water would snap closed over his head like some massive prehistoric fish, all bulging eyes and needle-sharp teeth and—

And, okay, he had to pull himself together here.

"Just call it, Meggy. I can do change if that's what you really want. Just...can you describe the change?" He wrenched one last smile out of a dwindling supply. Because he and Meg had watched *The Breakfast Club* together about a million times. Surely the *Can you describe the ruckus?* reference would remind her of why their friendship was worth saving. But she didn't smile back. She closed her eyes instead and breathed as if it were a task that required serious concentration. "Just tell me what you want."

"And then what?" She opened her eyes and Drew stared, shocked. Because her eyes were full of pain. Deep, thick, suffocating pain. Oh, God, she was drowning in it. What the fuck was going on here? He'd lost his bearings completely. "You'll be that? You'll be whoever I want? You'll feel what I want you to feel?"

"That's not what I meant." His tongue was thick, clumsy.

"What did you mean then?"

His inner scales swung wildly, terror and anger, panic and loss all fighting for control of his throat. "Damn it, Meg, just say it! Just tell me! What the hell do you want from me?"

"No." She shook her head slowly. "I think the right question is, what do you want from me?"

"Us," he said promptly, relieved that he knew the right answer. Because this was unquestionably the right answer. "You, me, the couch, the work. Minus the argument." He paused then went with honesty. Because this was Meg, even if she was temporarily hard to recognize. "Plus the sex, if possible. That's a bonus, though. It's not a deal breaker."

"Because sex is awesome but trivial?"

"Well...yeah."

"Inconsequential? Casual?" She smiled and the edges were breathtakingly sharp. "A sweaty little workout between friends, no strings attached?"

"Well, not exactly. I mean, I'd prefer that if you're sleeping with me, you're not sleeping with anybody else."

Like E, for example. "But otherwise, sure. Why not? You said we had to make room for something new. Why can't this be our new?"

He stepped into the space between them and the air practically vibrated against his skin, all tension and anger and uncertainty. But potential, too. Potential and history and, yeah, love. It was all there, hanging thick in the air as he reached for her. She didn't move, didn't flinch, just let him touch her. She let him comb his fingers into the cool, slippery spill of her hair. He lifted it, a little entranced at the sight of it running through his fingers like sunshine.

"It didn't have to mean so damn much, Meg," he murmured, and met her gaze head-on. "It changed things, yeah. But it didn't have to change us."

"It didn't change us," she said softly, and his throat tried to close. Because the words were right. The words were exactly what he wanted to hear. But that mouth of hers—that gorgeous, generous, curvy mouth? It was white with the control she was exerting over it. She was fighting with superhuman strength and Drew knew without question that he didn't want to hear whatever she was forcing herself to say.

"Meg, don't—" he began and stepped back, his hands up as if to ward off a bullet or something.

"The sex didn't change us." She gave her head a single, hard jerk that sent her hair flying behind one shoulder with a web-fine glitter. And Drew was dazzled, hypnotized into standing still and letting her take aim. "I did. I fell in love with you and I changed everything."

He stared, ears ringing, head light and shocked. That toxic stew of confused emotions roiling around inside him disappeared, and suddenly he was empty. Blank. Scoured hollow. "You...what?" he managed, his lips numb, his heart still.

"I fell in love." She didn't smile. Her fingers were twisted together like live wires but her face was calm. Smooth. Serious. "With you. I'm in love with you, Drew."

Chapter 25

"No, you're not." He said it with an assurance and speed that ripped Meg's heart neatly in half. Thankfully, her self-control had always been tougher than her heart. He gave a startled half-laugh, like *man, you really had me going for a minute.* "Of course you're not in love with me. That's ridiculous."

"I know, right?" She drew the corners of her mouth up into a grim smile. "Totally ridiculous."

He shoved both hands into the crazy bramble of his hair and blew out a breath. "That's not funny, Meg."

"Believe me," she told him. "I know."

"You shouldn't even joke about—"

"I'm not. I wish I were."

He stopped, his mouth still open on whatever he'd been planning to say, his fingers dug deep into the post-afternoon-delight case of bed head he was rocking.

"Yeah, that's pretty much the reaction I had." She gave him the laugh this time, all *well, shit, right*? "You want the details now, I assume? The wheres, whens, hows and whys?" She shrugged and glanced down—direct eye contact with all that shock and dismay was a little much—only to discover that she'd buttoned her shirt crooked. Nice. "I can't tell you much but here's what I know."

She carefully undid her bottom button. Slid it into the correct buttonhole before moving on to the next. She didn't know why she was being so modest—at this point, Drew had seen it all, touched it all, and put a hickey on most of it—but for some reason she wanted to keep her skin to herself.

"Do you remember when you kissed me?" she asked. "Years ago, I'm talking about. That first time. At my dad's house, when Clara freaked out and we got arrested?"

"Yeah."

"And I told you that we weren't going to go there. Kissing and everything it might lead to? Not an option for us. Not then, not ever."

"I remember."

She was done with the buttons. She wished desperately for something else to do with her hands. For some valid reason not to look at him. She didn't want to see the naked shock and dawning unhappiness on that precious, funny face of his. She looked up anyway. Met his eyes with fierce courage.

"I didn't change my mind."

"Yeah, I think you did." The shock was fading into accusation now, and the bleeding halves of her heart wept. "I know you did."

"No, I didn't. My mind is completely firm on the question of you." She swallowed. "It's my heart that got stupid. Because I know you, Drew. I *know* you. I recognized you the minute I met you. I called it the night you kissed me that first time. I knew you could burn me down. One kiss and I knew you could leave me with nothing but ashes if I let you."

"Jesus, will you stop that? Will you stop talking about me like I'm a disease?"

"But you are," she cried, driven beyond care. "You are a disease to me!"

He stared at her, that expressive face white with shock and tight with hurt. She couldn't stop, though. She couldn't care. She had to get through this. He had to understand.

"I take sex seriously, okay? I even take kissing seriously if I'm doing it right. I can't give away my body without my heart being involved. It's who I am and there's nothing I can do about it. And honestly? I don't want to do anything about it. I hold myself precious. Because if I don't, who will? So if a guy gets in my pants, it's not because he told me he was worth it. It's because I decided he was worth it. Not just worth it, either, but worthy."

"Well, I've definitely been in your pants, so I must be worthy." He arched a brow. "Which makes me a worthy disease?"

"You're the exception that proves the rule."

He flinched. "Well, ouch."

"Oh, Jesus, I'm destroying this." She dragged a hand over her face, sucked in a breath that didn't really help and started over. "You're not a disease in general. You're my disease."

"Because we have epic sex."

She sighed. "Because I knew you'd be an incredible lover."

"And you were holding out for a shitty lover." He nodded wisely. "Yeah, I can see how that makes sense."

"I'm holding out," she said carefully, "for somebody who loves me back."

That shut him up. She should feel satisfied. It was hard to shut Drew up. But there was nothing inside her but pain. His, hers, it was hard to tell them apart at this point.

"You feel good, Drew. You feel incredible. You feel...addictive, okay? One taste and I wanted you like I wanted my next breath. Which was always going to make it tough for us to recover from this. To pretend like it was fun but nothing serious."

"Because you take sex seriously."

"Because, despite all my best efforts, my heart decided to take you seriously." He flinched again. She managed a jerky shrug in return. "But, yeah, I was willing to try. You're the most important person in my life, too, so I was willing to at least try to pretend it wasn't a big deal. It was my fond hope that someday, given enough time and effort, it really wouldn't be. Fake it till you make it, right?" She tried a smile. "But that option died the second I said yes to an instant replay here on the couch."

"Why?" He asked this with what looked like genuine bafflement. "Fun isn't a sin, you know. Why is saying yes to something delicious such a bad thing?"

"It's not." The memory of Drew's delicious blasted through her with punishing clarity. She took a moment to breathe, to let it recede. "But I didn't say yes—"

"Uh, yeah. You did. With enthusiasm. I'm not the

world's most perceptive guy but I'm not a rapist." He glared at her. "I'd have noticed no."

"That's not what I meant, Drew." She pushed her hair back with weary hands. "I said yes—with the enthusiasm noted—but not because I wanted to say yes. I just couldn't say no."

He absorbed that in brooding silence and she forced herself to go on.

"That's the problem, Drew. You understand that, right? You said it yourself—sex between us is a nice bonus but nothing essential. What's essential to you is our friendship. And I wish I could say the same but it would be a lie. Because I'm in love with you." He flinched one more time and her heart crumpled just a little further. "I want more than your friendship. I need more. I need you to love me back."

"Meg." He said her name like a plea, like a prayer, and pain spilled over the jagged edges of her heart to pool in her guts. "Meg, if I could love anybody—"

"It would be me." She nodded briskly. "I know. I believe that, I truly do. I don't know if that part of you died with your parents, or if you still have it and just can't find it." She shrugged. "It doesn't matter. And don't you dare apologize. If anybody's sorry, it's me."

"You?" He shot her a wary, sideways look. "What are you sorry for?"

"I'm sorry I didn't see this coming." A weary sorrow crept into the agony puddled inside her. She blew out a breath and let her shoulders slump. "I swear on all that's holy, if I'd known that my heart was sliding this way, I'd have stopped it. I'd have done whatever it took to shore it up, to reinforce the ramparts or whatever. But I didn't know. It took me by surprise. One minute it was Drew-and-Meggy, beers-at-Declan's, just-like-always. Then you were barreling across the bar toward me with murder in your eyes and I didn't recognize you. Then I didn't recognize myself, either. And it all fell apart from there." She lifted helpless shoulders. "I wish I could explain it better. I wish I could take it back. I wish I could undo it." Mortifying tears gathered in her throat, cinched it down to a stingy pinhole. "I don't want to lose you. I don't know how to live in a world where I'm not—" Her throat closed abruptly and she had to stop, swallow.

"Where you're not what?" he asked, and she couldn't even swallow away the constriction this time because he'd put aside all the accusation and the anger to look at her with pure concern. "A world where you're not what, Meg?"

"Where I'm not yours." She tried to smile at him but it was trembly and awful so she stopped. "I know you have friends by the dozens but I don't."

"Meg, come on—"

"No, don't. Don't start lying to me now. Not at this point." She realized belatedly that tears were streaming down her cheeks and she swiped at them impatiently. "People are hard for me. I don't make friends easily. Definitely not friends like you. Losing you—" She shook her head. "That'll be a tough punch to take. I might not stay on my feet. But you need to know that I'll get up. I always get up. So I don't want you worrying, or God forbid trying to help me up, okay? That'll be the hardest part for you. Letting me go. But that's exactly what you'll need to do."

"Good God, Meg, stop it." He took her by the arms, gave her a little shake. "Nobody's dying here. We can get past this. You're not losing anything." But they could both hear the uncertainty under all that brisk reassurance.

"Of course I am. I already have. So have you." His touch already felt awkward, both of them agonizingly aware of the distance between his intentions and her hopes. One more piece of her heart chipped off and she slipped carefully free. "We'll never be what we were. We already aren't. I'd really hoped we could find some way to..." Her hands were shaking so she folded them neatly together. "But we can't. There's no way around this. Bottom line? I'm in love with you."

He lifted his eyes to the ceiling. "Will you please stop saying that?"

"It hurts, doesn't it? Hearing those words and knowing they're not what you want them to be?"

He closed his eyes. "Touché."

"And knowing that you mean them? Genuinely? That only makes it worse for me. What makes it worse yet, though, is knowing that, because you genuinely do love me, you'd probably try to be in love with me if I asked it of you. You'd probably give it a solid effort. But if you're honest with yourself—really, brutally honest—you'll admit that that's not what you want. You don't really want anything more from me than my friendship. And the occasional afternoon delight when you're bored or horny." She smiled at him but didn't know why she was bothering. He wasn't looking at her. Probably never would again. "But I don't want your friendship, Drew. I want your heart. The occasional afternoon delight—epic as it may be—isn't enough for me.

"So listen, here's what we're going to do." She squared her shoulders and took craven refuge in her beloved bullet points. Everything looked more doable in list form, even heart break. "It's nearly six. So we're going to retreat to our separate corners and clean up. I still want those answers from E, and he's a cagey one. We'll want to look like responsible, sober adults rather than dingo-ravaged sluts."

He scowled. "We don't look like—" The sun had sunk low enough to turn the windows into mirrors and she tipped her head toward their reflection. He sighed. "Okay, we do. We look like dingo-ravaged sluts."

"And we're going to fix that before we go sweet-talk the truth out of your long-lost buddy."

"And when we've done that?" He slipped his fingertips into his pockets and rocked back on his heels. Studied her carefully. "When you've satisfied yourself that he's not an evil puppet-master who manipulated us into doing his illegal dirty work? That he's just an old friend making a fresh start?"

She refused to look away. "Then I'm going."

"Going?" He stared. "Where?"

"Away." She didn't even try to smile this time. "I need a fresh start of my own here, Drew. So do you. We're kind of co-dependent, if you hadn't noticed. And if the old life is right there, all tempting and easy, are we really going to build anything new?"

"New. You've been hitting that note all day." He scowled. "I hate new, Meg. I always have. New house, new school, new life. They always suck. New sucks. I didn't like it when I thought you were talking about E—"

She blinked. "You thought E was the new I was asking for?"

He shrugged. "Women love him."

"I don't."

"You think he's hot."

"He is. That doesn't mean I want to sleep with him." She shuddered. It would be like sleeping with a snake, all sleek muscle and cold-blooded strategy. "That wasn't what I meant when I said we had to make room for something new."

"I know that now." He sighed. "I like this new even less."

"I know." She suppressed the urge to pat his arm. Old habits died hard. She wondered if this one would die on its own or if she'd have to kill it. "I'm not that into it myself."

"Are you sure about this, Meg?" He lifted his eyes to hers and they were nakedly hopeful. "Are you sure we can't just...make room? Budge over, like you said, and make room for this?"

"I'm sure. I'll never get over this if we keep spending every minute of every day together." She didn't know if getting over this was even possible but she wasn't going to tell him that. He was in her blood at this point, in her DNA. He'd invaded her at the cellular level, and extracting him without destroying herself might not be an option. But living with the thing she needed most both inches away and yet utterly beyond reach? That was dying by torturous degrees, and would be even worse. "And if I don't get over this, I'm never going to love anybody else. More to the point, nobody's ever going to be able to love me." She lifted her shoulders. "Call me crazy but I still want that. I still want the fairy tale. I want what Bel and James have, what Will and Audrey have. I want somebody to love me like that, and I want to love them like that in return. You can't be that guy,

but maybe somebody else can be. If I don't leave here—
leave you—I'll never find out."

"So you have to go." He nodded slowly. "I get it, Meg.
I do. It makes sense. But I hate it."

"I know." Her hand rose of its own volition this time
but she caught it before she made contact. "I know, Drew.
Let's just get through tonight. One step at a time, right?"

"Right." He met her gaze, gave her that crooked half-
smile of his. She wondered if it were possible to die of heart
break. If so, she'd like to just get it over with because
surviving with this kind of pain didn't seem worth it.
"Because everything is better with bullet points."

For a single, stricken moment she simply stared. Two
seconds ago, she'd thought her pain intolerable but this?
This was an ocean of agony. A galaxy. Because, sure, she
might find somebody who loved her better, but would he
know her like this? Understand her like this? Could he walk
with her through a violent holocaust of pain and still find the
wherewithal to tease her about her love of all things
organizational?

She managed a garbled response—no idea what she
said only that he accepted it as English and passably
appropriate to the conversation—and fled.

Chapter 26

Meg wore unrelieved black. Drew would be tempted to think she was in mourning except that she looked good enough to eat. A shawl-collared jacket nipped in elegantly at her waist, then finished with a skirty sort of swish around her hips. There was probably a high-fashion name for that kind of thing but Drew didn't know what it was. He did know, however, that if her shoes weren't black and visibly expensive they'd have comfortably qualified as stripper heels.

And Drew ought to know. Back in the good ol' days, he'd made something of a study of stripper shoes. And strippers. He'd dated enough of them to know that shoes like Meg's were the exact opposite of sexy to the women who wore them. Walking in them hurt like hell, and dancing in them? Torture. Meg strode through the lobby of the Prince George Hotel as if they were running shoes, though, so they evidently weren't a problem for her.

No, the problem was all his. Because between the shoes, the jacket and a pair of skinny black trousers that clung demurely to every inch of those endless legs? Meg was pure, high-octane sex tonight. Drew wouldn't be a guy if he didn't notice. And Drew was definitely a guy. He noticed. He noticed everything about her. Everything, apparently, except the most important detail.

Meg was in love with him.

He followed her across the lobby at a sedate amble that gave him time to turn that thought over in his mind. To hold it there and really have a look at it. Because things had gone so fast earlier. Revelation, response, new plan, bam. Over and done. Beyond an initial burst of howling betrayal— which he felt perfectly entitled to, given the years-long ban on all things sexual that she herself had instituted—he hadn't felt anything yet. Didn't know what to feel. The whole thing sat inside him like a knot he couldn't undo.

He'd grasped the logic of her argument, of course, but he couldn't shake the feeling that there was more to it. Something she wasn't saying, some nuance he was missing here that, if he could only put his finger on it, would make that last puzzle piece fall into place. And, hopefully, unlock his brain, unfreeze his heart and let him feel the staggering loss he knew he was supposed to feel at the demise of the most important relationship in his life.

The memory of Meg's face—streaked with tears but calm and resolute—popped into his mind. And he felt...nothing. That strange desert inside him pulsed hotter and whiter, however, as if it were beating in place of the heart that had so far refused to acknowledge the entire situation. He wondered if he should be worried. He probably should. Except that nothing was wrong. Nothing he could put his finger on.

She stopped at the elevator bank and waited, hipshot, for him to catch up. And it was all so normal. Her coat was slung over one arm, her hair swept up into a dramatic braided crown, her eyes huge and painted all smoky. She was even tapping her toe, impatient as always with his tendency to mosey. She shot a cuff as he arrived at her side, glanced at a silvery bangle of a watch.

"Seven forty-two." She arched a brow at him. "He said eight?"

"For the last time, Meg, yes. He said eight." He tucked his hands into his pockets because they hadn't gotten the this-is-over memo and were itching to touch. That jacket was killing him, with its itty-bitty waist. The pale strip of skin tastefully exposed by the deep cowl neckline of whatever she was wearing under it didn't help.

Knee-jerk, he told himself. Because only a real ass deliberately entertained impure thoughts about a girl who felt more for him than he could feel for her. He poked restlessly at that desert-bright void inside him where all his emotions should be. A girl who felt more for him than he

209

could feel at all, evidently.

He glanced at her neckline again, at the silvery glitter of a necklace plunging deep into her cleavage. At the polished black stone at the bottom of that plunge, nestled warmly against her breastbone. His dick pulsed optimistically. Of course it did. Because when all else went numb, you could trust the dick to pick up the slack and feel all the feels.

"What did he say when you talked to him?" she asked with exaggerated patience. "Exactly."

"He said we should pick him up here," he told her, with similarly exaggerated patience. "At eight."

"Reservations?"

"He's taking care of it."

"You should call him," she said. "Let him know we're here."

"Chill out, will you?" He arched a brow but more for form than because he wanted to spar with her. "We're, like, fifteen minutes early."

"So? We're here. Why not at least check to see if he's ready too? Worst case scenario, we get to wait for him in the bar. Best case, though? We get a bonus fifteen minutes of interrogation time."

"You're awfully eager to get this party started."

"Soonest begun is soonest done."

He frowned. "Did you just quote *Mary Poppins* at me?"

"No, that's *well-begun is half done, otherwise titled Let's Tidy Up The Nursery.* But it applies. We hosed up the nursery, Drew. Time to clean it up."

"My point stands. You're awfully amped to tidy up the damn nursery. Why is that?"

She gave him a look that openly questioned his intellect. "Because I've had a shitty day, Drew. I'd like to just get it done."

"Yeah, well, my day hasn't exactly been a picnic, you know."

She eyed him with something close to disgust. "Poor baby."

"Come on, Meg." He stepped closer, lowered his voice. The entire lobby didn't need to be in on their conversation.

"You dropped the L-bomb on me this afternoon. You blew our lives to shit and didn't give me even thirty seconds to digest before you bought your plane tickets to the Bahamas or wherever."

"I haven't bought plane tickets anywhere yet, Drew."

"I was being metaphorical." He scowled at her. "My point is that this is a big deal and you're rushing it. You're rushing me. So will you just give me a damn minute?"

"Of course. Take all the time you need." She shifted her coat to the other elbow, folded her hands neatly together and arranged her face into patient, amiable lines. "Or fifteen minutes, whichever comes first."

"Nice. Very compassionate."

"My middle name." She dropped the face, glared at him and shoved her hands into her elbows. "Oh, fine. I'm sorry, okay? It's been a righteously shitty day and I don't have a lot left in the tank. And what I do have? I don't know if I can afford to give it away."

"I know, Meg. I know. It's just...can we go over it again?" He swallowed past the knot in his throat. "I know it's hard for you. It's not exactly easy for me. But I'm having trouble wrapping my mind around this whole thing and I think it would really help if we could just sit down over there at the bar, get a drink and go over it again. Just walk me through it, step by step, so I can—"

"I'm in love with you, Drew."

The words fell into the arid emptiness inside him without a sound. Without impact or even stirring the air.

"I'm in love with you," she said again, with something like her old wry smile in place. "That's why I had sex with you. Twice now, God help me. That's also why I can't have sex with you ever again. I'm in love with you. And you're not in love with me. Sleeping with you under those circumstances rips big, bloody hunks off my heart. But I can't tell you no, either." Her mouth twisted bitterly. "Obviously."

"I'm sorry." It was useless to be sorry, but he was. Not that he felt sorry. He didn't feel anything. But he hated that she was hurting.

"I know you are. I am, too." She sighed. "Any other questions? Or was that sufficiently clear?"

"No. Clear." He swallowed. Was this what it felt like when you woke up in the hospital and realized that you couldn't feel your legs? When a part of your body that was utterly integral to life as you'd known it just went dark? He should be feeling something here, shouldn't he? He groped desperately for some vestige of what they'd had, who they'd been. "It's just...I love you, Meggy."

She gazed at him for a long, taut moment, then said, "I am going to punch your stupid face for you."

"Would you?" At least then he'd feel something.

"No. Wallow in your guilt."

But she patted his arm just like she used to, all brisk and no-nonsense. Then her gaze shifted, and she straightened. Put on her for-the-public smile. And Drew knew that his fifteen minutes were up.

He turned and found E striding across the lobby toward them in a pair of perfectly tailored slacks and a sweater that looked like it had been hand woven by Peruvian orphans from the wool of virgin mountain sheep. He must've taken the stairs. Drew stuck out a hand. "E! Hey, good to see you!"

"Yeah, you, too." E shook, and pulled him in for a one-armed handshake/hug hybrid. "As for you—" He turned to Meg and gave her a leisurely up-and-down. "You look better than good. You look positively edible." He went the air-kiss route on her, both cheeks, very continental.

"Speaking of edible," Meg said, laughing while she accepted the kisses, "I understand you were in charge of reservations this evening?"

"I was. I had to make up for this morning's rudeness somehow, didn't I?" He didn't let her go but stood there, her elbows cupped in his palms. Drew wasn't sure he liked the familiarity but his smile was everything gentlemanly, and he divided it between her and Drew. "I considered several restaurants, but in the end I just didn't want to share the two of you this evening."

"No?" Drew cut Meg a glance but she was gazing at E with the perfect combination of curiosity and appetite. As if

E had just offered her a present, and it might be him.

"No. First of all, we're celebrating the ridiculous house I just beggared myself to buy."

"Right," Drew said. "Congrats on that, by the way."

"Thanks." He grinned. "Secondly, however, you both did me a favor yesterday—an enormous one—that I imagine has caused you a moment or two of uneasiness in the cold light of day." He quirked a brow in question and Meg gave Drew a laughing sideways look that said *busted*. He sent one back that said *I told you there was nothing to worry about.* "I owe you both a debt. And some answers."

"Drew doesn't believe in debt between friends." Meg sent him that switchblade smile of hers. "But I wouldn't mind some answers."

E laughed. "Which is exactly why I've taken the liberty of having dinner catered in my suite tonight. I think we could use some privacy for this conversation." He leaned forward to push the elevator call button. "It's too bad I didn't find the right home a bit sooner. Cooking is something of a hobby of mine, and it would've given me great pleasure to whip up something special for you in my own kitchen." He gave Meg a look of melting earnestness. "There's just something so intimate about dining at home, don't you agree?"

"Oh, absolutely." The elevator gave a soft chime and the doors slid open. E gestured Meg ahead of him and she threw him a laughing look over her shoulder as he and Drew followed her into the carriage. "Especially when the conversation is as substantial as the meal."

"I'm afraid I can't guarantee the meal, as it's not my own work. The chef came highly recommended but—" E gave a Gallic shrug and leaned back against a red velvet panel as the elevator slid upward. "But the rest should satisfy on every level."

Meg twinkled at him. "Words every girl loves to hear."

E gave an appreciative chuckle. "I do try."

The elevator came to a halt and the doors parted. Drew automatically put a hand on the jamb and stepped aside to let Meg out. E swished a gallant hand and said, "After you." He didn't, Drew noticed, do anything about actually holding the door, but why would he? Drew was on top of it. All E had to do was make the empty gesture.

Meg stepped out of the elevator, hips swinging, and E stepped out behind her, a hand in the small of her back guiding her toward his suite. Drew followed at his usual amble, a thoughtful and unfamiliar frown on his face. He hadn't seriously considered Meg's concerns that E was dangerous, but something here felt...off. The supposed debt E felt? The much ballyhooed answers he was ostensibly providing that required more privacy than a restaurant could provide? The heavy-handed flirting? It just smelled off.

He suspected it was that last one his gut didn't like, but he didn't know why it should be so. E was an incurable flirt, but so was Meg, in her own sharp-toothed way. She'd turned it on for hundreds of guys over the years and for hundreds of reasons, the vast majority of them non-sexual. Why should it stick in his craw to watch her play the game with E? She wanted her answers, and she was going to get them. Flies, honey, vinegar, et cetera. Besides, she was in love with him, not the other way around. It shouldn't matter to him who she smiled at, or who she wore those heels for.

And it didn't. Truly. That weird, white desert inside him was perfectly, aridly unconcerned with the exchange of naughty double-entendres in the elevator.

But at the same time, he knew that something was wrong here. It absolutely was. He knew it.

He just didn't feel it.

He didn't feel anything.

Chapter 27

Meg hadn't thought to imagine what E's suite might look like. She'd been preoccupied, plus she didn't care. But if it had crossed her mind to wonder what E's preferred digs might look like? She'd have come up with something awfully close to this—everything with a pedigree and every pedigree in its place.

He unlocked the door with an actual key—not the kind of thing most hotels had anymore—and ushered them into a gracious sitting area with high ceilings and buttery yellow walls. Plaster walls, of course, not drywall, because this was the Prince George and everything should whisper faintly of ancient money. A curvy sofa sat against the left-hand wall, its velvet slightly shabby, its bones stunningly elegant. It was a neat trick, aging well. Meg hoped she learned it before her time arrived.

"Very pretty," she said, moving forward to inspect the painting on the wall above the sofa. It was a Revolutionary War battlefield—blood and fear in every masterful brush stroke. Brush strokes that were plainly visible upon closer inspection. "Good heavens. This isn't a print. But surely it's not the original Trumbull either." She leaned closer, then turned back to lift a brow at E. "Is it?"

"I don't think so, no. A reproduction, likely by a student of his." He closed the door behind Drew and beamed like a teacher pleased with a star pupil. "You're familiar with John Trumbull's work?"

"Of course we're familiar with his work," Drew said. "Guy was blind in one eye, but his portrait of Alexander Hamilton was so good that some lady painter copied it for the ten dollar bill." He moved to Meg's side to inspect the painting. He smelled clean and faintly green, as always. Her

Susan Sey

heart tried to twist but she suppressed it with a ruthless
smile. "We'd hardly be American if we didn't love that
story."

"We do enjoy our underdogs," Meg murmured. Drew
was inches from her elbow. She'd give her right arm for just
one breath that didn't have him in it, but didn't want to give
E the slightest hint of discord between them so she stayed
put. "Land of the free, home of the long shot."

E smiled. "I've been here over a decade. One would
think I wouldn't need the reminder anymore but—" He lifted
laconic shoulders. "I always forget how plucky you
Americans are."

"Plucky." Meg judged that she'd endured Drew's
proximity long enough and stepped away to continue her
survey of the suite. "I like it." A tri-panel window graced the
far wall, large for the era though small by modern standards.
Come daylight, the view was likely spectacular—horse-and-
hound country for miles.

"You should," E said. "It looks good on you."

"Everything does," Drew said. "That's Meg for you."

She manufactured a light laugh and moved over to
explore a graceful archway in the center of the right-hand
wall. "I beg to differ. The early two-thousands were...let's
call them an awkward phase, shall we?"

She poked her head into the alcove inside the arch and
found a tiny but extremely functional kitchenette on her right
and a tidy bathroom dead ahead. The door on her left stood
open just a hand's width and she leaned unabashedly
sideways to peer in.

"Awkward? You? Come now." E chuckled. "I don't
believe it."

"Oh, you should. I got all my height over the course of
a single semester. Of sixth grade." Behind the door was E's
bedroom, of course. The bed was massive, a four-poster
ocean of pillowy goose down and starched sheets, the
headboard huge and elaborately carved. Very grand.
Practically royal. She bet E adored it. She turned to him and
smiled. "I was taller than every single teacher I had,
including the men. Plus I had no idea how to dress myself."

216

His eyes drifted from her heels to her hair, lingering over the deep vee of skin she'd covered with nothing but a necklace. "You clearly figured it out."

"Didn't she?" Drew stood in the center of the room, next to a square table covered in a crisp white tablecloth and set for three. "You should see her closet. It's got its own ZIP code."

Meg laughed and joined him at the table. She carefully chose the chair across from his rather than beside. "It's true. When it comes to clothes, I have no self-control."

The carpet swallowed E's footsteps as he crossed the room and picked up the bottle of wine breathing on the table. "I like a woman with a healthy appetite," he said, his eyes light and laughing. He tipped the wine into her glass, then into Drew's. He filled his own and lifted it. "To satisfaction."

Meg refused to let herself even look Drew's way. Satisfaction was both a liquid hot memory and an unattainable dream, and she had no desire to involve herself in a war she couldn't win. At this point the best she could hope for was a surrender on her own terms. She refused to spend the rest of her life looking at Drew like a dog stares at the door when its owner is away.

"To satisfaction." She tapped her glass to E's. "And to whatever comes after."

Drew rolled his eyes. "To cryptic toasts." He tapped his glass to theirs. "Now let's eat, because it looks like E's gone to a lot of trouble to set this stage."

"Table." E's smile was benign. Amused. "I set the table."

Drew smiled back, easy as always. "Oh, please. If you don't start speechifying about sharks and laser beams and volcano lairs in a minute here, I'm going to be disappointed. Meg's going to be downright crushed." He sipped his wine. "Plus these hors d'oeuvres look amazing and I'm starved." He dropped into his chair, threw an ankle over his knee and studied E over the rim of his wineglass with expectant eyes. "Well? Curtain's up, E, and we've got our popcorn. Time for the big reveal."

E laughed. "I forgot how much I liked you, Drew."

"I'm an easy guy to forget."

"You underestimate yourself."

He might've read her mind. Because Meg wished desperately that Drew would be easy to forget, but somehow she doubted it.

E rounded the table, pausing to draw out her chair. She smiled her thanks and sank into it. Gave Drew a round-eyed *what the hell are you doing* face, to which he gave a lazy shrug. He was getting the party started, evidently, and on his own terms.

E took his seat between them and waved an inviting hand over the pretty plates of nuts and fruit, cheese and crackers that studded the table like little islands of delicious.

"I said I forgot how much I liked you, Drew," E said. "Not that you existed." He chose a pecan, smeared it with a bit of honeyed goat cheese. "I always knew I'd circle back around to you one day."

"Did you?" Drew picked up a celery stick, drew it through a puddle of pesto-laced hummus. He bit in with relish, his teeth very white. "How interesting."

"I agree," Meg said, and dropped an elbow on the table to lean in. To aim the little recorder in her necklace E's way. Because this *was* getting interesting, and she wasn't a security expert for nothing. Meg never showed up to a party empty handed. "Let's hear more about that, shall we?"

"Of course." E selected a cracker next, smeared it with some sort of fruity compote and topped it with a bit of cheese sliced so thin she could see through it. He offered it to her. "You should taste this fig butter. It's amazing."

She took the cracker and set it on her plate. "You know what I think is amazing? That you happened to run into an old friend with exactly the skills you needed at exactly the moment you needed them."

E's eyes danced at her over the rim of his wine glass. "As amazing as the fact that said friend was in possession of his own friends who also happened to have exactly the skills I needed?"

"Exactly."

"I love your suspicious little mind." He leaned back in his chair, wineglass dangling elegantly from one hand, a small smile playing around those gorgeous lips. He nodded her toward the cracker. "Seriously, Meg. You need to taste that."

She picked up the cracker and set it on his plate. "Why don't you have that one?"

His smile bloomed. "My goodness. You really do think I'm Dr. Evil. I haven't slipped you a mickey, darling. I've simply offered you a rather spectacular fig butter."

"And I'm appreciative. Spectacular fig butter is hard to come by."

"No kidding," Drew said. He helped himself to a bunch of glistening red grapes. "I had some fig butter last week that was utterly pedestrian. No imagination."

Meg kept her eyes on E's. "I hate an unimaginative fig butter. Plus?" She leaned in just far enough to let the deep cowl of her shirt fall enticingly open. "Everybody knows you shouldn't take candy from strangers."

"Do they?" E's eyes dropped to her cleavage and lingered there. Or at least where her cleavage would be if she had any. "So a man can't hand-pick the choicest morsels from the table for his lady anymore?"

"Well, I guess he can," Drew said. "If he finds a lady who's willing to risk waking up on the floor of his dorm room minus her underpants and plus a venereal disease."

"Charming." E picked up the cracker. He toasted her with it and popped it into his mouth. Closed his eyes and savored. "Satisfied?"

"Depends." Drew smeared a cracker with fig butter and topped it with another translucent wafer of cheese. "Are we getting to the laser-beam equipped sharks soon? Because I'm getting bored." He paused to chew and swallow. "Damn, Meg, that really is amazing." He smeared another cracker, cheesed it and handed it over. "I'm about to change your life. You're welcome."

E frowned at him. "I'm changing her life, thank you very much. That fig butter was my find." He turned to Meg. "Well?"

"For God's sake." She ate the cracker. "Yummy. Now about those sharks?"

"That's it?" E stared. "Yummy?"

Meg regarded him with sympathy. "You shouldn't eat your feelings, E."

"I don't eat my feelings." He frowned at her. "I simply appreciate good food. Decent wine. Classic art."

"Beautiful women?" Meg offered.

"Expensive couches," Drew said.

"Live-in help," Meg said.

"Old money."

"Pure-bred dogs."

"Corgis." Drew laughed and helped himself to another cracker. "Definitely corgis."

E sighed. "This entire evening is wasted on you two."

"What? No!" Drew popped a couple more grapes. "We love theater, don't we, Meg?"

"We do. But I think we're being a little interactive for E's taste." She smiled. "I'm getting the idea that this was supposed to be a one-man show."

"Oh." Drew considered that. "A monologue."

"And we're going all improv on the poor guy." She gave Drew sorrowful eyes. "We are a bad audience."

"Terrible." Drew poured her more wine. Topped off his own glass. "The worst."

"Okay, let's pay attention." She turned cooperative eyes to E. "Go ahead. We're ready." E lifted a very patient brow and she said, "You're right. One more thing." She nudged the honeyed goat cheese toward Drew and stage whispered, "Try that. It won't change your life but it might make you think about taking it to Vegas for the weekend." She turned back to E and smiled brilliantly. "Okay, ready. Hit us."

Drew fig buttered another cracker and passed it to her in exquisite silence, his eyes attentively on E. She accepted it the same way. E sat back in his chair, threw an ankle over the opposite knee and studied them.

"Well, I must say, you're making this very easy for me."

Drew threw her a look that said *are we supposed to*

answer, or is this the monologue? She gave him a tiny shrug and turned her attention pointedly back to E. Drew sighed and followed suit. In spite of the roaring pain of the past few hours and the unimaginable loss of the hours ahead, a laugh bubbled up her throat. It tickled her nose and tugged mercilessly at her mouth. God damn but Drew was a good time. She was going to miss his stupid ass.

Her throat tried to seize up at the very idea so she shoved it away and concentrated on the situation at hand.

E lifted his wineglass for a leisurely sip. "I was prepared to feel quite guilty about this."

Again, Drew cut her a questioning look. This time she gave him the *pay attention* face, with some *for God's sake* eyes thrown in for good measure. She turned back to E, all expectation.

"It gives me no pleasure to threaten either of you," E said. "I do hope you'll believe that. Just like I hope it won't come to that." He smiled at them, and it spread over his perfect face like an oil slick, all rainbows and damage. "A little cooperation, and we can put all this behind us. Perhaps we can even be friends."

Meg's stomach went light. The mask was slipping. Here came the crazy. She'd known it was there. She'd felt it, hadn't she?

"Maybe we can," she said. Leaned back and prepared for the worst. "Why don't you tell us more about this cooperation you're interested in?"

Chapter 28

"It's quite simple, really," E said. He produced a shiny silver thumb drive and placed it on the white tablecloth between them. It gleamed there like a bullet. "I want Drew to upload the contents of this thumb drive to the NoVD servers via Edward Valor's laptop." He smiled. "Tonight."

Drew glanced at Meg. She was gazing at the thumb drive like it was a poisonous snake. "What's on it?" he asked.

"Short answer? Evidence that Valor tampered with the Secret Service data stored on his servers."

Meg closed her eyes and moaned softly. Drew couldn't blame her. She hadn't predicted exactly this but she'd been sniffing the right direction. God damn it. Meg's gut was rock-solid. With the notable—and disastrous—exception of letting her fall in love with him, when had it ever been wrong?

About never, that's when. When was he going to learn to listen?

"On this thumb drive is evidence," E went on, "that Valor fabricated a key piece of intelligence upon which the Secret Service based a decision that sent half a dozen field operatives to their deaths, not to mention another half dozen in-country assets. Evidence that he did so in full knowledge of the probable consequences. But best of all? It contains evidence that he then erased—or attempted to erase—all traces of that key data in an effort to sabotage the poor analyst who made the call." He gazed fondly at the thumb drive. "It's beautiful work, if I do say so myself. Very subtle, very skilled. Shadows here, traces there. Nothing damning in and of itself, but taken as a whole, it adds up to undeniable proof that Valor sacrificed his honor and his principles—not to mention a dozen innocent men—in pursuit of a personal vendetta against a coworker." E shook his head sadly. "A shame, that. But war does terrible things to a man's mind. Not all of our conquering heroes return home precisely intact."

Drew glanced at Meg, and found her gazing at E with utter calm.

Meggy had her game face on.

A jolt of love—pure and incandescent—streaked across the void inside him, jagged as a bolt of lightning. Gratitude followed like thunder. Because this wasn't Meg's problem. He was Meg's problem. Thanks to his terminally poor impulse control and some fifteen year old guilt, he'd destroyed their friendship, broken her heart and let a Dr. Evil wannabe into their lives, all in a single weekend. At this point, she had every right to stand up, dust her hands and walk out that door. To leave his sorry ass to deal with the fallout of all those crappy decisions. Her departure was already scheduled for first thing in the morning. She ought to just bump it up a few hours and let him swing on this.

But was she running? Hell, no. Meg was sticking. Suiting up. Going to war. For him, with him, beside him. In spite of everything he'd done to her, in spite of all the ways he'd failed her, she had his back this one last time. Wonder crackled through that desert-bright void inside him, as dangerous as unharnessed electricity.

As he watched, Meg straightened her shoulders and slid her chair back to face E more squarely. "That's a big ask," she said mildly. E arched a brow and she held up placating hands. "We're not saying no. But a little more context would be helpful."

"Context." Drew nodded and leaned forward, elbows on knees. "Yeah. I mean, if that was the short answer, what's the long one?"

E ignored him, studying Meg with appreciation. "Would your curiosity survive the knowledge that I've surrounded us with so many scramblers that NASA itself couldn't get a signal in this room? That no wireless gadget of any stripe functions at all anywhere from here to the elevator?" He leaned forward to place a finger on the soft lapel of her jacket, the same jacket that had been driving Drew nuts all night.

"Hey!" Drew jolted forward. He didn't know what he intended to do, just that the sight of E's finger tracing that delicate vee of pale, exposed skin was intolerable. Meg didn't look away from E or shift away from his touch. She only lifted a staying hand to Drew, who grabbed the reins on this shocking surge of murderous intent and forced himself back into his seat. If Meg said she had it, she had it. But Drew wanted blood in his mouth.

E traced the glittery thread of Meg's necklace from her throat to the shadowy invitation of her cleavage. He took the heavy black stone that glowed there in elegant fingers. He lifted it, turned it to the light and murmured, "Fascinating." He brought his eyes to hers. "Your work?"

"I told you I'd learned to dress myself," Meg said drily. "Not that I'd learned to trust anybody. Precisely the opposite, in fact."

"Rings on her fingers and bells on her toes. And a nifty recording device between her pretty breasts." E laughed and lowered the stone to her chest, let his fingers drift deliberately a few inches afield as he nestled it carefully back into place. Bloodlust rose in Drew's throat again like bile and his hands curled into fists against his thighs. E withdrew his fingers bare seconds before Drew made up his mind to break them off. E flicked one of Meg's dangly earrings and sat back to watch it tick-tock beside the clean line of her jaw. "Those, too, I assume?"

"But of course." Meg tipped him a sparkling look. "Tell me, how confident are you in your scrambling devices?"

"Very. I didn't choose to spend fifteen years with the Secret Service, but I was hardly fool enough to waste them. Your pretty earrings are recording nothing but static tonight, Meggy."

"Those guys do have some serious kung fu, electronically speaking," she conceded. "And I'll admit, I haven't cracked it yet." She smiled. "But I plan to. Soon."

"Not soon enough for tonight."

"Eh." She shrugged, unconcerned. "Win some, lose some. It's staying in the game that counts." She showed him her teeth. "Recordings or not, we're still a long way from taking our balls and going home."

E turned to Drew. "I can see why you love her so. Are you quite, quite certain she's off limits?"

"Quite," Drew murmured, and he was. Quite.

"But you're just chums." E's smile went silky, predatory. "You're really not—how do the kids put it these days?—hitting that?"

"Your dickish tendencies are showing," Meg said crisply.

"Apologies," E said, not taking his eyes from Drew. "It's just that I've never seen a truly platonic relationship in the wild before. It's a bit like finding a unicorn."

"Yeah, it's all rainbows and glitter up in here." Drew smiled grimly. "You get used to it after a while."

"Is that what happened?" E studied him with something akin to pity. "You got used to her?" He shook his head. "Shame."

Drew blinked at him, struck. Was that what had happened? Had he just gotten used to Meg? Stopped looking at her? Or maybe just stopped seeing her?

No, not her. Realization dawned with excruciating clarity. Or not just her. He'd stopped seeing himself, too. Because what had blown up between them last night hadn't been impulse. Drew made probably 75 percent of his decisions on impulse, so he knew what that was. It was a whim and a leap and a hoo-yah free-fall into whatever came next.

What had happened between him and Meg last night hadn't been like that. It had been more like a lightning strike in a forest that hadn't burned in years. And that was the thing, wasn't it? Forests were supposed to burn. They were made to burn. There were seeds that only opened at, like, 2,000 degrees or something. Forests died if they didn't burn, choked to death on their own fallen leaves.

So he and Meg had burned. Finally. They'd burned themselves to nothing but a circle of scorched earth. For

225

Christ's sake, Drew was still all but smoking. The fire lived in his bones now. He understood this with sudden and perfect certainty. Whatever he and Meg had lit last night was forever.

Which was exactly why Meg had to leave. He understood that, too. Truly, he did. They couldn't keep burning each other down like this, not if there was no love to grow them up again afterwards. Or not enough love. Or not the right kind of love. But he wondered, had lighting the fire destroyed them? Or was it that they'd lit it too late? That they'd let that shocking want between them accumulate like forest detritus until there was too much to burn off with a safe, civilized little fire? Until it had burned so murderously hot that it only destroyed and didn't renew?

He wanted to ask Meg about it, to see what she thought. Only he couldn't. After tonight, she wouldn't be around to gut check his crazy ideas. After tonight, she'd be gone. He glanced across the table at her, found her gazing back at him. Her game face was still firmly in place but her eyes were just for him, and they said *courage*. A spark of agony crackled across all the numbness inside him. Loss looming large. The Novocain of shock wearing off. The pain waking up. God help him.

"Yeah, I guess Meg and I are a bit off the beaten path, friendship-wise." He drew on that old rusty well of easy and forced a lazy shrug. "It works for us, though."

"Does it really." E slid his eyes Meg's way. Sent her a smooth smile. "Darling Meg. If you're ever in the mood for a friendship that trends a trifle warmer, I do hope you'll remember my number."

"I'll keep it in mind." She crossed one long silky leg over the other and propped an elbow on the table. Studied E closely. "For now, let's circle back around to that long answer. I'd like to hear more about why we're framing Edward Valor for a crime he didn't commit." She paused, arched a brow. "We are framing him? I'm reading that correctly?"

"Oh, we are. We're definitely framing him.

"Why?"

226

E's smile was brilliant. "Because he's a right git."

"Oh, well, then." Drew helped himself to the candied almonds. "By all means, let's see the guy disgraced, impoverished and imprisoned."

E gave the thumb drive a lazy spin on the tablecloth. "Let's."

Drew shook the nuts in his hand and considered E lounging across his chair, all silky menace. "Okay, understand first of all that I'm not standing up for the guy. I'm willing to file him under Major Dick just for driving that stupid monster truck. But torpedoing his career, his reputation and his future? Just for being a jerk?" He shook his head. "I don't know, man. It seems extreme."

E sighed and topped off his wine. He lifted an eyebrow toward Meg. She shook her head. Drew nudged his glass forward. "Yeah, hit me. I have a feeling this is going to get complicated."

E shrugged and tipped wine into his glass. "What decent story isn't?"

"Fair enough." Drew picked up his replenished glass, waved E forward with it.

E leaned back in his chair and studied them gravely. "So I wasn't completely honest with you last night."

"No." Meg didn't bother to make it a question, or to feign shock.

E smiled, indulgently amused. "*Mais oui*. My apologies. You see, the Secret Service did, in fact, remove me from a situation that had become...untenable, let's say, and in a dramatic hail of rubber bullets, too. That much of last night's story is true. But I was never their mole. I was spared the indignity of ingratiating myself to penny-ante hackers, of scrounging for rumors and chasing gossip in order to keep my handlers happy." His lips curved in a smile that didn't spell amusement to Drew. "No, I had the privilege of legitimate employment. I was—and am—a bona fide Secret Service employee right here in Virginia. And have been these past fifteen years or more."

"Holy hell, you're a Secret Service agent?" Meg's eyes were huge. Drew doubted she was feigning shock this time either.

"Oh, heavens no. Merely an analyst. I can only assume that it amused somebody powerful to demand that I repay my debt to society by protecting the very society I'd endangered with my...extracurriculars." E lifted his glass to her. "Here's to poetic justice."

He drank, eyes dancing over the rim of his wineglass at her. He was enjoying her, Drew realized with a shock of dismay. Genuinely enjoying her, and that felt very dangerous. He didn't want E's appreciative amusement in the same county as Meg.

"As it happens," E went on, "the work suited me. Who knew? And for several years—eight, ten even?—it was fine. Enjoyable, even. I was quite a valuable employee, as you might imagine, given the Secret Service's predilection for hiring upstanding citizens such as yourselves. I provided a certain perspective that they distinctly lacked."

"I'll bet," Drew said. Because what set the great hackers apart from the merely good ones was the ability to inflict breathtaking damage without even a twinge of conscience. Which was why Drew had been a good hacker—very good—but E had been unquestionably great. The Secret Service probably *had* appreciated his perspective. They didn't usually hire sociopaths. God.

"Then Valor joined up," E said, his lips flat, his eyes bright.

"Wait," Drew said, "Valor's a Secret Service agent?"

"He is."

Meg frowned. "I thought he was the Chief Security Officer at NoVD."

"He's that as well." E leaned back, a professor preparing to launch his favorite lecture. "You see, the Secret Service sifts through massive amounts of real-time data on a twenty-four hour basis, Meg. Field agents and informants stream it in constantly. There's no way human beings could make sense of it in time to do anything useful with it, so we have computer programs that identify patterns in real time and bring them to analysts like myself, who then decide what's actionable and what's static. It requires far more fire power, electronically speaking, than is practical to house in our own office space. So we contract it out to server farms all over the country. Their stacks are on the job twenty-four/seven, crunching raw data and streaming us the results."

"And one of these data farms is at NoVD," Drew said.

E pointed a finger at Drew as if he'd won a prize. "But of course the Secret Service can't leave security up to the server farms themselves. Not when American lives are dependent on the integrity of that data and the intelligence we cull from it."

"Of course not." Meg's eyes were narrow, thoughtful, and Drew could all but see the words *business opportunity* looming over her head in a cartoon bubble. Good old Meg. So dependable.

"Every facility we use agrees to create a VP or a CSO position or the equivalent with a very narrow set of job responsibilities—maintaining unimpeachable security on each and every one of their servers that we use." He spread his hands. "And in return we issue them a Secret Service agent to fill that position."

"So the data you work from is stored at NoVD," Meg said, her wheels still visibly turning. "And Valor is the agent in charge of securing it."

"Quite. The integrity of that data begins and ends with Valor but at the end of the day? He's a glorified babysitter." E smiled. "Quite the come down for a bona fide American war hero, no?"

"Quite," Drew said. "A little fact that you mentioned to him every chance you got, I assume?"

"What? And exacerbate an already difficult working relationship?" E spread innocent hands. "You wound me."

"You two didn't get along then?" Meg asked.

"Not through any fault of mine." E sighed. "But evidently, it was a great affront to a man with Valor's credentials to serve alongside a degenerate such as myself."

"Was it?"

"It was." E smiled bitterly. "The man's a West Point graduate and a decorated combat veteran, you see. He's also fluent in Russian, Ukrainian and Chechen. He was brilliant in the field. And if he'd only thought to invest in proper bloody footwear, he could've stayed there."

Meg blinked. "Footwear?"

"He underestimated a Chechnyan winter." E shook his head. "Badly. Cost the gentleman his toes, which ordinarily wouldn't be an insurmountable problem but—"

"Wait, his toes?" Drew stared.

"Frostbite." E waved this off. "But it also cost him his military career, as the Army Rangers require a full complement of digits."

"Of course they do," Meg murmured.

"They sent him home and the Secret Service snapped him up," E went on. "They do love their Boy Scouts. But they love their rules just as much and refused to put the toeless bastard in the field where he clearly belongs. So they put him in charge of my unit instead."

"Where he discovered...you?" Drew ventured.

"Me." E smiled. "My very presence was an assault on propriety, of course, not to mention an insult to everything he'd sacrificed his toes for." That smile went brittle, sharp. "Imagine a hero like that serving alongside a spoiled, amoral, entitled brat such as myself? A common criminal whose mummy and daddy bought him a sweet deal over jail time? If the Secret Service thought I was in any way valuable, it was dead wrong. And if it thought I was to be trusted? Well, now, it was just stupid into the bargain, wasn't it? And Edward Valor, American Hero, wasn't going to stand for that. He would neither eat, sleep, nor breathe until I was exposed for the parasite I so obviously was."

Drew resisted cutting a troubled glance Meg's way, but only barely. Because that wasn't the *Reader's Digest* version of Valor's opinion. That was a direct quote, memorized word-for-word, and brooded over to an unhealthy—and possibly dangerous—degree.

"He meant to see me out of a job, the bastard." E linked his fingers over his belly and leaned back comfortably. "Now I didn't care the job particularly, but it was the principle of the thing, wasn't it? Nobody tells me what I can or can't have. What I do or don't deserve." E smiled at them, but his lips were tight, and the skin was pulled taut over his perfect bones. Taut enough that the twisted and wrong underneath showed, if only for a wavering second. Then he pulled in a sharp breath that smoothed away the fury, left only the beauty. "I may be a criminal, after all, but I'll be damned if I'm common."

"No," Meg murmured. "You're certainly not."

"I'd been planning a shift to private industry anyway." He gave a deliberately negligent shrug. "Excellent money in private security, as Meg well knows."

Meg tipped her head in assent but stayed wisely silent. This conversation was beginning to smell like gunpowder and Drew had the breathless impression that a single careless word could blow them all to kingdom come.

"But I do have a bit of a temper." E admitted this with charming chagrin. "And Valor had roused it. So I decided to indulge myself." His smile was crooked, boyish. "I do that sometimes. It's possible that I *am* a bit spoiled." He gave them a lazy shrug and went on. "I decided to hang around a bit longer. Not forever, you understand, just long enough to turn the tables. To see him disgraced. To put him out of a job." He smiled and Drew felt the chill all the way to his bones. "Revenge truly is a dish best served cold."

"That's what they say." Drew kept his face carefully interested. "How cold are we talking about here?"

"Five years, give or take." E selected an apple slice, bit it crisply in two. "The long game is a specialty of mine."

"I'll say." Meg rounded her eyes appreciatively. "Have you had Drew in mind for the last play all along? Or was that just lucky?"

"Patience, darling, you're skipping ahead." His smile was warm, indulgent. Drew felt faintly ill. He fought the urge to hurdle the table and shield Meg from even the sight of it. "For the first few years I did nothing but lay a foundation. I looked up a few old friends from my hacking days, put my oar in here and there. Nothing that would leave hard evidence, mind you. I just shared a bit of data here or made a decision there that resulted in some Secret Service misfires and the plumping of a few suspicious pockets.

Nothing actionable, but definitely the sort of thing that would stand out like a beacon if you were looking to reveal me for a spoiled, amoral, entitled brat, out to enrich himself at the expense of justice."

"You had him jumping at shadows," Meg said.

"If you like." E lifted his glass to her. "Or, put another way, I allowed him to create a statistically significant pattern of bias against me."

"You set him up," Drew said. "You undermined his credibility."

"Of course I did. And he made it so easy that it was actually a bit dissatisfying." His mouth twisted. "All I had to do was provide even the flimsiest appearance of wrong-doing and he was all over me." He shrugged. "But you can only cry wolf so many times before people begin questioning your judgment, even if you are a war hero." His sigh was deep and satisfied. "So I took my pleasure in the work. I'm a patient man, and I built my trap slowly. I built it expertly." His smile bloomed. "Then I sprung it."

Chapter 29

"Did you?" Drew stretched out his legs, crossed his ankles. "How?"

"I let him catch me."

"In what?" Meg asked.

"In a mistake." He waved his wineglass negligently. "I won't bore you with the details. Suffice it to say that a week or two ago, I made a decision that resulted in significant loss of American life. Bad press. Very ugly."

Drew raked his memory of the headlines and frowned. "Wait, was this that thing in the Ukraine? With the rebels or the separatists and a shipment of guns or ammunition or—" The details skated away but the impression of blood and smoke was indelible. "I read about that."

"Of course you did." E's smile was smug. "The suits were understandably displeased. They called Valor onto the carpet about it yesterday, and he in turn called me onto the carpet. The ensuing discussion was...let's call it lively."

"And the result?" Meg asked. She looked as sick as Drew felt.

"It all came down to a single piece of data." A small smile played around his lips and he leaned in.

"Really." Drew tipped his head.

"Indeed. Data that, interestingly, disappeared."

"Disappeared?" Meg asked. "How?"

"Well, that's the question, isn't it?" E set aside his wine glass and gave the thumb drive another careless flick. "The intel was unquestionably there when I made the decision. But at some point between making the call and accounting for it to the suits—" He spread his hands. "Poof."

"Which means?" Drew said.

"One of two things," E said. "First? Either the data

never existed and I'm lying to cover my ass and protect my criminal friends—"

"—which is the story that Valor will tell," Drew said.

"Oh, he did." E grinned, delighted. "He really did."

"And the second conclusion?" Drew asked. "The one I assume you're endorsing?"

"The second conclusion is that Valor, who's always hated me, has finally blown a gasket and framed me." E lifted his wineglass to the light, inspected the deep red glow with satisfaction. "He planted that pivotal piece of data which led me to an awful, and ultimately tragic, decision—"

"—in a desperate bid to finally open the Secret Service's eyes to the disease that is you," Meg finished, and that odd emptiness inside Drew pinged again. Disease. She'd called him a disease, too.

"Precisely." E set his wineglass on the tablecloth and folded his hands. "Of course I've been suspended since the incident occurred—all passwords and privileges revoked while the drones go over every scrap of my work with a fine-toothed comb. Every log in, every key stroke, every email."

"Which means you're on record as having no opportunity to cover your tracks or support your case," Meg said.

"Exactly as I'd planned." E lifted the thumb drive, let it gleam in the light with the mesmerizing beauty of a snake. "Because I didn't need access to the system. Not as myself, anyway. I had an ace up my sleeve." His smile was chilling, and Drew felt it all the way to his spine.

"Drew," Meg said softly. "Drew was the ace up your sleeve."

"He was. Has been ever since I learned that the DC Statesmen had secured James Blake, international sports star, to make America fall in love once and for all with football." E laughed softly. "Pardon me, soccer."

"And where you have one Blake brother—" Meg said.

"—you have them all," E finished. "Hence the ace up my sleeve." He studied Drew with amusement. "You had real potential once upon a time, Drew. Solid skills and a refreshing enthusiasm for the game, plus some oddball creativity and a flair for theater. You might've been somebody. But those brothers of yours?" He curled his lip. "They ruined you."

Drew smiled at that. His brothers had saved him. "Did they?"

"All that loyalty, all that honor? What was that thing you used to say?" He snapped his fingers, searching for it. "About share and share alike? Your fight being my fight?"

"Family first," Drew told him helpfully.

"What we have, we share," Meg said.

"Your fight is my fight," E said. "Right. That was it." He laughed. "It's quite a privilege to be a Blake. Quite a responsibility, as well. And you said it yourself—for a time there, I was your brother." He tipped his head, studied Drew with cold eyes. "My fight was your fight. My trouble was yours to share, and you left me to die on the loading dock of the 2nd Parliamentary Bank." He tsked. "For shame, Drew. For shame."

"But you didn't die," Meg pointed out.

"But Drew didn't know that, did he? All he knew was that he'd watched his best friend—his brother—shot to death. Watched him bleed out on the concrete, then went home to his cozy bed and his living, breathing brothers, none the worse for wear." E's smile was uncut evil. "He carried that burden of guilt, the horror of that fundamental failure of character in his heart for fifteen years. But he also carried a debt, a debt of honor and brotherhood. And all I had to do to call it in was rise from the grave and ask for a favor." He leaned forward to pat Drew's knee. "You're the good sort, Drew." It didn't sound like a compliment and Drew didn't take it as such. "You made it so easy."

E turned his attention to Meg. "And you were equally predictable. You have a suspicious little mind."

"One of my best qualities," she returned evenly.

"Indeed. Unfortunately, you overrode your instincts to protect your best friend who, let's face it, isn't great at keeping himself out of trouble. Which, of course, I knew you would." He caressed the stem of his wine glass. "Predictability is never a good quality, Meg. You should work on that." He turned to include Drew. "You both should. But not right at this moment." He smiled. "Right at the moment, you should both continue to be the cooperative little sheep you've been thus far. Just follow instructions, children, and you'll wake up in your chaste little beds tomorrow morning with all this behind you."

A thread of uneasiness uncurled inside Drew. Both. He didn't like that. In fact, he hated it. He wanted Meg as far away from this shit as possible. So he forced himself to sit back, to hook an elbow over his chair back and regard E with his customary lazy good humor. "And if we don't?"

"Then your darling Meg goes to jail." E's smile was a slow curl of triumph. "I have her fingerprints all over Valor's car, all over the ductwork between his office and the conference room. You wiped all trace of us out of the system but—" He dropped his eyes, ran them the length of Meg's legs and smiled. "—she's the memorable sort. And Justin remembers her."

"The kid from the door." Meg's face was ashen, resigned. "We tailgated him into NoVD."

"We did indeed. And Drew and I were just as unmemorable as you might think, given young Justin's absorption with your legs. But, interestingly, he remembers your legs *and* your face. Well enough to pick you out of a photo array without a trace of hesitation." E shrugged modestly. "Given the day you had at work yesterday, Meggy, it wouldn't be a stretch to spin those little facts into some jail time."

"Day at work?" Drew frowned at Meg. "What does that mean?"

She waved him off with a hand that told him everything he needed to know. E had enough to make good on his threat. He could hurt Meg. Might even be looking forward to it.

And suddenly that weird waiting void inside Drew, the vacuum-sealed emptiness that Meg's declaration of love had left inside him? It shattered. It simply imploded, and what had been waiting outside the bubble roared in like a storm surge. It broke over him in a towering wall of dirty water, studded with all kinds of unlikely shit. It battered and spun him, lashed him with dizzying waves of despair and hope, love and hate, fear and courage, loss and gratitude.

And grief. Great aching waves of it crashed over him without mercy. Grief for every home he'd left, for every friend he'd abandoned, for every pet he'd given away when the new place didn't allow them. For the brother he'd lost when Will stepped into their father's shoes. For the brother he'd lost when James stopped playing a game and began earning their daily bread. For the parents who'd bled to death in a heap of twisted metal on a sunbaked highway in west Texas. For the boy who'd built a clean, bright space around his heart so he didn't die from the pain. For the man he'd become, who observed his life with the amused detachment of a movie-goer instead of plunging himself elbow-deep into the messy guts of it and living.

But most of all? For Meg. For brilliant, courageous, loyal Meg. For the woman who saw him for exactly the coward he was, and loved him anyway. Who'd taken all that astonishing courage in hand and told him so. Who would tear her own heart out and leave with integrity rather than stick around and allow him to discard the most precious thing he'd ever been given because he was too damn stupid to recognize it for the gift it was. Who nevertheless refused to let him stand alone against a threat.

Who loved him.

And he loved her back.

The knowledge slid into the chaos inside him like warm oil, smoothing out the bitter chop, settling the waters. He loved her. Not as his best friend, not as a brilliant colleague. He simply loved her. It had been waiting outside that aching space inside him all this time. That heat smoking in his bones that he'd mistaken for lust? It was love, just waiting for him to find the courage to open his eyes. To open his heart. Which was funny when he considered that he'd always pictured her as the fortress, when he was the one with a fucking clean room around his heart.

But it was gone now, that space, smashed into nonexistence by the idea that somebody—anybody—would harm her. Rage prickled through him, hot and consuming. But terror ran underneath it like a black river because if anything happened to her...

Drew sucked in a breath, refused to follow the thought any farther. Nothing would happen to Meg. He wouldn't allow it. He couldn't survive it so he wouldn't allow it. He didn't allow himself even a glance across the table at her. He was too raw, too battered by all the emotion rushing roughshod through the tender places he'd spent decades protecting. But he brought her up in his mind's eye—long and slim and elegant, that sharp-edged face and that funny up-turned nose smack in the middle of it all. The spill of sandy-silky hair that she kept under wraps, the endless legs that she didn't. The bullet-proof courage and the bone-deep loyalty. The slender thread of vulnerability tying it all together. The roaring fire of her love.

He'd burned her down. She'd said so. But she'd burned him down, too. They'd burned each other down and he'd known it hadn't been ordinary. It had been fucking transcendent, only Drew was too afraid, too detached to understand it.

Well he understood it now. He didn't deserve it. He doubted he ever would. But he understood this—it was precious and he would protect it with his dying breath. He would protect *her*. And if that was all he could do, he'd make damn certain it would be enough.

He said, "Give me the thumb drive."

Chapter 30

"Drew, you can't do this."

He strode across the lobby, his face grim, his long legs eating up the distance with purpose. Meg scurried after him, her heart knocking anxiously in her chest. "Drew, I'm serious. You can't do this. It's wrong. You don't need to protect me. I'm fine. I have lawyers. Good ones. Expensive ones. Nobody's going to touch me. You don't have to do this!"

He strode on, utterly unaffected. She finally hooked a hand through his elbow and dug in her heels. "Drew, stop."

He stopped so suddenly that she stumbled. Then his hands were under her elbows, steadying her. She gazed up at him, startled into silence.

"What do we say in the Blake house, Meg?" he asked softly. "What do we say about this kind of thing?"

"No." She shook her head, and the tears she'd been fighting all night crawled up her throat. "This is not your fight."

He smiled, his old crooked, funny smile. "Of course it is. You're my family, Meggy. You're mine." He brought up a hand, cupped her cheek with a tenderness that clamped her throat shut completely. She had to close her eyes against the pain. He cleared his throat, smoothed a hair away from her face and put his hand carefully back under her elbow. "We're going to talk more about that later. A lot more. But for now all you need to know is that your fight is my fight. Anybody who takes aim at you takes aim at me. We're in this together, so stop arguing, will you?"

She shoved back the tears and the pain and the longing, and opened her eyes. "For God's sake, Drew, what you're talking about is illegal."

Drew smiled at her. "Announce it to the whole building, why don't you?"

She lowered her voice to a tight hiss. "It's illegal. Not to mention immoral and vicious. He's destroying a man, Drew. Systematically, methodically, purposefully. He's fucking gaslighting the guy! Because of some name calling? Jesus! Now I don't want to go to jail any more than you do but—"

"You're not going to jail. I won't allow it." He turned her toward the door and shoved her into the dark parking lot. The air was mild and wet, like fall was having a summery flashback. Everything smelled like damp leaves as he propelled her across the parking lot to his Blazer, opened the passenger door and practically tossed her inside. He circled the hood, gave it a fond pat before sliding into the driver's seat and firing up the engine. He tossed his phone into her lap. "Family meeting in half an hour. Make it happen, will you?" He sent her a look across the dark truck. "Get Clara, too."

"Clara?" Meg stared at him. "You want my psychic twin in on this?"

"Family is family. And you're not going to jail, Meg. But not because I'm cooperating with E." He tossed the thumb drive in her lap, too. "Hold onto that, will you?"

She gazed at him, the thumb drive in one hand, his phone in the other, her brain spinning in useless circles. "But you said—"

"I know what I said. But if E had scrambling devices all the way to the elevator, it's totally possible that he also had listening devices all the way to the lobby."

"Of course it is." Meg blinked at her sweaty fists. She had to start thinking here. "God, of course it is."

"So I made it sound good. But you can take this to the bank, Meggy." He threw the Blazer into reverse and backed out. "Nobody's going to jail but E."

* * *

"Well, I'll hand it to you, little brother," James Blake drawled an hour later. He was sprawled across the cushions of Drew's black leather couch like he'd been melted there, all shaggy blond hair and lazy grace, one big hand draped carelessly on the knees Bel had curled into his lap. Meg wasn't a huge sports fan but even she enjoyed watching James play. All that laziness exploding into lethal athleticism the instant it met a soccer field? It was just so unexpected. "You sure know how to have yourself a weekend."

"Yeah, thanks." Drew shrugged modestly. "It's not strippers and scotch but it gets the job done."

"I want the timeline again," Will said from the other side of the sectional. Meg sat in the center of the U-shaped couch with Drew and she didn't have to turn Will's way to feel the waves of hostility he was radiating. She refused to flinch, but holy crap, he was a scary bastard when he had his game face on. And when that game face was aimed at you? That was some terrifying shit right there. She swallowed as quietly as possible.

"Thanks to me, E had Valor's office all to himself for about fifteen minutes last night. He used the time to build himself a backdoor into a Secret Service database via the guy's computer," Drew began.

"Thanks to me," Meg put in. "Thanks to me, Drew."

Everybody ignored her, exactly as they'd been doing for the past half hour. Drew leaned forward, his linked fingers dangling casually between his knees. "This backdoor is programmed to open exactly twenty-four hours from install and to stay open for a single two-hour window, after which it'll shut itself and self-destruct, leaving absolutely no trace that it ever existed."

"Wow." Jillian sat between Will and Audrey, an ethereally beautiful teen in what Meg had to admit was definitely designer peasant wear. She frowned thoughtfully into the middle distance. "That's no one-off exploit. He must be good. Really good." She shifted her focus to Meg, and the impact of all that brain power zeroed in on a single target was terrific. It was hard to believe sometimes that there was no biological relationship between this brilliant girl and Will. "He's that good?"

"He's that good," Drew assured her. "At this point, we

have approximately—" He checked his watch. "—three hours until this backdoor opens. By the time it closes, I'm supposed to have uploaded the contents of this thumb drive to the NoVD servers, and in doing so destroy an innocent man."

They all took a moment to eye the thumb drive sitting innocuously atop a crooked stack of magazines on the coffee table between them.

"Or else Meg goes to jail." Audrey looked to her for confirmation. "Right?"

Meg opened her mouth but Drew put a hand on her knee and got there first. "That's what E's threatened, yes."

Will addressed her directly for the first time since Drew had started talking. "Does he have enough on you to make that happen, Meg? Outside of the prints?"

Meg forced herself to meet those cold eyes directly. "He might. I was pitching a new company on Friday and the CIO was...let's call it opposed to women in technology."

"How opposed?" Bel asked.

"Decidedly. He flat out told me that even if I was good enough to hack the Secret Service itself—he actually name checked the Secret Service—my lady hands were still getting nowhere near his precious system." She refused to let herself look away from Will. "I, in return, implied that I was exactly that good. Then I might've called him a tool, wished him luck and gone to meet Drew for a beer."

"Oh, Meggy," Clara sighed. She was on James and Bel's side of the couch in what Meg assumed she considered staying-in-on-a-Saturday-night wear. It looked like something Greta Garbo would throw on to answer the door. Minus the turban. Plus the feathers. "That temper of yours."

"I know." Meg smiled tightly. "You don't win over the patriarchy calling people tools."

"Or implying that your resume includes hacking the goddamn Secret Service," Will snapped.

"Is it enough?" Audrey asked him. She reached across Jillian to touch his knee. "Is Meg really in trouble?"

"Ah, hell." He leaned back and rubbed both hands over his face. "She could be. I mean, it's all circumstantial but spun a certain way? Added all together?" He dropped his hands and sat up. Met Meg's eyes, and she felt the chill all the way to her bones. "Yeah, it's a bad picture."

"But it's my picture." Meg rose. Her knees were iffy but they held, thank God. She smoothed her jacket with damp hands. "There's no evidence against anybody but me. This isn't your fight, none of yours. It's mine."

"Sit down, Meggy," Drew said.

She ignored him, spoke to Will. "I have excellent lawyers, and believe me, I pay them enough to—"

"I said sit down." Drew's voice had an unfamiliar snap in it this time, and she let the shock run through her with something like joy. He wanted a fight? Fine. She'd give him one. She was ready to tear this bandage off, damn it. Right now. Maybe she'd bleed to death, maybe she'd survive it. Either way, at least it would be over.

"And I said no." She spun and shot a finger at him. "This isn't your fight. This is my fight. My problem. My mistake. And I'll be damned if I'll let you make it yours— make it your entire family's—in a fit of misguided guilt!"

Drew studied her for a long moment. "Fine," he said. "Stand if you want to. But you're going to regret those shoes in about five minutes." He turned back to their audience and said, "So that's about the size of it. Any questions?"

James and Will exchanged a long look. Meg would have stalked off but she was trapped behind that look like it was an electric fence or something. Finally Will said, "Okay. Here's what we're going to do. First, we're going to get our lawyers with Meg's, see what we can do about—"

"Will, no," Drew said. Will didn't look up from his phone, just continued scrolling his contacts for the stable of attack dogs he kept on retainer. "Don't bother your lawyers. Not yet."

"What, you have a better idea?"

"I do, actually."

Will snorted. "Better than blood-thirsty lawyers? Because blood-thirsty lawyers are always—"

"Yes."

"—a good idea." He looked up and frowned. "Really?"

"Yes." Drew smiled at him, that sweet, crooked smile that always made Meg narrow her eyes. Because this was how he started playing people, with that guileless smile that said *I am absolutely harmless, and even if I weren't I'm too lazy to make the effort.* "I have a plan."

"You do." Will looked at James, nonplussed. James offered a tiny shrug. Will looked back to Drew with palpable skepticism. "Is it as good as the plan that got you into this mess?"

"Maybe." Drew slid an elbow over the back of the couch, purely unconcerned by the glittering edge on Will's voice. His smile went from sweet to amused. Meg didn't buy it. Not for an instant. She'd been suckered by that nothing-to-see-here smile more than she cared to remember. "Maybe not."

"Damn it, Drew." Will slapped a hand down on the coffee table. The stack of magazines jumped. So did Meg. "This isn't a joke so stop screwing around and pay some fucking attention here, will you?"

"Easy, son," James said to Will, then turned to Drew. "Come on, buddy. Family first, right? Your fight is our fight?" He sat up long enough to give Drew's shoulder an affectionate cuff. "Plus you know how much Will loves to put his dukes up. He's a family man now. Doesn't get to bust his knuckles so much anymore."

"Amen," Audrey muttered. Will scowled at her.

James continued speaking to Drew. "This here is his golden opportunity to crack some heads. He's looking forward. How about you be a sport and let him at it?"

"Be a sport?" Will's lip curled. "No, Drew, how about you just be quiet and let the grown ups work? Because we've got real trouble here and—"

"My trouble," Meg snapped. She couldn't do this for another minute. Bad enough that Drew underestimated himself so badly half the time. Watching Drew's brothers do it, watching him let them was intolerable. She'd had enough. "This is my trouble, and I'll take care of it. I can take care of myself, you know. I've been doing it for fifteen years without any help from the famous Blake brothers and I

244

expect I can do it for a few minutes more." She snatched up her coat and purse. "Goodnight, gentleman. It's been memorable. Feel free to continue shouting in my absence."

"Why does she sound like she's leaving?" James asked Will. "Like *leaving* leaving?"

"Because she probably is." Will scooted his knees to the side to make room for her grand exit.

"And who could blame her?" Audrey lifted a tiny foot, put it to Will's knees and shoved them back into place. And there went the grand exit, damn it. "What with the way you're making the family so appealing."

Meg glared at Audrey, who was too busy scowling at her husband to notice. Will scowled back at his wife. Meg wondered if the air itself would spontaneously combust. Will and Audrey were kind of a volatile combination at the best of times. Jillian sighed and scooted herself farther into the couch cushions, out of the line of fire.

"She *should* leave." Bel said from the other side of the sectional. Meg just closed her eyes, breathed and reached deep for strength. "Faced with this family situation? Please. Any girl with half a brain would be out the door like a shot."

James' voice was smug. "And yet here you sit, Mrs. Blake."

"That's different," Bel told him. "I'm in love."

"So is Meg." He paused. "Isn't she?"

Meg's heart gave an agonized leap inside her and she opened her eyes. She had to get out of here. Now. She spun away from Will, only to find Drew on his feet and in her face. Damn it, now she was doing it. Underestimating him. But he always moved so much faster than she expected. Faster than he led people to expect he could. She narrowed her eyes. He did that shit on purpose. She knew he did.

"Get out of my way."

"Nope." He put both hands on her shoulders and shoved her back onto the couch. He didn't shove her hard. Not even close, actually. But shock folded her knees and she landed with a huff and a bounce. He shot a finger at her. "Stay." She stared, open mouthed and utterly beyond words.

He turned to his brothers. "Will. James. I love you both.

245

You know that, right? You saved my life in so many ways. I owe you both more than I can ever repay."

Will shifted uncomfortably. "You do not."

James smiled. "Shut it, Will. The man's making a speech." He snuggled himself more comfortably into the couch, wrapped an arm around Bel's shoulders. "Go on, son. Be grateful for Will's sacrifice some more."

Will scowled. Drew smiled. "I *am* grateful for Will's sacrifice." He sent that sweet smile James' way. "Yours, too." James shrugged modestly. Bel flicked his ear.

"Ow."

"He mostly raised himself," Will told Meg. "So this massive sacrifice he's talking about is nothing more than feeding and clothing his ten-year-old ass. And what half-way decent person wouldn't—"

Audrey reached across Jillian to flick Will's ear.

"Ow." He clapped a hand to it and glared at her.

"You're interrupting." She turned back to Drew with a dazzling smile. "You were saying?"

He grinned his thanks and turned back to Meg, who was still sitting on the couch, shocked and silent. "Don't listen to Will," he told her. "Times were tough in the Blake house once upon a time. We had trouble aplenty just keeping body and soul together for a while there. Keeping the family together was another heap of it, I'm sure. Lord knows we didn't need to make trouble of our own, but James had a taste for it. And Will?" He shook his head. "That boy had a downright talent. As for me, I've always been more the watch-from-the-sidelines type."

"One of my favorite things about you," Meg said instantly, hope springing up inside her. "And as we're dealing with a certifiable sociopath here, may I point out that this would be a bad time to break with tradition?"

"I do love a good show," he continued, as if Meg hadn't spoken. "But that's the thing right there."

"What is?"

"How much I love a show. Because you watch shows. You don't do anything. You don't have to. You just...watch. And from a nice, safe distance, too. And that, Meggy mine?

That's no way to live."

The river of terror inside her roared, drowning out the hope and threatening to spill over its banks. "But screwing with E on this is a good way to die," she pointed out. "Because—did I mention?—he's insane."

"I know. Believe me, I know. I've always known. I don't know that I could've put my finger on it exactly when we were kids, but I knew he wasn't right. And frankly? That was what I liked about him."

"What, his psychopathy?"

"No. Well, yes, actually. If by psychopathy you mean that ability of his to sincerely not give a shit about anything or anybody. I was attracted to that as much as the skills and the charisma and the money. Damn, but I wanted that for myself."

Meg's heart ached inside her. "To not give a shit?"

"Exactly. Because in those days, I just hurt. I *hurt*, Meggy. Every bit of me, all the time. It was just this constant grinding ache in my gut, and I wanted what E had. That numbness. For years, I wanted that more than anything."

James made a small, pained noise. Even Will looked troubled. And Meg understood. Every family had its roles, and the Blakes' were more rigid than most: Will was the fighter, James was the super star, and Drew was the lover. The beloved. He was the sweet-tempered baby boy who glued it all together, who found the humor in everything. Who created humor when none existed. Whose charm was so universally irresistible that loving him was sometimes the only thing they all had in common.

On the other hand, Drew was right—he didn't actually participate very much. But he was wrong if he thought that meant he didn't matter. His role in the family was utterly vital. He was the Greek chorus of the Blake family tragedy, running the action through that infallible moral compass of his and churning out the pithy commentary that helped everybody understand what the hell was going on. Who sussed out what it all meant, and where it fit on the landscape of their hearts and in the story of their family.

The discovery that he wasn't untouched by the grief that

had derailed the rest of them, that he hadn't been cheerfully unaffected by the unimaginable loss they'd all lived through? That he, too, had lived all those years in a haze of chronic pain but had smiled so well that they'd bought it? It had to be a devastating blow to the brothers who'd raised him. Who'd done their best by him. Who'd thought—hoped? Prayed?—that maybe he was okay.

"I got pretty good at it," Drew said. "The numbness. Not E-quality good, but good enough. I spent years not feeling much of anything, honestly. I built this space around my heart and kept everything—everybody—outside of it. It seemed better. Safer, for sure. Then E pointed his gun at you."

"Metaphorically speaking," Meg said quickly. She threw an automatic hand Will's way. "There were no actual guns." Will subsided. Christ. She wasn't even really family but he'd been halfway out of his seat already and on his way to murder E. She blew out a tight breath and turned back to Drew, who didn't look any less dangerous. Her heart gave an uncertain thud inside her.

"Yeah, so that happened," Drew said. "And suddenly, that numbness? That safe distance I liked to keep? Gone. Shattered. Like it had never existed. I swear on all that's holy, Meg, I wanted that guy's blood in my mouth."

"Drew, please." The fear she'd been squashing down for hours rose up and choked her. Made her voice small and pathetic and shamefully unsteady. She didn't even care. She just had to keep him safe, and if that meant tossing her pride in the gutter in front of his entire family, so be it. "I love you."

"I know." He dropped to the couch beside her and gripped one of her hands in both of his own. "I know, Meg, and I—"

She spoke over him. She knew how he felt about her and respected it. She just couldn't bear to hear it again. "No, I *love* you, Drew. And E will destroy you without a second thought. Because winning is what he does. It's all he cares about. It's all he needs. But you're what I need. You. I don't need you to love me back but I do need to know that you're okay. I need to know that you exist, that you're healthy and heading toward happy. If I'm going to survive this, I need that. I know you can't give me everything I want, but you can give me this much." Tears were streaming down her cheeks, and they tasted like defeat. She was so tired. "You can back the fuck down on this. You can grow up tomorrow. You can let Will be Will on your behalf one last time." She gripped his hands and leaned in desperately. "You can give me that much, can't you?"

"No." His hands were shaking. Or maybe hers were? She honestly couldn't tell. Couldn't think about it over the roar of pain and the hiss of terror filling her head. "No, Meg, I can't."

"Why not?" she cried. "God, Drew, why not?"

"Because I'm in love with you."

Chapter 31

Something inside her broke. She felt the snap, the slide and the shatter. The noise she made was almost feral with pain.

"No, you're not." She dragged at her hand, desperate to take it back from him. "Of course you're not. Jesus, Drew! You'd lie to me? About that? Do you really need to get your way so badly?"

"I'm not lying to you." His grip on her hand was like iron. "I'm in love with you, Meg. It's the truest thing I know."

Pain scrabbled inside her like an animal in a trap, unreasoning and wild. "But you said—"

"—that I didn't love you back. That I couldn't." He shook his head grimly. "I know what I said. I was stupid and wrong, okay?" He leaned in, caught her gaze and held it. And she saw truth and fear sharpening every edge of his face into something both foreign and somehow familiar. A spark of hope flew into the darkness of her panic, bright and fleeting, and she stopped fighting, mesmerized.

"I was in love with you even then," he told her. "I think I always have been. I just couldn't feel it. I couldn't feel anything. I haven't for years."

His smile was wry, self-mocking. "Then E came along and implied that he could hurt you. That he *would* hurt you, and because of me. And there went the numb, like I said. Years and years of self-preservation, blown to smithereens by love."

Joy struggled against caution inside her, and she put a hand to her throat, to the jagged bump of her pulse. Her fingers were shockingly cold against her skin. "Love."

"Love." He renewed his grip on her other hand, the one

he refused to surrender. "It's some destructive shit, love." He dropped his eyes, studied her hand inside the cradle of his. "Dangerous. And it hurts."

"Aw," James said. "Our little boy's all grown up."

"Shut it," Will said mildly. "Can't you see the man's making a speech?"

"Which is probably why I've avoided it all these years," Drew went on as if his brothers were invisible. "Because I remember exactly what loving me cost James and Will. I remember exactly what loving my parents cost me. Losing somebody you love? It's like accidentally cutting yourself. And then you're standing at the kitchen sink and you've got a dish towel clamped to your hand and you're telling yourself it's going to be all right, that it's probably not that bad but the blood's spurting out to the beat of your own damn heart. And you know that this shit might kill you. It hurts, Meg. It's terrifying."

"I know," she whispered. God, did she ever.

"But it didn't kill me. It didn't kill any of us. We survived. And maybe love costs—a lot—but if my brothers taught me anything, it's that love isn't just survivable. It's survival. It's the thing that makes survival worth it, anyway. And when love came knocking at their doors again, they didn't hide from it. They weren't afraid. They just jumped for it."

Bel cleared her throat pointedly. James muttered, "We were maybe a little afraid."

"But just a very little," Will said quickly.

"Women will always love pirates," Audrey said, apropos of nothing. Meg didn't care. She was fixed on Drew, her mouth dry, her head light, her heart tumbling uncertainly inside her chest.

Drew shook his head. "Then love came for me. You came for me, and I...didn't. I didn't jump. You did, of course. The instant you figured your shit out you took an immediate flyer because, Christ, you're fearless. You're kind of magnificent. You know that, right?"

She opened her mouth then just shut it again. His smile was small, crooked. "All that gorgeous courage," he said wonderingly, "and I failed you. I let you down. But my brothers didn't raise a coward, Meg."

"Damn straight," James murmured. Somebody sniffled. Bel? Audrey? *Will?* Meg had no idea. She didn't even care. She was too busy trying to listen over the wild clatter of the blood beating in her ears.

"So I'm reaching for you now. I'm jumping." He lifted his eyes to hers and what she saw there sent everything in her sailing. Her insides just flew up in a jumbled rush of hope and joy. "I know I don't deserve you. But I also know that you're mine. You're not just in my heart; you are my heart. You're part of it. The best part, probably. So believe me, delivering E's ass kicking with my own boot isn't a sacrifice. It's an honor and a privilege. But it's also my duty. You're mine." He ghosted his knuckles down her cheek with a tender reverence that closed her throat. "I know I haven't inspired much confidence in the ass kicking department, but I do know how to take care of what's precious. I can live up to your love."

"But you don't have to!" she cried, fear taking the lead once again. "Don't you get it? I'm already yours." She reached a shaky hand to him, brushed aside the thick tumble of hair that always fell into his eyes. "I always have been. You don't have to live up to anything. Let's just release the lawyers and live happily ever after."

"I can't do that, Meg." He lifted his eyes to hers and she caught her breath. Those warm laughing eyes were cold and filled with fury. "He threatened you. He threatened what's mine, and a man doesn't back down and let somebody else take care of what's his."

"God damn," Will said. "Our little boy *is* all grown up."

"What did I tell you?" James said.

"Don't encourage him," Meg snapped. "Either of you."

"We're not encouraging him," Will said in tones of deep satisfaction. "We don't have to. Because that there is a well-raised young man."

"Sure is." James plopped a foot up on the coffee table. "And I, for one, am looking forward to hearing this plan of his. Kid's always had a flair for theater. I bet it's good."

Drew grinned. "It's sort of awesome, honestly."

"Is it?" Meg glared at him. "Does it involve you and your brothers taking stupid risks while I sit at home with the wives biting my nails?"

"Hell, no." Drew's grin spread into something brilliant, though that black menace still shifted like lava underneath. This capacity for violence felt so strange in him, and yet it wasn't jarring. It was like the bass note that anchored the chord, she realized with a pulse of wonder. It balanced out his inherent optimism and native good humor, salted his personality into something complete and mature. This is who he was always meant to be. A good man, a sweet man, a kind man with the strength and the courage to protect his own.

"I have to stand up for you, Meg. But I don't want to stand in front of you. I want to stand up with you. I want to stand up beside you. I know who you are—I love who you are—and I'd never ask you to stand down. But you can't ask me to either. We'll do this together." He dipped his chin, caught her gaze and held it. "Okay?"

"You need this," she said. Acceptance dawned slowly, reluctantly. "This is what you need to be who you are. To become who you're supposed to be."

"Yeah." He considered it. "Yeah, I do."

She slid a hand around the nape of his neck, threaded her fingers into the thick, glorious silk of his hair and dragged his mouth to hers. She poured everything into that kiss—all the fear, the love, the joy, the hope and the need fighting inside her. She gave it all to him like a confession, like a promise.

"Then okay." She pressed her forehead to his, her eyes closed, her heart fragile and bare. "It's yours."

"I won't let you down, Meg." He wrapped his hands around her wrists, strong and warm and solid. "I swear it."

"I'll hold you to that." She drew back, threaded her fingers through his. "Now. Let's hear about this plan of yours."

"Right." He pulled in a breath, met her eyes directly and said, "We have to hijack the movie."

She blinked. "We have to...what now?"

"Hijack the movie. Because everybody's got a movie rolling in their head, right? I'm guessing E's is a spy/thriller/espionage thing, with E as the persecuted hero. And he's just about to force feed the villain a big ol' mouthful of comeuppance."

"Sounds about right. And we're the villain?"

"Oh, no. That's Valor. We're nothing but extras."

"We're extras?"

"One step up from warm bodies. Our only purpose in this movie is to plant the smoking gun, then die like good little soldiers when the script calls for blood. Demoralizing, isn't it?"

Meg considered that. Maybe it was the lack of sleep, but this was actually starting to make sense. "We have a sucky part," she decided.

"And we're idiots for taking it." He shook his head grimly. "But that nonsense is over, Meggy. Starting right now."

"Because we're hijacking the movie?"

"Because we're hijacking the damn movie. E's script sucks. I'm doing a rewrite."

"Well, good for you. But you have to realize that no amount of rewriting can change the fact that they have my fingerprints in that ceiling?"

"Oh, I don't need to change the facts," he said cheerfully. "I only need to change what they mean."

"I don't think you can do that, actually."

"Sure I can. According to E's script, see, those fingerprints mean that you pulled an illegal pen test at NoVD last night. My script, however—while readily admitting that you were in that ceiling last night—maintains that you were there on purpose and with full permission."

She eyed him doubtfully. "Your script says that."

"It can." He all but wriggled with excitement and Meg couldn't help but smile. He was so damn contagious. "Trust me on this, Meggy. People don't care about what happened; they only care about why it happened. Truth is nothing but the most plausible why."

"It is?"

"Of course! I mean, think about it. Something insane happens—a kid dies, a plane crashes, a bridge falls into the river—and what's the first thing we do?"

"Call 911?"

"Exactly! We immediately start talking about it! We tell some stranger the story of this incomprehensible tragedy we just saw or survived. We tell everybody about it, in fact. Eventually we get kind of good at it. We give it a beginning, some rising action, a climax and a resolution. Maybe we have to nudge the facts around a little but nobody's going to argue because we're all desperate for this thing to make sense. And if you tell it right, this thing—this incomprehensibly tragic thing? It can. It can make sense. It can fit into your life like it was always supposed to be there. Like it belongs. Whichever story does that the best? Whichever story makes the most sense out of the random facts? We call it history." He shrugged. "All we have to do to win here is tell the best story." He gave her knee a comforting pat. "Lucky for you, I'm an excellent story teller."

"The best," she said automatically. Because he was. He was the best storyteller she'd ever known. He'd been making sense out of random events his whole life, hadn't he? For himself and for his brothers. He'd built a career—a lucrative one—out of spinning strangers' facts into the kind of charming, bite-sized stories that the public ate up like potato chips. If anybody could write them a win here, it was Drew.

He was, she realized slowly, a superhero, albeit a nontraditional one. And stories were his unlikely superpower. She gazed at him like she'd never seen him before, like he'd unexpectedly ripped open his shirt to reveal himself as Superman. He might as well have.

"So what do you say?" He gave her an encouraging smile. "Want to write some history with me?"

Her heart tried to overflow and she pressed a hand to it. He was right. Love really did hurt, even when it was right and good. She wouldn't give it up for the world.

"I do," she managed. "More than anything."

Drew turned to the family—to their family—and said, "How about the rest of you? Are you in?"

"Always with the ridiculous questions," Will sighed. James rolled his eyes.

"Just try to keep us out of it," Audrey said. "I dare you."

"I'm not taking that dare," Drew said. "I've tangled with you before." He turned to his niece. "Jillian?"

Her face—so like Audrey's—lit with surprised delight. "You have a part for me?"

"Of course I do. Kind of an important one, actually."

"You see, Will?" She shot her de facto father a triumphant look. "Drew thinks I'm responsible. Drew thinks I'm useful. Drew thinks I can handle myself in the world."

"Drew thinks a lot of things." Will's eyes went narrow and he turned them on Drew. "But if he thinks he can put my kid in harm's way—"

Drew lifted both hands. "Easy, Dad. She doesn't even have to leave the house."

Will subsided and Jillian's mouth went sulky. "Aw. This is a computer thing, isn't it?"

"Yeah, but it's sort of dirty, so you might like it. You blew up in Russia recently, didn't you? Your style blog, I mean?"

"I had a nice little bump there, yeah."

"I need a few hot Russian girls with big ambitions and flexible morals. Any chance you know somebody?"

She laughed. "I work in fashion, Drew. How many do you want?"

"How many can you get?"

She pulled out her phone and began thumb typing with lightning speed while Will scowled at the screen over her shoulder. She stopped typing, scowled back and rose. Sailed out of the room, nose in the air.

"I didn't say a word!" Will frowned at her back. "Seriously, how was that my fault?"

Audrey sighed like she was considering another ear flick.

Drew turned to Clara. "How about you? Are you in?"

"Of course I am." She smoothed her...was she seriously

wearing a feather boa? Meg shook her head in fond wonder. "What can I do?"

"I need you to tap your Secret Service contacts. FBI wouldn't hurt, either. We need a couple of big wigs who are willing to listen to our version of this story. The higher up, the better. The more responsible they are for public image, the better. Can you get me a meeting?"

"On it." She rose with her usual grace and sailed to the door, cell phone in hand.

"Speaking of meetings." Drew turned to Will next. "Can you get me in touch with Garrett Dain?"

Will huffed out a short laugh. "What do you want with that asshole?"

"Will, be nice." Audrey patted her husband's knee. "Garret's a lovely young man. He just hates you, that's all."

"Does he?" Drew sighed. "I was afraid of that."

"Why?" Will glared. "Because people just hate me?"

"Nothing personal," he murmured. "Occupational hazard, I'm sure." Meg almost smiled at that. "But I really was hoping you could introduce me to the guy. Valor's not the trusting sort but I need him to trust me."

"And Dain connects to this how?"

"Would you believe that he played for Army the same time Valor did? They were soldiers and teammates. Next best thing to brothers, I'm thinking. And if you could get Dain to vouch for me—"

Will pulled a hand down his face and turned to his wife. "Audrey, I'm going to need you on this one."

Her smile was dazzlingly smug. "Because Garrett Dain hates you."

"True enough. But he loves the money I'm going to get him. And you know what else he loves?" He sent her a smoky look that Meg felt in her knees somewhere. Jesus, was that what Will kept buried underneath all the shark? No wonder Audrey was so smug all the time. "My wife." He rose and held out a hand. "So come on. Let's go to work."

Meg watched them go. James' stocking foot tick-tocked lazily on the coffee table and Bel just watched Drew, one brow arched, a small smile on her elegant face.

"Well, boss?" James grinned at Drew. "What've you got for us?"

"It's a touchy one. It involves hero worship and the potential corruption of innocent youth." Drew paused. "It'll also probably get you a beer."

Bel smiled. "The holy trinity of things James lives for."

"You'll probably have to invite said youth to practice with the DC Statesmen," Drew warned him. "He's smart and he won't sell his virtue for cheap. Not even to you."

James squinted at him. "Is he a talented amateur, or my eventual replacement?"

Drew considered the server from Declan's that he had in mind for this little job, remembered the fluid ease with which he'd moved, the way it had always reminded him of James. "Possibly door number two," he admitted.

James sat up, interested. "Hot damn, my knees are killing me. When do we start?"

Drew checked his watch. "Now wouldn't be bad." He explained briefly what he wanted and sent them off. Then he turned to Meg. "As for you."

"As for me?" She considered him, deeply intrigued by this new take-charge Drew. A thin thread of arousal vibrated in her belly, buzzy and low, like a plucked guitar string. The same string, she realized suddenly, that he'd twanged at the bar the other night when he'd gone plowing through the crowd toward her with murder in his eyes. Evidently she liked Drew all grown up. How very interesting. "You have a job for me...boss?"

His smile was slow, slinky. "Ask me that again later."

"I will." She smiled back, sharp and shiny. "Oh, believe me. I will."

He blinked, then cleared his throat, visibly reeling his thoughts back in. She'd give a lot to know where they'd wandered. Later, she told herself. She'd definitely follow up on that later.

"For now?" he said. "Here's what I need from you."

Five minutes later she was staring at him in open-mouthed astonishment. "Jesus God. You really do believe in my skills, don't you?" She opened her hand, gazed at the thumb drive in her palm. "You really think I can do a convincing job on all that in the next, what, two, two-and-a-half hours?"

He put a finger under her chin and dropped a kiss on her mouth. "I know you can. You're a ballsy girl, Meg, and your skills are incomparable. Make it look good, will you?"

She grinned and gave in to the sweet rush of tackling an impossible challenge. Of tackling it, smearing it into the turf and generally making it her bitch. Adrenaline bubbled up inside her like the tide lapping its way up a white sand beach, all heat and friction and promise. "Oh, Drew. I make everything look good." She stood, gripped the little bullet of metal in her hand, already running code in her head.

"You sure do." He gave her bottom a fond pat. "God, do you. Now get lost. I have work to do."

* * *

Three hours later, Meg appeared in the doorway of Drew's suite. She all but danced across the room, the thumb drive aloft, victory all over her beautiful face. Drew grinned back and held up one finger.

"It's a lot to ask, I know," he said into the phone clamped between his shoulder and his ear. He listened for a moment. "Believe me, I know that, too. We were like brothers once, me and E. Until we weren't. So, yeah, I know exactly what you're up against here, Valor. I'm up against it, too."

Meg bounced at his elbow, and rolled both hands in a *hurry, hurry* gesture. At some point, she'd scrubbed her face, traded in her crown of braids for a simple ponytail and ditched the couture in favor of an ancient College of William and Mary sweatshirt, running tights and flip flops. Even her bare toes wiggled with impatience.

"Bottom line? E wasn't my brother and I was stupid for thinking he was. But I'm older now. Smarter. Meaner. And I have one hell of a lot more at stake. I know you don't know me from Adam but you know Garrett, and Garrett does know who I am. He knows my people, and—" He listened, then barked out a laugh. "Nobody likes Will. Not at first. But does Garrett trust him?" Another pause. Then he smiled. "Yeah, that's my brother. He's not easy-listening but there's nobody I trust more when the shit starts flying. And believe me, Valor, the shit has started flying here. I have your back on this. Or I will, if you'll let me." He paused to listen, then closed his eyes in relief. "Keep an eye on your inbox." He opened his eyes to jack a questioning brow at Meg. She nodded impatiently. He grinned at her. "Documentation forthcoming. I think you'll be impressed."

He clicked off and tossed the phone into the jumble of papers and screens and keyboards covering his desk. He rolled his stiff neck, knuckled gritty eyes and turned his attention to Meg.

"You did it?" he asked.

"I did it." She threw down a quick victory boogie that boosted Drew's flagging energy considerably. "I did the hell out of it, Drew. And with—" She checked her watch. "—twenty-two minutes to spare! I am a genius. A goddamn bona fide genius. Contact Mensa and tell them to bow the fuck down, because I rule."

He reached out and snagged her into his lap. "You're the queen of coders." He took the tail of hair hanging down her back, wrapped it around his fist. "You win at ass kicking." And he lifted her into his mouth.

"No lie." She linked her hands behind his neck and fell into that kiss with enthusiasm. "I like winning, Drew."

He slipped his free hand under that sweatshirt. Found a whole lot of bare, silky skin. "Me, too," he breathed. "Let's win some more."

She glanced at her watch beside his ear and scooted off his lap. "Just over an hour until the window closes," she announced. "And I don't know how long this upload is going to take. Let's work."

"Aw." Drew sighed. "I was just getting into that."

She held up the thumb drive. "You can watch me upload this." She smiled, and it glittered like a blade. "Think of it as foreplay."

He gazed at her, lust and wonder twining together

inside him. "You really did it?"

"I did."

He eyed her speculatively. "I don't suppose you'd let me upload that while you crawl under this desk and—"

"—and blow you?" She laughed. "That's your fantasy, not mine, and pedestrian to boot. I expected better of you."

He thought about that. "You're right. Not my best work. I can do better."

"Of course you can. You think about it. I'm going to upload this beast."

"I'll watch." He smiled and patted his knee. "Make yourself comfortable."

She narrowed her eyes. "This is delicate work, Drew. I can't be distracted."

"I won't lay a finger on you." He held up innocent hands. "Swear to God."

"Oh all right." She sighed indulgently. "If it'll make you feel better." She snatched up the thumb drive and danced over to his laptop. She leaned down to plug it into the USB port, and her bottom was right there, so pretty. He curled a slow hand around the back of her thigh.

He smiled. "One thing."

She froze but didn't move away from his hand. "I knew there'd be a catch."

He slid his palm up her hip and slipped an experimental finger under the waistband of her running tights. "Take these off first?"

She threw an incredulous look over her shoulder at him. "You want me to take my pants off? How is that not distracting?"

He made a show of linking his fingers safely together behind his head. Kicked out his legs, crossed them at the ankle and leaned back. Very casual. "Your call."

She planted her hands on her hips. Ran skeptical eyes over him, from his obediently occupied hands to the enthusiastic welcome pushing at the front of his jeans. Then she grinned. "You've got yourself a deal, mister."

He'd gotten more than a deal. He'd gotten himself a damn miracle. But he only grinned back. "Nice and slow,

Meg. Nice and slow."

Drew decided he really did like winning.

Chapter 32

Declan's Pub attracted a decent lunch crowd for a Monday. Drew hadn't expected quite so much company, actually. Lila had done him a bigger favor than he'd thought when she'd granted him and Meg this snug little corner table for as long as they'd wanted it. He flapped a napkin across his lap and smiled down at what smelled like a very respectable bowl of beer cheese soup.

"Are you seriously going to eat that?" Meg sat across from him, her eyes narrow and accusatory.

He stopped, spoon in hand. "I was thinking about it."

"Right now?"

"It's lunch time." He spooned up some soup. "I'm hungry." He closed his eyes to savor it. "And this is a damn fine beer cheese soup. My compliments to the chef. I wonder if they make it in house?"

Meg ignored her own steaming bowl and dug into that burglar's paradise she called a purse. She pulled out her phone and slapped it on the tablecloth beside her bowl. Her untouched bowl. She scowled at Drew's silent phone, similarly positioned.

"Relax, Meg." Drew blew on his spoon. "He'll call."

"That's what you said yesterday. That's what you said again this morning."

"I didn't say when he'd call, just that he would. Guy's a mystery wrapped in an enigma. Don't fence him in." He nodded toward her bowl. "Eat your lunch, kiddo. You'll want your strength."

"Oh, shut it."

She picked up her silent phone and double checked that the ringer was on. Then Drew's phone buzzed. He angled it toward him with one finger, inspected the screen.

"Is it him?" She dropped her own phone with a clatter and half-rose from her seat.

Drew lifted an eyebrow. "Nice game face, Meggy."

"*Is it him*?"

He grinned. "Sure is."

She reached across the table, twisted a hand in the collar of his sweater and dragged him half out of his chair, too. "Answer. It."

"Maybe if you'd stop trying to strangle me, I would."

She let him go and he smoothed his sweater. Pushed his bowl carefully out of harm's way and scooped up his phone before Meg decided to punch him.

"Hello?" He spoke into the phone. "E? Well, my goodness." He smiled at her across the table. "Were you serious about that whole I-hope-we-can-still-be-friends thing? Because I have to admit, I'm surprised to hear from you."

He winced and pulled the phone away from his ear. E's fury buzzed into the air, loud enough to turn heads at surrounding tables. Meg grinned at him. Drew put the phone back to his ear.

"Are you sure it's wise to discuss this over the phone?" he asked gently. He paused to listen. "We're at Declan's, grabbing lunch. And FYI, the beer cheese soup is surprisingly—" He pulled back to inspect the screen. "Huh. He hung up on me." He shrugged and set the phone down beside his spoon. Returned Meg's grin with one of his own. "E's had a difficult morning."

"Has he?" She drew her soup bowl closer and began eating with enthusiasm, her appetite evidently restored by victory. "Did Valor not get canned after all?"

"Not remotely. According to E, that investigation's been dropped. He's spent his morning being questioned about something else altogether."

Meg shook her head. "Now that's a shame. But what's it got to do with us?"

Drew smiled. "That, Meggy mine, is what E would like to know." He polished off his soup. "I imagine he'll be here any minute to find out."

She sat back, patted her lips with her napkin. "You know what? That was a good beer cheese soup. Excellent, in fact. You were totally right."

"As I so often am, Meg." Drew sighed contentedly. "As I so often am."

Ten minutes later, Declan's heavy wooden door swung open, ushering in a brisk blast of fall air. It fluttered a few tablecloths and turned a few heads. Kept a few heads turned—females ones, mostly—because, well, E had a way of filling up a doorway. He stood there, framed in a rectangle of daylight like an old west gunslinger—his suit sharply cut, his shoulders impressively wide, his eyes cold and murderous in that perfect, perfect face of his. A terrible joy spurted up inside Drew, roared forward to meet that murderous rage. It ran through his veins with something akin to pleasure, and he came to his feet on a hot shock of adrenaline. Waved a deliberately casual hand to E, who jerked his chin in acknowledgement and stepped off the landing.

Lila sailed by, a bar towel pinned around her waist like an apron, a tray of pints and soup bowls on her shoulder. Drew threw out a hand to flag her. "Hey, Lila, any chance of another chair?" He tipped his head at E arrowing through the crowd toward them. "Looks like we might have that third for lunch after all."

She paused to toss a glance E's way. "Didn't stand you up, then? Mr. Shoulders?"

"Dependable as the sunrise, that guy."

"I'll have another chair sent over." She fished a fresh set of silverware out of the jumble on her tray, bent at the knees to deposit it on their table and lowered her voice to a murmur. "And if this goes wrong in any way, if any of my people—or God forbid my pub—should suffer as a result of whatever debacle this is I've agreed to? I will take it out of your hide, Andrew Blake. And your wallet." She straightened and sent him a brilliant smile. "Anything else?"

Drew met her eyes squarely. "I've already asked too much."

"It's true," Meg said. "We owe you."

"No, I've owed you. And now we'll be square." Lila shifted her tray more comfortably onto her shoulder. "Still, try not to cock up my pub, will you? Cheers." And she sailed off. A server arrived at their table with a chair before the crowd had even swallowed her up.

"We needed another seat over here?"

"Hey, Josh. Yeah, thanks." Meg smiled up at the kid, the same server Drew had fist bumped the other night for having his back against Lila in the Great Purse-Holding Debate. "We didn't think our friend would make it but—" She stopped as E arrived at the table. "—here he is." She rose, held out her hands to him. "E! Such a lovely surprise!"

Josh melted back into the crowd with that nimble grace that had always reminded Drew of James. He frowned. It was probably why his subconscious had landed on Josh when he'd needed an innocent youth for James to corrupt in the name of justice. He sighed. He hoped to Christ this worked. If it didn't, he really would have a lot of making up to do, and not just to Lila.

E took Meg's hands and bussed her cheeks while his eyes continued to steam murder. That itchy, answering hunger curled Drew's hands into fists. He prayed he'd get through this without actually punching anybody. At least he thought that was what he was praying for. But violence whispered in his mind, slipped through his veins like blood, beat in his ears with his pulse. This man had threatened Meg, and the sight of his hands on her, his cheek brushing hers? It had Drew thinking that a good, filthy brawl might be just the ticket. Drew made a lot of money, after all, and his lifestyle was relatively modest. If need be, he could probably just buy Lila another bar.

E turned to him and held out a friendly hand. "Sorry to interrupt your lunch, old man."

Drew took the hand for a hearty shake. "Not at all." He gestured E toward the chair Josh had just dropped off, then took his own. "We were just finishing up but we're not in a hurry, are we, Meg?"

"Of course not." She sank into her chair and crossed her legs with a silky whisper. "We always have time for trouble.

Particularly when that trouble belongs to an old friend." She nudged her empty soup bowl away and gave E very concerned eyes. "What seems to be the problem?"

"I think you know quite well what the problem is." E's teeth were very white. Shiny. Dangerous. He ran his eyes over her with deliberate care and she sighed.

"I'm not wired today, E. I save that for special occasions."

He maintained a pointed silence until she held out both hands, palms then backs. She turned her head side to side to show off naked lobes, then drew her scarf aside to reveal a bare throat. No jewelry, no bugs.

"Satisfied?"

"Not quite." He arched a brow at her collar and she sighed. Leaned in and plucked her shirt away from her chest so he could see straight down it. That thirsty rage inside Drew prickled up his back and over his scalp. Settled into a thorny glow in his fists, which he kept under the table, just to be safe.

E leaned back with a slim smile. "That wasn't as much fun as it could've been."

"No kidding," Meg said. "You suck at this kind of thing. Do women really sleep with you?"

"Oh, dear, yes."

"Yeah, I guess they would." She considered him. "Face like that? Plus the shoulders? You probably get plenty." Her smile was full of pity. "But I'd be very surprised if anybody came back for seconds."

He shrugged and nodded at her phone. "May I?"

She slid it across the table to him.

Drew did the same with his own phone. "You want to look down my shirt, too?"

E ignored that to inspect both phones. Apparently satisfied, he powered them down and set them face-down on the tablecloth. "Your handbag, Meg?"

"Have at it." She reached under her seat and hauled it out. "Be forewarned. There's lady equipment in there."

"I'll hardly go into decline at the sight of a tampon." E pulled it closer and shoved a hand in. Gave it a thorough rummaging.

"I was talking about my pepper spray but, hey, they're your eyes. Keep bashing around in there."

"It's not that I don't trust you." He slid the purse back toward her with an easy smile.

"It's just that you don't trust us." Meg took her purse back, her smile equally easy.

"You're right. I don't." His smiled faded. "Because my instructions were very simple. Upload the evidence against Valor during the two-hour window I provided."

"A two-hour window during which you would be busily visible elsewhere, thus unquestionably alibied on the off chance that somebody was smart enough to track down the back door in the first place," Meg said with an eye roll. "Yeah, yeah. We got it. Insurance upon insurance. Good plan. Well done."

"It *was* a good plan," Drew put in. "Really good. You should talk more about it. Go into detail." He leaned forward to nudge the breadbasket E's way. "Would you mind speaking into the breadsticks?"

"Cute." E flipped open the napkin, selected a breadstick and bit in. "Honestly, you two. All you had to do was follow instructions, then go about your stupid, complacent lives. You could forget we ever met. Was that really so hard?"

"Of course not." Drew propped an ankle across his knee and leaned back to give him a friendly smile. "We just hate you, that's all."

"Did you really think it would work?" His gaze on Drew's face was steady, with a hint of true curiosity. "Did you really think you could alter the contents of that thumb drive and I wouldn't know?" He laughed softly. "I know your work, Drew. Even on your worst days, even under insane time pressure, you were above the sort of hack job you uploaded on Saturday night." He turned to Meg, pointed the breadstick at her. "So I suppose I have you to thank for that little mess."

"You said to upload the contents of the thumb drive." She smiled. "You didn't say we couldn't add a little *fuck you* to it."

E laughed with every appearance of genuine amusement. "If that's the best fucking you've got, it's a wonder people sleep with you, either." He let his eyes travel leisurely down the length of her legs. "Though I suppose you get the occasional one-off on the strength of those alone." His eyes came back to her chest. "And I do mean alone."

The urge to spill blood gripped Drew by the throat and he swallowed it down with an effort. "You checked on the upload?" he managed. "When? We barely got it finished inside the window!"

E chuckled. "Insurance upon insurance, Drew, remember? I was working with amateurs, and reluctant ones at that. Did you really think I wouldn't build myself a peep hole to spot check their work?" He shook his head. "It took about twenty minutes to undo your girlfriend's hack job." He leaned back, divided a glance between them. "It was quite satisfying, actually. Almost as satisfying as watching Valor get shit-canned this morning."

Drew stared at him. "You said they dropped the investigation. You said you'd spent the morning being questioned about something else."

"I lied." His amusement vanished, and those silvery eyes were murderously cold again. "Everything went exactly as I'd planned. Valor was stripped of credentials, his security clearance revoked. He was escorted out of the building by nine this morning, his personal effects in a cardboard box. I spent the rest of the morning making his office my own." He leaned back and that urbane amusement dropped over him again like a mask. "I also made a few phone calls."

Meg shot Drew a glance across the table, then turned wary eyes on E. "What kind of phone calls?"

"I truly wish this could've ended differently." E's sigh was deep. Drew might have almost thought it heartfelt, except that he knew E didn't have a heart. "I did try to avoid this. Remember that, will you?"

Drew's pulse ratcheted up a gear, and he and Meg exchanged another glance over the breadbasket, this one less worried and more panicked. "You tried to avoid what?"

E looked across the bar and hiked his chin. And Drew's

heart ground through several more gears because a pair of men caught the signal and rose. Both were wearing government haircuts and neat suit jackets that had clearly been tailored to accommodate shoulder holsters. Drew had been in enough trouble over the years to recognize them for the cops they were. And to recognize what their presence here meant.

Somebody's ass was under arrest.

And E wasn't worried about his own.

Chapter 33

The two cops arrived at their table, meaty hands folded politely in front of them. Dark haired, dark eyed, thick necked, they were virtually identical. One's suit was charcoal, though, where the other's was navy.

"Meghan Wise?" Charcoal asked.

Drew shot a glance at E. E gazed back with palpable regret, but smug satisfaction moved in those eyes. Drew looked at Meg next, and she blinked back at him in undisguised, open-mouthed horror.

"That's me," she said faintly.

"Secret Service." Navy reached into his suit coat and flipped out a badge. Drew didn't miss the lethal gleam of a holstered handgun against the crisp white shirt when he did so. The guy moved back half a step, gestured politely toward the door. "If you'll come with us?" Charcoal didn't move. Neither did Meg.

"Why?" she asked.

"We just want to have a conversation, ma'am," Navy said. "But I doubt you want to have it in public."

Meg looked back at Drew, splayed shaking hands on the table, and prepared to rise. Drew put a hand over hers, stopped her. "Is she under arrest?" he asked.

Navy hesitated, glanced toward E. "Not at this time."

"Then she's not going anywhere," Drew said, and sat back. "You want to talk? We can talk right here." He leaned around the two sets of massive shoulders to search the crowd for Lila or Josh. "I'll have a few more chairs brought up."

E sighed. "Don't be a child, Drew."

"Meg's not leaving this bar."

"Oh, fine. What about a private room, then? A snug? They have those in Irish bars, don't they? That's a thing?"

Drew frowned at him. "There's a back room, sure."

"We'll chat there, then." He tipped his head toward the agents who were starting to draw curious looks from the neighboring tables. "As I'm assuming that you'd like to maintain at least some semblance of personal dignity in front of your..." He surveyed the room with benign distaste. "...friends."

"Fine." Drew rose, tossed his napkin on the table and jerked his chin at Meg. She rose also, her purse in two white-knuckled hands. "Let's have that chat."

E slid his chair back, a smile of deep satisfaction on his perfect face. "Oh, let's."

She stared at him, then at Charcoal who'd clamped a hand onto her elbow. "Wait, he's coming?"

Charcoal ignored her, but E actually chuckled. "Oh, Meggy. I wouldn't miss this for the world."

She scowled at him. "Don't call me Meggy."

"I don't believe you're in any position to give orders," E said. "Meggy."

She pressed her lips flat and let Charcoal propel her toward the bar. Navy made a move for Drew's elbow. Drew stared him into thinking twice about that, then fell in behind Meg without assistance. Navy shrugged and took up the rear with E.

Drew felt eyes following their strange little parade all the way to the bar, where Lila was pulling pints.

"Uh, Lila?"

She took in his entourage and hiked a curious brow. "Yes?"

"My friends and I need to have a...private conversation. Any chance we can borrow your back room for a few minutes?"

"Surely. Will you be needing any service? Shall I send Josh—"

"No, just the room." He gave her a weak smile. "Thanks, Lila."

"Cheers." She went back to pulling pints and Drew nodded Charcoal toward a door tucked into the corner at the end of the bar.

"Through there."

Charcoal opened the door and thrust Meg in. Drew followed, and Navy held the door for E. E stepped forward, then stopped abruptly just inside the doorway. Navy put a hand on his shoulder and finished the job. E stumbled into the room and Navy stepped in behind him. Clicked the door shut and put his back against it.

"Hey, E," Edward Valor said. He was seated on a sagging green couch that had seen better days, elbows on his knees, fingers linked together between them.

E smiled faintly, the picture of bemused surprise. His eyes told a different story, though. They flew around the room lightning fast, registered the man and woman sitting on either side of Valor. Faces impassive, hands neatly folded, the strangers still somehow radiated the kind of power and authority reserved for high-ranking officers of the law. Very high. Drew fought a grin.

"Well, now, what's this?" E drawled. He hiked a regal brow. "I believe I saw you fired earlier today, Valor."

Valor ignored that and nodded E toward a wooden chair that looked like it had served in several wars. "Have a seat."

E looked askance at the chair. "I'll stand."

"Suit yourself." Valor straightened a pile of manila folders on the dingy coffee table at his knees. "Before we get started, why don't I introduce you around?" He tipped his head to the woman on his right. "This is Special Agent in Charge Moira Green, head of the Secret Service's Electronic Crimes Task Force. I'm sure you know the name?"

"Of course," E murmured and gave her a nod. "It's been on my paycheck for years, though I've never had the pleasure of her acquaintance."

"It's no pleasure, Mr. Silver," Green said crisply.

E smiled politely. "As you like."

Valor tipped his head toward the man on his left. "And this is Special Agent Beauregard Jeffs, FBI liaison to Interpol."

Jeffs didn't speak at all, only regarded E with cool, hard eyes. E—wisely, to Drew's way of thinking—remained silent, only gave the man a nod, which was not returned.

"So," Valor said and patted his knees. "E. It's no secret that I've been concerned about you for some time now."

E lifted a lazy shoulder. "You've always been concerned about me, Valor. I offend you personally. But I believe my record speaks for itself."

"It certainly does." Valor's eyes fixed on E with a flinty intensity that made Drew think he must've been one hell of a soldier once upon a time. "You're talented. Extremely so. Unfortunately, you're also a narcissistic sociopath."

"Excuse me?"

"Delusions of grandeur," Valor informed him. "Excessive need for praise? Singular lack of ability to form deep or lasting relationships due to—"

"I understood the words, Valor, thank you." E ambled over to the chair he'd just refused. Dropped into it with smooth grace. "Just not as they apply to me. Because I assure you, SAC Green, Agent Jeffs, I'm in excellent mental health." He shifted his eyes to Green, sent her a look of melting earnestness. "Unlike Mr. Valor who seems to be suffering from an advanced case of post traumatic stress."

Jeffs and Green continued to study E like a bug under a microscope. Valor went on as if E hadn't spoken.

"On the other hand, you're a more than competent hacker with above average language skills and an insight into the criminal mindset that the Secret Service values very much. For a long while, you were also relatively stable. Stable enough that we felt it was worth the risk to keep your talents in house. But over the past three to five years, your performance deteriorated to the point that I became convinced that it had finally happened."

"What had happened?" E asked with the patient indulgence normally reserved for cranky toddlers.

"That you'd finally switched teams." Valor's face didn't change but suddenly Drew half-expected to see his breath freeze into visible puffs of fog. The guy's rage burned that cold. Yep. One hell of a soldier. "We never deluded ourselves that you served the United States, E. We knew that you served only yourself, and the instant somebody offered you a sweeter deal, better money, or a more interesting challenge, you'd throw us under the bus without a second thought."

"Valor, please. Stop right there. You're embarrassing yourself." E gave a sympathetic laugh. "SAC Green, Agent Jeffs, I don't know under what pretenses Valor's brought you here, but you must know that he was fired this morning. Terminated for having deliberately and knowingly falsified intelligence in an effort to sabotage my career. So for him to bring us all here and lodge these outrageous accusations when I've suffered quite enough at his hand—"

Valor spoke over him with implacable calm. "Acting on these concerns, I exercised my right as your superior to covertly monitor your electronic activities, both personal and professional, for the past two years."

E went stiff. "I beg your pardon?"

"In the course of doing so, I discovered that you had amassed an extensive dossier on Andrew Blake, with whom you'd been known to associate during your criminal days." Green and Jeffs lifted their eyes to Drew, who gave them a cheery finger wave. They turned their attention back to E without comment. Drew grinned at Meg over E's head, and she rolled her eyes at him. Then they both turned their attention back to Valor. Because taking in a show together had always been one of their favorite things.

"I contacted Mr. Blake and discovered him to be unaware of E's presence in the area, or of E's surveillance. I informed Mr. Blake of my concerns."

"Which were?" Jeffs asked. His voice was low and smooth and very, very frightening. Drew was impressed.

"Sociopaths, when they finally decompensate, often exact revenge for slights real and imagined, recent and far past. And as Blake had walked away from the very bust that put E in Secret Service custody in the first place, he was a textbook example of somebody E might target. As was I, being E's current superior and perceived roadblock to success. E intended to destroy my career in repayment for that blockage, and he planned to use Blake to do so."

"How so?" Green asked.

"Under the guise of friendship, he coerced Blake into a

compromising situation. He then threatened to harm Ms. Meghan Wise, Blake's friend and sometime business partner, if he refused to plant the evidence that would destroy my career." He nodded Meg's way. To Drew's delight, she merely lifted a business-like chin. God, he loved her in hard-ass mode.

"At my request, Blake and Wise—both extremely skilled hackers in their own right—"

"White hat hackers," Meg put in with a smile. She produced a couple of business cards from thin air and slid them across that disreputable coffee table toward Green and Jeffs. "Specializing in corporate security. We're the good guys."

"That they are." Valor's habitual grimness lifted just long enough for him to meet her eyes with appreciation and the slightest whiff of...interest? Drew's amusement faded and he moved to Meg's side. Gave Valor some pointed eye contact that said *mine*. A smile ghosted through Valor's eyes and he gave Drew a minuscule shrug that said *message received*. But Drew had the distinct impression that the guy was keeping an eye on the situation just in case.

Valor went on. "At my request, they cooperated with E's demands fully. They participated in what amounted to a penetration test at NoVD. A successful pen test, as it happens, that gave E the opportunity to build a backdoor into the Secret Service database on site. E then gave Blake a thumb drive containing evidence he'd concocted of my supposed crimes, with instructions to upload it when the backdoor opened 24 hours later while E was alibied elsewhere. He did so. But not before amending its contents."

"In what way?" Green asked.

"The data E created was masterfully crafted, each piece meticulously date- and time-stamped to integrate seamlessly into the existing data as if it hadn't been added on but had always been there. I simply had Blake and Wise rough it up, add some date and time inconsistencies that would lead a skilled and observant investigator to question the data's integrity."

"Why would you allow the upload at all?" Jeffs asked.

"Why not simply take E into custody when he demanded Blake's and Wise's cooperation?"

"Because at that point we didn't have any hard evidence of the crime," Valor said. "We had a thumb drive wiped clean of prints, a very complicated web of motivations, and my word against E's. But given his psychological limitations, I knew we could have something much cleaner and more damning if we were simply patient and steadfast. And I was right.

"Within minutes of Blake's upload, I captured evidence of an unknown user logging onto the system. This user immediately began cleaning the data that Wise and Blake had dirtied up. I monitored and documented his every move, and was able to trace the user back to an IP address. Within hours, the Secret Service was able to confirm that this IP address was being used exclusively by E during the time frame in question. I hate to use such a hackneyed phrase, but we literally caught him red handed."

E stared, his face white. "You have nothing." He gave a contemptuous laugh. "Except perhaps a mental illness of your own."

"And once we tied E to that specific IP address," Valor went on relentlessly, "we were able to connect him to several other questionable activities originating from that same address. And discovered exactly where E's new loyalties lay, and what he'd sold them for."

Valor drew a handful of photographs from a folder and spread them on the coffee table facing E. E barely glanced at them, but Drew tipped his head for a good look. Damn, Jillian had done some fine work. He didn't know if he should be impressed or concerned that she'd been able to fulfill a request for morally flexible Russian girls quite so easily but he wasn't about to complain.

"We have sworn affidavits from each of these women—or should I say girls, as the oldest is barely sixteen and the youngest just twelve?" Valor's lip curled in faint disgust. "Each of them was victimized by a human trafficking ring that imports girls from the former Soviet Union, mostly the Ukraine. They were told they'd be working as models and actresses, of course, but it was a different story once they'd landed in a strange country with no money, no language skills and no passports. They've given sworn testimony, each of them, detailing parties they attended over the past six months at which they were forced to have sex with various men who'd provided classified government information to their handlers. None of them hesitated to pick E from a photo array."

"Oh for goodness' sake." E studied the photos dutifully and sighed. "I've never seen these girls before in my life."

"He was paid in cash as well." Valor plucked yet more papers from another folder and fanned them out on the coffee table. "He prefers Euros to either the American dollar or the Ukrainian hyrvnia, and likes them deposited directly into the Bahamian bank account referenced in these statements."

Drew resisted the urge to high five Meg over E's head. She'd created these documents from scratch, and under serious time pressure. Girl was amazing.

"You'll note how neatly the dates of the deposits correspond to several of the more questionable decisions he's made at work over the past two years," Valor said.

E leaned forward to inspect the papers. Sat back dismissively. "While I don't doubt that somebody is quite pleased with his bank balance, I'm afraid it's not me. I don't own that account, or any other overseas."

"We also have a sworn affidavit from a young man." Valor's voice was low. Calm. Almost gentle. "A Joshua Ibor?"

"Really, Valor." E laughed, but it was tight. "The girls were one thing but if you're implying that I'm also buggering a boy—"

"I have no interest in your sexual proclivities, E. But I do have a sworn statement from Mr. Ibor supporting each of the aforementioned allegations," Valor said. "He claims that the two of you met in a chat room some months ago, fell into the habit of exchanging porn and pirated software. You developed a mentor/mentee relationship which concluded with your dispensing some career advice that Mr. Ibor found troubling. So troubling that he risked bringing it to our attention."

"And what am I supposed to have said that this young man found so troubling?" E leaned back, amused, and folded his arms.

"According to the statement, you advised him to pursue a job in government intelligence because, while the pay was useless, there were other benefits."

E eyed him, amusement gone cold. "Such as?"

"Sex, money and drugs."

"What? No rock and roll?"

Valor ignored this to read from the paper in front of him. "*If you have the stones to steal it, the nerve to sell it and the brains to be discreet about it, you can be balls deep in pussy, coke and Euros just like I am.*" He met those cold eyes with unflinching satisfaction. "I'll spare you the rest of the conversation, but rest assured, we have all of it."

Drew knew exactly what Valor had. He'd written it himself, hadn't he? James had gotten Josh-the-server to sign his name to it, but this supposed testimony was all Drew's work. He was kind of proud of it, actually. Creative writing had always been a strong suit.

"Why on earth would I put a sentiment like that to paper?" E laughed, though it sounded strained to Drew. "Even if I had done such a thing—which I haven't—what kind of idiot would claim it in a chat room?"

"A narcissistic sociopath," Valor returned. He consulted the paper again. "*You're so full of shit*, Ibor writes in response to your claim." He lifted his eyes to E's again. "And that narcissistic streak of yours replied with dates, incidents, and links to specific newspaper articles covering the fallout of the information you sold. Of the decisions you purposefully blew that cost innocent men their lives."

"Valor, be reasonable. Of course I've blown calls. We all have. But each and every call was made in good faith, and based on the best data available at the time." E sent a careful glance toward Green and Jeffs still flanking Valor on the couch, and hesitated as if choosing his words. As if laying the truth on a crazy person was a touchy business, and he wanted to proceed with care. "Okay, listen." He steepled his fingers and pressed them to his lips for a centering moment before continuing. "Men die in this line of work, Valor. I know that's difficult to swallow, given everything you've sacrificed to protect them. To protect us all. But it's a hard world, and in spite of our best efforts, innocents do die." He spread helpless hands, the pain of the world all over that perfect face. "And we want there to be a reason. We want somebody to blame, if only so we can feel like we fixed the problem. That we fixed something. But sometimes there simply isn't anybody to blame."

There was a long, taut silence that gave Drew a bad moment. Because the way Valor was gripping his knees suggested that he would very much like to put his fist right in the middle of all that condescending sincerity E was dishing up.

"But sometimes there is somebody to blame." Valor's face—as opposed to his hands—remained smooth and professional. "And this is one of those times. Because all of these chat room interactions I've mentioned? Ibor kept screenshots. The person with whom he was communicating used the same IP address you used to check up on Blake's and Wise's work last night." Valor flipped the folder shut. "The data is quite clear."

At that, E shut his mouth, a move that Drew appreciated. What was it Meg always said? Upon arrest, you shut the hell up? E had clearly arrived at the conclusion that his arrest was imminent and he was taking her sage advice.

Drew edged a shoulder in front of Meg anyway. Because E had to know that—while Valor had been today's mouthpiece—Drew was the one who'd just handed him his ass. And if E decided to screw wisdom in favor of drawing a little blood on his way down, he wouldn't aim for Valor. He'd aim for Drew, and for maximum damage.

So, no, Drew wouldn't mind at all if E happened to overlook Meg's presence for the next few minutes here.

E rose slowly to his feet. Valor came to his feet as well. By the door, Charcoal and Navy put their hands under their jackets. E ignored them all, and turned blazing eyes to Drew.

"You unimaginable bastard," he said softly. "You did this."

"Not me." Drew kept his hands loose, his face impassive. But he kept his weight on the balls of his feet just in case. "You did this to yourself."

"You did this to me," he said again, "because of her." He spit the word like it was poison, and Drew put Meg just a little farther behind his shoulder. "Because I wasn't properly respectful to your ugly girlfriend, you think you can set me up?"

Behind him, Meg made an impatient noise. "This guy is such an asshole." She elbowed Drew aside and stepped forward. Drew's heart crashed into his ribs but he didn't reach for her. He wanted to, of course. He wanted to throw himself in front of her like E was a live grenade. But he didn't want to remind E of how very effectively Drew bled when Meg hurt. So he didn't reach for her. But it cost him. Christ, it cost him.

"Seriously," Meg went on, contempt freezing each syllable into an individual blade. "Can you even hear yourself? You built an entire nightmare for this guy!" She threw a hand Valor's way. "You undermined his confidence, smeared his reputation and gaslighted him relentlessly for years. But nobody believed for a second that he'd gone bad, and you know why not? Because the guy's a soldier. He's got honor. He's freaking built out of honor. He'd sooner wipe his boots on the American flag than lower himself to fight with the likes of you."

Drew glanced at Valor, who was staring at Meg like he'd never seen a woman before—all wonder and want. And just a trace of guilt. Drew willed the guy to mind his game face. God knew, he understood the impact Meg could have on a guy, but Valor needed to get his shit together. Because Meg wasn't entirely correct. Guys made of honor could lie. They didn't lie well, or easily, but they could do it so long as it served the greater good. But it didn't sit easily on those Captain America shoulders and Meg's spirited defense of his character had twisted that guilty knife. And it was showing.

Luckily everybody seemed too engrossed in the show

Meg was putting on to notice. As well they should, because his Meggy put on one hell of a show.

"And for you to stand there like some innocent victim and accuse me and Drew of doing the same to you?" Meg laughed with incredulous spite. "Good lord! We were good people who tried to do a good thing for an old friend, and in return you made us weapons in your personal war. We didn't do shit to you, but if we had? There's not a court in the land that would convict us. You deserve everything you're about to get, E. You deserve worse." She turned to Valor, magnificent in her rage. "Tell me you're charging him in Russia, too. He's still got citizenship there, right? He can go to the Gulag?"

Drew surprised himself with a laugh. "Goddamn, I love the way your mind works."

Valor blinked at Meg. "I think I do, too."

Drew scowled at him. "Do I have to say it out loud?"

"Nope." Valor lifted both hands. "Loud and clear."

"Good." Drew dropped an arm across her shoulders. Accepted without comment her sharp elbow in his ribs as the price for public posturing. Worth it "Okay, so I'm warming up to this Gulag idea. Is that still a thing?"

Valor chuckled. It sounded rusty, like he rarely used it. "Not since 1955 or so. But if the US charges don't keep us busy enough, I'll look into it. You have my word."

"Your word," E said with slick contempt, "is worth exactly shit. But it's all you have against me, isn't it? Because all this?" He flicked a contemptuous hand at the papers still spread across the coffee table. "It's just a vengeful little fantasy cooked up by an old enemy. So go ahead. File your charges. But just know that when you're done, I'll have your job. And Green's and Jeffs' as well. It'll take my lawyers about two seconds to shred everything these two idiots concocted." He flicked that hand Drew's and Meg's way. "But I'll have all of you wrapped up in court for the next century or so. I'll bankrupt each and every one of you—not to mention your precious US government—in legal fees alone." E's smile spread like gasoline, oily and lethal. "In absence of anything like a confession, which I obviously don't intend to provide, you'll—"

"Oh," Drew said. "About that. I meant to mention. You already confessed."

Chapter 34

E stared at Drew for a moment, blank with surprise.
"Of course I didn't."

"Sure you did." Drew gave a happy sigh. "You were so busy peeking down Meg's shirt that you forgot to open your silverware."

"My silverware?"

"We bugged it. We doubted you were planning to eat so figured it would be safe enough. Though I've got to say, it gave me a bad moment when you ate that breadstick. I thought you might decide to order lunch after all, and then we'd have been screwed."

Drew could all but see E replaying their conversation in his head, groping his memory for his exact words. Saw the moment he remembered what he'd said. *My instructions were very simple. Upload the evidence against Valor during the two-hour window I provided.* The mask of civility barely held against a blast of unhinged rage. Drew glanced uneasily at Meg but she was grinning at E with fierce delight.

"Aw, don't feel so bad," she crooned. "You grew up rich, that's all. In your world, you can buy whatever you need whenever you need it. But all those other things? The things and people you don't need?" She poofed her hands. "Invisible."

"Which is how," Drew put in, edging his shoulder subtly in front of her once again, "you end up making terrible, career-ending confessions to bugged spoons."

"Which is how," Valor said, "you end up going to jail."

"Oh, I'm going nowhere. But feel free to arrest me, if you really must." E held out his wrists for the cuffs, supremely unconcerned with the battle in his confidence about the war. "Let's get on with it, shall we?" He smiled at

Drew. "I'm sure my lawyers will have a field day with this supposed confession you claim to have. I'm sure they'll also enjoy this so-called evidence you've cooked up."

"Oh, I'm sure they will." Drew smiled back. "They just love billable hours, lawyers do. And this much evidence? In such a tangle? They could spend years straightening it out." Drew's grin grew. "Years that we'll spend enjoying our freedom, mind you, while you enjoy nothing but the inside of your prison cell and the warm regards of large men who like pretty faces."

"It's a point," E said thoughtfully. "I doubt I'll see the inside of a prison cell, of course, but on the off chance that I do?" He leaned to the side, caught Meg's eye and smiled. "Kiss me goodbye, won't you, darling?"

He snatched Meg out from under Drew's arm between one heartbeat and the next, so fast that Drew simply let him. He stood there and watched it happen in slo-mo, like a car accident unfolding before his eyes in a single time-stalled moment. He watched, helplessly frozen, as E drove his fingers cruelly into the loose swirl of Meg's bun and dragged her up against his body. She gave a startled yelp, and E took vicious advantage, wrenching her mouth open and plunging his tongue inside. It was a rape of a kiss, a twisted aberration of affection, and it struck Drew like a bullet to his gut.

A bullet that shattered the deep-freeze and sent time jerking back into motion. Suddenly everybody was moving, and with dizzying speed. Valor hurdled the coffee table. Green and Jeffs leapt to their feet. Charcoal and Navy sprinted forward, guns drawn. But Drew beat them all. He tore Meg from E's grip, sent him stumbling into Charcoal's arms. He set Meg away from him, just far enough to run terrified hands over her arms and shoulders, over her face and her hair.

"Jesus, Meg. My God." His hands were shaking. So was she. Her whole body vibrated under his hands. A hank of hair hung down in front of one huge green eye and an ugly red scratch scored the soft skin of her throat. He touched it with a single fingertip, traced it with exquisite gentleness from the underside of her jaw to where it disappeared into

285

the pretty scarf she'd pulled aside to let E inspect her for bugs. Rage welled up inside him like blood in a bullet hole but he clamped down on it. Tried to speak with something like calm. "Meggy, are you all right?"

"Yeah." She blinked up at him, shock receding behind a towering wave of something that he slowly recognized as rage. Meg wasn't shaking from fear or shock. Meg was shaking from pure, high-test rage. "Yeah, I'm good." She brought the back of her hand to her mouth, pulled it away and frowned at the bright streak of blood it left behind.

"Holy Christ." Drew stared. "You're bleeding. He hurt you." A rage filled him that eclipsed Meg's entirely. He thought he'd had his temper clamped securely down but it snapped its leash with an abrupt pop. He heard it in his head just like that—*pop*. He spun back to E, his elbow already cocked and ready to fire like a fucking gun. But Meg caught it. Stopped him. She was the only thing that could've. That cool, shaking hand dropped his rage like a bucket of ice water.

"No, Drew. He didn't hurt me." She stepped forward. Studied E like he was a math problem she'd just figured out. Blood welled on her lower lip and she dashed it away. "He hurt you. I was just the weapon. You were the target."

"Of course he was." E gave her an ugly smile, perfectly unconcerned with the drawn guns Navy and Charcoal had aimed at his midsection. "Believe me, if it's sex I'm after, I have any number of more interesting—not to mention more attractive—options. But I could hardly let Drew escape from this contretemps unscathed, now could I?"

He shook a dark tumble of hair out of his eyes and swiped a wrist across his own mouth. It came away streaked with Meg's blood. He smirked at it, then up at Drew. Sweat gathered on Drew's spine and his palms itched with violence. The need to break something seized him by the throat and shook savagely. Because that was Meg's blood on E's wrist.

"Believe me, I took no more pleasure from that kiss than she did." E turned that smirk Meg's way. "Probably less, in fact."

Rage roared anew, filled Drew's head like a swarm of killer bees. He pulled in a breath, but the oxygen only fed the fire. It raced through his veins like a tidal wave of violence and he finally just gave himself over to it with a terrible joy.

"Drew, no!" Meg snatched at the back of his sweater and hauled. He stopped, fists clenched, his entire self trembling on the slippery edge of violence. He struggled to focus. To hear her over the rage that was filling his head, clawing inside his chest. Because Meg was talking to him. She was asking him something. Asking *for* something. And while seeing E's blood on his knuckles was more important than his next breath, it wasn't nearly as important as giving Meg whatever she wanted.

So he fought the rage, dragged himself back from that razor-sharp fall and said, "What?"

She held out her purse. "Will you hold this a minute?"

He blinked down at it, then up at her. And suddenly, he understood. Meg wanted the swing.

Everything in him roared up and refused. The beast of his anger snarled and snapped, its appetite awful and desperate. He stared at her, willed her to take it back. To allow him the dark pleasure of shredding his knuckles for her honor. But she only stared back, silent and unmoved.

And he knew she was right to ask. Because E had used her. Worse, he'd disregarded her. To him, Meg had been nothing but a hammer, the fist to Drew's unprotected gut. And, yeah, maybe Drew had felt that fist all the way to his bones. Maybe the pain was ringing there still. But he'd only been hurt. Meg had been stripped. Devalued. Dehumanized. If anybody deserved the one swing he had a feeling Valor would allow them, it was Meg.

"Drew?" Her eyes were soft with understanding, implacable with need. She knew what she was asking. She knew what it would cost him, and she was asking anyway. "Will you hold my purse please?"

"Of course." He took the purse, his hands still shaking with appetite denied. He cradled it in his arms like their firstborn child and stepped aside.

Meg flashed him a look of pure love and fierce

gratitude. He had just enough to time to catch E's moment of utter confusion before Meg turned and swung. Girl was built long and lean. Her reach was excellent, her form even better. She should probably write her trainer a thank you note because her right cross was a thing of beauty.

E went down like a bag of hammers.

Regret seized Drew's gut in a bitter fist, then let go. It just released, left him clean as air, light as joy. Because Meg was standing over E's slumped figure like a Valkyrie, shaking out her fist and clearly praying for him to get up. To give her the barest pretext of a reason to hit him again.

Valor considered E lying there on the floor. He tucked his fingers into his pockets and said, mildly, "Oops."

Navy holstered his gun with an air of faint regret. "I was really hoping I'd get to shoot him."

Charcoal knelt and zip-tied E's wrists. Muttered something that sounded a lot like, "Get in line."

"Beg pardon," Meg said, perfectly straight faced. "My hand slipped."

"Understandably." Green had Meg's business card between two well-manicured fingers. She tucked it into her briefcase and exchanged a speaking look with Jeffs, then turned to Valor. "We trust you have the situation in hand?"

"Yes, ma'am," Valor said. "Thank you both. I can take it from here."

"I'm sure you can." Green watched the agents haul E to his feet and muscle him out the door. "We'll be in touch." She and Jeffs followed the agents, leaving Valor alone with Meg and Drew.

For a long moment, nobody spoke. Finally, Valor said, "Listen, I don't want to know how you did what you did. I truly don't. In fact, I'm pretty sure I'd be legally obligated to prosecute you if you told me, so please don't." He held out a hand. "Just know that I'm grateful."

Drew shook his hand. "Here's hoping that we don't have to see one another or speak of this ever again."

"Amen," Valor said. But his eyes drifted to Meg. "I'm sure you're still recovering from that little slip of the fist a minute ago so I won't offer to shake. But if you're ever in the market for a job or...anything else—"

"Watch it," Drew said. "I feel a slip coming on myself."

Valor flashed his teeth in a smile that was startling as much for its warmth as for its unexpectedness. He produced a business card and dropped it into the purse Drew was still holding. "Just keep that," he told Meg. "And if you ever need anything, either of you? Don't hesitate."

He pulled a faintly military about-face, and marched out the door.

Meg watched him go, then turned to Drew with a grin so bright, so genuinely delighted, that it dazzled him. "Well, I have to say, you sure know how to show a girl a good time. That was fun."

Fun. Drew studied her. She meant that, he decided slowly. She actually thought they'd just had fun. An answering grin sprouted in his heart, climbed across his soul and spread over his face.

"Okay, that settles it." He stood there, grinning at her in goofy wonder. "We're getting married."

"Well, my goodness." She laughed and spread a hand across her chest. "Was that a proposal?"

"You know what? I think it was."

A nervy shock zipped from his hands to the top of his head. Because Drew had proposed to a great many women over the course of his adult life, but never seriously. To be fair, nobody he'd proposed to had ever taken him seriously. In certain circles, in fact, he was sort of famous for the flirty-fake proposal. Lord knows his sisters-in-law had given him enough crap about it over the years. As well they should, considering the sheer number of times he'd proposed to each of them.

But the instant the words left his mouth, Drew had known that he meant this one. He wanted Meg to marry him. He'd never wanted anything more in his life, and God knew he'd wanted for a lot of things over the years. But he'd never wanted anything the way he wanted Meg. He wanted her in his bed, in his heart, in his life. He wanted to give her babies and a home, he wanted to give her a ready-made family full of brothers and nephews and all the trouble that came along with them. He wanted all that, and her. Only her.

"Yeah," he said, a jangling hope falling into the love and the relief already swirling around inside him. It all banged around in there like an insane one-man band. "Yeah, I'm definitely proposing. Will you, Meg? Will you marry me?"

"Well, as it happens—" She tipped her head and studied him, joy filling up those huge green eyes. "I think we're already engaged."

"We are?" He blinked at her.

"I think I asked you, though."

"You did?"

"Sure. I said, 'Will you hold this a minute?' And I held out my purse. Which is as good as asking a guy to marry you, if I understand correctly."

"And I took it." He gazed down at the satchel still as snug in his arms as a sleeping baby. He lifted his eyes to hers, comprehension dawning. "I said yes?"

"You said yes." She stepped forward, took his jaw in two shaking hands and laid her lips to his. "Didn't you?"

"Bet your ass I did." Love for her bubbled up inside him. Slid over his patchwork heart, and made him whole and clean and hers. "I'll always say yes to you, Meggy."

EPILOGUE

One year later

Meg's feet were killing her. Her arches wept and her toes had gone numb hours ago but her shoes had nothing on the freaking vise clamped around her torso. Why did women do this to themselves? It was torture, plain and simple.

She smiled down at the cleavage—the honest-to-God cleavage—that her corset had magically manufactured. Oh, right. That was why.

And it might be torture, but it was worth it. Totally worth it. A girl only got married once, after all, and the glassy-eyed shock on Drew's face when he'd gotten a load of her in this dress? Of the unprecedented boobage it had provided? Priceless. Watching that formidable brain of his kick into high gear, though? Watching him visibly hatch ideas on the myriad ways they could enjoy what was now spilling out of the top of her dress? Beyond priceless.

He was beyond priceless. He was scary smart—though sneaky about it, which she admired—loyal all the way to his bones, and he made her laugh. Even when nothing was funny. Especially when nothing was funny. It was a rare gift, that, and Meg was no fool. Her *I do* had been utterly without hesitation. As had his, which was nice. She tipped her head onto his shoulder as they sailed through the night toward the Annex in a darkened limo.

"I can't wait to get home," she murmured, her head pleasantly muddled from just half-a-glass of champagne too much. The perfect amount of too much. Damn but this had been a perfect night.

"Yeah?" He threaded his fingers through hers and laid his cheek against her hair. It crunched, the way bridal hair did. "Anxious to get me out of my tux, are you?"

"Definitely." Something stabbed into her kidneys and she shifted, resigned. "Because I can't get out of this corset by myself, and I know you won't help me until we've properly enjoyed it. Which will necessitate the removal of your tuxedo. Stat."

"I do love you, Meggy." He pressed a kiss to her crunchy hair. "I also love that corset. I'm sorry but I do."

"Enjoy it now, then. I have plans to ritually burn it later. Because holy hell."

He drifted a palm up the boned bodice that kept her from slouching the way she desperately wanted to and traced the lush curve of breast rising up out of it like bread dough. "Holy hell," he agreed reverently. "You looked like a princess today, Meg. Seriously. Disney couldn't have drawn you better." He dipped a finger into the dark cleft between her breasts. She'd never had that before, that interesting little cleft. Maybe she wouldn't burn the corset, after all.

"You know," he said thoughtfully, "I've always wanted to do a Disney princess."

She sighed. "Again with the pedestrian fantasies."

"What can I say?" She could feel his smile against her hair. "I'm a guy."

"Well, we can give it a go," she said doubtfully, "if you really, really need to do Disney, so to speak. But you should know that it took me about five minutes to find my own feet once I put this thing on. I almost had to get married barefoot." She patted the vast quantity of tulle that exploded from her waist all the way to her toes. "Send a postcard if you get lost."

Drew sighed. "I see your point."

"Micah said I looked like the cake."

"From the mouths of babes." Drew chuckled. "I think Bel did that on purpose."

"I know she did. She and Audrey were totally in cahoots on that one." She scowled. "First Audrey convinced me that only tall girls can pull off giant dresses—"

"Which is totally true," Drew pointed out. "This dress would've eaten Audrey alive. God love the girl, but she's about as big as a minute."

"—and then Bel copied the damn thing and made a cake to match."

"With flowers, though. And it was delicious." That finger drifted across the edge of her bodice again. "Just like you."

"It was a good cake." Meg sighed, too happy to scowl. "Bel knows her yummy and Audrey knows her pretty, and they threw us one hell of a party." She snuggled closer to him, her throat suddenly tight and hot. "I love your family, Drew. I really, really love them."

"Good. Because they're yours now, too. What we have, we share, right?"

She wanted to say *right*. She wanted to answer. But the joy clogged her throat and she could only nod.

The limo eased to a halt in front of the Annex's huge veranda. Golden light spilled from the ground floor windows but all was dark and quiet upstairs. Which was no surprise, given that the boys had spent the preceding six to eight hours eating themselves into sugar frenzies then dancing themselves sweaty. Micah had thrown in a boot-and-rally for good measure. Meg had been impressed but Bel had just rolled her eyes and said, "That kid. Cripes." Presumably they were all upstairs now, sleeping it off like Romans after the orgy.

Drew said, "Wait here." He got out of the limo, then came around to her door where he helpfully hauled Meg and her dress onto the driveway.

"Thanks." She grinned at him. "I was like a cork in a champagne bottle."

"No problem." He swept her into his arms.

"What the—Drew!" Meg whooped as he carried her up the porch steps, the chilly fall air swirling around them in a crackle of dried leaves. "How did you even find my legs?"

"I guessed." He hip checked the door open and carried her across the threshold with all appropriate ceremony. "Got lucky."

"No kidding," Will said. He and James were waiting for them on the landing of that *Gone With The Wind* staircase Meg liked so much, still mostly in their wedding wear. Will had ditched the jacket, leaving him in a black vest and turned-back cuffs. James was down to shirt sleeves and a pair of suspenders. Something cracked open inside Meg at the sight of them waiting there, something warm and fierce and forever. These were her brothers now. She had brothers.

"That's some bride you've got there, little brother."

"You know what?" James gave her a narrow up and down. "My bride has a cake somewhere looks just like that."

"I know she does." Meg tried to scowl but just couldn't manage it. Drew put her carefully back on her feet. "I'll be speaking to her about that."

"You're prettier than the cake," James assured her, his smile lazy, his eyes sparkling. "You win at pretty." He turned to Drew. "You really did pick a good one."

"Thanks." Drew slung an arm around her shoulders. "Speaking of brides, why don't you both go find your own? This one's mine and I'm taking her upstairs now."

"Not so fast, cowboy." Will rose, tucked his thumbs into his vest pockets. "We've got something for you."

"Better than the fact that my wife's wearing too many clothes and has specifically requested my help in getting rid of them?"

Will shrugged. "You can burn the corset later."

"Dude!" James gave Will's shoulder a backhanded slap. "You had to burn the corset too? Is that a thing?"

"It's a thing," Meg informed him.

James chuckled. "I thought it was just Bel. Who knew it was a thing?"

"Every woman who's ever worn a corset," Will said, then turned back to Drew. "So, about this thing we've got for you?" His eyes laughed, something Meg wasn't sure she'd ever seen before from Will. "Trust us. You want this."

"Do I?"

James laughed outright, and rubbed his hands together. "Yeah, you do. You both do. You really, really do."

Drew and Meg exchanged a look. Finally she shrugged and said, "I guess we do."

Moments later they were in Will's mahogany-and-leather home office seated on the deep couch across from his boat-sized desk. James perched on the arm of the couch and Will leaned back against the front of his desk, a plain yellow business-sized envelope next to his hand.

"First off? I heard from our buddy Edward Valor today," Will told them. "Update on E's trial."

Meg stiffened, and Will waved her off.

"It's good news. They're done with discovery and have decided to charge him with murder. Six counts, premeditated. First degree."

"For the Secret Service agents who died when he deliberately made the bad call he meant to pin on Valor," Meg said.

"Exactly," Will said. "It was by far the strongest charge and the best evidence. Which means that all the more...let's call it tenuous evidence that Drew cooked up?"

"The sex parties and the bank accounts and the on-line bragging and Valor backing it all up?" Drew asked.

"Otherwise known as Jillian and James coercing young people to bear false witness before sworn officers of the law?" Will's mouth was grim. "Your dearest wife fabricating paper trails and bank accounts? Your dreaming up chat room conversations from thin air and planting them all on E? My abusing a client-agent relationship to persuade Valor to cooperate with all of the above? Clara putting her professional reputation on the line to put enough fire-power behind Valor to make it all work?"

"Yeah," Drew said cheerfully. "That."

"All that," Will said, "has disappeared."

Relief was a cool rush inside Meg. She'd never been quite comfortable with having manufactured evidence against a man, even one as wholly guilty as E. Plus what she'd built had never been intended to hold up in a court of law. Drew's plan had always been to simply hammer at E's temper, to pile on accusation after outrageous accusation until he finally cracked and said something incriminating. Which, thankfully, he had.

"The only charges they're pursuing against E are the ones he earned all by himself," Will said. "So you can enjoy your honeymoon secure in the knowledge that all our little sins—necessary as I admit they were—are officially off the books. E's getting only what's coming to him, and not a shred more."

"Well, that is good news." Drew slapped his knees and prepared to rise. "But it's not nearly as good as enjoying that corset before we have to burn it, so if that's all—"

"It's not." James put a hand on his shoulder and shoved him back onto the sofa. "Patience, son. The best is yet to come."

Will picked up the envelope beside his hand, ran it through his fingers and smiled. It was that sharky smile that always made Meg's pulse do a nervous little dance, and tonight was no exception.

"Valor sends his best wishes, by the way." Will tapped the sharp edge of the envelope against his palm. "He's sweet talked his old buddy and my problem child Garrett Dain into ponying up a couple of season tickets for you both on the Ravens' fifty yard line as a wedding present."

"How thoughtful," Drew murmured, and glanced at the envelope. "Are they in there?"

"Where, here?" Will held up the envelope like he was surprised to find it in his hand. Meg narrowed her eyes. Nothing surprised Will. Nothing. "No." His smile spread and she swallowed. Reached for Drew's hand. "This is our present, mine and James'. To the two of you." He glanced over their heads at James, his pale eyes dancing with unholy amusement.

James outright laughed, then slapped Drew's shoulder. "Enjoy the honeymoon, son."

He rose and strolled toward the door.

"Do that," Will said. He laid the envelope precisely in the center of his gleaming desk and followed James. The door snicked shut behind them and Drew looked at Meg. She looked back. They both looked at the envelope resting on the desk.

"What is it?" she asked.

"Hell if I know." Drew rose to inspect it, hands carefully behind his back. "Nothing written on the outside."

"For heaven's sake." She shot to her feet and snatched it

up. "I'm sure they didn't give us anthrax for our wedding, Drew. I'm opening it."

"Right." He dropped a hip onto the edge of the desk and peered over her shoulder at the envelope. "I'll watch."

She smirked at him and ripped it open. "Coward."

"If it's explosive, I'm counting on your skirt to protect us."

She considered that. "It probably would, actually."

He nodded her toward the open envelope. "Well?"

She took a breath and shoved her hand inside. Pulled out a brushed metal thumb drive that gleamed like a bullet in her palm. She met Drew's eyes for a long moment, then they both shot around the desk. Drew got there first—longer legs, plus no giant skirt—and woke up Will's laptop. She was just a beat behind him and plugged the thumb drive into the USB port. They both dove for the mouse and this time Meg won.

"Damn it," Drew said. "You're fast."

"I'm motivated," she said, and accessed the drive's contents. "It's a video file."

"I see that." He peered over her shoulder at the screen. "Dated almost exactly a year ago?"

"Should we open it?" she asked.

"Why not?" Drew shrugged. "We're using Will's own computer. If it's going to blow up, it can blow up right here."

"Good point." She clicked it open and hit play. "This is—" She frowned. "This is the back of the Annex."

"That's my truck pulling up." Drew leaned closer.

"Is this—" Meg tipped her head, then comprehension hit like a hammer. "Oh my God. Drew—"

He whooped and yanked out the thumb drive. Snatched her up in his arms, tossed her over his shoulder fireman-style and headed for the door.

"You said you erased it," Meg told his back, her cheeks burning, her skirts flouncing.

"I did." Drew booted open the office door and sailed across the foyer where Will and James sat side by side on a leopard print bench, laughing like the demented. Drew took the stairs by easy twos. "Guess I wasn't quite quick enough on the draw, now was I?" He didn't sound particularly unhappy about it, either.

"I can't believe your brothers gave us a sex tape for our wedding," she muttered as Drew hit the top of the stairs and all but sprinted for the bedroom.

"No, you can't believe that our brothers gave us our sex tape for our wedding," he said. "But you're going to." He gave her bottom a fond pat. "We'll thank them later." He tossed her onto the bed where she landed with a breathless bounce. He ran his eyes over her with all the sleek hunger of a predator and the gleeful anticipation of a good man with a naughty imagination. "You can thank me now."

She spat a flounce of tulle out of her mouth then came up on her elbows to glare at him. "Oh, yeah?"

"Oh, yeah." His eyes caught and held on the breasts her bodice now only barely contained. Her heart tripped into a heady little cha-cha but she arched a cool brow.

"For what?"

He came forward slowly. Planted one knee and then the other in the jungle of her skirt, caged her between those long thighs and dropped one elbow onto the bed above her shoulder. He put his mouth one exquisite whisper from the shell of her ear. "For knowing when to take my time?" he suggested, and ran a leisurely palm from her hip all the way up to her bodice. Her breath backed up in her lungs and her entire world constricted to the tip of the clever, clever finger that was now tracing and dipping and playing along the lacy edge where dress met skin. "And for knowing when to get down to business."

Meg blinked. He'd tucked something cool and small into that interesting dip her corset had manufactured. She peered down and found the little thumb drive nestled neatly into her cleavage. She looked back up at him. His smile bloomed brilliantly.

"In case imagination fails," he told her helpfully. "When you're expressing your gratitude for my particular brand of awesome."

Love bloomed just as brilliantly inside her. "I think I've got it covered," she said.

And she did. For the rest of their lives, she did.

* * *

Thanks for checking out my Blake Brothers Trilogy! I hope you enjoyed the ride! Looking for your next romance fix? Check out www.susansey.com to see what's new!

About the Author

Susan Sey lives and writes in St. Paul, Minnesota, with her wonderful husband, their two charming children and a whole lot of snow. In addition to producing smart, sexy contemporary romances on an annual basis, Susan also maintains a guinea pig, attempts Irish dance and occasionally wrestles her children into wigs. (Really. It's a long story, though.)

She loves ice cream, her family and happy endings, though not necessarily in that order. She does not enjoy laundry, failure or mowing the lawn, but rises to the occasion as necessary.

Want to connect with Susan? You can find her at www.susansey.com, where it's just a hop, a skip and a click to finding her on Facebook, Twitter and signing up for her newsletter.

Or you can just shoot her an email at susan@susansey.com. She loves a good letter.